Sword Masters

Selina Rosen

The Green Spirit Project
(Exertus Spiritus Viridis)

At Dragon Moon Press, our carbon footprint is significantly higher than average and we plan to do something about it. For every tree Dragon Moon uses in printing our books, we are helping to plant new trees to reduce our carbon footprint so that the next generation can breathe clean air, keeping our planet and it's inhabitants healthy.

Sword Masters

Selina Rosen

www.dragonmoonpress.com

Sword Masters

Copyright © 2008 Selina Rosen
Cover Art © 2008 John Kaufmann

All rights reserved. Reproduction or utilization of this work in any form, by any means now known or hereinafter invented, including, but not limited to, xerography, photocopying and recording, and in any known storage and retrieval system, is forbidden without permission from the copyright holder.

ISBN 10 1-896944-65-5 Print Edition
ISBN 13 978-1-896944-65-4

ISBN 10 1-896944-67-1 Electronic Edition
ISBN 13 978-1-896944-67-8
CIP Data on file with the National Library of Canada

Dragon Moon Press is an Imprint of Hades Publications Inc.
P.O. Box 1714, Calgary, Alberta, T2P 2L7, Canada

Dragon Moon Press and Hades Publications, Inc. acknowledges the ongoing support of the Canada Council for the Arts and the Alberta Foundation for the Arts for our publishing programme.

Printed and bound in Canada
www.dragonmoonpress.com

This is a work of fiction. Names, characters, places, and incidents are the products of the author's imagination or are used fictitiously and are not to be construed as real. Any resemblance to actual events, locales, organizations, or persons, living or dead, is entirely coincidental.

For my dear friend Eva who went through hell and came out the other side only to have to go back again.

May her nightmares not have been in vain.

From the Sword Masters Charter

To be a Sword Master of the Jethrik a man's ability and his integrity must be beyond question.

He must be familiar with all weapon styles and be prepared to fight on any battlefield.

He must be pure of heart, having never been convicted of any crime.

He must never use either weapons or skills for anything but the most noble of causes.

He must be tall, physically perfect, healthy, and nimble of foot.

He must be wholly human, being in no way related to any Katabull.

He must be always truthful in his dealings with King and Country.

He must swear to serve loyally the country of Jethrik even if the candidate be from out country.

He must fully understand our ways and our customs.

No woman, whether she is out country or Jethrik, will be considered for a post as a Sword Master.

1

It was that time of year again, and Master Darian greeted the challenge with a mixture of joy and dread. Every year hundreds of men—none of them ever much more than boys with an attitude—showed up to try out. They all wanted to be Sword Masters. A good fifty percent of them Darian never even saw because they got weeded out on their height, or their weight, or because they had some physical abnormality that excluded them from the program. Every year some tried to sneak by the judges. They stuffed paper in their shoes and rocks in their pockets, sucked their guts in and lied about their ages.

After the initial weeding out, Darian gave them a good looking over. He asked them a few questions and cut their number by half yet again.

They all wanted to be Sword Masters because of the glory and honor associated with the title. They didn't know what it was like to kill a man, or to have him try to kill you. They didn't realize that it wasn't fun; that it wasn't necessarily glorious.

But Darian knew, and he could tell by talking to the boys, by watching their reactions as he questioned them, which ones had what it took and which didn't.

Darian looked the candidate in front of him up and down. He was all arms and legs, and he would have made the six-foot height requirement easily; however, he would have barely made the one hundred fifty pound minimum weight limit. He was dark haired and dark eyed with bronze skin. Obviously at least one of his parents was out country, but he was most likely full blodded Kartik. That wasn't a problem as long as he swore to uphold the laws of the country and serve it. If he could fight, Darian didn't care where he came from. Still, he stuck out like a sore thumb amongst the blond-haired blue-eyed cadets, and this in itself could pose a problem.

"So, boy... what country do you hail from?" Darian asked, although he was sure he knew.

"I'm Kartik, but I have lived here off and on most of my life," the boy answered without blinking. "I know your language, your customs, and your laws."

"And you want to be a Sword Master?" Darian asked.

"I already am a master with a blade," he answered. "I wish to serve the king and to fight the Amalite horde. I don't care about a title."

"Of all the bloody cheek! So you're already a Sword Master, and you want us to send you out right now I suppose!" Darian laughed loudly. "Send you alone maybe—out to the front lines. Maybe you could teach our boys a thing or two."

The other recruits laughed.

"I didn't say any of that, Sir," he answered unblinkingly. "I want to learn all that you can teach me. However my father taught me never to hide in false modesty. It is a *fact* that I am already one of the finest swordsmen you will ever know."

"Well... we'll just see about that, boy." Darian looked the boy up and down and realized he already carried a sword on his back. It was in the right position, too. He also already had his own armor—black studded leather pants and vest. The bright multicolored gambeson he wore underneath it screamed island born as much as his coloring did.

"Follow me." Darian motioned with his finger.

The boy fell in behind him following him to the practice ring.

Old Justin started to stand up; it was normally his job to test the new recruits. Darian motioned Justin back into his seat—he had other plans for this braggart. Darian looked around and noticed Gudgin, one of the second-term recruits, leaning against a practice pole watching the proceedings.

"Gudgin, come on down here and check this 'swordsman' out."

Gudgin rubbed his hands together and grabbed a practice blade from the rack. Darian handed a similar weapon to the boy. The recruit took a second to check the weight and length of the blade.

Darian placed the boy in the ring with Gudgin and stepped back out of the way. "Lay on!"

Gudgin ran at the boy, no doubt bent on teaching him a lesson he wouldn't soon forget. He swung a good hard blow at the boy's head, expecting it to connect, but his opponent caught the blade and struck back so fast and so furiously that Gudgin found himself protecting his own head. A second blow from his opponent's blade caught him in the ribs and made them burn. A third hit him on the chin and knocked him off his feet. When he looked up through glazed eyes, the boy was standing over him, his blade at Gudgin's throat.

Gudgin looked at Darian and shrugged. "A lucky blow."

The boy helped Gudgin to his feet, although it was plain to see that Gudgin was having trouble taking the stranger's hand. Gudgin was good. Considered by most to be the best of the second term cadets. He didn't like to lose to anyone. He certainly didn't like losing to a scrawny, out country greenie. He shook the boy's out stretched hand grudgingly and walked away to lick his wounds.

Darian stroked his chin and looked at the boy's eager face. "You *are* good. You need a little refining, but there is no doubt that you have talent. Where did you learn to fight?"

"As I said, my father trained me," the boy answered.

"And just who was your father, boy?"

"Jabon the Breaker," he answered proudly.

All noise in the arena suddenly ceased, and all eyes turned to look at the boy.

"Your father is Jabon the Breaker?" Darian asked in disbelief. "Jabon The Kartik Waster?"

"I just called him Dad," the boy said with a quick smile. The smile faded just as quickly when he continued. "My father is no more. Killed by some ignoble Amalite scum this last spring, as was my own mother in my youth. Her death made your cause his, and his death now makes your cause mine as well," the boy said with passion.

Darian looked the boy up and down. He definitely held himself like Jabon. He fought like Jabon. There was one way to be sure the boy was telling the truth about his parentage.

"Show me your right hand."

The boy held it up; the right pinkie finger was missing. It wasn't a reason for rejection at the school, and hadn't been ever since Jabon the Breaker had come to their door.

"Let me see your sword," Darian said.

The boy whipped the sword from his back in one fluid motion and handed it to Darian. Darian took it by its hilt and spun it around. Like the sword of his father before him, the bone of the missing finger was resined into the hilt. It was some strange custom which had been handed down from generation to generation in their family. Some tribal ritual. Jabon had been a wild man, and his son didn't look any more refined. However if the boy could fight half as well as his father had, he could beat their best.

"Your father was a very great man and a good friend to me. He never mentioned that he had a son," Darian said.

"After my mother died he was very grieved. He left me with his sister to be raised, and he came here to fight. I believe it was only after he had killed a great many Amalites that he was able to deal with my mother's death. Only then did I become something other than just a painful reminder of all that he had lost. He finally came for me and started my training. We lived part of the time here and part in Kartik. We spent a lot of time at sea."

Darian nodded, he could understand Jabon's actions. He had lost his own dear wife too young. At least Jabon's wife had given him a son. Darian's wife had died in childbirth leaving him a daughter who he had no idea how to turn into a lady.

He looked the boy up and down again and smiled. "What is your name boy?"

"Tarius," he said.

"Well, Tarius, Jabon the Breaker's son, consider yourself this season's first recruit. You are in," Darian said.

The boy's whole face seemed to light up. He grabbed Darian's hand and started pumping it up and down. The Kartiks didn't shake hands the way the Jethriks did, and it was obvious that this was a rather clumsy attempt by the boy to show that he knew their customs.

"You won't be sorry, Sir. I'll work very hard. I will kill many Amalites."

The boy had a good, strong honest grip. There was an innocent purity that shone from his almost too pretty face that Darian knew was—at least in part—deceptive. This boy had already lived, he had loved, and he had killed. Of this Darian was sure. He pried his hand away from young Tarius with an effort.

"Harris!"

A young boy, barely fifteen, ran forward. He had a clubfoot, and working at the school was as close as he'd ever get to being a Sword Master. Darian had taken him in and supplied room and board. In return the boy worked all day running errands for the cadets and doing chores around the academy. Harris showed his gratitude for having a place to sleep and food in his belly with his eagerness to please.

"Harris, show Tarius to the barracks."

Darian turned back to the long line of candidates. He had a lot more to go through and not all decisions would be as easily made as the one concerning young Tarius, son of Jabon the Breaker.

Gudgin walked up to Darian. He watched as the foreigner picked up his bags and started to follow the crippled boy.

"I would never criticize your judgment, Master Darian..."

"Then don't," Darian said moving towards the line of candidates.

Not taking the hint, Gudgin followed. "I feel I must say... Sir, he made me look like a rank amateur back there!"

"And this is a reason to throw out his request for admission?" Darian laughed. "Better yet, maybe we should have the man shot through with an arrow! Calm down, Gudgin. Be a sport and be glad he's on our side."

"*Is* he on our side then? He doesn't look like us. He is from out country. His look is freakish, all that black hair, those black eyes of his. He's all arms and legs... he looks like a devil or worse. Such skill in one untrained is unnatural..."

Darian laughed at him. "He's not untrained, boy! Don't you get it? His father trained him, and his father wasn't one of the best—he was *the* best. The best we ever had. I don't care what he looks like, and I don't care if he's a foreigner. As for the hair, he'll get it cut just like all the other recruits."

Tarius looked at the barracks and said. "This won't do... I'll get my own quarters. I have money..."

Harris laughed. "When I said you must stay in the barracks, that's what I meant. You *must*; it's the rule. Just like the hair cut and the uniforms. Will there be anything else, Master Tarius?"

"No. Thank you. And, Harris, I am no man's master. If you help me, then I shall help you. That is the way of my people."

Harris smiled broadly at the fellow. He liked him; *yes* he liked this strange fellow a lot. Harris was different and felt an instant connection with this man who was also *so* different. Harris had no idea what Tarius was talking about. He was *talking* to him, and that was a big deal to Harris. Most of the boys in the academy didn't talk to him at all unless they wanted him to do something for them or were calling him names.

"Whatever you say. I have to go now." He bowed and turned to leave.

Taruis snapped, "Do not bow before me!" He sounded almost angry. "I am not a god to be worshipped. Never lower yourself to me for it is to me an insult."

Harris nodded, started to bow again, caught himself and ran off in confusion. He didn't know where Tarius came from, but he was pretty sure he wanted to go there.

Tarius looked around the room and was more and more unhappy. There would be twenty-five recruits in here. It would make things a lot more difficult—if not impossible.

Slowly the new recruits filed in. They seemed to all purposely pick the bunk furthest from Tarius. They were all staring. No doubt because Tarius was different from anyone they had ever seen before. So was the black studded leather and colorful Kartik gambeson. The gambeson came down to Tarius's elbows and could be seen through the "v" in the neckline of the chest and torso armor. The armor was light and easy to move in, and Tarius had practically grown up in it. In fact, Tarius had no regular clothes, only more pieces of armor. Tarius's long black hair was unkept and floating every which way. Yes, the Kartik youth must be quite a sight to these Jethrik boys. Tarius sat on the bunk and looked down at the floor, suddenly feeling very self-conscious and vulnerable.

When most of the bunks were full, Master Justin walked in with Harris at his side.

"There are many rules you will be expected to follow if you are to become a Sword Master of the Jethrik, and you will learn them all in your first term here. These are the rules for the barracks. You will only be told the rules this once, and after that you will be expected to remember. Breaking the rules of the barracks is grounds for dismissal, so listen up." Justin cleared his throat and continued.

"First, a swordsman must be always clean. Clean in mind, clean in deed, clean in person. You will bathe weekly, and your clothes and personal effects shall be kept clean and in order. There is no excuse for untidiness." He looked right at Tarius when he said that last bit, and Tarius squirmed. "Second, a swordsman can not afford to be careless. If you break something through your carelessness, it will be your duty to restore it in its entirety. Third, no food, drink or women are allowed in the barracks," Justin said. "If you have errands to be run or any other incidentals, young Harris will attend to them. Meals will be served three times a day in the mess hall, morning, midday and evening. If you are late for a meal you will not be fed until the next one, so I suggest you don't tarry. Uniforms and bed linens will be picked up once a week for cleaning on Friday afternoon. These will only be picked up if they are lying in a bundle at the foot of your bed. Failure to clean your uniforms or bed linens is reason for immediate dismissal."

Rules upon rules! Tarius wasn't used to rules, especially not Jethrik rules, they seemed strange and uncalled for. Tarius's father had sworn by this academy—by these people. Tarius had to trust that Jabon had been right, and that belonging to them was the best way to fight the Amalite Horde, but right now Tarius just wasn't so sure.

"All that said, I suggest you prepare for the evening meal. Directly afterwards you will go to the main hall where you will be given your uniforms, and..." again he stared at Tarius, "...proper hair cuts. You have a few minutes to put your things away, and then Harris will show you to the mess hall."

Finally finished, the older fighter turned on his heel and left.

"Hey, cripple!" a big red headed boy screamed at Harris. "Come over here and help me unpack my gear."

The lame boy limped over to help, and the red headed boy purposely tripped him. Tarius had been sitting on the bed, but was standing in an instant.

"Let the boy be!" Tarius said, glaring at the redhead across the expanse of the room.

The boy took several steps towards Tarius and stopped. He laughed and said, "What sort of a man are you supposed to be?"

"Just leave the boy alone. Let him do his job in peace," Tarius said as if already bored with the whole situation.

The red-headed boy closed the distance between them quickly. He glared into Tarius's face. "I asked you a question. What sort of a man are you?"

Tarius silently caught the antagonizer's gaze and held it, a smile curling the Kartik lips ever so slightly.

The red-headed boy stopped in mid stride. The cold black eyes of this wild stranger seemed to glare through him. He raised his fist even as a fear he couldn't explain gripped his very soul.

"Go ahead; do it," Tarius hissed through clenched teeth.

Although fear gripped the young man's throat like a vice, he could not deny this dare. He swung on the strange boy who challenged him in front of a room full of his peers.

Tarius grabbed the much larger boy's fist mere inches from impact, twisted quickly, pushed back and brought him to his knees. Tarius grabbed the boy's elbow with his other hand, forced his arm straight and shoved down hard. The boy let out a scream, and Tarius stood away letting him fall to the floor.

"You Kartik freak! You've broken my sword arm!" he screamed in pain.

Some of the other boys moved in for a closer look. Not so close though that the stranger might get the idea that they were challenging him.

Tarius looked up at them and gave them a wild, untamed look, and through clenched teeth hissed out. "I'm the sort of man who isn't afraid to fight for what I believe is right! I'm the sort of man that would just as soon kill you as put up with your crap."

"Help me!" the boy on the floor screamed. "Someone help me! My arm is broken!"

"It's not broken," Tarius assured him. "I'll put it back in place—if you apologize to the boy."

"Apologize to a servant!"

"Or I leave you like that," Tarius assured him.

"I'm sorry," he spat in Harris's direction.

"Your apology lacks sincerity," Tarius hissed.

"For all the gods' sake. I'm sorry! I'm sorry!"

Tarius put a foot in the wounded boy's armpit, grabbed his hand and gave a quick yank, pulling the dislocated arm back into place.

The boy all but passed out from the immediate relief, but feeling better, he was mad all over again. He jumped up and glared at Tarius.

"You used magic on me," he accused.

"He used Simbala on you," a tall, thin boy said, edging from the back of the crowd. "It's a Kartik marshal art form." They all looked at him and he shrugged. "I've seen my father and my brothers practice it."

With much mumbling they all went back to their unpacking. Tarius had picked the bed at the end against the wall, and not too surprisingly the bed next door was still empty. Suddenly the boy with knowledge of Simbala walked over, threw his stuff on the bed and started unpacking.

"I'm Tragon," he said, turning and holding out his hand to Tarius. Tarius took the offered hand and shook it much in the same way he had shaken Darian's hand, and Tragon smiled. He was obviously taking the 'shaking' part literally.

"My name is Tarius."

Tragon laughed. "Everyone knows who you are already. My father fought with your father at the battle of Riksdale. My father is Kliton of Brakston Ridge."

"I believe my father spoke of him," Tarius said. It was a lie. Jabon never talked of the men he fought with in the Jethrik, not by name anyway. They weren't his people any more than they were Tarius's, and while he cared for them as comrades in arms, he had never felt like he was a part of them. It was only their common cause that brought them together. A common enemy that Jabon couldn't fight on his own then, any more than Tarius could fight it alone now. The Amalites and their horrors were the world's problem, and their annihilation the duty of any decent fighter.

"My father said your father slew five hundred Amalites at the battle of Riksdale," Tragon said.

"I doubt it was that many," Tarius said with a slight smile.

"Even half that many would be a great feat," Tragon said excitedly.

Tarius looked at Tragon and realized suddenly that this rather handsome young man was neither afraid nor intimidated. He wasn't as ignorant as the others and so believed he had nothing to fear from Tarius. He seemed to *want* to be close to Tarius, and this could be problematic.

———◆———

Dinner had been nutritious and tasteless. The uniforms were plain blue puffy pants, black stirrup boots, and plain long-sleeved white tunics, which offered no protection at all. Tarius was accustomed to wearing armor as clothing, and this stuff made Tarius feel almost naked. Normally in the Kartik this would have been no problem, but under the circumstances this was the last thing Tarius needed.

The haircut was worse. What protection did Tarius now have for the head area? What padding for a helmet? Everything these people did seemed to make no sense at all.

Tarius lay fully clothed on top of the bedclothes, the sword drawn and lying beside the fighter. The lights were doused, and Tarius lay alone in the dark.

Tarius's mind raced. *What the hell was I thinking? I can't pull this off! I'm the only woman in a room with twenty-four men. A room where no woman is allowed. These people's ways are strange; they are crazy! Women are treated like a different species here. How can I hide my secrets from all these people when I live with them? Thank the one who has no name that they didn't make us strip!*

She looked over at where Tragon lay on his bed. *He's followed me around like a puppy all night. I wonder if he knows. He damn near came in the shower with me. No locks on the doors; it's only a matter of time till I get caught. All this bathing... what a waste! I'll have to find some other place to bathe. I am caught up in my father's curse. Forced to live with these strange, basically stupid people, hiding all that I am so that I can do my part to weed the Amalites from the world, and gain my revenge.*

"Tarius, you asleep?" Tragon asked in a whisper.

The sudden sound of his voice had made her jump, and her hand had automatically gripped her sword. "No, I'm not," she answered.

"I can't sleep, either," he said. "It's not easy is it?"

"What?" Tarius asked not understanding the question.

"To be the son of a great fighting tradition. Every male member of my family has been a Sword Master of the Jethrik. My father, my uncles, my two older brothers—all have been great warriors. My father is a Knight, and doubtless my brothers would have been knighted as well if they hadn't died in the Battle of Garrison. I am all that's left to carry on the tradition. I... I'm afraid. If I don't make the cut, I will disgrace my household. I'm not very good. In fact, I'm sort of clumsy. I am also afraid of dying, and I have no wish no desire to fight."

This was the reason the boy had been drawn to her, because he felt a camaraderie. They both had their fathers reputations to live up to, but it was fair to say that Tarius didn't really understand the boy's problem. "You should go into farming and raise sons who might carry on your great fighting tradition."

"And disgrace my family!" Tragon gasped in disbelief.

"Why would that disgrace your family?" Tarius asked. "People can fight or they can't fight. It's in you, or it's not. If you die without producing children, then the line dies with you and no good fighting people can ever come from you again."

"Wow! You really *are* a foreigner," Tragon scoffed.

"If you were to marry a woman who came from a good fighting line but couldn't fight herself, then chances are your off-spring would be very good fighters," Tarius explained.

Tragon laughed almost too loudly then. "Women fighting! Women don't fight."

"Kartik women fight," Tarius said plainly. She was surprised at how utterly ignorant of Kartik culture these people were. After all, Orion Harbor was less than a days ride from here and it was always teaming with Kartik sailors and traders.

"Oh, now you are pulling my leg," Tragon said.

"No I'm not. My own mother was a fine swordswoman until an Amalite thug ran her through," Tarius said.

"If you say so." Tragon yawned sleepily. "If I don't become a Sword Master I will disgrace my family, my father will never forgive me, and I will be disinherited. Penniless, with no skills to sell."

"You only *think* you have problems," Tarius mumbled.

"What's that?" Tragon asked.

"Relax. The more you think about fighting the worse you will be at it. It has to come from somewhere within. You see your sword as an inanimate object, something separate from yourself. Your sword must become part of you. As if your arm continued on past your fingers. As if the blade were a mixing of bone and flesh and steel. When you feel as if you have lost a part of yourself every time you sheath your sword, then the rest will come naturally."

When Harris woke them for breakfast the next morning, Tragon looked over and found that Tarius was already gone. He dressed hurriedly and rushed to the mess hall to find Tarius already there, obviously freshly bathed, dressed, and looking so wide awake that Tragon decided that at least for the moment he hated him. Even wearing the academy uniform Tarius stuck out like a sore thumb. So dark, so different, his sword on his back. If nothing else none of the rest of them carried steel. At least nothing more than a small dirk at their waist.

When they were all seated breakfast was brought to them. Tragon sat across from Tarius.

"What time did you get up? Are you trying to make points or something?"

Tarius shrugged, stuffing food in his mouth however it would go down. He didn't bother to answer Tragon.

Justin walked up behind Tarius and cleared his throat. "Tarius?" Justin addressed him.

"Yes, Sir," Tarius answered.

Justin picked up the fork and put it into Tarius's hand.

"Make us all happy by learning to use a fork and spoon as well as you use a sword," Justin half scolded. He walked away, and Tragon laughed.

Tarius glared at the boy, who fell silent, then looked around her at everyone else, obviously studying how they were eating. Then she quietly copied them, though it seemed a horrible waste of effort to her.

Tarius watched out of the corner of her eye as Darian entered and started talking to Justin. They were looking at her, and she squirmed inwardly. She was afraid at any minute they would figure her out. If only she at least looked like the others, but she didn't. She was Kartik, and she looked and acted Kartik. She didn't even eat like they did.

"Well, how are they doing?" Darian asked.

"Fairly well, all and all. Tarius is going to be a problem, Darian. He's *too* different," Justin reported. "Last night there was an altercation in the barracks. Young Derek tripped Harris, and Tarius took exception. On top of everything else, he is apparently a follower of the nameless god. The altercation ended with Tarius dislocating Derek's arm using Kartik Simbala. He only repaired it after Derek apologized to the boy."

"That sounds like grounds for dismissing Derek, not Tarius," Darian said.

"He sleeps in all his clothes with his sword across his chest. He eats with his hands. He's strange in a way I can't quite put my finger on, and I'm afraid the others will never accept him," Justin said.

"Kliton's son, Tragon, seems to have accepted him just fine."

"Then what of the sword, Darian? None of the other boys are armed yet. It must be intimidating for them knowing that Tarius, who can pull their arms out of socket like it was nothing, is also carrying around a bastard sword with—of all things—his *finger* in the hilt."

"The boy has lived by the sword, Justin. The sword is literally part of him. You only have to look at the scars to see that. Yesterday when he was still in his own clothes I noticed that the skin between the point where his gambeson ends and his vambraces begin is scarred with a dozen different cuts. There's a small one on his chin, and look at his throat! Someone literally cut the boy's throat. It's a wonder that didn't kill him outright. I would no more take that boy's sword from him than I would lay my own weapon down."

"All right, then I'll speak the words we all never spoke about the boy's father. There is something unnatural about him," Justin said lowering his voice still more. "There was something unnatural about Jabon, and there is something just as unnatural about his son—if not more so. They aren't *like* us, Darian! For the gods' sakes, they cut off their fingers and put them into the hilts of their swords!"

"Give me twenty men as unorthodox with as much skill and as good a heart, and I'll have an army that will grind the Amalites into sand," Darian said. "Let this bunch learn to deal with diversity from Tarius. Let Tarius learn our ways from them. In the end, we will all be the same people. All will have gained from knowing one another. I learned much from Jabon and so did you. I only hope that he learned something from us as well."

2

Tarius looked at the book in front of her in panic. She hadn't counted on this, hadn't counted on this at all.

She listened intently as the teacher at the front of the room lectured, and the other students interacted with him. He liked to teach by asking them questions, having them answer, and then telling them whether they were right or wrong. He seemed to especially enjoy it when they were wrong.

"Young Tarius?"

Her head snapped up at the sound of her name. "Tell me, then, what would you do?"

"The grain clearly belongs to the man who grew it and stored it. The man who stole the grain is a thief and should be punished."

"How?"

"I would order him to work for the farmer in the spring until he had done enough work to make up for what he had taken," Tarius said.

All the other students laughed.

Tarius shot a heated look around the room, and slowly the laughter died down.

The teacher, Edmond, obviously a man of books and not of swords looked at them all and smiled, then picked a young man named Burgis. "So, Burgis... why are you laughing?"

"The penalty for theft is death; everyone knows that," Burgis said.

"You would kill a man because he was hungry?" Tarius asked, defending her answer.

"He broke the law!" Burgis spat back at Tarius.

"He stole grain, not even that much, obviously he doesn't mean to resell it," Tarius said.

"It wasn't his..."

"Which is why I said he should have to work off what he stole," Tarius said.

"You don't understand our laws, foreigner," Burgis said.

"Actually," Edmond said as if shocked, "Tarius is correct. As a Sword Master of the Jethrik, you will occasionally be asked to patrol, and on these patrols you will sometimes be asked to settle local disputes. For some of the more remote villages you will be their only access to the law, and you must judge these cases carefully. Because of the small amount of grain that was taken, it is obvious that the man does not mean to sell it for a profit. You didn't even bother to ask important questions such as *Does the man have a family?* If he does, who will provide for them when he is killed? How does it serve the community to kill this man who was only trying to feed his family? The normal course is to make the man

20

work on the village roadways for six weeks, but Tarius's answer is even more just. Let the man work for the person he has stolen from. People's lives will be in your hands; your ethics must be perfect. You must follow the spirit of the law, not follow it to the letter. That is the reason for this class, because out there you will not just be protecting the kingdom, but protecting what the king stands for. If you make a cruel judgment it will reflect on the king and the kingdom, as well as destroying the lives of people whose only crime might be that they are hungry."

The class only lasted for an hour, and then they were dismissed. As the others walked by, Tarius could see that being right in class hadn't helped her popularity any. Not that she cared one bit. The further away they stayed, the less likely they were to learn her secrets.

―•◆•―

Arvon shook the hair from his eyes. Now a full-fledged Sword Master, he wore his hair as he wished. "That the one?" Arvon asked, although the boy was kind of hard to miss. Like looking for a black cat in a white room.

"That's him," Darian said.

"He's just a boy, and starving at that," Arvon said.

"He is Jabon's son," Darian said.

"Jabon the Breaker?" Arvon asked in hushed reverence upon hearing the name of one of his heroes.

"The same. Boy even has his finger in the hilt of his sword like his father."

"But still... He's just a boy!" Arvon balked. He felt like a schoolyard bully being asked to teach some wise ass a lesson.

"Approach him as if he is only a boy, and he will make you look a fool. He took Gudgin out like it was nothing for him, and he wasn't even warmed up yet. He fights like his father—wild and yet calculated. He needs some refinement, and I figure you're the only one who can teach him anything he doesn't already know. Who knows? You might even learn a few new tricks yourself."

―•◆•―

Tarius set the book down on a bench and went to join the others in line waiting for instruction. Darian came over and pulled Tarius out of line.

"Follow me, Tarius," Darian said.

Tarius nodded and followed him across the yard to where a young man, somewhat older than herself, stood holding a practice sword.

"Tarius, I want you to meet Arvon. He will be in charge of your training from now on."

Tarius looked from Arvon to where the others were being paired up to second term students. "No offense, but I don't want to be treated differently than the others." She looked Arvon up and down. It was evident by the scars on his forearms and cheek that he was the veteran of many battles. His hair was blond and slightly longer than the cadets were allowed to wear. He wore a sleeveless white tunic.

"Tarius, quite simply put, I can't afford to constantly be nursing the injuries you would make on second term students..."

"My father always said there is something to be learned from even the slowest man," Tarius said.

"If you're afraid you can't handle Arvon..."

That was all it took. Tarius was looking for a practice weapon before Darian had a chance to finish his thought.

"Take your sword off, Tarius," Darian instructed.

Tarius reluctantly took the sword from her back. She put it on a bench close by, but then couldn't quite walk away from it.

"No one will touch your sword, Tarius," Darian promised.

Tarius nodded and went into the practice ring with Arvon where he was stretching. He told Tarius to do the same. Tarius went through the stretching exercises, and Arvon laughed.

"Am I doing something wrong?" Tarius asked glaring at him.

Arvon laughed louder and slapped Tarius hard on the back. "Not at all! I just never saw a man with so few bones in his body. So... you ready?"

Tarius nodded, and without warning Arvon slung his wooden blade at Tarius's head. Tarius caught the blade and easily slung it off.

"Ah!" Arvon said with a smile, jumping back and taking a more protective stance. "So, you are good."

Tarius smiled back. She liked Arvon instantly. Here was a man who understood the sword; who loved it as much as she did. They were a pretty even match, and as Darian had predicted Arvon was learning as much from Tarius as Tarius was learning from him. When it was time to go to lunch, they both seemed reluctant to stop fighting.

Arvon sat with them at lunch, and as Tarius and Arvon talked on and on and on, Tragon felt more and more lost and afraid. He hadn't done so well in the arena. In fact, one of the second term boys had said it was sure to be the first time in Sword Master history that a recruit had impaled themselves on their own practice blade. As if that weren't bad enough, no one had bothered to tell him that the cloth covered wooden practice blades actually *hurt*. He had knots and bruises everywhere. Tarius had a knot over his right eye, but it didn't seem to bother him at all.

There was no way Tragon could make it in. There were twenty-five of them now, but in two weeks they would cut them down to fifteen. If you didn't make the cut you could always try again, but very few were ever accepted if they didn't make it the first time around. His father would never let him live it down.

He had to make it in. But how? He wasn't worried about the academics. Book learning came easy to him. But he'd never pass the sword part unless by some miracle he stopped tripping over his own feet.

Arvon excused himself and left, and Tragon moved closer to Tarius. "So, how'd you do?" he asked, even though he knew.

"I did all right." Suddenly Tarius looked sullen. "Not that it matters."

"Why do you say that?" Tragon asked in disbelief.

Tarius picked up the handbook then put it down slowly. "I can't read or write. Not even my own language," Tarius whispered. "I surely can't read *this*! I'll be out as soon as I flunk the test."

Tragon smiled. All was not yet lost. "I've got an idea."

———•◆•———

They sat in the courtyard after the evening meal. It was the middle of spring, and the days were getting longer and warmer. It was turning out to be almost as hard to teach Tragon to handle a sword as it was to teach Tarius to read and write. Tarius had tied Tragon's feet together with a string in order to try and improve his stance.

Tragon shook his head and dropped his sword. "That's it. I'm done in." He looked at Tarius eagerly. "Am I getting any better at all?"

"Most assuredly," Tarius said, although she wasn't at all sure that he was improving fast enough to make the cut.

"He looks better to me," Harris said, nodding appreciatively. Tarius was his hero, his champion. Tarius protected him from all the pompous little asses who wanted to kick Harris around. In return, he was devoted to helping Tarius do anything he wanted done.

It was Friday night, and they had the weekend off. A bunch of the other students walked towards them on their way into town.

"Tragon!" Derek yelled. "We're going to the pub. Want to go with us?"

Tragon looked at Tarius. "Want to go?"

"No, I have too much to do," Tarius said. She knew the invitation didn't extend to her. She watched him walk away.

"They're all jerks anyway," Harris said, patting Tarius on the shoulder. "I'll help you with your reading."

"That would be good." Tarius and Harris sat down on a bench under a tree. Harris was actually a better teacher than Tragon was. He was more patient and explained things better. Tarius liked Tragon, but realized that he was mostly self-serving. It was fine as long as she was helping him, but when he was supposed to be helping her he was always in a big hurry.

After about an hour she put down the book. "So in all fairness I should now teach you the sword. After all, that was my deal with Tragon, who ran off to leave you to do his work. So what do you say?"

Harris automatically looked at his foot. "I can't fight. I'm a cripple."

"What utter crap!" Tarius arched backwards and jumped to her feet in one fluid motion without using her hands. A feat that always delighted the boy as was evident by the smile which leapt to his face. She reached down and helped Harris to his feet. "If a clumsy oaf like Tragon can learn to fight, anyone can."

"I can never be a Sword Master," Harris said.

"No offense, but your country's rules on who can and can not fight are idiotic. You can allow someone to fight, but if they aren't a fighter in their heart, what good is it? Then you tell someone else they can't fight. Yet if that person is a warrior at heart, then you're an idiot. Come now; I'll teach you. I can tell you have a fighter's heart."

Tarius pressed a practice sword into Harris's hand and walked around behind him to show him how to hold it. With her hand on his she started to move the blade through the air, carefully whispering in his ear all the little tricks and movements as they went. It wasn't the way she was teaching Tragon; he wouldn't have stood for it. It was, however, how her father had taught her.

She put the front of her legs on the back of his. "Now, move your feet with mine."

He nodded, the concentration making wrinkles in his forehead. "I can... I can do it, Tarius!"

"See? I told you. You have a bad leg, so we fight around it. Use it, it's part of you, part of what you bring to the fight."

He nodded. He knew exactly what she meant. Knew what she was trying to do. She was teaching him to move around the leg. To move it less. To make the rest of his body compensate for it. Soon she moved away from him, took up her own practice blade, and started to spar with him. When they took a break Harris looked at Tarius his face beeming and said, "I don't think I have ever been this happy or felt this normal."

"You see my friend, you were born for the sword."

They fought with very few breaks till it was almost dark.

Periodically, Jena's father sent her to stay with her aunt so that she could teach Jena to be a proper lady. Jena hated it. As soon as she walked through the front gates into the courtyard she took off her shoes and put them with her bag on the ground. She took the pins out of her hair and let it roll down her back, then she undid the top two buttons on her dress. As she drew in a deep cleansing breath, she heard the familiar sound of practice swords clanking somewhere over to her left. Curious, she went to investigate. Most of the boys went home or to the bars on the weekends, but some of them were poor or lived too far away to go home, so they stayed even on the weekends and breaks.

She recognized Harris immediately and was both shocked and excited. She had seen the boy wistfully watching the swordsmen training all around him, obviously wanting to be part of what was going on, and knowing that he could never be. Before she even looked at the man Harris was fighting with she liked him. Then she turned to look at Harris's opponent, and her heart literally skipped a beat. He was the most beautiful man she had ever seen—dark and strong and mysterious.

She had thought she would die an old maid. No man had ever caught her fancy. She'd never had any desire to pair with any of the young swordsmen her father paraded in front of her on a regular basis in his futile attempts to get a male heir. But this man held the other half of her soul.

Get over it, Jena you're acting like a giddy girl who's never seen a handsome man. Breathe, Jena, breathe. He's just a man!

Suddenly Harris spotted her. He waved the sword high in the air. Jena was very fond of Harris. She'd never had any siblings and treated him like a little brother instead of the hired help in spite of what her father said. She mended his clothes, and when she made cookies she always made sure he got a handful right after they came out of the oven. Because of this she had the boy's complete devotion.

"Jena! Jena! Did you see me? I was *fighting!*" Harris shouted.

Jena walked forward and looked shyly at the stranger.

He nodded at her and lowered the practice weapon he held to his side. If possible, he was even more beautiful up close.

"Jena, Tarius is teaching me how to fight! Tarius is the best fighter here, even better than Arvon," Harris said.

"I wouldn't say that," Tarius said modestly.

Jena smiled at him. "So, you must be Tarius."

"And you must be Jena," Tarius said smiling back.

"Oh!" Harris said, seeming to suddenly remember his manners. "Tarius this is Jena, Darian's daughter. Jena, this is Tarius, son of Jabon the Breaker."

Tarius looked at her, and in that moment Jena felt absolutely naked. Something about his eyes just seemed to look right through you. Damn! She even liked his scars.

"I ah... I suppose I'll see you around. If you're as good as Harris says, you're no doubt a shoe-in around here."

"Not unless he can learn how to read," Harris said helpfully.

Tarius glared at him.

"Sorry," Harris apologized ruefully. "Hey, Tarius! Jena can help. Jena taught *me* to read."

"I'm not much of a teacher," Jena said shyly.

"*Please* help him, Jena. Tarius is my good and true friend. I don't want him to have to go away," Harris pleaded.

Jena wanted nothing more than to keep the strange man close. "Yes, of course I'll help him. If you'll just fetch my stuff from up by the front gate and take it to the house."

"Sure!" Harris ran off to do her biding.

"I don't want everyone to know I can't read," Tarius said, a bit embarrassed. "I don't want to put you out."

"It's no problem really and I won't tell father. He'll just think I'm helping you study. Come back to the house with me," Jena said taking Tarius's hand.

"Is that allowed?" Tarius asked.

"I don't worry too much about the social rules. You don't plan to violate me, do you?" Jena asked with a faint smile.

Tarius looked flabbergasted. "Most certainly not."

"Then come on!" Jena led Tarius to Darian's house, which was part of the academy grounds.

Harris ran in a few seconds later, nodded at Jena, and ran Jena's bags to her room.

"I, ah... I don't usually run around without my shoes on," Jena said nervously.

Tarius just shrugged as if he didn't notice, and Jena decided that this might turn out to be a very real problem. Tarius just didn't seem to be noticing her at all.

They sat down at the kitchen table, and Jena started teaching Tarius to read.

Darian had been down at the pub, and he had to admit he'd had probably one more pint of ale than he should have. Still, he could swear that his daughter—the same girl who had shunned every advance made by every worthy prospect he had shoved her way—was sitting alone at his kitchen table with the best young swordsman he had ever had the delight of helping to train.

There were cups of something hot before them, and they were obviously in deep conversation. How had this happened?

"She's just helping him to study," Harris said at his elbow, obviously making sure that Darian knew there was no hanky panky going on.

Darian smiled down at the boy. "How long has he been here?"

"A couple of hours," Harris said. "They haven't been doing anything, and they haven't been alone; I've been here."

"Harris, I'm not worried about my daughter's virtue," Darian said in a low voice. "In fact, for the first time I'm actually hopeful."

Harris smiled back at him. "I think they like each other."

"In that case, let's make ourselves scarce and let nature take its course."

"It's getting late. I'd better get back to the barracks. Thanks so much for your help." Tarius stood up and grabbed her book off the table. "If I pass my test, it will be mostly because of your help."

"Well thank you very much, but it would seem that Harris and... what did you say your friend's name was?"

"Tragon."

"It seems that they had already started you in the right direction. All you need is practice. It's really not as hard as it seems. I'd be only too glad to help you any time that you have a spare moment." Jena followed Tarius to the door. "You're... You're not as young as the others, are you? I mean you look younger, but you're not."

"I'm twenty-three," Tarius said. She looked at Jena, saw the smile on the young woman's face, and stiffened as an entirely too familiar feeling swept over her. She quickly pushed it down and fumbled quickly with the door latch. "Thanks... Thanks again." Tarius quickly fled out the door closing it behind her. She took a deep breath of the spring's crisp fresh air and felt no better. Tears welled up in her eyes, and she found herself running across the compound. She hit the wall running, jumped on top of it in a single bound and then dropped down on the ground on the other side. Behind the wall there were woods. She ran into them as the tears poured and her chest heaved with the heaviness of her loss. Then all pain was forgotten as she embraced the night.

They hadn't thought they were in any danger. They had thought they were safe; that was what made it so horrible. That they hadn't been ready for it. Jabon had gone out to hunt, leaving his wife and child safely in camp with the rest of the pack—or so he thought. No one knew that an Amalite raiding party had landed. No one was prepared. The Amalites were like a curse, a blight on any land they touched. They believed that their gods wanted them to conquer the world. They would subdue a country and then force conversion on the people of the land. Those who did not convert were killed. The Amalites' beliefs were perverse and repressive, and their people were filled with a vile hate fueled by the belief that anyone who did not believe as they did was evil and should be killed to appease the gods. There was no bargaining, no reasoning with them. They came, they saw, they killed, they perverted, they repressed, and then they moved on. They were a constant source of evil in the world, but no one had considered that they would cross the sea. The people of Kartik had felt safe.

The boats landed, and the screaming zealots rushed off and just started killing everything that stood in their path. There weren't many of them, and the great Kartik army had quickly driven them back into the sea, but not before they had killed most of her pack.

So much blood! So much blood you wondered where it all came from. She remembered her mother and the others fighting valiantly, but the Amalites just kept coming, driven by fear and hate, more afraid to stop than to go forward. An Amalite sword finally ran through her mother's chest. Tarius was standing behind her, and she saw the sword come through her back. Even at the tender age of five Tarius had seen death before, and she knew her mother was dead. She didn't even have time to grieve before a sword sliced into her own throat, and she was left for dead. She wasn't, but even her own father thought that she was. She could still hear his awful scream of horror.

They stacked her with the dead. They all thought she was dead, and they stacked her in a pile with the dead to be burned. There were bodies on top of her and bodies beneath her, and she couldn't cry out. She couldn't move; she was trapped. Trapped with the dead, the fire... they were lighting the fire!

Tarius woke up screaming and found herself sitting alone in the middle of the woods. She sat up and wiped her hands down her sweating face, then she started to cry. Her clothes were torn, her sword was in her hand, and there was blood on it, on her face, and on her hands. The shredded remains of a rabbit lay on the ground beside her.

She listened carefully and heard a stream. She got up, walked to the stream, and washed her face and hands, cleaned the blood from her blade and what she could from her shirt. *What does it mean? What does any of it mean? Why think of that? Why remember it? Why dream it? Why now?*

There were only a couple of tears that weren't in the seams, and she could probably patch those. But she only had two uniforms, and there were bound to be questions asked about how this one had been shredded. She stood up and started walking up the creek. It ran through the town, so if she walked upstream she'd eventually come to the academy.

The bindings around her breasts were killing her this morning. So she stopped, took off her shirt and then slowly unwound the cloth, exposing her breasts to the air for the first time in days. She was lucky she wasn't too well endowed, or this whole thing would have been impossible from the start. She took a deep breath thinking how great it felt. Shirtless, she still slung her blade over her back carrying her shirt and the wrappings in her hand. When she got close to the academy she'd do it all over again.

Is it really all worth it? For what? To help people that I don't know... That's not why I'm doing it. I do it to stop the Amalite horde from crossing the sea. I do it for my homeland, for Kartik. I do it to honor the memory of my mother who died young at their hands, and my father who they wouldn't allow to enjoy his old age. I do it for my people who have been hunted and cursed by the Amalites from the day they came into being. But it hurts to care about people...

What had her father said over and over to her? *"It hurts to lose people you care about, but it hurts more to have no one you care for."*

He was always worried about her. Worried that she shied away from relationships with people, preferring the company of horses. But she had dropped the barriers of her heart, she'd fallen in love with Janice, and Janice had rejected her love. She hadn't returned her love, in fact she had been repulsed by it.

The same way that Jena would be repulsed if she knew Tarius was a woman and not a man. Of course in Janice's case it hadn't been the *woman* part that had repulsed her.

A quick sniff of the air told her that she was downwind from a privy, and from the stench of it, no doubt it belonged to the academy. After all, one hundred or more people made a lot of shit. She stopped and rewrapped her breasts, silently praying that someday there would come a time when she could be all that she was without fear of rejection. For now she would play the game. She put her shirt back on and started walking again. As the smell got stronger, she saw the stables. She could go through the stables and get almost to the barracks without being seen by anyone but the grooms.

She jumped the fence into the pasture in an easy stride and started for the stable where she walked inside without being noticed. One of the horses whinnied, and she stopped to pet his dapple-gray nose.

"What a good boy." She talked to the horse, stroking his big neck and shoulders for several minutes. She'd had to sell her own dear horse to book passage from Kartik. She missed him; he had been a good and true friend. But he'd gone to a good home with one of her pack brothers. "I'll never fit in here. I'll never fit in anywhere," she told the horse. "I don't care. I have my steel. What other love do I need?"

"It won't keep you warm on a cold winter's night," a stranger's voice rang out.

Sneaking up on Tarius was the wrong thing to do. This stranger hadn't finished speaking when he found Tarius's blade at his throat. He jumped back a little and held up his hands. "I presume by the speed with which you draw steel, and by your coloring, that you must be young Tarius. Darian has told me much about you. All good."

Tarius looked him carefully up and down. Deeming him no threat, she returned her sword to its sheath.

"I see you have me at a disadvantage, as I do not know your name," Tarius said suspiciously.

"Do you think I come to steal horses?" the stranger asked.

"Doubtful. From the look of your hands, I'd say you've never turned an honest day's work. You don't carry yourself like a swordsman; more like a noble," Tarius answered. "If you'll simply state your purpose, I will gladly tell Sir Darian of your presence here."

"So you think I'm up to no good then?" he asked.

Tarius looked him up and down again. He was a medium-sized man with a head full of blond hair and a well-kept red beard. Tarius was thoughtful.

"I must admit I can't guess your purpose. I only know that I have never seen you before," Tarius said. "Who knows but that you are some Amalite spy..."

He laughed loudly then. "Ah, young Tarius, you are no sleeper! I will let you off the hook. For, you see, I am King Persius."

The boy nodded in his direction and said by way of apology, "Please pardon my ignorance, Your Majesty. However you must realize that I didn't expect to run into the king of the entire land in a barn full of horse crap."

The king laughed. This boy was far from intimidated by him. It was just as obvious by the way he held himself that he did not feel humbled in the king's presence. He remembered what he had read about one of the Kartik religions.

"Are you a follower of the One Who Has No Name?" he asked curiously.

"I am," Tarius answered without blinking.

"Then why do you come to serve me as a swordsman of the Jethrik?"

"Because all is one. The Amalite are a wound on the planet that will spread if it isn't taken care of. When you have a wound on your leg you don't bind your arm. If we stop the Amalites now, here, then they won't spread. I serve you because I believe in your cause, on the day I do not believe in your cause, then I will no longer serve you."

"You won't swear fealty then?" the king asked, a bit taken aback.

"Why would you gather good and honest men around you, and then ask them to follow you blindly? If that be the case why not take any sort of man? Don't you surround yourself with good strong men of good character so that if you make a mistake someone will be there to stop you from destroying the country?" Tarius countered.

The king smiled. This was a good man; a man whose council he could use. A man of good and pure judgment. Such a man was a rarity, and Persius made a mental note to keep in touch with this one. The king liked Tarius, but there was something different about him that went beyond that fact that he was definitely out-country bred. Persius couldn't quite put his finger on it. Something in his mannerisms—in the way he held himself.

"And what do you think of a monarchy?" the king asked.

"It is a shame that people must be governed. However I have seen the justice of men ungoverned. Their compassion does not exist, and there is no pity. The poor go hungry. The strong act in moments of passion and execute their prisoners without a trial. The innocent die cruelly at the hands of ignorant beasts who long to kill what they do not understand."

Persius smiled then; he thought he knew what was different about Tarius now. The boy was queer, a lover of other men. It wasn't a problem. It wasn't widely accepted among the Jethriks, but it was tolerated. They weren't the Amalites, so there was no law against it. It wasn't even grounds to keep someone out of the academy as long as they didn't conduct their perversions on academy grounds.

"What do you think of a king?"

"If a king is good and just, then the kingdom will have a time of peace, or if forced to war will be victorious. If not, then all shall parish," Tarius said. "That is why good men must rise up and smite a bad king."

"And what sort of king am I, Tarius?"

"If I did not think you were a fine king, I would not be here now."

The king laughed loudly now and moved to pat Tarius on the back. "You are indeed the only truly honest man I have ever met. All day long people tell me how great I am. If I were to ask you what sort of man I am, what would you say?"

Tarius looked confused. "What do you mean, Majesty?"

"Am I a better man than you are?"

"No, and no better than the crippled boy who works in the bunk house. All people are equal; only our natures set us apart. Good and Evil—those are the only differences that matter."

"And you love only your blade, is that right Tarius?" the king asked.

"I was talking to a horse, Sire," Tarius explained. "Telling him, if you will, my woman problems. If it's not too presumptuous of me, what are *you* doing here, Sire?"

The king laughed. "Well, if you must know, I occasionally like to come by and check out how things are going around the kingdom. Keep in touch with the people. I think that in order to be a good king, one must remain a part of the whole. I must remind myself that I *am* the same as the stable man, the Sword Master, and the crippled boy who works in the bunk house."

Tarius nodded with appreciation. "That is very wise."

They walked out the front doors of the stable, and an escort of five guards fell in behind them. The king saw the puzzled look on Tarius's face. Obviously he didn't understand why the king's guards hadn't been with the king.

"Sometimes I like to talk to horses, too," the king whispered in Tarius's ear.

Tarius laughed.

Darian watched as the king walked across the courtyard with Tarius at his side, and his guards walking closely behind him. The king's personal guards were all of the order of Sword Master as well as knights, and so to walk behind one still in training must have chapped them good.

Tarius would go far in the kingdom, and with the gods' good graces, he'd go far with Jena, as well.

3

Darian looked at the list in front of him. It was never an easy decision, but this batch of recruits had very few clear-cut culls among them.

The council that decided who went and who stayed consisted of Darian, Edmond, Justin, and five Sword Masters who had helped in the training up to this point, including Arvon.

"OK let's start with the one who should be easiest. Tarius?" Darian asked.

"At this very moment I know that Tarius can beat my best," Arvon said. "He holds back out of courtesy to me, because he likes me."

"I agree," Justin said. "When I sparred with him he out-classed me in both speed and style. I admit I had my reservations about him, but he is a fine young man who, in spite of his many differences, tries to fit in."

The other fighters were all in agreement. Edmond was silent.

"Edmond?" Darian asked at length.

Edmond took in a deep breath. "He didn't pass his written exam. He did very well in class; his oral presentation was superb."

"How bad were his scores?" Darian asked, worried.

"Don't tell me we are even thinking of denying Tarius acceptance into the academy because of bad grades!" Arvon said angrily. "He is unequaled in skill with weapons of all kinds. We are fighters; we should be able to fight first."

"We are also arbitrators of justice, and as such we can not be ignorant," Darian said. "How bad were his scores?"

"Bad," Edmond said. "He missed questions he got correct in class. He's not stupid by any stretch of the imagination, but his writing is barely legible. He might even have gotten some of the answers correct if I could have read what he'd written. Actually, I think he's illiterate. I'm sure that he knows the law, and he's most certainly virtuous."

Darian remembered the nights Tarius had been sitting with Jena studying under candlelight. The times he'd seen him under a tree in the courtyard going over the book with Tragon or Harris. If he had just been studying all that time, there was no way he would have failed the test. Edmond was right. Tarius hadn't been studying for the test; he had been learning to read and write.

"If you gave him that same test orally he would pass with flying colors I have no doubt of that," Edmond said. "However a Sword Master must be able to read."

Darian turned to the servant standing at the door. "Go and fetch Jena."

They all gave him a puzzled look. Darian shrugged and didn't bother to explain himself.

The servant returned with Jena in tow.

"Yes, Father," she said sweeping into the room.

Darian flinched at the sight of her. Her hair was undone, there were no shoes on her feet, and her dress had been pinned up on one side till it was almost indecent. She looked like one of the serving girls from down at the pub instead of a noble's daughter. He stood up and walked to the side of the room with her.

"What's wrong?" Jena asked.

"Have you been teaching Tarius to read?" Darian asked in a whisper.

"I can't say," Jena said looking at her feet.

"That means 'yes.'" Darian shook his head in worry.

"Are they going to kick him out?" Jena asked in a panic. If they cut him, he wouldn't hang around to try again. He'd go back to Kartik, and she'd never see him again, she knew this as well as Darian did. "You can't let them do that, Father," Jena begged in a whisper. "He couldn't read at all when he got here, not *at all*. He learns quickly, and he's learning more all the time."

Darian nodded, then smiled. "I don't suppose you'd be opposed to tutoring the boy, then?"

She shook her head quickly.

"All right, go on then."

Jena left, and Darian sat back at his place at the table. "Tarius can obviously read and write a little, or he couldn't have answered any of the questions. I have just talked to Jena, and she has said she would be happy to tutor the boy. Does any one have any objections to Tarius's entry if he learns to read better?"

"I have none at all," Edmond said with a smile.

The list didn't get any easier as they went on. Finally, there was only one more spot, and two candidates left—Tragon and Derek.

"Derek is the better fighter, there can be no doubt about that," Arvon said and the other fighters all agreed.

"However Tragon had a perfect score on his written exam. The only perfect score in this batch I might add, while Derek's scores were barely passing," Edmond said. "In fact, Derek's scores were not much better than Tarius's, and as we all now know, Tarius is just learning to read."

"Derek has the will to fight and the strength," one of the men said. "I don't think Tragon has either. I think he's here because he feels he must be here, not because he wants to fight."

"I agree," Darian said.

"Derek is ill mannered, and we already have the likes of Gudgin to deal with," Justin said. He had voted against Gudgin and lost. He hoped that they would look at their past mistake and not repeat it this year. Justin knew the importance of unity among the Sword Masters. It was why he had originally objected to Tarius, and it was why he objected to Derek now. He had admitted he had been wrong about Tarius, and now he hoped that Darian would admit he was wrong about Derek.

"Gudgin has calmed, and in time so will Derek," Darian said.

"But Tragon is already a gentleman, and not without skill. He is getting better, and he will continue to improve," Arvon said. "There is merit in what Justin says. We can teach a man to be a better fighter, but how can we teach him to be a better man if he doesn't have the right metal to begin with?"

The discussion went on for what seemed to Darian to be hours. Surprisingly, it was Edmond who finished the controversy.

"It seems to me that the choice is simple. We will be pairing these men off into teams. As has already been stated, Derek has trouble getting along with others. We currently have a man before us who is way ahead of his brothers academically, but weak in the sword. We have another who out classes all with his sword, but who failed the written part of the test. Am I the only one who sees that by pairing these two men together we will have the most perfect team of Sword Masters to ever ride for the king?"

All agreed, and Tragon was admitted into the academy.

They watched as the number of recruits in the room went from twenty-five to fifteen. They said good-bye to the friends they would miss, and encouraged them to try again, but none of them dared to show how glad they were not to be cut until the others were gone.

It was Burgis who let out the first scream of triumph. This had been his fourth attempt at getting in, and he could not contain his excitement. After Burgis it was perhaps Tragon who celebrated the loudest.

Tarius lay back on her bunk and watched them all as they whooped and hollered. She smiled and relaxed for the first time since she had taken that damned test, but she didn't feel like celebrating. She felt sorry for the ones who didn't make it, even for Derek who was a big, stupid jerk. She wasn't even supposed to be there; she was lying to the world. She had taken the place of someone who *did* belong there. She comforted her guilty conscience by reminding herself of how stupid their rules for admittance were.

After a few minutes they decided to go in to town and find a pub they could terrorize.

"Come on, go with us," Tragon pleaded, pulling at her arm. "I owe my good fortune to your good teaching and your help. Please come! I'll buy you a drink. Hell! I'll buy you a hundred," he said throwing his hands in the air and spinning around.

Tarius laughed. "If it's all the same to you, I'll pass. Maybe some other time, though."

"I'll hold you to that," Tragon promised.

Tarius watched them go feeling sorry for whatever pub they landed in that night. Then she got up and went to her locker. She pulled out her own clothes, wiping the mold off the leather. She looked around quickly to make sure she was alone, and then changed. She slung her sword over her back and walked out into the courtyard. She would go into the woods tonight. She took in a deep breath enjoying the smell of the dirty leather garments. She had missed the feel and the smell of them, the dark hiding her in the night. She moved on quietly, sneaking around everyone she saw. She was good at this—at not being seen. It was a game she had played for years. She saw Darian suddenly step out of his house, so she jumped and rolled into cover, coming up in a crouching position with sword in hand, just because it was part of the game.

"Are we under attack?" a voice asked quietly from behind her. She pivoted quickly and saw Jena standing there. Jena stooped to pick up some strawberries she had dropped out of her skirt, smiling broadly at Tarius saying all too clearly that she knew exactly what Tarius had been doing.

Tarius sheathed her sword and moved to help Jena pick up the berries. "I was... I was... I'm sorry I startled you."

"I figured I'd better say something quick before *I* startled *you*," Jena said.

They reached for the same berry, and their hands touched. Their eyes locked for just a moment, and then Tarius looked away and moved her hand. When all the berries had been picked up, Tarius got straight up in one fluid motion and put down her hand to help Jena to her feet. Jena took it willingly and held it tight long after Tarius had helped her up. She purposely caught and held Tarius's gaze.

"I'm glad you're staying..."

"Your father tells me I am to study my reading and writing. That you have once again volunteered to help me. I will be forever in your debt," Tarius said, gently trying to take her hand back. Jena wasn't letting go.

"Is it true what they say?" Jena asked looking at the missing finger.

"That my finger is in the hilt of my sword?"

"Is it?" Jena asked.

"Yes, it is," Tarius said.

Jena made a face. "Did you cut it off yourself?"

Tarius nodded simply.

"You know, of course, that's insane. Don't you?" Jena asked with a smile.

"So I've been told."

Jena kissed Tarius's cheek and finally let go of her hand. Then, suddenly shy, she turned to walk quickly away. At the steps to the kitchen she turned. "Do me a favor, won't you?"

"Anything you ask," Tarius said.

"Don't whack anything else off." She ran inside.

Tarius frowned hard and started walking in the opposite direction. "Well, there isn't much fear of that as I've got nothing to whack off," Tarius mumbled under her breath.

She liked Jena because Jena didn't give a damn what everybody else thought. She wore what she felt like wearing, or didn't wear it as the case might be. She spoke even when she wasn't spoken to. She laughed freely and sincerely, and she was beautiful in a way that few women were. For one thing, she still had all her teeth. Her long hair was almost always flying wildly about her head, and her blue eyes shone with pure mischief.

She could fall in love with Jena, and it was obvious that Jena was developing feelings for Tarius. There was only one small problem. Jena thought she was falling in love with a man. Tarius was a lot of things, but a man wasn't one of them.

She felt even more guilt than she had earlier. The Sword Masters' guild deserved her deception because they had stupid rules, but Jena didn't deserve it. Tarius supposed she could do things to purposely make Jena hate her. The problem was she didn't really want to. She enjoyed being lavished with Jena's attention. It was her curse that she had this thing for Jethrik women. No doubt because Jethrik women would reject her, when Kartik women would and had fought over her.

It was all crazy. Her affection for Jena could ruin everything she had worked so hard for. It could do nothing but hurt Jena and would only make Tarius crazy. Yet she was walking around on air because Jena had kissed her cheek.

All proof that what everyone says about me is true. I am crazy.

She took a run at the wall, cleared it, landed on the other side and ran off into the night.

Arvon looked at Tarius. He liked him. Mostly, he had to admit, because he was just so damned pretty. Arvon was sure the boy was every bit as queer as he was, and he couldn't help but feel attracted to him. Still, right now the little shit was pissing him off. He was holding back as if Arvon couldn't handle everything he had in him. Arvon was pretty sure the boy was right, but he still wanted a chance to try.

"Is that all you got, pretty boy?" Arvon chided, trying to make Tarius angry. Tarius's fighting didn't change, so Arvon threw a blow harder than was usual in practice. It barreled its way through Tarius's defenses and connected just above the eyebrow opening Tarius's head. Tarius stepped back and put a hand to his forehead, wiping the blood away.

"You fight like a girl!" Arvon screamed at him before he noticed how badly Tarius was bleeding. He hadn't meant to really hurt the boy. He started to call for help, but suddenly Tarius was all over him, and it was all he could do to defend his head as the practice blade slapped into him again and again and again. Next thing he knew, he was on the ground, his head spinning, his blade gone, and Tarius was pounding him in the face with his fists.

"Never say that again! Never say I fight like a girl! My mother was a swordswoman, and she could whip your queer butt. So don't say it like it's bad!"

It took three men to haul the enraged boy off of him. Arvon's nose and mouth were bleeding, his head was spinning, and he didn't know how much of the blood was his and how much was Tarius's. One thing was for damn sure; you didn't want to make the little shithead mad. There was something else he knew without even thinking about it. If Tarius hadn't been restraining himself, he, Arvon, would be dead. If Tarius wanted you to be dead, you would be. The boy was a killer by nature.

Medics were called in to attend to both of them, and Arvon noticed with self-loathing that they were putting stitches in Tarius's head. He looked at his practice sword, thinking that a padded weapon—even thrown too hard—shouldn't have done that, and noticed that the padding had ripped away leaving bare wood. He should have checked for that before he geared up. He felt like a total heel, especially since it was Tarius who was getting reprimanded by Darian.

"What the hell were you thinking!" Darian screamed at Tarius.

"You heard him. He purposely provoked me," Tarius defended. He didn't even flinch as they stitched him.

"He was testing you. You might have killed him," Darian scolded.

Tarius looked at him then, and the look on his face told Arvon that he was truly ashamed of what he had done. Arvon could only imagine what *his* face must look like.

"I'm... I'm very sorry, Master Arvon," Tarius said.

Arvon nodded back, angering the medics who were trying to attend him. "It was my fault, Tarius, and I who should apologize. First for my callous words, and second for my blade, which I see only now was unpadded and has inflicted damage on the most beautiful face in the academy."

"And I'm sorry I called you queer."

"That's quite all right; I am quite queer," Arvon said, and laughed in spite of the fact it hurt.

When they were all patched up they stood up, met each other in the middle of the practice ring, and hugged.

Arvon was sent off to recover for the day, but that was not to be Tarius's fate. Master Darian walked over and handed him a fresh practice blade. He had one in his own hand. Darian answered the question on Tarius's face.

"Let's see how you fare against the old man. And let me warn you, if you molly-coddle me the way you have been Arvon, or if I get the slightest feeling that you are patronizing me, I won't call you names. I'll kick your ass."

Darian had longed to spar with the boy ever since he arrived. Tarius didn't disappoint him. Darian was a worthy opponent for the youth, but by no means an equal one. Tricks he used to get through the boy's defenses only worked once. Tarius had moves Darian had never seen before. Had he not been hurt, Darian doubted he could have gotten him as many times as he did.

Finally, when they were both exhausted Darian held up his hands. "Enough! You wear me thin." He walked up to Tarius. "Do not let your anger rule your blade," he said in a raspy whisper as he tried to catch his breath. "I know there is great anger inside you, and you have a right to be angry, but that anger will not serve you in battle." Tarius nodded silently. "I'm very sorry. Sorry that I hit Arvon. Sorry if I have disgraced you."

Darian laughed. "You don't by any chance think that's the first time in the history of the academy that a sparring match has turned into a real brawl, do you? You don't put men together and have them fight without it occasionally getting personal."

Tarius nodded.

"Go get cleaned up and go to dinner."

Tragon sat down across from Tarius. "That was some fight! What did he say to you?" Tragon asked, starting to eat even before Tarius could answer him.

"He said I fought like a girl," Tarius said picking at the food on her plate.

"Is that all? Everyone's been saying he made a pass at you."

As if to add credence to Tragon's statement, Gudgin and some of his buddies walked up to the table.

"You and Arvon have a lovers spat today?" Gudgin teased.

"Jealous because you want my ass all to yourself, Gudgin?" Tarius spat back, not looking up from her plate.

Tragon laughed in spite of his best efforts, spitting potatoes back into his plate.

"Why, I ought to kick your little queer ass!" Gudgin said.

Tarius jumped to her feet. "Maybe you'd like to try." Today she was just tired of it all. Tired of being tested by every dog and his brother. Let all the bastards who wanted to, come and try to take a piece out of her. Let it be done and over with once and for all.

"Wow! What the hell has he been eating?" Tragon mumbled, picking up his plate and quickly moving out of the way.

―・◆・―

Jena had come to the mess hall looking for Tarius, having heard from her father of his injury. She had tried to stay away, but she just couldn't. She had to make sure Tarius was all right.

As she walked in she saw Gudgin gearing up to hit Tarius in the face. "Come on, butt monkey, let's see what you have!"

Jena knew what butt monkey meant, and she took immediate offense. She had seen the way Tarius looked at her. It was obvious that Tarius liked girls.

She walked up and took hold of Tarius's arm. She looked at the cut above his eye and the growing purple ring, then she glared at Gudgin with real hate. She let go of Tarius and poked Gudgin in the chest with her finger.

"Oh, big man! Fight with him when he's already hurt. You disgusting pig!"

"Leave me be! This is between we men. If Tarius can be counted as a real man."

Tarius gently took hold of Jena's arm and pulled her back to him and away from Gudgin. "You watch how you talk to her, or I'll spit you," Tarius hissed.

"Why, does she help you with your knitting?" Gudgin taunted.

"I'll..." Tarius started to move forward and Jena stepped in front of him. She wrapped her arms around Tarius's neck and kissed him full on the mouth. Tarius kissed her back and she felt like her whole body was on fire.

Jena pulled back from him with more than a little effort and said in all the voice she could find. "Now, you can stay here and fight with this idiot, or you can come with me." She took hold of Tarius's hand and started leading him towards the door. Tarius followed her without argument. Jena turned in the doorway and glared back at Gudgin.

"Now who's a big ole butt monkey?"

They disappeared to the wolf-whistles of the entire room.

Gudgin picked his jaw up off the floor, and he and his friends went back to their seats.

Darian and Justin, having been informed by one of the servants as to what was going on, ran in just moments too late. Everyone tried to act as if nothing had happened.

"Harris!" Darian screamed.

The boy ran over obediently.

"What happened?"

Harris filled him in... "Then she kissed him, and they left together."

Darian looked at Justin. "You deal with Gudgin however you see fit. I'll go find Tarius and my daughter."

———•◆•———

Jena dragged Tarius into the courtyard.

"You didn't have to come save me, you know," Tarius said. "I can take care of myself. I'm certainly not afraid of Gudgin."

"I know," Jena said. She stopped walking and turned to face Tarius. "You like me, don't you?"

Tarius swallowed hard and nodded her head silently.

Jena wrapped her arms around Tarius's neck and kissed her again.

Tarius didn't fight it. She wrapped her arms around Jena and pulled her closer. She ran her hands up and down Jena's back as they kissed. It felt good to have a woman in her arms again. It felt good to touch Jena.

Suddenly reality kicked in, and she pushed Jena away. "I... I can't. We shouldn't be doing this. I'm ruining your reputation. I have respect for you and for your father. This is wrong, I am not even of your country."

"I don't care about that, and my dear father would like nothing better than for you and I to marry and have lots of little sword babies," Jena said with a smile. She looked shyly away, then turned back and looked deep into Tarius's eyes. "Tarius, I love you."

The word echoed in her head, causing instant and intense pain. She loved Tarius, but she didn't love *her*. Jena loved this person that Tarius pretended to be. She could never love the person that she was. It hurt. It hurt not to be able to tell her the truth and hear her say that it didn't matter. It hurt not to be able to give Jena what she needed. But before she knew what she was doing, she had spoken from her heart instead of her head.

"I love you, too," Tarius said softly. Jena moved to hold her again, and Tarius grabbed her hands. "But it won't work. Can't you see that?"

Jena shook her head wildly. "No! I love you, and you say you love me. What could stop us from being together?"

"More than you can imagine. I am not the man you think I am, Jena...."

She would never know whether she would have told Jena the truth or not in that moment, because that was when Darian had found them.

"Would you spoil my daughter's good name then, Tarius?" Darian boomed accusingly.

"In no way, sir," Tarius said.

"Then get back to the barracks. Perhaps the hit you took on your head has made you temporarily mad. We will talk of all this in the morning."

"Yes, sir," Tarius looked at Jena once more and then left at almost a run.

———————

"What were you thinking! Kissing him... and in the mess hall in front of all the swordsmen for the gods' sake!" Darian scolded. "I think maybe you need to go back to you aunt's house for a while..."

"Don't send me away from him, Father. I love Tarius, and I believe he loves me."

"If that's the truth, then a little time apart won't hurt anything," Darian said with a smile. He hooked his daughter's arm in his and started leading her back towards their house.

"You do like him don't you, Father?"

"He is like the son I never had, but if you make yourself too available to him, you will lose him," Darian warned.

———————

Tarius stared at the ceiling in the dark. It was all too much. Maybe she should just leave. Leave tonight; get the hell away from it all. Every day the web of lies became more complex, and every day it was hurting more people. Most of all the lies were hurting her.

Jena loved her; she loved Jena. It was an impossible situation.

She didn't belong here. She belonged with her pack. But the bloody Amalites had killed her pack, and the few who were left had scattered across the Kartik. She was alone. Forced into a world that neither wanted nor understood her.

In the Kartik, same sex couples were commonplace. In a Katabull pack there were more same sex couples than there were heterosexual ones. They procreated through mixed pairing, and no one even thought about it. It was the way life was. But the packs had scattered, and the Katabull were spread out across the island of Kartik. Soon there would be none of their kind left in the world, and the Amalites would have done what they set out to do concerning the Katabull.

She got up, careful not to wake the others, and snuck out of the bunkhouse. She ran the length of the courtyard, once again jumped the fence and made off into the woods. She headed for the creek.

———————

Tragon had known for weeks now that his friend had a habit of late night excursions that sometimes didn't end till dawn. He had the feeling that Tarius did something on these excursions that made him a better swordsman. A secret ritual maybe. Tragon wanted to be a better swordsman. Obviously, the way to do that was to copy Tarius. If Tarius was doing some magic ritual that was helping him, then Tragon wanted to do the same ritual.

Tonight was the perfect night to follow his friend, as both moons were full and would give him plenty of light, but he soon found that he could not keep up with Tarius. Fortunately, he was a good tracker; his father said he was one of the best. He found Tarius's trail easily because he was doing nothing to cover it. It wasn't long before he heard a noise up ahead, and he quickly dove into a bush scratching his face and hands in the process. He peered through the bush and could see Tarius some fifty feet ahead. He was standing on a rock beside the creek.

Quietly, Tragon moved closer. He knew he had to be careful not to get caught because whatever Tarius did out here was very private. If it weren't, Tragon would surely have been invited along. Tarius didn't want *anyone* to know his secret, so if he was going to learn what that secret was, he was going to have to be very careful and very quiet. He managed to get within twenty feet of Tarius without detection. Apparently the sound of the water was concealing any noise that Tragon was making.

The creekbed here was one large slab of rock. Erosion of the weaker strata had left a hole about the size of a small cart and about as deep in the rock. It was constantly filled with clear, clean water.

Tarius started to undress.

Ah! Some sort of cleansing ritual, Tragon thought.

Tarius took off his shirt, and underneath he was wrapped in a white cloth.

Ah! Some sort of magic cloth.

As the last of the cloth dropped away, Tragon had to bite down on his tongue to keep from screaming out. The best swordsman in the guild was not a *man* at all! It didn't make any sense. Was this the secret of Tarius's great prowess, that he was a she?

Maybe he just has over-developed breasts; they aren't very big. I've heard of men having breasts before. It would be pretty embarrassing. If I had them, I'd tie them up, too...

Then the pants came off, and it was obvious that Tarius was not now—nor had she ever been—a man. And not only was Tarius a girl, but she was a girl with a very nice body. She got into the water, which came up to her neck, and just soaked. No doubt trying to relieve the pain of the beating she'd taken that day.

I've slept by her every night; how could she fool me? How could she fool the whole kingdom? Because no one expects a woman to be any good with a sword. What do I do now? Tell Darian? They'd kill her; she's beaten them all. Hell, she kissed Darian's daughter! They'd definitely kill her—if they could, which I doubt...

She crawled out of the water then and lay flat on the rock. The weather was warm, and no doubt the rock felt warm compared to the cold water she'd been soaking in. Then it happened. At first he thought it was a trick of the light and he blinked twice to clear his vision. She was changing. The skin on her forehead and shoulders was thickening. She moved into a sitting position, and he could see that her jaw had thickened as well. Her canines were protruding. He muffled a gasp, and her head swung to face him. Dark brown eyes with elongated, cat-like pupils stared at him only a minute, and then the beast was on its feet and coming for him.

He jumped up and ran. He could hear it growling and the deep huffing of its breath as it pursued him, then something jumped on his back and he was going down. Going down beneath something that weighed a good twenty pounds more than Tarius.

The creature spun him around, and as he looked into the eyes of the creature, he was sure he was about to meet his brothers.

"What the hell have you done?" the creature cried in agony.

The voice was if possible even more rasping, but it was still Tarius's voice.

The creature shook him like a child might shake a rag doll. "What the hell have you done?" it asked again. Although it was more an accusation than a question.

"I followed you. I wanted to know why you were such a good fighter. I thought that you were coming to do some magic ritual. I had no idea..." He trailed off, afraid to speak the words.

"That I was Katabull, or that I was female?"

"Neither." Tragon realized he must sound as scared as he was. He also realized he had wet himself. *No sense*, he decided, *in playing the hero*. "Tarius, if you understand me, please, please... Don't eat me."

The beast smiled at him then, and he saw his friend in the beast's features. "You should be so lucky." She got off of him and sat on the ground beside him. She made a face, moved and pulled a twig from her seat. "What the hell am I going to do with you?"

He started to crawl away. She let him move about three feet and then grabbed his leg and pulled him back easily.

"You know everything about me. You could get me thrown out of the academy, perhaps even killed."

Tragon sat up beside the beast. "Why... why would you want to be in the academy? Wouldn't you rather be with your own people?"

"Don't you think I would be if I could? My people are scattered in every land now. My own pack is mostly gone, killed by the Amalites. That is why I want to join you. To destroy them before they can do to other peoples what they have done to mine. Your people feared us, you made us outcasts, but at least you didn't hunt us and kill us. At least you accepted our right to exist. The Amalites would deny all but their own kind the right to even live. If your rules weren't so stupid, I wouldn't have had to lie to anyone, and maybe Jena would have fallen in love with me for who I am and not who she thinks I am."

"So you really don't like men the way they were teasing you about tonight, you *do* like girls but *you're* a girl, so that means your still queer as Arvon," Tragon said in a confused tone.

"Thank you, Tragon, that was very helpful," Tarius said.

"So, are you going to kill me then?" Tragon asked carefully.

Tarius looked at him through animal-like eyes. "Are you going to tell on me?"

Tragon thought about it only a moment. "No. I wanted to learn your secret; it's obvious now that it's not something I can cash in on. However, there is talk that they plan to pair us together when we go out into the field. Since I don't like pain, or even the thought of death, how stupid would I be to turn down the chance of riding with the Katabull? I won't even have to get sweaty unless I just want to."

"Good." Tarius stood up and went to retrieve her clothes and sword.

Tragon followed her, watching her dress.

"Doesn't that hurt?" he asked of the way she was wrapping her breasts.

"Well, it certainly doesn't feel good," Tarius said. "Of course I'll have to tighten it after I change back."

"Couldn't you change back now? You're kind of... Well, scary this way."

Tarius smiled at him then, a very scary, toothy smile indeed. "Can't. Once I transform all the way I have to eat raw flesh or blood before I can change back."

"Oh! Isn't that lovely? If you don't mind, I'll just head back now."

He watched as the creature ran off into the night. It was a lot to keep quiet about, but his silence would mean he lived, and if he talked... Well, Tarius would probably kill him first. If someone else caught her, let them expose her. It wasn't going to be him. How did it serve him? It didn't, and he wasn't in the habit of doing things that might get him killed if there was nothing in it for him.

4

Darian watched them playing in the courtyard with no sense of joy. Tarius and his class were well into their second term. The country was deep at war with the Amalites, and keeping the second year students quiet was a daily chore. They all wanted to go fight on the front. Tarius was worse than the others.

It was their spring break, and while most of the students had gone home to help their families with much needed crops at this time of war, a few had stayed. Among them were Tarius who had no home to go to, and Tragon who seemed to be afraid to get too far away from Jena. It was obvious that Jena's heart lay with Tarius, but Tarius was impossible to read. On the other hand, Tragon was obviously in love with Jena, and she didn't even know he was alive.

It seemed to Darian that Tarius tried to push Jena towards Tragon on a regular basis, and the more he did it, the more deeply Jena yearned for Tarius. It hurt Darian to see her this way, and he didn't understand Tarius at all. It was like he purposely fought his feelings for her.

It was a big awful mess.

For now Harris, Jena, Tragon and Tarius played ball in the courtyard like four kids with not a care in the world. The game kept their minds off the very real problems here and at the front.

Tarius grabbed the ball in midair, and as he came down Jena tackled him to the ground. She used any excuse to touch him, and at least for the moment he seemed only too willing to oblige. They laughed as they rolled on the ground, and Darian could see the hurt in Tragon's eyes. Jena never encouraged Tragon's advances. He knew where he stood, but that couldn't have made him feel any better. It must seem to him that his friend was always to best him at everything.

The king looked at the motley entourage and grimaced. Persius tried to be diplomatic because Jero was the most powerful of the six barbarian kings, and he didn't want to provoke him when he might very shortly need him as an ally. Jero thought he brought Persius great honor, but unfortunately Persius was neither in the mood nor prepared for Jero to honor him in the barbarian's own special way. Persius had a war to attend to, and a country to try and feed when the enemy was setting whole fields on fire.

More to the point, considering the problem Jero's presence brought, most of his good fighting men were in the field.

"Good king Jero! There is no swordsman currently in my palace who can best your champion, so there would be no contest," Persius said from his perch on the throne.

"If you forfeit, we win, and your kingdom is mine..."

"Whoa, whoa, whoa! Wait just a minute! That is your law, not ours," Persius said quickly.

"I bring you great honor, and you throw my deed into my face. You have no honor. Your kingdom is weak, and we shall overtake you," Jero said.

Damn touchy, these barbarians. Persius drew in a deep breath. What an unbridled mess! On most days the barbarian's threat would have meant nothing. However at this particular moment, he was down to a fistful of personal guards. Everyone of any prowess in battle had been sent to the front, leaving the capital city basically unguarded. In retrospect, not a very bright thing to have done.

Jero chose this moment to show up with fifty armed soldiers. They could rip the city to shreds before they could be contained, if they could be.

"Not understanding your laws, I spoke too quickly. Let me talk to the captain of my guard. I will have an opponent for your champion to fight at sunset and a great feast in your honor as well."

Jero and his entourage bowed, pounding their fist against their chests, grunted and left the throne room.

"Rutson! Send for Darian! I think he has a man who can champion us."

It was not his choice to make. The king had asked for the boy by name. Darian watched Tarius walk from the bunkhouse with his sword on his back and his helmet under his arm, wearing the armor he had come to them in.

Jena was crying and hanging on Darian's arm.

"Send anyone else, Father, but don't send Tarius. I beg you!" Jena pleaded.

"Daughter, let me go!" Darian shook her hand off. "If you are going with us, dress appropriately."

"I'm going, but I'm not watching," Jena said. Then she ran to Tarius, threw herself into the boy's arms, and started crying, pleading with him to decline the fight.

Darian threw up his hands. He gave up. There was no turning Jena into a proper lady. Trips to her aunt's house only seemed to bring her back more determined than ever to have Tarius on her own terms.

Tarius got into the waiting carriage, but Jena wouldn't let go. She sat beside her as they waited for the others.

Jena's tears cut Tarius to the core. "Jena, please stop. I will be fine. Look at me. I'm not afraid, why should you be?"

"I'm afraid *because* you're not afraid. Because you are a *moron*. You don't have the good sense to be afraid." Jena cried, drying her eyes and wiping her nose on the back of her hand. "All you think of is the great honor that has been bestowed on you."

"I will always be doing this because I am not a careful man. See how much better a husband Tragon would make you than I?" Tarius said.

"For the hundredth time... It is not him I love. It is you. Only you. You said you loved me, too, once. Remember?"

Yes, and that was a huge mistake I have regretted daily since. I should have used my head to stay my heart and my tongue, Tarius thought with a sigh.

Tragon stepped into the carriage then. It was obvious by the look on his face that he had heard what Jena said, but this wasn't the only reason he was white as a sheet. He was to be Tarius's second. Tragon had already begged her not to pay any attention to Jena's pleas. "If I fight in your stead, Tarius, I will die as surely as you will live to fight another day."

Tarius had assured him that she had no intention of declining the fight.

When Justin and Darian climbed into the carriage the driver took off.

It was a royal carriage. *Very nice,* Tarius decided. If she was riding to her death, at least she was doing it in style. Her death would certainly solve a lot of problems. She sighed again, she wasn't afraid, she was too conceited for that. She was sure she was going to win. What was bothering her had little to do with the imminent battle and everything to do with the blond girl who sat beside her hanging on her arm and soaking her armor with her tears. Tarius had no idea at all what to do about Jena or the way she felt about her. However, death seemed like the easiest way out.

It took them the better part of an hour to reach the castle.

It was a grand palace with four towers that kissed the sky. It was made of hand-cut stones, none of which were smaller than a man. The castle had been built over a period of nearly a hundred years, added on to by three different kings, and redecorated inside and out at the whim of the queens. There was no moat, but the main gates were made of six-inch thick oak boards, and would be a deterrent to any attack. Truth was, the castle was so far in country that it had never had to stand against a siege.

They were escorted through the courtyard and into the main hall. Darian leaned down to his daughter.

"For the gods' sake, Jena, show a little pride. Let go of the boy's arm, and for once in your wretched life act like a lady," Darian scolded.

Tarius cringed when she heard Darian's harsh words to his daughter. Tarius didn't want Jena to change. She wanted Jena to stay just the way she was. Yet she knew if she continued to spurn Jena's affections the way she had, there was a very good chance that Jena would become the woman her father wanted her to be, thinking it was the only way anyone would ever love her.

Tarius purposefully moved and took Jena's arm, linking it through hers, so that it looked more proper. Then she leaned down and whispered in Jena's ear, "Don't ever change, Jena. You are perfect just the way you are."

Jena very purposefully became a drag on Tarius's arm till they were far behind the others. She stopped and turned to look at Tarius.

"See? Why do you say things like that and then push me away? I don't understand you, Tarius."

"Why do you have to make things so hard?" Tarius sighed. "You know how I feel about you. I have told you. It is my curse that I can't give you what you want; I wish that I could, but I can't. I can't be who you think I am. Can't you just fall in love with Tragon? He does care so very deeply for you, and he'd be good to you. He could give you what you want."

"No he couldn't, he's like all the rest, he'd want me to change into what he wants and in the meanwhile he would never be who I want, because I only want you. How do you feel about me, Tarius? Tell me; you may go out there and die to save a foolish king's honor, so tell me truthfully. How do you feel about me?" Tarius looked at her. "I do love you, Jena. But love isn't a magic word that makes things right. You and I could never be together. I could never fit into your world, and you will never fit into mine."

Jena didn't let her say any more. She slung her arms around Tarius's neck and kissed her, good, long and hard, and Tarius couldn't help but kiss her back.

Darian seemingly appeared out of nowhere, grabbed Tarius by the shoulder and started pulling her away. "Oh, for the gods' sake, Jena! He's got work to do! Don't turn his mind to all of that."

―――◆―――

The feast was almost as big as her opponent. She didn't eat at all. She watched him carefully as he gorged himself. A fight to the death, and he was eating and drinking like it was his last meal—which Tarius vowed it would be.

However, if she died in the fight that would sure save everyone a lot of grief.

Darian sat to the left of the king this night, while Tarius, acting as King's Champion, sat on the right. It was a great honor that was completely wasted on Tarius. Jena sat beside Tarius, picking at her food and mumbling little things about how stupid Tarius was for any number of reasons. Tarius just sat there grinning at every derogatory thing Jena said to her. Why did the damnable woman have to be so stinking appealing?

Persius forced a smile for the barbarian king as he leaned towards Darian and said, "He's really got our jewels in a vice. Makes me wonder if the bastard wasn't fully aware that every good swordsman in the kingdom was away on campaign."

"Your best swordsman is here, my king. Tarius will take him easily," Darian assured the monarch.

"Let's hope so. The gods' alone know what these animals will do if he loses." Persius smiled then. "I hear there may be a match there," he said nodding his head in the direction of Tarius and Jena. "Of course, only if Tarius wins tonight."

"My daughter is very smitten by the lad. He, however,seems reluctant. I can't tell you that I would be disappointed by such a coupling," Darian said.

―――――◆•◆―――――

When the barbarians were so liquored up they could hardly walk they called for the battle to begin. The barbarian wore no helmet, so Tarius brushed hers aside when Tragon handed it to her.

"Tarius! In the name of your god!" Tragon said, offering the helmet to her again.

"My god has no name," Tarius said with a smile, "and I will need no helmet. I will win, Tragon."

Tragon nodded. He looked at Jena and hated himself for the thought that came into his head. "Fight well, my brother."

Jero walked over and looked Tarius up and down. He laughed. "What insult is this? You send a boy who doesn't even shave to fight my champion?"

"He is of age. He is of the Kartik people, and they do not shave. He is young and small, yes, but well skilled as are all my Sword Masters. Your champion will find him a worthy opponent."

"Your ego will lead only to your ruin. My champion shall hack this boy to pieces," Jero said.

Persius looked at Tarius. He was like a wild animal ready to spring. "Let the fight begin." Persius raised his hand and a horn was sounded.

Jero's champion didn't wait for the horn to quit sounding. He ran full speed at Tarius, wielding a sword easily twice as big as the one Tarius carried. Tarius stood there till the giant of a man was almost on her, then stepped smartly out of the way. As the man passed her she swung the flat of her blade into the back of his legs, and he went crashing to the earth. Tarius stood back in a ready stance and gave the man time to rise and face her.

"Damn it! He is his father's son," Tragon heard Darian tell the king.

"The man is roughly three times his size, and he's playing with him!"

The man was mad now, and he ran at Tarius, swinging just as soon as he was within sword range. Tarius caught the blade easily, forced it down, and then slid her blade up his till it sunk neatly into the meat of his shoulder. She quickly drew her sword all the way across his shoulder and jumped back.

The barbarian finally seemed to realize that he could not intimidate this opponent. When next he approached Tarius it was with skill instead of strength. But instead of standing calmly to meet the attack as she had with the first two, Tarius screamed like someone posessed and jumped in the air, bringing both feet to rest in the big man's chest. At nearly the same moment that her feet landed on the man's chest, her blade slid quickly and precisely across the man's neck, cutting the man's throat completely and evenly. Without seeming to have stopped, she completed the vault over her opponent's dying body, and landed on the ground facing his back. Both her feet were firmly planted on the ground, and her blade was at the ready, but all she really had to do was jump out of the way when he fell. Which he did in stages, first his head and then his body.

Tarius bowed to the king then wiped her fingers down her blade clearing it of blood, flipped her fingers in the air to clean them, and wiped the remainder on her pants.

Tragon wasn't sure how he felt.

The crowd went wild, and Tarius looked at Jena just in time to see her peeking out from behind her fingers. She looked at Tarius and started to cry again—this time in relief.

What the hell am I going to do about you? You are ruining everything, and you don't even know you're doing it! Tarius thought.

Jero broke the cheering with angry words. "It is a trick! Foul magic!"

Persius was undaunted. "You make excuses for your kinsman's bad swordsmanship. There is no magic here. Do you not know that all Sword Master's of the Jethrik fight as Tarius does? It is why we are the mightiest kingdom in all the land."

"If my witch should say that there is magic in his blade..." Jero started.

"Then your witch would be a liar. Have you so little honor that you will not admit to defeat? My man was a better swordsman. No more and no less. The competition is over. Let us remove the body and continue with our merry-making as good allies should."

Jero reluctantly agreed. The body was removed, and the party went on.

Tarius sat down beside Jena and started to eat.

"How can you eat when you have just killed a man less than ten feet from here, even as his corpse is removed?" Jena asked in disgust. "When his blood is still on your hands!"

"Well, I couldn't eat *before*, it would have made me sluggish," Tarius explained calmly.

"That's not the first man you've killed is it?" Jena asked.

"Not by a long way." Tarius laughed. "Now it's I who don't understand you. I thought you wanted me to win. I thought you didn't want me to die."

"I didn't. Thank the gods you're all right." Jena was confused. "But shouldn't you feel some remorse?"

Tarius shrugged. "He would have killed me. Now take Tragon. There's a man who has never killed and will feel sad when he does."

Jena slapped at Tarius playfully and smiled in spite of herself. "You really are the most awful person I have ever known."

"That is rather my point, dear lady."

"I have never in my life seen a swordsman such as Tarius," the king said to Darian.

"Nor have I. Not even his father was as good as he is," Darian said.

"He's extraordinary!"

"He's not human," a soft voice spoke behind them. It was Old Hellibolt, the palace mage. Persius' father had put great store in the old man's council. Persius more or less ignored him.

"Not human!" Persius laughed. "He is Jabon the Breaker's son."

"Who knows for a surety that Jabon was human? And only the blind would believe that thing is male!" Hellibolt was gone almost as quickly as he had appeared.

"What did he mean?" Darian asked.

Persius shrugged. "Who knows? He grows more senile by the day. These days it seems that he is constantly feeding me some riddle or making some prophesy of doom." He turned his attentions to young Tarius. "Good Tarius, do you find the food to your liking?"

"Aye, Sire," Tarius said. "I am sorry to be such a glutton."

"Nonsense, my boy, you have earned it," Persius said. "You are by far the finest swordsman I have ever seen, Tarius."

"Thank you, Sire," he said.

Persius looked hard at the boy. Damn! He was a pretty one. Old Hellibolt was right; *he did* look like a woman. Persius found him oddly attractive and quit looking at him for that very reason. He had four wives—all beautiful women, and he was well pleased with them. He was not now and never had been attracted to men. For this reason Tarius made him uncomfortable. *Damned old fool!* He never would have thought it if Hellibolt hadn't said something.

Suddenly Tarius was on his feet, and the chair he had been sitting in was unceremoniously thrown to the floor. Steel crashed above Persius head, and he looked up just in time to see Tarius's blade pressed hard against a blade which would have crushed Persius' skull.

Tarius pushed the attacker off his blade and then pushed his blade forward hard to catch the attacker in his side. This seemed to do nothing but anger the attacker who slung his blade into Tarius. Tarius countered, but not before the blade had hit.

The attack had caught Tarius off guard. She hadn't expected an attack, much less that they could sneak one past the king's two guards standing just a few feet behind him. She wouldn't make another mistake, and she wouldn't play games. She brought her blade up and blocked the blow coming for her head, spinning his blade. She used the momentum to carry her blade to the man's chest. She jabbed upwards just under the solar plexus, plunged up into the man's heart, then twisted leaving nothing to chance. Tarius threw the man off her blade, and he fell to the floor, convulsing for a few minutes before he died.

"What treachery is this?" Persius demanded getting to his feet. He stared at Jero. "Explain yourself."

"He was the brother of my champion. He must have been upset. I assure you he acted on his own," Jero said quickly.

"This man is a liar," Tarius whispered to the king. "He is filled with deceit. There is no honor in him. If he was angry over his brother, why go after you? Why not kill me?"

Persius nodded that he understood what Tarius was saying. "Better a guarded truce than none at all," he whispered to Tarius.

To Jero he said simply, "Let's pray no one else should decide to defend his blood, or I'm afraid there will be none of you left by dawn."

He drew his own sword from its scabbard on his side and held it out towards Tarius. "I know it is not your custom to bow down before any man. Therefore stand erect and let me bestow upon you the honor of being one of my knights." He tapped his sword on both of Tarius's shoulders. "Now go to the infirmary, and my own surgeon will attend to your wound, Sir Tarius."

"Thank you, Sire," Tarius said nodding her head.

Jena took her by one arm and Tragon by the other, and they started to lead her towards the infirmary. A servant was leading the way. "Come on ya mighty bastard," Tragon said only half joking. "It's not enough that you best us all at the sword, but now you have become a knight before any of us have even made Sword Master."

The surgeon looked at the wound through the pants and rubbed his hands together. "Ah! It's going to need stitching." He sounded damn near giddy about the prospect. As the king's surgeon he most likely didn't really get to treat anything more than the staff's occasional scrapes and burns. "All right, off with your clothes.'

"No," Tarius said plainly. "Stitch it through the hole."

"Young man...." the doctor started.

Tragon cleared his throat. "That's 'Sir'."

The doctor looked more than a little surprised. "Sir, then. You can't expect me to stitch your wound through the hole in your pants!"

"I'm not wearing any under drawers," Tarius explained quickly.

"I'll leave the room," Jena said shyly.

"You may if you want, but I'm not taking my pants off." Tarius was on the verge of panic. She was pretty sure that a doctor was going to notice right off that she didn't have a dick.

"Why ever not?" the doctor asked.

Tarius couldn't think of a lie quickly enough, but thank the Nameless One that Tragon did.

"It's against his religion. He's Kartik, don't you see? A follower of the Nameless God. They don't take off their clothes in front of others, not even their own spouses. They only undress in total darkness. I've been his sword brother for almost two years now, and he doesn't even shower with the rest of us."

"I can't promise to do much of a job through your pants," the doctor said.

"Just do it," Tarius demanded. She could feel the blood running down her leg and filling her boot. It hurt, and she felt weak. If she passed out, there would be no keeping them from undressing her.

He gave her some powder—in spite of the fact she told him she didn't need it—that was supposed to help with the pain, but all it did was make her head fuzzy. She still felt every damn punch with the needle. Jena was standing in front of her, and she seemed to come in and out of focus. That was the last thing she saw—either blood loss or the drugs knocked her cold.

She woke in the morning with a pain in her head to match the one in her hip, and she promised herself she'd never let them give her any of that powdered crap again. She reached for her sword and grabbed flesh instead.

She opened her eyes carefully. She was clean, dressed in her academy uniform, and Jena was wrapped all around her. Jena's arms were around her waist, Jena's head was resting on her chest, and her own arms were around Jena. Jena stirred, stretched, and looked up at Tarius. She answered the question that was on Tarius's mind in a sleepy, sexy voice.

"Your sword is under the bed."

"How..."

"Tragon cleaned and dressed you. He did it in the dark so as not to break your custom. You were pretty out of it with the powders by the time we got you home."

Tarius realized she was in Darian's house no doubt in a guest bedroom.

"You should not be here," Tarius said in a sad, low voice.

"I don't see you letting me go," Jena said.

"All the more reason that you shouldn't be here." Tarius didn't let her go even then. She moved and kissed the top of Jena's head. "You are ruining everything, don't you understand that? I had things all planned out, and you are ruining them. Men would fight for your love why can't you go after one of them and leave me alone?"

"I only want you," Jena said quietly. "And I don't believe that you *really* want me to leave you alone, or I would, no matter how much I love you."

"But you don't really love me, and I shouldn't love you."

"Don't tell me how I feel, Tarius, and why shouldn't you love me? What's wrong with me?" Jena asked forlornly.

"There is nothing at all wrong with you Jena, you are perfect. It's me, I'm what's wrong. I'm no good for anyone. Steel is all that really matters to me, Jena. Strong metal, limber flesh, and the skill to use them. That is all that I am, and all that I will ever be."

"And all that I will ever be is the woman who loves you," Jena said.

"Dammit, Jena, you don't even know who or what I am. I have secrets, Jena, so many secrets, dark secrets. There are things that you will never know about me. Things that I will never tell you. Will you be happy like that?" Tarius asked angrily. "Happy knowing that I have secrets which would rip you apart? That you will never truly know me?"

"If I am with you, I will be happy." Jena ran a hand down Tarius's cheek. "Nothing else matters to me anymore, Tarius."

"But I will be gone most of the time when my training is finished. There is a war and soon I will be sent there. I may never come back..."

"You will always come back, Tarius, and I will always be waiting for you. My heart tells me this."

"If you keep doing things as stupid as crawling into my bed, no other man will have you, and you really will be stuck with me," Tarius scolded.

"I would give my whole self to you this very minute willingly if you would only have me," Jena said unashamed. She moved so that her head was just above Tarius's, and Tarius pulled her down to her in a long, passionate kiss.

She wanted her. Her god help her she wanted this woman. Her hand found its way up Jena's nightdress, and she started to caress her flesh even as her tongue probed Jena's hungry, eager mouth. Reason and logic fled, passion stole her good sense, and in that moment she just forgot how impossible the whole situation was.

Darian stormed in unannounced, took one look at the scene and started screaming at Jena, though why the whole thing was somehow Jena's fault alone Tarius didn't really understand. "Jena, for the gods' own sake! Must you act like a common whore!"

Jena untangled herself from Tarius and jumped from the bed

smoothing her clothes as she did so, as if swift movement would somehow make Darian believe he hadn't seen what he had seen. She looked at her feet knowing that it probably wasn't going to work.

Tarius for her part seemed to be temporarily frozen to the bed.

"The man doesn't want you! How many times must he tell you this? How many different ways? Do you think this kind of thing will be kept silent forever? No good man will have you if you keep this up. Why do you think Tarius isn't interested? Only because you throw yourself at his feet; because you act like the lowest harlot at the pub."

He kept going on, and Jena just stared at her feet, looking sadder and more confused by the minute.

Tarius looked at her. *Damn I want you! I want you more than my sword. More than a stupid title and more than I want to kill my enemies. I've fooled everyone else. Who's to say I couldn't fool you? You've never been with a man, and I've been with plenty of women. I know I could please you. Everything else I have done—all the other deception has been for everyone else. Why couldn't I do this for me? She loves me; I love her. It could work. I can't stand to hear Darian talk to her like this, not when he's so wrong. Not when it's all my fault.*

Tarius jumped to her feet, and almost fell down. Jena caught and held her; she was a strong woman. Maybe strong enough.

"You are wrong, Darian. There is nothing wrong with Jena, and it is not that I don't want her. Only that I do not deserve such a woman as she. She is perfect, and practically anyone would make her a much better husband than I. I am wild and unkempt if left to my own. What you see now is what the academy has made of me, and when my schooling is done I shall return to my old form. The hair will grow back; the leather will go back on. I'll bathe when I please and come and go without cause or warning. But since she seems determined to have me, and since I would have no one—least of all you—defame her, then I will have no choice but to marry her."

My God what have I done?

Apparently Jena was as shocked as she was because it seemed to take her a moment to realize what Tarius had said. When she did, she hugged her so hard she almost sent them both crashing to the floor.

Darian just stood there with his mouth open for a minute. The he laughed out loud. "It had never occurred to me before. Your own mother was a woman of the sword. No doubt Jena does seem a "perfect" woman to you."

"So, what do you say old man?" Tarius asked. "Will you give me your fine daughter for a wife?"

"Yes, Sir Tarius, I will," Darian said beaming with pride.

5

"You did what!" Tragon screamed, angry and shocked to his very core. "You heard me."

They were off in the woods behind the academy.

"Then you are crazier than I thought, Tarius. Crazier than anyone thought. How the hell do you think you're going to pull this one off? Don't you think she's going to notice that you don't have the necessary equipment?"

"I've made love to many women, many times. There are other ways to please women..."

"Queer women maybe, but Jena isn't queer. She thinks you're a *man* for the gods' sake! You know how I feel about her, damn it! How could you do this to me? I'll rat you out, I swear I will. I'll tell her all about you. I'll tell them *all* about you..."

Tarius grabbed him by the throat and lifted him off the ground. When Tragon looked down he was looking into the face of the Katabull. "And before they kill me, if they can—which I doubt—I will kill you and take her away to the Kartik with me. That's a promise," Tarius hissed. "I love her, and no one—least of all you—is going to stop me from having her."

"I hate you!" Tragon said with real venom, trying to squirm free of Tarius's grasp. "I feel like you have stolen everything which should have been mine, and you don't even belong here! Not at the academy, not even in our country! I wish I had told as soon as I found out. Then none of this would have happened—not to me and not to Jena."

"Nothing has happened to you except that you weren't ejected from the academy. As for Jena... she is not your property or your worry." Tarius put him down, fixing his collar with an expression on her face she knew put fear into the hearts of men. "Try to betray me, Tragon, and I will make damn sure you pay."

The look of fear on his face as he turned away from her rather detracted from the impact of Tragon's silence as he stomped away from her. He was mad, but she knew he wouldn't say anything. Tragon worried about nothing quite as much as he worried about his own neck. And Tragon didn't really love Jena, he wanted her because he was a rich boy of privilege who'd been handed everything he ever wanted, and he didn't like to be told no. At one time Tarius had believed Tragon loved Jena, but now she knew he didn't. If he truly loved Jena, he'd do more than rat Tarius out, he'd kill her in her sleep.

Tarius would kill for Jena, she'd die for her, if this weren't true she'd have walked away from the woman and never taken all the chances she was taking now.

She knew it was crazy. She just didn't seem to be able to stop herself.

After Tarius had hunted and returned to her human form she walked back onto the academy grounds, and Jena met her, immediately wrapping her arm around Tarius's waist. Tarius draped an arm over Jena's shoulders.

"How did he take it?" she asked.

"He'll learn to live with it in time. I imagine if he thought he could take me in a fight he would have hit me."

"Everyone will be coming back tomorrow," Jena said. "Classes start. Father says you have to go back to the barracks and continue your training."

"It's only right..."

"But you're a knight now, Tarius! That's better than a Sword Master. You're not healed yet; how can you be expected to practice?"

"I don't want to be treated differently. Not because I'm going to marry the headmaster's daughter, and not because I'm a knight. I want to finish my training and go to the front with my brothers. I want to help drive back the Amalite horde; hopefully annihilate them completely. Their history is a tapestry of murder and death. They will never stop until either we or they are all dead. We must do more than defend our borders. We must go into their land and burn them out in the same way that they burn us out. We must give back better than we get. Only then will there ever be rest in the world. Only then will there be peace."

"I wish... I don't want to be separated from you."

"And when they are utterly destroyed, you won't have to be," Tarius promised.

Tarius limped into the arena practice sword in hand only four days after having been wounded. Most of the accomplished Sword Masters were on the front, and that left students to train students. Since Tarius was the best one there, Darian had been having her train the new recruits as well as her fellow cadets.

Tragon greeted Tarius in the middle of the circle with a bold hug. Tarius gave him an odd look, and Tragon answered her unasked question.

"I didn't sleep much last night. What I said to you... I don't hate you. You're right, she wouldn't have loved me even if you weren't in the picture, and at least this way I don't have to think of some other man dirtying her."

Tarius nodded. "Good. Then we are still allies." Tarius hugged him back then.

Tragon walked off to practice with Justin, and Derek walked into the ring. He had made the cut this time, in a time of war they lowered their standards, but his attitude wasn't much if any improved. He was from one of the rich families of the kingdom, and he really thought that his money should get him special treatment. That just didn't happen at the academy.

"So, golden boy, what happened to your leg?" the red-headed boy asked Tarius.

"He saved the king and was knighted," Darian answered from behind Derek. "So that would make Tarius *Sir* golden boy to you."

Derek seemed to boil inwardly at the realization that the outland Tarius now held a title.

In their practice fights, Derek tried to use Tarius's limited mobility. He even tried to strike the wounded hip. He became more and more frustrated as he realized none of his blows were going to connect.

"Do you want me to teach you, or do you just want to keep trying to hurt me?" Tarius asked. This only seemed to make Derek madder, and he tried even harder to hit Tarius. "You waste my time, boy. Give me someone over here who wants to learn."

Another of the first year students walked over, but Derek wasn't done yet. He ran at Tarius in a rage. Tarius sidestepped, and as the boy started to fall on his face Tarius hit him good on the back of his legs.

"See? I told you," Justin said to Darian as they watched the scene. "He's no good." Derek's manner had only confirmed what Justin had always said about him.

Darian noticed that Harris was getting wonderful, vicarious pleasure watching Tarius whip the boy over and over again while hardly working up a sweat. Still, Darian knew there had to be an end to it. Finally, he walked over, stepped in front of Derek, and took the practice blade from the boy's hand easily.

"You were cut the first time you were here because you seemed to have trouble getting along with others. If you do not change your attitude immediately, you will find yourself cut again. Just because you made it to the final cut doesn't mean you get to stay no matter what you do. You act out once more, and you're out of here."

"I'm sorry, Master Darian," Derek said, bowing low. He walked out of the ring, past Harris who stuck his tongue out at him daring him to make a scene.

Darian saw him out of the corner of his eye and shook his head at him. Harris looked crushed. Obviously he had decided that he had the perfect opportunity to torment his tormentor, and Darian had taken it away.

When the class was over Harris and Tarius stayed behind to continue Harris's training.

Darian watched them work from the shadows.

After about thirty minutes they put away the equipment. Harris ran off to do his evening chores, and Tarius started for the courtyard, no doubt to meet his daughter.

Darian stepped out of the shadows, almost but not quite startling Tarius.

"Harris... He's quite the swordsman," Darian said.

Tarius looked at him, no doubt trying to see by his features whether he was angry that he was training Harris or not. "Every person with a passion for steel should have the right to learn it. He is as good as any of the second term students and better than most of the first."

"Maybe because you have been training him all along. I'm not blind, Tarius. Didn't you think that I would notice that the lad was putting on a fighter's muscles, and that his movements have become less clumsy?" Darian asked.

"It is a shame he can not be a Sword Master," Tarius said.

"He can't join the academy; this is true. He can never have the title, but if he continues to learn from you I have no doubt that Harris will be a Sword Master." Darian smiled and patted Tarius on the back. "Seeing him fighting makes me wish I had thought to train him myself. That I had seen past his crippled foot and found his abilities. Were it not for you he would have gone from being a crippled boy to being a crippled man, happy to do thankless tasks for arrogant men. Now he'll want more, and you have given him the tools with which to demand more. Your ways are odd Tarius, but may the gods forgive me, I sometimes believe they are far kinder and wiser than ours."

Darian turned to walk in the direction of the main hall, and Tarius watched him go with a smile.

"I hope you mean what you say, old man," Tarius said under her breath. She grabbed two practice swords looking around to make sure the theft was not detected. Then she limped out the door and into the courtyard. Jena met her by the back gate that lead into the woods. Jena hugged her, and they kissed.

"You sure you're up to this?" Jena asked.

Tarius nodded. She took Jena's hand and led her to a clearing she and Harris had made in the woods a few weeks earlier. Tarius preferred the woods to the practice arena, and she and Harris had decided to build their own "practice arena." She had assumed she would only be fighting Harris here, but last night as Jena and Tarius sat in the courtyard watching the new recruits play at fighting with tree branches and the likes, Jena had planted another seed in her head.

"I always wished that I could fight," Jena said wistfully.

"Why don't you then?" Tarius asked.

"Women aren't allowed to fight. In fact, women aren't allowed to do most things that are fun or have any meaning," Jena said, stretching her bare feet into the grass in front of her.

"What a stupid country this is! How stupid to make women believe they can be nothing but what men wish them to be. If you want to fight, then you should fight," Tarius said with passion.

Jena laughed. "This is why I'm mad about you, Tarius. Why I had to have you. No other man understands me; they all think I'm daft. You treat me... Well, like an equal." She smiled a sly smile at Tarius then. "So, are you going to teach me to fight?"

"Of course," Tarius said. "You're my woman, and any woman of mine will have to be able to wield steel."

"If my father finds out he'll kill us both. You know that, don't you?"

If your father knew any of the things I'm hiding from him he'd kill me, she thought. *For this he will merely scream a lot.*

"Then we won't let him find out," Tarius whispered with a grin.

———◆———

She put the blade in Jena's hand and put her own hands over Jena's. "Just let my hands guide yours... No, don't fight me; let me be in control. Let the blade become an extension of yourself." She lay her head on Jena's shoulder and temporarily lost track of what she was doing when she got an eye full of Jena's ample and wonderful cleavage. *You could sure as pain never bind this woman flat.* She shook the thought from her head and continued the lesson, whispering directions into Jena's ear as they went. Soon she was having Jena follow her legs in the same fashion she had taught Harris.

Finally Tarius faced her. "So... Are you ready?"

Jena nodded, her determination apparent by the set of her chin.

"Then lay on," Tarius said.

Jena slung her blade at Tarius weakly, obviously aiming more at the weapon than at the warrior who held it.

"Harder, Jena, harder, and at me not my sword," Tarius said.

"I'm afraid I might hit you!" Jena protested.

"Ah! You cut me to the quick! Do you think me so unskilled that a fighter on her first time out will strike me with anything but air? Do your very worst. I promise you, you will not hurt me."

Jena took Tarius at her word and came at her with conviction in her blade. She was made for the sword; Tarius could see it in her eyes. She knew something of technique as well, having watched sword fighters her entire life, and she was strong. Strong enough and fast enough to make Tarius work to keep her promise. She took direction well, seeming to know immediately what Tarius meant. Her blows came harder and faster and with more accuracy.

It was almost dark when their blades locked up. Blade to blade, chest to chest, Tarius looked down into Jena's determined face and had never felt more desire. She grabbed Jena's blade and threw both blades to the side. Then she grabbed Jena and fell backwards onto the ground, bringing Jena down on top of her. She kissed her hungrily over and over. She rolled, putting Jena under her and rubbed her body across

Jena's. Her heart was pounding so loud she could hear it. Jena's mouth hungrily received her kisses, long and deep. Jena's hands ran over Tarius's back. If she felt or was worried about the wrappings it didn't show in her body language. Tarius's hands fumbled at the lacings on Jena's dress, and Jena eagerly helped her. But when Jena tried to undo Tarius's pants, Tarius grabbed her hand and held it.

"I only want you Jena," Tarius whispered. "Only you."

She let her lips travel down Jena's body, and Jena forgot about anything else.

Later, they lay in each other's arms on top of Jena's dress. Jena was tired and almost asleep in Tarius's arms. "I don't understand, Tarius... Isn't there something that I could do for you?"

Not without blowing your whole world to pieces, Tarius thought.

"That *was* for me. Do you think that I didn't have any pleasure from it?"

"But, don't you want to..."

"No."

"Don't you want me to..."

"No."

"But..."

Tarius silenced her with a kiss. Then said in a whisper. "Don't make everything so difficult. Can't you just be happy?"

"I am happy," Jena laughed. "But I don't understand..."

"You know... I have told you. I am different from other men. If you want someone you will always understand, then you should have chosen Tragon..."

Now it was Jena who silenced Tarius with a kiss. "I love you, Tarius. You're right, you're different, and it's exactly because you are different that I love you. If you are truly happy with our lovemaking, then I am ecstatic."

"I am happy," Tarius said and smiled. "Very happy."

She frowned then. *I'm too happy. It can't last; it never does. So I will enjoy it as long as it does and hope that I can take her with me when the time comes. Hope that her love truly is without bounds. That there comes a time when I can tell her without losing her.*

Arvon and his sword brother, Brakston, had just ridden in. Arvon had taken an arrow in his leg, and he had come back to recover from his injury as was the habit of unattached Sword Masters of the Jethrik.

Brakston helped him to dismount. "The grooms will attend our horses. I'll take you to the surgeon. The sooner you're well the sooner we can get back to the front."

"Oh, and we wouldn't want to miss a minute of that! Wading through mud and guts and gore. Food that a starving rat wouldn't touch. All the lovely diarrhea from drinking dirty water. Not to mention the wonderful arrows, swords and axes people are always throwing at you." He clapped his hands together in mock anticipation. "Oh, let's do hurry and get back. I don't want to miss either the rat season or the plague." He coughed loudly and ended up bent over spitting vile looking stuff from his mouth. Brakston went to his side, helped him to a bench, and then helped him to sit. He placed his hand gently against Arvon's head.

"You are running a fever again my friend."

Arvon laughed. "Ah, that would explain why I've lost my attraction to war."

Brakston looked at him. He knew exactly how his sword brother felt. They had all fantasized about the glory of it all, but there was no glory in the death that had faced them on the front. They'd make a little headway one day only to be pushed back the next. The rains had come, and with them came disease and mosquitoes the size of small birds. Arvon's wound had seemed a simple one compared to others, but a bad infection had set into it, and he'd become sick. It soon became evident that Arvon was going to have to leave the front or die, and he couldn't go alone. Brakston couldn't really say that he was sad about having to be the one to bring Arvon home.

"You'll get some help. You'll feel better," Brakston promised. "Rest for a minute."

Arvon saw Tarius and Jena sneak in the back gate holding hands. From their rumpled appearance, it didn't take a genius to figure out what they'd been up to.

Arvon sighed deeply. "Ah, there goes the end to one of my most beautiful fantasies."

"Huh?" Brakston looked in the direction that Arvon was looking and saw the couple. He laughed. "Not hard to guess what those two have been doin'."

"My point exactly, and I was so hoping that he wanted me as badly as I wanted him," Arvon said.

Brakston laughed. "Quit, ya old puffta... Tarius!"

Tarius looked up quickly, first with the startled look of one who has been caught, and then grinned and ran towards them. Tarius hugged first Brakston and then Arvon.

"Oh, sure, hug me now you young cad, when I know what you've been doing with this young woman," Arvon said. He looked at Jena who stood just behind Tarius with a huge grin on her face. "So, I see you finally chased this young man till he caught you."

Jena took Tarius's arm beaming happily. "We're getting married."

Arvon held a hand over his heart. "Ah! Woman, you slay me."

Brakston nudged Tarius with an elbow. "I suppose you better be marrying her if you were doing what I think you were doing out in the woods. The old man would have your hide, you know that don't you?"

"When is the big day?" Arvon asked.

"Soon, before I ride out on my internship," Tarius said. "I graduate in less than two months, you know."

"No I didn't," Arvon said. It made him feel old. He was glad to be back at the compound, away from the war. Back among familiar things and people.

"Tarius, would you help me take Arvon to the surgery..."

"You're wounded then, Arvon?" Tarius asked.

"Oh yes, and the infection has given him the fever," Brakston said.

Tarius moved then to help Arvon to his feet, and it was then that Brakston noticed that the boy was limping himself.

"What happened to you, lad? Didn't do that playing with your girl in the woods, did you?" he teased.

It was Jena who slapped him hard on the shoulder. "That's enough of your mouth, Brakston," Jena said. She moved to help Tarius with Arvon. "I'll have you know that Tarius was hurt saving our good king from a barbarian."

"You saved the king?" Arvon said looking at Tarius in awe. "Then you're not just wearing spurs because you have lousy out-country manners?"

"You horse shit!" Brakston popped Tarius on the shoulder so hard he almost sent all three of them to the ground. "You've been knighted!"

Tarius smiled but said nothing.

"See what a fine teacher am I? How my students become knighted before they even graduate from the academy?" Arvon said.

"See how the fever has gone to his head? We better get him to the surgery," Brakston laughed.

They started helping him to the surgery. He wasn't the first Sword Master to come in this week; three others had all come back from the front wounded. Two of them had died.

"It must be getting bad," Tarius said more than asked the two Sword Masters.

Both men looked at Jena.

"Jena is no faint heart, Arvon," Tarius said knowing what he was thinking.

"I am aware of that," Arvon said, but he wasn't about to fill her in on all the gory details. Not when very soon Tarius would be slung into the middle of it. Unless he was mistaken, there would be no internship for these boys. They would be shipped right to the front where their skill both with weapons and leadership were needed. "You, you know what war is, Tarius. You have lived through the horror. I really hadn't. I'd been in a couple of battles. The kind you hear about—the glorious battles where everyone dies clean, and in an afternoon the battle is over. This just goes on and on and on. I don't have to tell you, Tarius; you know what I'm talking about. I was sorely prepared. I'm still not prepared." He lowered his voice. "I don't know if I can go back."

Tarius whispered also. "Then why should you go back? Stay here and train men to fight. You have done your part. Find yourself a mate; fall in love. Live before you have to die. Who would deny you that?"

Arvon nodded then smiled at him. "I could have loved you, Tarius."

Tarius laughed. "Ah, you are full of the fever. You could never love me! I'm a filthy wild little bugger. There is no air of refinement about me. You, my friend, need a gentle man."

Jena left to tell her father that Arvon and Brakston were there, and that Arvon was wounded. Tarius stayed with Arvon while Brakston went to find the surgeon who had apparently gone home for dinner.

"So tell me how you saved the king, Sir Tarius," Arvon said. He lay back on the soft bed. "Damn! That feels good, now go on tell me." Tarius told him the story, and Arvon laughed. "You are indeed worthy of the title, Sir."

"The title annoys me," Tarius said.

"And Jena?" Arvon asked with a smile. "How did you win her favor?"

"Apparently by trying over and over again to get rid of her," Tarius said in a far away tone.

Arvon laughed again then coughed. "I will have to remember that one."

Tarius grew tired of leaving her friend there to suffer with no help. It wasn't as if she knew nothing of caring for wounds. She got up and started taking Arvon's pants off.

"Tarius! And you an almost married man, too," Arvon teased.

"Would you stop it." Tarius laughed. The pants came off, and she was no longer laughing. The dressings were filthy and stunk like death.

She carefully removed the filthy dressing. The arrow had gone through close to the bone. It had been removed properly, but improper care and improper cleaning had left the wound to become a mass of oozing green and yellow puss with red leech lines running in every direction. She didn't say anything. She just went to the sink and drew a bucket of water, grabbed some soap and a rag and started cleaning the wound. Arvon didn't complain that it hurt him, and Tarius knew this was a bad sign.

"It's bad isn't it?" Arvon asked.

"Well, it isn't pretty," Tarius said managing a smile. "Don't they cauterize wounds on the front?"

"There's no building a fire out there. There's nothing but rain day in and day out. Besides there's never time. There aren't enough medics, and very damn little in the way of medical supplies," Arvon said. He sighed and added. "I don't even know why we're fighting."

"That's because you haven't seen what the Amalites do to a land.

No one who doesn't conform to their perverted rules is allowed to live. People like you and me are killed first because we are immoral, and don't conform to their idea of 'normal.' They are like locusts; they creep in at your borders eating at your land, and before you know it there is nothing left of you. They send their filthy missionaries ahead first. People ignore them because they seem harmless. The missionaries look for the lost ones in a community—the ones that don't have families or homes. They promise them a better life, and so slowly they take over from the inside. They find your weaknesses and your strengths and report their findings to their leaders. When they finally strike, their people are on both sides of the line, and you don't know who the enemy is. They are evil to the very core of their being . Their primary belief is that anyone who doesn't believe as they do is evil, and therefore they are under no moral obligation to treat us any better than bugs. Their history is littered with slaughter and death. *That* is why we fight; we have to kill them. We have to kill them before they can kill us, because given half a chance they will kill us all. Have no doubt of that."

"They should have you speak to the troops, Tarius, the men need to know what they are fighting against and for," Arvon said.

Tarius just nodded silently.

Tarius had been taught how to bind and tend wounds as a child in Kartik. She knew that the Jethrik ways were different than Kartik and certainly different from the way the Katabull did things, but there was still no sign of the surgeon, and she got the impression that Arvon was running out of time. She found a piece of wire and some alcohol. Then she secured a piece of cloth to the wire. First making sure she had left no sharp edges hanging out, she dipped the cloth into the alcohol. If it ran into the wound easily, that would mean that it was rotting instead of healing.

"This is going to hurt a lot," Tarius said.

"Thanks for telling me," Arvon said with a forced laugh.

Tarius poked the swab into the wound gently. Yellow and green puss immediately erupted from it, and instead of screaming in pain, Arvon let out a sigh of relief. The smell was awful, and Tarius almost threw up. She ran the swab through the wound several times. It was no wonder Arvon was running a fever.

He was all over filthy, so Tarius undressed him and started to give him a sponge bath as much to clean him off as to reduce his fever.

"Ah! My dream come true," Arvon coed.

"Shut up, ya blaggard, or I'll leave ya set in your own filth," Tarius said but not without a smile.

His fever was bad, and he shook with the cold. As soon as he was clean, Tarius dressed his wound and pulled one of the surgery's tunics on him. She covered him with blankets and wondered where the hell the surgeon was.

"Crawl in with me, keep me warm," Arvon said through chattering teeth.

Tarius laughed as she cleaned up the mess she'd made. "You really are incorrigible."

"Do you really only like women?" Arvon asked.

"Yes, sorry," Tarius said with a smile. "If I liked men, I'm sure I'd go for you in a heartbeat. However, I'm afraid you would be gravely disappointed in me," Tarius said.

Brakston walked in then. "Where's the surgeon? He said he'd meet me here."

Tarius shrugged. "I cleaned it up and dressed it the way I was taught. I'm sure the surgeon will want to do it all over again when he gets here."

"It feels better all ready," Arvon said. He was starting to get tired.

"He hasn't kept any food down in days. Water either for that matter," Brakston said.

Tarius nodded. "I'll go get him broth then." Tarius left.

Brakston watched him go. "He is a puzzlement that one. Looks like a kid, yet he knows so much more about everything than I do."

"His life has been a hard one," Arvon said.

The surgeon swept into the room then, and ran to Arvon's side. "I'm sorry it took me so long. It's the leg, isn't it?"

Arvon nodded. "It's all right. Tarius has seen to it."

The surgeon looked at the dressing. It was different than he would have done it, but it worked the same way. "Well, he seems to have dressed it properly. Let's just see the leg." He peeled the dressings back, and a frown darkened his face. "The infection has spread; the leg will have to come off."

"You'll not take my leg," Arvon said.

"I'll give you something to kill the pain." He walked over and started mixing powders.

"Isn't there some other way?" Brakston asked.

"I'm afraid not," the surgeon said.

Arvon looked at his partner with panicked eyes. "Don't let them take my leg. I'd rather be dead."

"He will be if we don't take the leg," the surgeon promised. He got out a huge knife and a saw.

"No, no!" Arvon cried. "Please don't do this! Brakston, don't let them do this."

"I want you to live..."

"Without the leg he won't live," Tarius had stepped into the room. She looked at the surgeon. "The leg will heal. It was filthy; I cleaned it. If we keep the wound clean and dry, there is a chance that it will heal."

"Sir Tarius, would you challenge my skill as a surgeon? I tell you this man will die unless we remove his leg," the surgeon said.

"And he will die if you do remove his leg," Tarius said. She looked not at the surgeon but at Brakston.

"Listen to me. I have seen what happens with wounds like this, and I have seen what happens when they take a man's arm or his leg. His chances are better with the leg than they are without it." Tarius moved to stand between the surgeon and Arvon.

"Sir Tarius," the surgeon started in a patronizing tone. "I know you have your friend's best interest at heart, but if he doesn't have this surgery soon..."

Arvon took hold of Tarius's pants leg, and Tarius looked down at him. "Tarius, a thousand blessings on your head, and on that of your fine lady. My gratitude and loyalty till the day of my death if you save my leg from this butcher."

The surgeon took a step forward with his knives and his saw, and Tarius drew steel.

"The only thing that will be cut off this night is your head if you come one step closer to my friend," Tarius said with venom. "He will live, and he will have both legs."

Brakston drew his blade. "Tarius, good brother, hear me. The surgeon knows what's best in this matter."

Tarius saw the servant in the back take off running, no doubt to go and get Darian. She didn't care. Arvon was her friend, her mentor, and he had made a pledge to her like no person ever had.

Darian and Jena ran in one door as Justin ran in the other.

Darian reviewed the situation keenly. "What's all this then?"

"Arvon needs surgery, and Tarius won't let the surgeon touch him," Brakston explained. He didn't know what to do. Who was wrong? Who was right? The doctor said Arvon would die without surgery. Arvon didn't want the surgery. Brakston didn't want Arvon to die. Tarius said he was as likely to die with the surgery as without it. Brakston was tired, hungry and confused. He knew only one thing for a certainty he did not want to fight Tarius. For one thing, Tarius was his friend, and for another he knew he could not beat Tarius in a sword fight.

"I don't want my leg cut off," Arvon said.

"As long as he doesn't want his leg cut off, I'm not going to allow anyone to do it," Tarius said.

"Jena," Darian said under his breath, as if just realizing she had followed him. "Go back to the house. This is a matter between men."

Jena shrugged and didn't move a muscle. She even had the bad manners to speak. "It's Arvon's leg; it should be his decision," she said.

"Daughter, this is a matter between men," Darian said hotly.

"But she's right," Arvon said. "It is my leg."

"He's filled with fever from the infection. His judgment is skewed! You can't allow him to make this kind of decision now. It must be done for him," the surgeon said.

"Tarius, step aside. The lad will die without the surgery," Justin said in a calm voice.

Tarius stood silent, sword still drawn and ready. It was obvious that he didn't mean to back down.

Darian looked around, carefully trying to weigh out the situation. Arvon was a fighter—a man who didn't want to even consider living without both legs. The surgeon was a proud man who didn't want his decision challenged by the likes of this out-country barbarian. Brakston was war, road- and worry-exhausted, and didn't really know what was right.

That left Tarius. Tarius had made up his mind. They'd have to kill him to go against his will, and Darian doubted that he, Justin and Brakston together could take him. In fact, he was *sure* that they couldn't.

Besides, as Darian remembered it, Tarius was right. Most men who had amputations died anyway from the shock.

Justin looked at him, obviously anxious for him to make a decision.

"Arvon does not want his leg removed. We all know that none of us can beat Tarius in a fight, and with Tarius as his champion I believe that Arvon's decision will have to stand," Darian said. "Surgeon, put your tools away."

Brakston's steel went back into its sheath, and Tarius's was sheathed at once.

"Fine, but I can tell you I'll have nothing to do with this," the surgeon said. He glared at the out-country wild man. "You think yourself a better surgeon than I. Fine! Let his death be on your head." He stormed out.

Darian motioned with his head for Justin and Brakston to leave, and they did so without question.

Tarius redressed Arvon's wound and covered him. Then he walked over and got the mug of broth he had brought for Arvon. It was still warm, so he helped him to sit up and handed him the mug, which he emptied gratefully. When he had finished it Tarius helped him to lie down. When Tarius set the mug down, Darian motioned for Tarius to join him and Jena.

Jena and Tarius both squirmed, not quite sure which offense they were about to be scolded for. Both were hoping against hope that Darian didn't know about their little romp in the woods. If he knew about either the fighting or the sex, they'd both be in for a beating.

"Can't you just once act like a lady and keep to your place?" Darian said in an angry whisper to Jena.

Jena and Tarius looked at each other and sighed a heavy sigh of relief knowing that they hadn't been caught. Jena even managed a sly smile, and Tarius, red faced, looked quickly away.

"I'm sorry, Father," Jena said.

"Are you really, or are you just telling me what you think I want to hear?" he asked suspiciously.

"Why the former of course, Father," she said sarcastically.

"See that's what I'm talking about, Jena. You're a woman, as such your job is to do as you're told," Darian said.

"She has her own thoughts and ideas," Tarius said hotly. "She's a woman, not a toad. Her thoughts and feelings are as valid as any man's, maybe more so."

Darian literally tugged at his hair. "Ah, Tarius! Can't you see what you are doing? She is bad enough already, but you encourage her to be even worse! It's as if you prefer her because she is head-strong and messy."

Tarius smiled unashamed, "I do."

"You are mad! You are both quite mad and iritating! You expect the whole world to change for you!" Darian ranted.

Oh, you have no idea how true your words are. If only the world would change for us, then I could be who I am, and Jena could be who she is, Tarius thought.

"Look at you, Jena! No shoes, and your hair looks as if you've been rolling around in the woods!"

Again Jena and Tarius looked at each other with hidden meaning.

"And you Tarius, you can not continue to throw yourself into the middle of things like this. If you are wrong, then Arvon's blood is on your hands."

"No, his blood will be on the hands of an Amalite archer, and at least I will know he died with a full spirit," Tarius said. "I will stay with him till he is well."

She looked at Jena then. "You'll see, he'll live, and he'll have both legs."

"I only hope you're right, or we'll all have to hear about it forever," Darian said. "Come along, Jena."

Jena moved to embrace Tarius, and they kissed.

"Oh, would you just come on!" Darian smiled in spite of himself. "You two bring constant shame upon my head!"

The next three days were rough. Tarius didn't get much sleep. Arvon shit himself at least a dozen times, and Tarius had to clean him. Each time a humiliated Arvon apologized and Tarius told him to forget it. Tarius forced liquids down Arvon and wiped his brow with cool water. When the fever got too high, Tarius swabbed Arvon's entire body to bring his temperature down. Just before dawn on the third day, the fever finally broke. Arvon had been talking out of his head for most of the night, but as the first lights of dawn slid in the surgery's upper window, Arvon spoke clearly and crisply, startling Tarius out of a near sleep. Tarius rose from the chair she'd been sleeping in and went to Arvon's side.

He was looking at the light that streamed in the window. "My mother was a creature of infinite wisdom and beauty. I often wondered what she saw in my father, who was but a plain and simple farmer." He turned to look at Tarius. "She used to say that in the mists of a fever you saw crazy things, but you also sometimes saw things the way they truly were. Now this is a funny thing you see, because I always believed that I got all of my father's traits and none of my mother's. Yet last night I was sure I saw my own dead mother."

"That's not too odd. I often see my parents in my dreams," Tarius said.

"Ah! But this was odd because I wasn't asleep at the time, and I was looking at you," Arvon said thoughtfully.

Tarius laughed. "Now that is rich. You mistook me for your mother?"

Arvon nodded, troubled now, and not sure of the thought he had been so sure of only moments before. He went on with quiet deliberation. "Yes. I thought you were my mother because, for a moment, you looked just like her."

Tarius left Arvon's side and went to get the glass of water she had drawn earlier.

"See, I haven't told anyone this, but my mother was Kartik," Arvon said.

"Ah! I thought I noticed a bit of the island in your features," Tarius said. "See, I knew we were brothers in more ways than one."

"Well, yes, that's just the thing. Because, you see, my mother said she was Kartik, but in reality she was of a much older people." Arvon looked at Tarius hard then, although Tarius didn't notice, being too occupied with trying to get the overfull glass of water to Arvon. It was too much trouble, so Tarius stopped to take a sip. "You see, Tarius, my mother was the Katabull."

The glass fell away from Tarius's mouth and crashed on the floor, sending pottery shards everywhere. Tarius looked at Arvon in stunned silence.

"Well that explains why the arrow did so much damage," Tarius said.

"So. Was my vision right, Tarius? Are you, the greatest swordsman of the Jethrik, the Katabull?"

Tarius sat on the edge of Arvon's bed carefully. "Yes, I am the Katabull."

"And are you a man or a woman?"

"Did you mean the oath you swore to me?"

"Yes, I did," Arvon said.

"Then yes, I am a woman," Tarius said cautiously.

"Does Jena know?" Arvon asked, lowering his voice still more.

Tarius's features took on a tortured look as she answered. "No. She's young and inexperienced; she knows nothing of the Kartik people, and I make up things about our culture and my religion to cover myself and my methods."

"Do you love her?" Arvon asked.

"With all my heart and with all my soul."

"How long do you think you can fool her, Tarius? How long can you fool everyone including yourself? It's a dangerous game, my sister."

"I know that. But I've made love to her, and she was none the wiser."

"And what about you? How long are you going to be happy to never have her touch you?" Arvon asked quietly.

"I can't deny my longing for her touch, but I would do anything, absolutely anything, no matter what the sacrifice, to be with her," Tarius said.

"What happens when she wants more than you can give her, Tarius?" Arvon asked gently. "She thinks you're a man."

"I am a man in every way that matters," Tarius said. "I look like a man. I fight like a man. I can satisfy her. What else does she need?"

"*It* my friend. Eventually she's going to want *it*, and you ain't got *it*."

"I'll worry about *it* when the time comes," Tarius said. "I have to live for today. None of us may have tomorrow. I know it's wrong to deceive her. I tried to run her off—you know that I did. But she wouldn't go. Look at it this way. Any other man here would make her miserable, tie her up and gag her. Only with me can she be the person that she truly is."

"I'm not judging you, my dear friend. I only know what happens when one tries to live in a web of lies. Eventually one strand comes down, and then the whole weaving falls in on itself. Only know this; if there should come a day when that should happen to you, I will be there for you in any way that I can be."

6

Two months later they were graduating, and Arvon walked to the ceremony. Everyone said it was a miracle.

The ceremony bored Tarius almost as much as the new uniforms annoyed her. She longed to be back in the black leather she'd grown up in instead of the blue and white gambeson and chain mail shirts with metal pauldrons they were issued. It was cumbersome and noisy. They had practiced in it for months, and she was used to it, but knew she could do better without it.

Jena met her directly after the ceremony, threw her arms around Tarius, and they hugged. Jena made a face. Apparently she didn't like the armor any more than Tarius did. They started walking towards the courtyard away from the great hall. Most of the new Sword Masters would be going home with their families for a massive celebration. Tragon's family had big plans; he'd been telling them about it for weeks. Family and friends had come from all over the kingdom, and they would be having a three-day feast.

There would be no such celebration for the orphaned Tarius. They would save their celebrating for the next month when she and Jena would be married. Tarius wasn't looking forward to that ceremony and would be glad to have it over with. The ceremony would make Jena happy and the sooner the better. Tarius knew she and Tragon would be sent on their internship soon afterwards, and the way things looked now they would spend their "internship" on the front.

Harris rushed to catch up to the couple. He squeezed in between them, putting an arm around each of their shoulders.

"Are we going to fight?" he asked eagerly.

"I hadn't thought of it," Tarius said. She looked around Harris at Jena. "What do you say?"

"I have to change; I'll meet you there." Jena dislodged herself from Harris and ran off towards her father's house.

Harris looked down at his feet suddenly.

"So, what's on your mind?" Tarius asked, she could read him like a book.

"You'll be going away soon," he said.

"But I'll be back," Tarius said. "My wife will be here, and you my brother, you are my family now, Harris."

Harris nearly glowed then, and her words seemed to give him the courage to say what was on his mind. "You're a knight, Tarius, you should really have a squire."

Tarius felt like an absolute idiot. This was quite obviously what the boy had been hinting at for weeks. It hadn't occurred to her before now, because she simply didn't think in those terms. "So I am. I suppose I should really have a squire then, and since I have already trained you and know you to be as fine and good a person as I have ever known, and as good with a sword as any Sword Master, I suppose you should be my squire."

The boy pulled back, took Tarius's shoulders in his hands and looked her square in the eyes, "Do you mean it, Tarius?"

"Yes, my brother, I do."

Darian saw Jena run into the back of the house in a beautiful gown befitting the fiancée of a knight and Sword Master. A short while later, he saw her come out in something that looked like it had been cast off by a scullery maid. He wondered what she was up to, and having nothing else to do for once, he followed her.

Jena ran into the field and happily picked up her weapon. Tarius had been letting her spar with Harris, but today Tarius was going to spar with Harris first and he told Jena so. Jena looked somewhat disappointed. She sat on a log and watched Tarius bend over and shed the hated chain mail.

"Don't worry, my love, your time will come," Tarius said with a smile.

Jena smiled seductively, "You know I hate waiting."

Darian heard the familiar sound of practice swords. Up ahead of him he could just make out a clearing. As he got closer he could see Tarius and Harris fighting with Jena sitting to the side watching them. From the looks of the well-beaten dirt they played here hard and often. There was no doubt that the crippled boy no one had wanted had turned into a fine swordsman. His daughter seemed totally wrapped up in what Harris and Tarius were doing. She was happy, and thank the gods she had found someone who not only accepted the fact that she wasn't cultured but actually appreciated it.

Then something happened that literally made him weak in the knees. Jena took up a blade and started to fight with her intended. What was more, from the way she fought it was obvious that this wasn't the first time she'd had a blade in her hand. He watched with feelings of both dread and pride.

But it was so wrong! Women weren't supposed to take up steel. It was an unwritten but widely understood law. Women made life, they weren't supposed to take it. It went against the very laws of nature.

But she was good. Damn good, and not just for a girl. She was graceful and strong. She knew where to throw a blow, and when she went against Harris instead of Tarius she matched him blow for blow.

Darian watched them practice for several minutes. Then the youngsters took a break. Jena and Harris sat on the downed log and Tarius lay on the ground with his head in Jena's lap. Jena looked at the lad, and her love for him shone through every fiber of her being. It had been years since anyone had looked at him like that. Not since Jena's mother had died, leaving him to raise their baby daughter as well as he could.

He was a man, he knew nothing of raising babies or young women, but Jena was all that he had of her mother, and he couldn't bear to be parted from her. He'd done the best he could, but it was no small wonder the girl acted the way she did or even that she had a lust for steel. She had grown up in a swordsman's academy for the gods' sake! What chance did she have to learn to be a lady? A few weeks at her aunt's whenever Darian thought she was becoming too wild and woolly. Ruefully, he realized that it hadn't been enough. Not if he really wanted Jena to be a lady of refinement like her mother.

But Jena was happy, and she'd found a man who accepted her for all that she was. Who loved her for the person she was, and not what he could make of her.

Darian should stomp into the field and condemn the three of them. He should order Jena to stop these lessons. He should let Tarius have it for inflicting his strange ways on his daughter. And he should give Harris living hell for helping and for keeping their secret from him. Truth was, he just didn't feel like it.

It would be an act, a show, inflicting on them what he knew other people expected. Truth was, he was proud of all of them. Besides he doubted very seriously that either Jena or Tarius would bow to his wishes or even pretend to, no they'd argue with him and he just wasn't up for it. Quietly, he turned and walked back to the house without saying a word. It was easier to pretend like he didn't know.

Tarius now lived in the house with Darian and Jena, and most mornings found Jena mysteriously missing from her bed. Darian knew if he looked in Tarius's bed he'd find her there, so he just didn't look.

It was early on a weekend morning, so the banging on the door aroused him from his sleep. It was a messenger from the king. He handed a note to Darian, clicked his heels and left.

The letter was for Tarius, and Darian feared what it was. He stopped outside Tarius's door, and he heard what sounded like scuffling coming from the other side. Knowing those two, it was just as likely that they were wrestling as making love.

He knocked on the door, and it was suddenly quiet on the other side. In a few seconds Tarius opened the door a crack. Seeing it was Darian he walked out, fully dressed—if obviously hastily so—his sword on his back. He closed the door quickly so that Darian shouldn't see into the room.

Darian handed Tarius the message, and Tarius opened it carefully. He read the letter twice to make sure.

"Well?" Darian asked impatiently.

"The troops morale is at an all-time low. The king will ride into battle and take over command of our forces. He wants me to serve beside him. To command." He looked up from the paper. "Tragon and I will leave with the king at the end of this next week."

Darian was surprised. Tarius seemed less than pleased with the honor. Then he saw the boy's eyes go back to the closed door and knew why.

"Harris will be going with us," Tarius said thoughtfully.

Darian nodded. "I had expected as much. It's Jena you're worried about."

"I want to marry her tonight," Tarius said quickly. "That will give us a week together as husband and wife. I don't plan to die. But if I should, I don't want to leave her unmarried with no pension." Tarius added almost to himself, "Damn it all, she has ruined everything."

"Why's that?"

Tarius looked at him and smiled. "Because before her all I ever loved was my steel. All I ever longed for was battle and a chance to revenge myself on my enemies. Now none of it matters to me as much as just being able to look at her."

Darian smiled. "I thought as much. May the gods watch over the man who comes up against one who has everything to live for. I will get the Shaman; you tell Jena." He motioned his head knowingly at Tarius's door, and Tarius blushed.

"I don't ask her to come to me; she just does," Tarius said in an embarrassed tone.

"I know. After this evening it won't really matter where she's been sleeping these last few weeks." He smiled and left.

They had put the ceremony together quickly, and Tragon wished to the gods that they had forgotten to invite him all together. He was happy when Tarius chose Harris to stand with her instead of him.

Jena looked more beautiful than ever, all dressed from head to toe in swirls of dark blue cloth. She never even looked at him; she had eyes only for Tarius who wore her armor as was traditional of a warrior in her country. Besides that, the only thing that wasn't traditional for a Jethrik ceremony was the giving of a token. The betrothed gave to one another a thing of significant personal value to them. Tarius gave Jena the gold chain she always wore. It had belonged to her father and had a coin on it marked with strange letters and symbols, the origin of which Tragon could only guess at. Jena gave Tarius a necklace of blue and white beads that had belonged to her mother. It was very sweet and made Tragon mad as hell.

By all rights he should be marrying Jena. He could make a proper lady of her and give her things that Tarius never could both physical and monetary.

The feast was magnificent, but Jena and Tarius didn't stay long enough to really enjoy it. No doubt the barbarian had dragged Jena off into the woods to do whatever filthy thing she did to her to keep that stupid grin on Jena's face all the time.

"So, Tragon!" Darian popped him on the back. "Are you excited about your internship? Not many new swordsmen have as their first assignment riding with the king!"

"Yes, sir. Very excited and honored," Tragon said. *And that's the only reason I don't rat the twisted beast-girl out. Tarius's fighting skill will keep me alive and give me the position and prestige I never would have had on my own riding with anyone else. Tarius will be made a captain in a week, and so I will be made a captain. When she's made a general they'll make me one as well because I'm her partner. I've even heard a rumor that I will be knighted soon just because they like to keep the partnerships even. I may have lost the girl, but I'll get everything else that Tarius can get for me. I'll keep her filthy little secret as long as it serves me.*

"You'll watch his back won't you?" Darian asked. He knew of Tragon's not very well hidden feelings for Jena and sometimes wondered if Tarius's worst enemy on the front might not be his own partner.

"If he dies, I shall fall next," Tragon said. *Because if they can kill Tarius, there will be no hope for any of us.*

Harris was drunk, and he was funny. He was doing stupid tricks that Tarius had no doubt taught him to impress a bunch of wide-eyed young ladies. Just then, he was balancing himself on one hand, and Tragon couldn't help but feel jealous. Tarius had never bothered to teach him either hand-to-hand combat or Simbala. She had wasted all her time training this crippled boy. In fact, he got the distinct impression that she actually preferred Harris's company to his own.

Tragon glared at the room of idiots. Here they were, celebrating the marriage of two women. The marriage of one of their gentle countrywomen to the Katabull. A shape shifter who was as animal as she was human.

Arvon snuck up on him unexpectedly. "A copper for your thoughts."

Tragon all but jumped out of his skin. "She should have been mine, Arvon," he hissed.

"Ah! But she didn't *want* to be yours," Arvon said.

"So I've been told," Tragon said bitterly.

Arvon glared at Tragon's back. Tragon didn't know that Arvon knew about Tarius, but Arvon knew that Tragon knew, and he didn't trust Tragon because of it. Arvon owed Tarius a debt he could never repay, and anything that might cause her a problem he saw as his own threat. He could see Tragon stabbing Tarius as she slept, and he'd told Tarius so. Tarius had just laughed.

"He is my friend, my partner. He wouldn't have been allowed to stay in the academy if it hadn't been for me. He knows that; he told me so himself," Tarius had said.

"You're marrying the woman he loves."

"Thinks he loves. Tragon doesn't really love anyone besides himself. She's beautiful, and he wants to possess her. That's not the same as love."

"And yet you trust this man?" Arvon had said skeptically.

"He knows that I can get him up the ranks just like I kept him in school. He knows that as long as I am alive, he has a better chance of staying alive," Tarius had answered.

Tragon observed the merry makers with no joy, and Arvon, still at his back, whispered in his ear, "Tarius saved my life. If any harm were to come to her, or if her secrets were to suddenly leak out... Well, I wouldn't take too kindly to that. I'd have to take revenge on whoever had caused her harm." Arvon put a meaningful hand on Tragon's shoulder, just to remind him of how much bigger he was than Tragon.

Tragon stiffened. "You know Tarius's secrets?"

"Let's just say that any beast can smell its own kind, and that Tarius isn't the only one who broke the admittance rules." Arvon said and let out a low, not very human growl that made the hair on the back of Tragon's neck stand on end. Arvon walked away, leaving him alone.

The growl was one of the few Katabull traits Arvon had, but Tragon didn't have to know that.

Tarius had taken Jena to a large rock by the creek. There she had made love to her long and slow, but of course still didn't remove her clothes own or allow Jena to touch her.

"Tarius... We are man and wife now, surely..."

"I don't want to risk impregnating you before I go into battle," Tarius said. She'd worked on this excuse for months, and it seemed to her to be a sound one. "I don't want you to go through it all by yourself. Nor do I want to miss the birth of my child. I want to be here for you."

"You wouldn't have to put your seed in me, you could..."

"That is forbidden by my god," Tarius said quickly.

"Then let me find some other way to give you pleasure. Let me give to you what you have given to me."

"Jena... Please, don't ruin everything, Jena." Tarius rose sadly to her feet and walked to the water's edge where she stood and stared into the surface of the water. She swallowed hard, trying to clear the tears that filled her throat. *Damn it, Jena! I want you to touch me so much I hurt, but it can't happen. Why can't you just be happy with what I can give you? Why do you force me to make up more and more and more lies, when all I want to do is to tell you the truth? When all I want to do is love you?*

Jena came up behind her and wrapped her arms around her. She slipped her hands up under Tarius's shirt, running her hands over Tarius's bare stomach. Then she kissed the back of her neck. "Is it wrong to want to please my husband? To want to feel all of his naked body sliding against mine? To feel him inside me?"

You are killing me, Jena! I love you, and you are killing me trying to please me. My god, help me! I love your touch! I want so much more from you. It's good that I'm going away, and the longer I stay away the better. You have ruined me, and now you're driving me crazy.

"Don't I make you happy, Jena?" Tarius asked sadly.

"Oh yes, Tarius, but..."

"Can't you believe me when I tell you that I am happy? That I have everything I need from you?"

"But, Tarius, other men..."

Tarius turned then and looked down at Jena angrily. "When will you learn that I am not other men, Jena? Other men would tell you how to walk, how to talk, what to think, and what to wear. Your pleasure in lovemaking would be the last thing on their minds. If you wanted another man, you should have married another man and left me the hell alone as I begged you to time and time again." Tarius jerked from Jena's grasp and walked into the woods.

Jena picked up her dress, wrapped it haphazardly around herself and went after Tarius. She had to run to catch up.

"Tarius, please. I'm just trying to understand. Just trying to do my duty to you."

"Your duty! Oh how very, very romantic." Tarius spat over her shoulder and sped up, so that Jena had to run to catch up with her.

"Damn it Tarius, you know that's not what I meant," She grabbed Tarius's arm, but he pulled away from her.

"Tarius... please listen. I love you; you're the only one I love. I'm sorry I upset you. I just wish I knew why you're so mad."

Tarius wasn't listening to her, so Jena ran and jumped on his back, knocking them both to the ground. She wrestled Tarius around till the wedding dress was tangled around them both, and she was sitting straddling Tarius's hips. "I said I'm sorry, you hard-headed Kartik bastard!"

Tarius laughed and Jena relaxed. He was going away in less than a week. The last thing Jena wanted was to fight with him. She stretched out on top of him, kissing his lips gently at first and then with more passion. "I have no complaint with you, my husband. I just don't ever want you to have any complaint with me. I want you to be fulfilled by me and only by me."

"I promised you today, Jena," Tarius grabbed the coin that hung around Jena's throat now instead of his own. "I will not touch another, and no other shall touch me. I gave you my word, and I meant it. I take my pleasure from touching you, from holding you. Your kiss. Your gentle caresses, it's so much more than I had ever hoped for. It's enough for me, why can't it be enough for you?"

Jena nodded silently, convinced at least for the moment.

"Perhaps we should get back to our party," Jena said with a smile.

"Perhaps we should have our own party here."

They had met the king's carriage and his entourage at the castle and been told their assignment. Tarius and Tragon, and of course this meant Harris as well, were to ride ahead of the carriage. It was a high honor. It was also incredibly dangerous, as it was the first place the enemy would hit if they were ambushed.

As they started down the road, Tragon told Tarius as much, feeling less charitable towards her by the minute.

Tarius was silent. She wore the hated chain and the too thick, too long, too dull blue gambeson. She wore her own helmet, a metal skullcap atop black leather covered with chain mail on the sides and back. She also of course carried her own sword instead of the standard issue.

Harris rode respectfully behind his knight and his Sword Master partner in spite of Tarius's protests. This was for him a day that he had never dreamed would come. He was riding off to do battle in the king's retinue. He, an orphaned, crippled boy, was squire to the fiercest knight in the kingdom.

By the end of the day Harris was feeling somewhat less triumphant. His butt hurt, and he felt like his balls were going to be pushed up through his lap if his horse went into a rough trot even one more time. Finally, they stopped to make camp for the night. The king's herald rode up to Tarius.

"Sir Tarius, the king requires your presence."

Tarius followed him back to the king's carriage.

Seeing Tarius outside, the king stuck his head unceremoniously out one of the windows.

"Good Sir Tarius, do me the honor of acting as captain of my retinue," Persius said.

"Sire, with all due respect, I must tell you that I am not qualified for such a task. This being in fact my internship..."

"'If you want to be safe, follow the man who bears the most scars,'" Persius quoted. He smiled at Tarius' shocked look. "I am not without knowledge of the world beyond my kingdom. Wisdom is wisdom, whether it be Kartik or Jethrik. Now, please take command of these men and of this camp."

"As you wish, Sire," Tarius said.

He positioned the king's carriage, the cooks' wagon, and the provision wagons in the center and placed the camp around them. Then he ordered the horses staked out on rope tethers around the edge of the encampment. There was much grumbling, but no one said anything directly to Tarius. Tarius assigned watches. Now this Tragon could handle. At Tarius's side he wielded nearly as much power as did Tarius, and Tarius always listened to his suggestions even if she didn't often use his ideas. When he barked out orders at Tarius's side people listened just as they would listen to Tarius. He didn't even have to take care of his own horse, as caring for his and Tarius's horses fell on the head of her squire, Harris. So Harris tended the stock while they were busy setting up camp.

It was almost dusk when he and Tarius headed for the cooks' wagon where the king sat in his portable throne.

The man who no doubt should have been captain of the retinue looked at Tarius. "So, boy, tell me why you have laid the camp out in this mess?"

"Connar, a little respect for Sir Tarius is in order," the king ordered.

"Yeah, that's, Sir Boy, to you," Tarius said without a smile. She took her helmet off and threw it top first on the ground as was her habit. "High rank in the middle out to lowest rank, which would be the horses. Horses have excellent hearing, dislike unfamiliar noises, and are usually skittish in unfamiliar surroundings. So, if the horses start making noise on any side, you go check for trouble. Also because the horses are tethered on individual lines instead of in a rope pen or on a single tether, it would be very hard for anyone to steal all our horses at one time."

"But it means you have to feed and water each horse individually," Connar complained.

"Takes time I admit, but it's not an impossible task, and this way if there should be a disease in one horse, it's not as likely to spread to the others. If you're not pleased, you may do it your own way tomorrow night," Tarius said. She'd really rather not make such decisions. However she thought this configuration, one she had learned not from the Katabull but from the Kartiks, was by far the best and most easily defended.

"Connar would not dare to usurp the authority of the man who his king put in charge, would you, Connar?" the king asked pointedly.

"Not at all, Sire. Mere curiosity, that's all," Connar said quickly. He looked at Tarius. "Your plan seems a sound one, and since I am to take the first watch I think I will retire for a short nap."

He walked away, and the king motioned for Tarius to come closer. When Tragon started to come with her, he waved a dismissive hand at him. Tarius covered the distance quickly.

"Tarius, when one is in command one does not ask people what they want to do. One tells them what they will do."

"I'm afraid I'm not very comfortable giving people orders," Tarius said. She sat on a rock and looked at the king. "The men don't like me, and I don't like being in command."

"Well, you'd better get used to it, Tarius. You are a fair man, with good common sense, and a hell of a fighter. You are a leader of men; of this I have no doubt. I have total faith in you," Persius spoke softly. "Besides, my personal retinue has forgotten their place. They have become sluggish and out of shape. I figure by putting an out-country freak such as yourself in charge they will all be humbled. Maybe they'll even work toward improving themselves so they won't continue to be shown up."

The next day when they rode out, gone were Tarius's issued armor and clothing. Once again she was clad in studded leather and gaudy Kartik gambeson. The only thing she had kept from the Jethrik armor were the pauldrons, which she tied on her gambeson. Around her waist she wore a blue and white sash to show her loyalty to the king, but other than that she looked just like what Persius said he wanted—an out-country freak. Intimidating to the men she commanded, and hopefully terrifying to their enemies.

"That's damn cheeky of you," Tragon said riding along side Tarius. "You could at least *pretend* to want to be like the rest of us."

Tarius smiled back at him undaunted. "I want to be me."

"No you don't, or you wouldn't be here at all. You'd be home darning some man's socks." Tragon realized just how resentful he felt when he saw how angry Tarius looked. Her dark features seemed darker, and he could swear that just for a second her eyes went to their Katabull state.

When she spoke to him, her voice was hardly more than a hissed whisper, and yet he had no problem hearing her at all. "If you ever say anything like that again, I'll split you."

The way she was looking at him, he had no doubt that she would, too. He had better hide his resentment and watch his mouth. He needed Tarius as an ally. As a friend she would let no one touch him. On the other hand, if he gave her any indication that he wanted to disclose what she was, he had no doubt she'd kill him just as easily as she would any other man.

He'd seen her kill only twice, but knew it didn't bother her. Knew it didn't make her lose sleep or worry her in the slightest. Tarius was a killer. You didn't want to make an enemy of someone who killed as easily as Tarius did.

He had to rid his mind of the hateful thoughts he was harboring for Tarius. He could ride Tarius's coattails to get where he wanted to go. If she was discredited, if she was found out, then she couldn't help him. Worse than that, if she were discredited, he would be as well. That was if Tarius would let him live at all.

He took a deep breath. "I'm sorry, Tarius. I'm afraid I'm still having trouble with the whole Jena thing. I know it's not your fault that she loves you, but I can't blame her, so I blame you, even though I know it makes no sense."

Tarius nodded, seeming to calm. "I think I know how you feel. If things were reversed I suppose I would feel the same way that you do."

Harris rode up on Tarius's left, moving from his position behind them. "Tarius?"

"Yes Harris."

"I thought you would want to know... I heard many of the men speaking against you last night. They think it is wrong that the king has put you over them. They say they'll not take orders from you for long, and..."

"Harris, my friend, know this... Men talk crap. They talk crap to impress each other, and they would talk crap about whoever was running things. They talk crap about the king when they dare. I'm just an easy target because I am strange to them," Tarius said. "Listen closely and inform me of what you hear and who is saying it. But let them talk all they want to. If I know who is talking, I won't be surprised if they should decide to follow their words with actions, but take heart my friend. The more they talk, the less likely it is that they will do anything."

Harris nodded, perfectly convinced of Tarius's wisdom.

About an hour later, the road narrowed and they were traveling through a much more densely wooded area. Tarius knew this meant there was a greater chance of ambush. Not that she really anticipated that a troop of Amalites would have gotten so far inland.

About two hours later she smelled smoke followed quickly by a smell that had been permanently etched in her memory so that there could be no doubt.

"Company! Stop and arm," Tarius screamed.

She sniffed the air; she could smell them. She truly had not expected them to be so far in country. She looked around, but saw no sign of them in the trees and no sign of them hiding in the bushes around the road.

"Keep watch," she ordered Tragon, and she went back to talk to the king.

"Sire."

He looked out the window of his carriage.

"I smell smoke and Amalites on the air coming from the north."

"There is a small village north of here," one of the king's councilors said from within the carriage as he looked at a map.

"Permission to take half the men and ride out to investigate," Tarius said.

"Permission granted," Persius said.

Tarius immediately started barking out orders. Who would go with her, who would be staying to guard the king and where they should position themselves. Then Tarius gathered her forces and rode off in the direction of the smoke at full gallop.

Harris was amazed at how the same men who had been talking "crap" about Tarius now fell in behind him, listening and obeying his every command. Harris even forgot his own sore and swollen balls as he raced his horse to keep up with Tarius.

As they got closer they could hear the screams of the villagers. Tarius split her forces in half, sending half of them to the other side of the village under the command of none other than Gudgin. Harris noticed Tragon hung back now, and let Tarius take the lead himself. Harris spurred his horse on. If Tragon would abandon Tarius, then Harris would fill the gap.

Tarius would attack from this end of the village first, and the other forces would close in as the Amalite horde tried to retreat, thus trapping them in the middle—hopefully on the outskirts of the village.

As they came into the clearing around the village, Harris saw that many of the structures were on fire. He also saw the horsemen and foot soldiers and heard the screams, but it wasn't till they were in the village itself that he saw for the first time how hateful were these Amalite scum. An old woman was running from the raiders trying to get to cover. One of them cut her across the middle and then trampled her beneath his horse's hooves as she lay dying. They were upon the scum before they were aware of it, their own carnage blocking out the noise made by Tarius and his men. Tarius broke from the rest, racing forward with his sword drawn. He dove into the fray first and had killed three of the Amalites before they were even aware of his presence. He killed four more before the rest of them even engaged. Then he dismounted, jumping first on his saddle and then flipping through the air to land on his feet. Harris saw the battle rage on his mentor's face, and for a second he froze. This was it. This was real, no fake battle with fake swords. He pulled his blade and ran into the fray. Tragon was nowhere in sight, and Tarius needed someone to watch his back.

Harris now knew that they must win. Tarius was right; they had to drive the Amalite horde back and utterly destroy them so that none of them would ever again darken the land. Harris saw dead villagers everywhere he looked, so that when he killed his first Amalite it didn't really even faze him. It didn't register when he killed his second or his third, either. They were to him like the bottles he had lined up on the fence to try and hit with a slingshot when he was a boy. Targets, no more and no less.

Tarius ran through the Amalites on foot, making it hard for Harris to keep up with her. She'd run up on a horseman, he'd lean down to run her through, and when he did she would easily duck his blow and drive her blade up into his heart. Then she'd jerk him off his horse and go after another. When the ground troops ran up, she was ready for them. She let out a scream that made the hair on the backs of necks everywhere stand on end, and then she ran at them kicking and slashing her way through, killing a man with every blow. She shouted orders to the troops behind her.

"Move up! Move up! Drive them out of the village!"

The Amalite horde ran in terror before her, and when they ran out of the village on the other side Gudgin's troop was waiting for them. The battle lasted for only an hour, and when it was ended every last man of the Amalites had been killed. They had lost four men, and three more were badly wounded. In the village more than half the villagers had been killed.

Gudgin rode up to Tarius and dismounted. He looked at Tarius and slowly he started to smile, then he ran up to Tarius and embraced her.

"You are a crazy bastard, Tarius, but thank the gods that you ride with us!" Gudgin released Tarius and he slapped her on the shoulder. "Never was there a fighting man such as you, my brother."

"We could not have left here victorious if not for your leadership this day, good brother. Go back with your men and get the king. Me and mine will help these good people tend to their dead," Tarius said.

Gudgin nodded, mounted his horse and left.

Tarius started barking out orders and soon all were busy either taking weapons and armor from the corpses of their enemies, or helping the villagers put out fires and bury their dead. They threw the bodies of the stripped Amalites unceremoniously into wagons. They would be taken far away from the village and dumped unburied in the woods. To the Jethrik this was a sign of great disrespect and loathing.

After the battle, Harris, like a good squire, had gone off to find Tarius's horse. It wasn't till he returned with the horse to see Tarius and another fellow throwing a dead Amalite into a wagon that it all started to hit him. Tarius turned to face him, and there was not one spot larger than an inch on Tarius's entire body that wasn't covered in blood. He looked at Harris and smiled, nodding his head in appreciation over the horse. He looked to Harris like some ghoul from a picture book.

All around them the villagers cried. There was not one of them who hadn't lost a good friend or a family member.

He saw again the body of the old woman he had seen killed by them. He looked from the woman to Tarius. "I had thought... I thought you were exaggerating about them, but the minute I saw them I knew how hateful they were."

"They kill because they think that's what their gods want them to do. They think that anyone who does not believe in the same gods that they do is evil and deserving of death. There could not be any more dangerous thought. There has never been a more hateful people. They kill everything that moves, and then they burn everything else. They destroy the world and everything in it for their gods' sake."

Harris nodded. If Tarius's words were meant to somehow comfort Harris, they did not. They did, however, reinforce in him a conviction to fight beside Tarius and rid the world of these bastards forever.

The king and his entourage rode in. Persius got out and walked among the people. After several minutes of looking, he finally found Tarius. "What a horrible slaughter!"

"Yes. And totally uncalled for," Tarius's voice was almost, but not quite angry.

"What do you mean?" Persius asked.

"There were twice as many villagers as there were Amalites. If they but had steel in their hands and had been trained to fight, they might have driven the horde off themselves. As it is, if we hadn't come along when we did, they would all be dead and the Amalites would have gained yet another stronghold in your country."

"What would you suggest?" the king asked.

"Only that you do this. Take one swordsman of any skill at all and send him to each village. Send him with weapons of any quality—anything is better than nothing, even farm implements can be used as weapons in trained hands—use the weapons we take from fallen Amalites. Then have him train the villagers. Let each village erect a watchtower and let them assign watches as we do in Kartik. Then your army will be as none before, for it will include every man in the kingdom, crippled or whole. In this way we can keep the Amalites from creeping into the center of the country. Keep them from burning our crops. Instead of it taking weeks for us to react to an attack, we would react immediately. Instead of your subjects cowering in fear, they could rest in the knowledge that they can defend themselves and their lands."

"You have given good council once again, Tarius. As you have spoken, so I will do. I will send a rider now to carry this decree back to the castle and then to issue it throughout the country. Who should I put in charge of the task?" He wasn't really asking, just thinking out loud, but Tarius answered him anyway.

"Who better than my own father-in-law, Darian, to choose swordsmen to train your subjects? And who better than Justin to help procure weapons?"

"It shall be done," Persius said. "Now if you would, Sir Tarius, please go wash the blood from your body. You look like a little Kartik devil."

"As you wish, Sire."

———◆———

Persius went to his carriage and crawled in. He got out a piece of parchment and wrote out his orders along with a brief account of what had happened. Then he sealed it with his signet ring and sent it off with one of his heralds, sending along a swordsman for his protection.

Then he leaned back in his seat. Never had he seen such carnage and death. He should have come to the front sooner. He'd had no idea the Amalites had been able to break this far in country. All his life he'd been sheltered from the brutality of war. Oh, he'd been trained to fight from a very early age, but till now there had never been any need for him to put his own person in danger.

"She gives very good council," Old Hellibolt said from his seat across from the king.

The king took in a deep breath. "Tarius is a man, Hellibolt. He comes from out-country, from Kartik, that is why he looks so feminine. But he is a man, a strong man. He is married to Darian's own daughter."

"Then Darian's daughter has married a woman," Hellibolt said conversationally.

Once again, Persius began to wonder why he had even bothered to carry the old charlatan along with him. True, the troops were always more at ease when they believed a soothsayer was with them predicting the way they should go, but Hellibolt seemed to get crazier by the minute. Tarius had just won them a major victory. He had been totally unconcerned about being covered in blood. He was the brightest thinker

Persius had ever known, and this old fool thought Tarius was a *woman*! He didn't want any more fuel added to the thoughts that already ran through his mind concerning the lad.

"You are a crazy old man," Persius said.

Hellibolt laughed. "You make a woman who is also a creature of the night the chief of your army. You knight it and take its council, and you call *me* crazy."

"Enough, old man, I'll not have you soil the reputation of such a fine fighter. Such a fine *man*," Persius started.

"I'm not trying to soil *her* reputation," Hellibolt interjected.

Persius glared at him. *If Tarius were a woman...* He shook the thought from his head. "Do not interrupt me, and never again speak aloud your evil accusation. To think a woman could fight better than any man in the kingdom is absurd. Keep your idiocy to yourself, or I'll have you beheaded."

Hellibolt shrugged. "As you wish. I will never again talk about Tarius's lineage or gender."

"Take care you do not, old man," Persius spat.

———◆◆◆———

Tarius followed the creek up a good long way. She sat on a rock and held her hands to keep them from shaking. After looking carefully around, she took off her leather, and after checking one more time she climbed into the creek. The day was warm and the water even in the shade was refreshingly crisp but not cold. The water ran red with blood, but not one drop of it was hers. She hadn't gotten so much as a scratch. She pulled her leather into the water and washed it. Then she got out of the water and pulled it on wet. Even if she had brought other clothes with her, she still would have had to wear the wet leather because it would shrink if she wasn't wearing it to keep it stretched to the right size. Of course this way, even with her undergarments, it would chafe her skin raw in the seams. She cleaned her sword and her sheath, then she sat down on a rock and used leaves to dry her blade. Her hands still trembled, and her mind raced back to the battle, playing back the moments that had happened too fast to be comprehended and processed at the time. It took longer to recall it all than it had taken to do it.

She was a little shocked. All this time she had thought that killing a bunch of Amalites would make her feel better about what they had done to her parents. To her people. She had thought that revenge would lift the anger away from her like a veil. But killing them hadn't changed the way she felt about being forced to live a lie, or how she felt about losing her parents. It didn't erase the vision etched in her mind of her Pack being slaughtered.

She realized only now that this was a pain that could never go away.

That no amount of killing, no amount of revenge, was going to remove the images. The memories of having the sword drawn across her throat, of being left for dead in a stack of bodies, the unforgettable stench of death. These were her legacy, a part of her. To lose it would be like cutting away a limb. They were part of her, as much a part of her as being Katabull. They had shaped her to the person she was as much as being female and loving women had done.

It was a horrible past, a past she wouldn't wish on anyone, but it was hers. It belonged to her, and it was the one thing no one could take away.

She looked at the creek. The water ran clean again. She was clean and her weapon was clean. In a few weeks the village would be repaired and from the outside no one would guess that a great slaughter had taken place there. But the hearts of every one of them who survived this day would remember. Not a one of them would ever be quite the same as they had been when the Amalite horde decided to descend on a village of helpless farmers and ranchers.

Many of those children, the ones that lived, would grow up as she had; parentless, with visions of death in their heads. They would learn to hate before they had even really learned to love, and they would never feel safe again.

And this cycle would never end till the last Amalite priest was laid to rest beside the last Amalite soldier.

She had been gone too long. There was work to do, and if she was to give out orders she must also share in the work. She got up and started the long walk back. Now the body started to ache at the work it had done.

No one respected a leader who never got their hands dirty, who put themselves up on a pedestal above others. If Persius wanted the real respect and admiration of his countrymen, he would crawl out of his carriage and start carting around dead bodies. He would help dig graves.

Riding into battle in a suit of armor no arrow could pierce, surrounded by men sworn to die before they let a hand fall on him, might look a grand gesture to a fool, but any person worth his salt could see through it. It was a show put on to boost moral. Nothing more and nothing less. Persius would sit on a horse twice as good as any of theirs. He would be surrounded by the best fighters in the kingdom. Then he would ride onto the battlefield where he could be seen by the most people, and he would bark out a few orders from the safety of his gauntlet of men. The troops would be heartened, and then he would quickly ride off the field before the real battle started. He would get in his carriage and go home to await the outcome.

The troops' moral might be boosted for a day, maybe even a week, but no more. But if he would get out and dig the latrine, then they would take heart. If he would shit in the latrine instead of in a china pot that someone else had to dump for him, then the men would believe he was one of them. They would feel good about fighting for the kingdom.

Grand gestures didn't win Tarius's respect, not the way small ones did. She looked at the beaded necklace around her throat and then quickly tucked it into her armor. Not to hide it, but so that it would be safe. She thought of Jena. She had missed her the moment she'd left her line of sight.

She tried not to think of all the many things that could go wrong with her relationship with Jena. She fantasized that she told Jena everything, and that Jena didn't care. That she said she had always known.

Too soon, she was back at the village and back to work. Tragon joined her. He hadn't bathed as she had, and yet he was relatively blood free. She hadn't seen him throughout the battle, but she guessed from the too clean look of him that he had hung back. She liked Tragon, but was all too aware of his many faults. She knew she couldn't count on him to watch her back. Harris, yes, but not Tragon. Tragon would always put his own life over any others.

Which was just one of many reasons he never would have made a good mate for Jena. When guilt poured into her brain like rain on her head she would have to remember this fact.

Harris ran up to work with her, and she realized he was almost as bloody as she had been. "There's a creek," she nodded with her head in the general direction. "Go and clean up; you'll feel better."

Harris nodded quietly and was obviously releaved to be able to get away for awhile.

"Listen up and pass the word on," Tarius yelled. "If you feel you need to wash, there is a creek on the other side of the village. Wash up, but be quick about it! I want the dead out of the village by nightfall." Tragon started to leave with several others, and Tarius caught hold of his arm. "You're hardly dirty at all, my brother."

"Is that a crime, Tarius?" Tragon asked with a smile.

"Depends on why," Tarius hissed. "Certainly you're not dirty enough to need a wash down. Help me with the bodies."

An angry retort died on Tragon's lips. He knew why he wasn't bloody, and so did Tarius. Yes, he had hung back, but what did it matter? Tarius was a one-woman slaughtering machine. Why should he risk life or limb when all he had to do was get out of Tarius's way and go in to finish off the ones she hadn't quite killed? There was no crime in playing it safe, and with Tarius taking all the risks, well, it just wasn't necessary for him to do so to make a name for himself. Especially since Harris seemed more than willing to take his place on the front line.

And if Tarius died... Well, Tragon would be there to comfort her widow.

Of course it would be better if she died towards the end of the war instead of the beginning. Better if she could protect him as long as possible.

Tragon answered Tarius in a lowered voice, eyes on the ground. "I'm sorry, Tarius. I'm... I'm ashamed to say that I was scared. I had never seen anything like that before. By all rights, we should be on our internship, handling disputes between villagers and minor skirmishes. I froze for a minute; I was scared nearly to death."

Tarius was a woman, and she had the compassion of a woman in most cases. Tragon hoped to appeal to the woman Tarius pretended not to be. He wasn't entirely successful.

"There's nothing wrong with being afraid, Tragon. We have all known fear. The only dishonor comes from what you do with your fear." She grabbed his chin and forced him to look at her. "Abandon me again, Tragon, and you had best pray that you never need me at your back, because I will not be there."

Tragon nodded silently. They went back to work moving bodies.

Tarius gently dressed the wound on Harris's arm. It was deep, but not bad enough to need sewing. He'd cleaned up as they all had, but his youthful features had lost the look of innocence that had lit up his face only a few short hours ago.

"You all right?" Tarius asked.

Harris nodded silently.

"You can tell me, you know," Tarius said finishing the last knot in the dressing. "Your arm will heal. You do know that, don't you?"

"I know... but... The Amalites! It's as if... I don't know how to put it. It's as if they don't feel our pain. As if they kill us as easily as they would slaughter sheep," Harris said. "These people held no weapons. They couldn't defend themselves. What good does it do the Amalites to kill them?"

"My father told me many truths, but there was one that stood out beyond all the rest. He said, 'Of two things take heed. A man who believes he is right, and proving that man wrong.' They need no other reasons."

Harris nodded, although he wasn't exactly sure what Tarius meant. They were alone at their tent. The other soldiers, even Tragon, were talking to each other and reliving the day's events. Naturally, each one was making himself sound better than the one before. Harris had tried to fit in, to get into their groups and talk, but they moved quickly away. In fact he noticed that they treated him almost exactly as they treated Tarius. He figured he was in good company, but no one liked to be shunned, and he didn't really understand it. Tarius was the hero of the day, and yet they avoided him as if he had plague.

"Why don't they like us?" Harris asked in a quiet voice. For the first time that day he sounded like the mere youth that he was.

Tarius looked across the camp at where Tragon talked easily with a group of the men. "I know how you feel. Let's tell it as it truly is but keep it between ourselves. Tragon was a coward today. Yet he is accepted and we are not. All because we were born different." Tarius lay down on the ground close to the fire, and she stared across the flames at Harris. "We have to earn every shred of respect we get because in their own way they are no better than the Amalites. They also despise people that aren't like them. I'm out-country, and I have strange ways they don't understand or respect. You are a cripple, yet you and I are better fighters than any of them. In their heads, we should be barely competent, so the fact that we are better than them mocks their beliefs, mocks their training."

"You are better, Tarius, but not me. I'm not better than they are! I couldn't be..."

"Do you doubt my judgment, Harris?"

Harris laughed. Tarius was his mentor, but he was also his only true friend, and Tarius did not intimidate Harris. "I doubt your eyesight. Anyone can see that my skill does not match that of any Sword Master..."

"Do you think a title makes you a better fighter?" Tarius looked at him and smiled. "Their titles make them quit trying, quit improving. You are constantly improving, constantly working at improving."

"But I can't run or jump like them..."

"You have learned to fight. You don't need to be able to run as fast or jump as high because you, my friend, have learned how to stand your ground and fight," Tarius assured him. "Now I'll hear no more talk of them being better. They are not better fighters than you, and they are certainly not better men."

Harris blushed red with embarrassment at Tarius's praise.

"Come, let Tragon and those idiots stay up talking and drink themselves sick. When the morning comes and we break camp to start out again, they'll wish they had as few friends as we do."

When they were settled into their tent, swords by their sides, Harris found that he was more tired than he thought he was. His muscles ached, and the wound started to throb but wasn't really painful. He yawned.

"Tarius?"

"Yes?"

"Do you miss her?" Harris asked.

"Yes. I miss Jena very much," Tarius said, feeling in that moment as if her heart were being ripped from her chest.

"I know you miss *her*. I didn't mean Jena. I meant... I meant your mother," Harris asked in a hushed whisper. "I was very little when my mother died, too. I still miss her. Is that wrong?"

"No, it's not wrong. I still miss my mother, and I always will. But that dreadful hole that was ripped in my soul when the Amalite bastards killed her was filled completely when I fell in love with Jena, when she fell in love with me. When you fall in love, you'll feel whole again as well."

"Maybe, but where will I find a girl like Jena?" Harris was only half teasing. Jena had been like a sister to him, but that didn't mean that he hadn't had a crush on her. He didn't think he could be happy with any fine lady who never took her shoes off or wrestled. He told Tarius as much.

"Go to sleep you rogue. You only make me miss her more," Tarius said.

Harris fell to sleep almost the moment he relaxed, but sleep did not come as easily to Tarius. She tossed and turned and was still awake when Tragon came back to the tent hours later. He smelled like bad rum and smoke, and from the way he fell into his bedroll she guessed he was drunk. He more passed out than fell to sleep. Doubtless, the villagers had treated the soldiers to some of their liquor stores. She supposed as captain she should have ordered them to sleep at a decent hour and rationed or even disallowed the alcohol all together. However then they'd all hate her even more. So let them drink themselves into a coma and stay up all night. She decided to start out at a quick pace in the morning and taper off towards midday.

She fell asleep thinking of Jena and woke in the morning with a deep longing that she couldn't shake. As expected, half the camp had a hangover, and it took them a little longer to get on the road. This was her excuse for double pacing the horses. Every once in awhile you could hear one of them retching, and she was glad to be riding in front. Tragon was a delightful shade of green, and after the first hour he succumbed. He reined his horse to a stop, jumped down, ran into the woods and started retching. The king's carriage called for the procession to stop, and Tarius was called back to the carriage.

"We're moving a bit slowly aren't we?" Persius asked.

"I... I'm trying to keep us at a medium pace, but several of the men—including my own partner—have fallen very ill," Tarius said.

Persius smiled knowingly. "Too much drink?"

"Aye, Sire," Tarius said.

"You should have ordered them to be moderate and to turn in early," Persius said disapprovingly. "It's your job to keep them in line, Tarius. Don't be afraid to give them orders."

"I thought perhaps that if they lived through this, there would be no need for any orders concerning drinking or long nights," Tarius said. "If I'm wrong, I will make it an order."

Persius nodded approvingly.

They rode on.

"You're a Kartik bastard," Tragon said to Tarius when he had endured yet another hour at a double time.

"Aye, but I'm a sober Kartik bastard," Tarius laughed.

"Serves you right for snubbing us," Harris added.

"Don't you start in on me, you insolent child!" Tragon groaned and leaned into his horse's neck.

"You'll get no sympathy from me. You have done this to yourself," Tarius said. "Perhaps you and your boyfriends will use a little more temperance in the future."

Tragon realized something then. "You don't drink, do you, you awful bastard?"

"No," Tarius said. "If you were me, would you drink?"

Tragon thought about it and decided that, no, he would not. If you were Tarius, and you got drunk, you might accidentally say or do something that would tell the world that you were a girl. Worse yet, you might get mad, turn into a beast, and rip some poor drunk's face off.

"No, I suppose I wouldn't," Tragon said.

Harris silently wondered why.

7

It took them the better part of two months to get to the front, mostly because they kept running into troops of Amalites. None of their scouts had reported activity so far in, so they'd had no idea how close the country was to being entirely overrun by the Amalites.

Persius was appalled. They had told him it was bad on the front, but they hadn't said a damn thing about the bastards being spread throughout the countryside. By the time they got to the front they had killed over a thousand Amalites, and had lost over one hundred of their own men. Tarius had replaced them with men from the villages they passed through, taking men who wanted to fight and were big enough and strong enough to handle themselves in battle. Tarius assigned one of the newcomers to one of the better swordsmen in the company to train. He outfitted them with the armor and weapons of the men they were replacing. At first there had been a great outcry from the men. It was customary to bury these things with the fallen soldier.

Persius himself had called Tarius to one side when he had first tried to implement this practice and explained the tradition to him.

"Sire, with all due respect, the Amalites are over-running your country," Tarius said. "My own sword was built by the hand of my dead father. In its handle is a finger which once graced my very hand. Yet should I fall in battle, I would not want my blade to be retired with me. Dead men can't swing steel, and they have no need for armor. Surely my brothers who have fallen would have felt the same way as I do. We are in danger of losing to the Amalites, in which case the whole world will likely be wiped out by them. Let us not let silly customs stop us from wining this war."

Persius then gave the exact same speech, using his own sword—also left to him by his father—as an example. From then on, the men had no problem stripping a dead comrade of his armor and giving it to the first willing man who could wear it.

They handed the spoils gleaned from the Amalites they killed out to the villages they encountered, thus arming still more men. Tarius gave each village a quick lesson in how to use a sword, how to use a club, how to use an ax, how to use a staff. She gave them instructions on how to keep watches, and what to watch for. Then they went on till they came to the next village. It slowed them down, but not too much, and meant that they left an armed and battle-ready countryside behind them and none of the enemy at their backs. Since it was Tarius's own way to come in from behind her opponent as well as in front, she expected the Amalites to try to do the same and she didn't want to find herself walled between two groups of Amalites with no way to retreat.

Persius noticed that the attacks came closer together with every day that they got closer to the front. More and more the attacks were not launched against hapless villages, but were aimed against the king and his entourage. No doubt word had gotten back to the Amalites that the King of Jethrik himself was coming to join the battle with over a thousand well-trained men.

Nothing could have prepared Persius for the actuality of the front. The heavy spring rains had turned everything to mud, and then a long dry spell had baked it dry. Where his men were camped and all across no-man's land, not a blade of grass stood. Even the trees seemed to be in distress. Trenches in the open served as latrines, and the flies and the stench were unbearable. Far in the distance he could see the smoke from the Amalites' campfires.

He got out of his carriage against the advice of council and immediately stepped in a big pile of horseshit. He shook it off his boot and walked up to meet Tarius. All around him the men who had been holding the king's ground set up a great roar, applauding his arrival and bowing to his presence. Persius nodded and waved as he walked up to Tarius who dismounted as he approached.

The stench of death wafted up towards them, and even Tarius was unable to conceal his disgust.

"Well, Sir Tarius, you have not steered me wrong yet. What by the gods do we do now?" Persius asked in a whispered panic.

Tarius looked around surveying all at once the condition of the camp, the condition of the men, and their strategic location to the enemy. He took in a deep breath and shrugged.

"The men are tired and weak from hunger and disease. We are completely in the open here without any cover. The smell is hideous, and in itself would kill morale. I say we wait for cover of darkness and retreat."

"Retreat!" Persius screamed. "Are you mad! To give up more land to..."

"Hear me out. We won't go far—just up to where we can't be seen—back into the woods where it is cleaner. We dig proper latrines and put a good meal in these men's bellies. Then before light we snuff out all our fires. When the Amalites awake in the morning, it will look like we have run off, but we'll be on horseback waiting for them. They will send in scouts of course, and we will quietly kill them and wait. Soon they will believe they have us on the run and come after us with every available man. We will meet them there in the woods with everything we have," Tarius said. "By nightfall we will be able to make camp where they are now."

Persius nodded with a smile. After a moment's thought, he nodded again and patted Tarius on the shoulder. Then he climbed up on top of his wagon, called the troops near and told them of the plan. The men cheered, delighted with such a bright leader.

"Do you ever tire of him taking credit for your ideas?" Harris asked in a whisper.

Tarius smiled. "Not at all. If the plan fails miserably they'll only have one person to blame."

———•◆•———

As soon as it was dark they started the task of moving camp. Tarius delegated authority, gave a bunch of orders, and got everyone moving. In the resulting turmoil, she and Tragon disappeared into the night.

"Do you want to tell me what we are doing?" Tragon asked riding up behind Tarius. When Tarius turned to face him, she was the Katabull, and Tragon almost fell off his horse. "Damn it, Tarius! You scared all hell out of me."

"We go to the enemy's camp. I will make a diversion." She smiled at him then, her long canines shining in the moonlight.

Tragon had forgotten how different she looked and sounded in this state.

"Yeah, I'll just bet you will," Tragon half mumbled. "So, what the hell am I here for?"

"Someone has to watch the horses," Tarius said.

"Why aren't the horses afraid of you? I'm afraid of you, and I'm not a stupid animal," Tragon said.

"Animals aren't stupid; they're simple. They have instincts that you humans have lost. I am the Katabull, as such I am more of their world than I am of yours. They know instinctively that I mean them no harm." She smiled again, and it made the hair rise on the back of Tragon's head. "Believe me, whatever I'm hunting gets plenty scared."

"So, where do I wait with the horses?" Tragon asked. "Because, quite frankly, I think this would be as good a place as any. Right here away from all those big, hairy-assed Amalites."

"Come on," Tarius ordered, and Tragon followed reluctantly. The closer they got to the Amalite camp the more it stank, and the more apparent it became that they weren't in much better shape than the Jethrik camp had been. Death, shit and decay. They were way too close for Tragon's comfort when Tarius finally stopped and dismounted. Tragon followed suit, and Tarius handed him the reins to her horse.

"What are you going to do?" Tragon asked.

She smiled—a look that literally turned Tragon's stomach. "Like I said. Create a diversion."

"A diversion from what?" Tragon asked in a whisper.

"From the fact that we are moving our entire encampment," Tarius hissed. She put the hood on her cloak up and walked towards the camp as if she belonged there. She was almost on the camp when a man keeping guard approached and stopped her spitting out a guttural sentence that no doubt asked her to give her name rank and purpose.

Tarius looked up at him and smiled. He almost had a chance to scream before she grabbed him by the hair of his head and dragged a dagger across his throat. She moved the rest of the way into camp unmolested, not really too big a surprise considering that the cloak she was wearing had been stripped from a dead Amalite. She walked right up to the fire where several men were warming themselves, her head down. She listened to them talk, not understanding a word they spoke, but understanding the emotion behind the words. Suddenly a man touched her arm, shaking it. She realized that one of them must have asked her a question. She removed the cloak in one smooth gesture and raised her head. The Amalites screamed. There were few things they feared as much as the Katabull. This was why they had tried to hunt them to the last child.

They ran away from her rather than at her, so she drew her blade and dove on them, chasing them through the camp, killing anyone she touched. She was the Katabull now, more animal than human, and an unbeatable force. She could see better than them, hear better than them, run faster, jump higher, and was ten times as strong. She grabbed a log from a fire on the unburned end and started igniting anything that would burn.

A man charged her with a glaive, and she threw the burning stick at him, catching his shirt on fire. He dropped the glaive and ran away screaming. Tarius sheathed her sword and grabbed the huge glaive. Then she started taking apart the rest of the camp with it, killing anyone who got close enough. When she tired of this, she dropped the weapon and tore through the camp grabbing screaming men and snapping their necks and slinging them aside like so much cordwood.

Then the first of the crossbow bolts whizzed past her, and she knew it was time to retreat.

———◆•◆———

From where he stood with the horses, Tragon could see the fires and hear the terrified scream of "Katabull!" as it was yelled throughout the camp. He could hear the sound of men dying. Occasionally he caught a glimpse of Tarius running amuck through the camp. Then suddenly she was at his side, covered with blood. She took the reins from his hand, mounted and was gone before he was even on his horse.

———◆•◆———

"By the gods! What is happening at the Amalite camp?" one of the captains asked.

"Tarius said he and his partner would create a diversion," Persius said with a smile. "It would appear that they have done so. Tell the men to work faster. We must be entirely moved by daybreak."

The captain moved away to do the king's business, and old Hellibolt took the captain's place at the king's side. "So, how do you suppose young Tarius is creating this... diversion?"

"What have I told you, old man? I'll hear none of your lies concerning Tarius. Besides which I don't care how he's doing it as long as it is effective."

If Tarius had been in her human form the night before, she would have awakened with stiffness in her joints. But she hadn't been human last night, and the only after effect of all that physical activity was the metallic taste of fresh blood still lingering in her mouth. She got up and took a long drink of water the minute she stepped out of the tent. Her leather was tight from the soaking she had given it last night washing off the blood, so she found some oil and rubbed it on her leather wherever she could reach.

"So, Tarius, do you ever take your clothes off?" It was Gudgin who asked the question. He wasn't trying to make her angry, in fact she and Gudgin had become rather close. He was a good leader and took her orders without question. Gudgin was ribbing her because he liked Tarius, it was his way of showing his acceptance of the foreigner.

"Not even to make love," Tarius answered, and Gudgin laughed.

"Quite some diversion you made for us last night. Care to tell me just what you and your partner did?"

"Just snuck in and started some tents on fire. Easy enough done. We were in and out before they were even aware of what was happening," Tarius said.

"So, do you think the king's plan will work?" Gudgin asked.

Tarius nodded. "Oh, aye, it seems a fine plan."

Tragon pulled himself out of the tent just as Harris ran over with a plate full of food for Tarius. Tarius thanked him and sat on a nearby rock. Tragon looked expectantly at Harris who in turn gave him a 'you've got to be kidding' look.

Tarius had almost finished eating when a page came running up as if a demon were on his tail.

"Sir Tarius! Amalite scouting teams approach. What are your orders?"

Tarius didn't look up from her food. "Tell the crossbow men to wait. Hold their fire until the scouts come into the cover of the woods. As soon as they're under cover, the crossbows are to open fire. Make sure none of them make it back out. Capture the horses if possible, but kill them if you have to. Nothing of the Amalites that comes into these woods is to leave to go back to their camp," Tarius ordered, and finished eating her breakfast as the page ran off. She put down her bowl and rose to her feet. She drew her blade and started to sharpen it with a whet stone. When she had run the length of the blade just three times on each side, she put the stone back in her pocket, sheathed her sword and put her helmet on her head.

Tragon took one look at her and swallowed hard. He knew this day there would be a hell of a battle. He knew it because he saw it in the way she sniffed the air, in the way her every muscle seemed to tense up ready to spring. She wasn't worried about the consequences right now, wasn't wondering whether she'd live through the fight, or whether they'd win or lose. In fact, Tragon doubted Tarius ever even considered that she could lose in battle. No, she had none of the nagging fears that the rest of them had. She lived to fight, and in battle none could equal her. She was truly in her element.

Tragon, on the other hand, was one bare nerve. He knew death could be waiting, and that his own indecision would likely bring about his doom. His lack of skill could get him killed. He had no blood lust; he didn't hate the Amalites, and he didn't even understand the reason for the war. So they wanted to take over. Was one king or one religion any worse than another? Tragon didn't think so. Tragon was here for one reason and one reason only. His father and his brothers had been Sword Masters, and he couldn't bring shame on the family name, not and hope to inherit. His father had never respected him, and he badly needed to gain his father's respect even if he gained it falsely, riding on the coattails of the she beast, hiding always in Tarius's shadow, hoping to avoid being hit or killed. Being pulled along in her wake, letting others believe that he was as brave and as powerful as Tarius.

It was only now when he stood poised on the brink of death that he doubted his plan. He might die, and what good was glory or respect or inheritance to a dead man?

"Are you ever afraid?" Tragon asked in a whisper.

"Only of losing Jena. I was afraid of bees until I was stung. I was afraid of snakes until I was bitten, and I was afraid of death until I had killed a man. Now I am not afraid of anything, only cautious. I certainly don't fear the Amalites. I don't fear them at all. My father says a brave warrior knows the day of his death. He told me that the day he died. I will not die this day," she said with the confidence of someone who truly knows their fate and knows that they have not yet finished their required task.

Tragon didn't know that. He didn't feel like he had any duty to perform. This was scary, and he wished with everything in his heart that he possessed even the courage to turn tail and run. At least that would be the truth. The real him. Tarius, he realized, was not the only one who had secrets.

They sat there for an hour, silent and ready. A second Amalite scouting party was sent out and then a third. Both times they dealt with them the same way they had dealt with the first.

Soon the entire Amalite army rode into the clearing, but not at a dead run. Slowly and steadily.

The royal page ran over, and before he could open his mouth to speak Tarius rode towards where the king sat astride his horse in full plate, probably even more uncomfortable than the rest of them. The king was to take the center unit in after Tarius had taken the right flank in. The left flank was to circle around and try to get behind the Amalites. To Tarius, who wished to utterly obliterate her opponent, it was always important that their retreat be blocked.

The page ran along beside Tarius. "The king wants to know when..."

"It's all right, boy. I'll talk to the king myself. Many thanks to you."

Tarius rode up to the king.

"Should we rush them now?" the king asked. "They seem in no hurry to charge us."

"Our archers have been instructed. Let our enemy come into range, we will call on the archers, and many of the Amalites will fall. They will become less sure of themselves. When I ride out, wait till we have engaged, and then bring your men in. When you have engaged the enemy force, Ramses will bring his men around and try to encircle them. The plan is working; why change it now?"

"Exactly right. Return to your place," Persius said with a rough salute. He wasn't used to the armor, and it showed.

"Take good care, Sire. It will do nothing for the men's moral if their king falls in battle."

Persius nodded his head.

Tarius rode back up beside Tragon.

"Why do they..." Tragon swallowed hard. At this point, he just wanted to have it done with. "Why do they not charge? Why do they approach with such caution?"

Tarius moved closer to Tragon; further away from Harris. "Katabull history is handed down verbally from one generation to the next," Tarius said in a whisper that Tragon had to fight to hear. "It is done so meticulously and with such care that very little has been lost. See, the Katabull come not from Kartik but from Amalite." She saw the shocked look on Tragon's face and smiled. "It's true, or at least it is what our history claims. We lived there in peace with the Amalites. Outcasts, we weren't allowed to live in amongst the natives, but we weren't hunted and killed, either. We lived by our laws, we lived on our own, and they left us alone. Much in the way the Katabull are treated today in your own kingdom. Not mistreated really, but not with the same rights and privileges of the common man. Such was our life in Amalite. Then the new religion came to the land. It promised things that people wanted, and it didn't seem to matter to them that everything the priests of this religion said sounded incredible. They wanted the things the religion promised.

"The followers were pests, but no one regarded them as a threat until the king clutched this new religion to his bosom. He made it the religion of the kingdom and ordered all the citizens to obey its oppressive laws. Those that would not were punished or killed. However the Katabull had never had the same religion as the Amalites, and had never been considered part of the people. The king and the priests were hard pressed to find a reason for the Katabull to be forced into conversion. None of them truly believed that we could be part of their religion any way, as we were not, and never had been quite as good as they were. We were also stronger and more powerful than normal men. It would take an army to bring down the smallest Katabull village. The king knew that he did not have the support he needed to raid the Katabull villages. They had never been part of the general populace, so why make them part of it now? They didn't want us to be part of their religion, and yet the fact that we wouldn't bow down to their gods angered them. The fact that we did things that they could not do, things that they wanted to do, made them still madder. The cunning king knew it wouldn't take much to stir the people into war against the Katabull because they already distrusted us.

"One night the king sent a company of men out to steal six children of noble families. They then killed the children, dismembered them, and spread their parts through the streets of a Katabull village. When the noble men found their children's mangled bodies, one of them "recalled" that he had seen a Katabull that night outside his home, and the rest—as they say—is history. The priests announced that their gods had ordered that all Katabull were to be killed. The Amalites descended on the Katabull villages in such numbers that even the Katabull could not fight them and had to flee their land. But they failed their gods when they failed to kill us out. We were forced to live in small packs in every corner of the world, but we were still very much alive.

"From that time till this, the Amalites have believed that if you see a Katabull at night, death will follow in the morning." Tarius smiled at the look of understanding that crossed Tragon's face. "They are afraid because they believe their own lie. They believe that the Katabull brings bad luck for them. Bad luck and death, and this one does. You always hate most that which you fear the most."

Tarius moved again, this time closer to Harris. She pulled her sword, held it above her head, and the archers perched in the trees above them nocked their arrows. She let the blade fall, and the arrows started to fly. The barrage of feathered death seemed to go on forever, but really only lasted a few minutes.

"Now!" Tarius screamed and started out of the tree line at a full gallop, her unit following close behind her, Tragon pulled along in their wake.

The Amalites were bewildered and terrified. They had been winning easily against their battered opponents, but these were not the same timid men they had been fighting. These were beasts. Beasts who hacked through them with a vengeance and surrounded them on all sides.

The first attack brought death from above as arrows rained down on them from archers hidden in the treetops. The first targets struck were the Amalite archers, making it impossible to shoot the crossbowmen from their perches. Then they started to take out their horsemen—especially any that appeared to hold rank. The second attack came suddenly. Mounted horsemen ran at them, hitting their right flank hard and heavy. Then, even as they sent their left flank in to save the right, shield men ran out hitting them in the middle. The shield men were followed by men with pikes and spears, and behind them were the horsemen waiting till their footmen made a hole in the Amalites' shield wall. Then their own shield men opened like a wave and this new batch of horsemen descended on them like locust. When they tried to retreat, they found that another troop of horsemen had come in behind them, and still the enemy's arrows rained down.

They had seen the Katabull at night, and death had followed the next day. As it was written, so mote it be.

Persius' sword and armor were nearly as bloody as that of his chief warlord. Many good men had fallen, but for each one that they had lost, a dozen Amalites lay dead by the sword, the arrow, or the battle-ax. Persius held his sword high above his head and let out a triumphant scream.

Tarius did the same, as did all the men.

Tragon did it, but didn't feel it. He had a nick on his left leg, and he felt sick to his stomach. He looked at his blade; it was bloody, for this time he had truly fought. He'd had to fight just to survive. He'd nearly been killed a dozen times, and he was badly shaken. He got off his horse because he was afraid he was going to vomit. Just as he felt the bile rising in his throat, he saw Harris and Tarius jump off their horses and run to embrace each other. They were real warriors. This carnage was what they lived for. They made him even sicker, and he threw up.

Tarius took three quarters of the able-bodied men and rode on to the Amalites' camp, making sure there was no one to follow them. They couldn't afford to leave the enemy at their back. They spent the remainder of the day caring for the injured, burying their dead, and stripping the Amalites' bodies. The next day they rose early and rode on till almost dark, trying to reclaim as much ground as possible.

On Tarius's instructions their badly wounded were sent to the nearest village to recuperate.

"Why carry the wounded with us?" Tarius had asked Persius. "It does them no good; they can not heal on the battlefield. Load them into wagons with the spoils stripped from our enemies, the weapons, and the armor. Send them to the nearest village to heal. Hand the weapons and armor out to the villagers as payment to nurse our men. Then choose from the villages enough men to make up for those lost in the battle and have them come back to base camp. We will leave a quarter of our men here to deal with the remaining dead, train the new men, and prepare to defend this area should we be pressed back. Meanwhile, let us move on to push the Amalites back. When we have won the next battle, we will pull this detachment of men up behind us to hold our ground. If we need them, they will never be more than a day behind us. We will send pages out four times a day, and they will likewise send them out four times a day. In this way we will always know what is going on there, and they will always know what is going on here. If we feel we need part or all of this force for reinforcements, then we call on them. In the meantime they can be training the new recruits and refining their own skills since we will leave the poorest of our fighting men behind at base camp. Only take care not to let them know that we have chosen them to stay behind because of their lack of skill. Point out to them that it is because they are such grand fighters that we have left them—a much smaller group—to guard our retreat. In this way they will try hard to be worthy of your respect."

Persius gave out the orders, but the plan of action was Tarius's to the very letter.

Three days later they encountered another Jathrik troop. The men were battered and battle weary. They were up against an Amalite force possibly half the size of the one they had slaughtered a few days ago. The men were all sick with fever from the mosquitoes that seemed to be everywhere. This camp, like the other one, was filled with the stench of death and human waste. Again their first order of business was to move camp, but this time they didn't even bother to wait for cover of darkness. Tarius feared that the disease would spread through their own ranks if they didn't move and do it quickly.

It seemed to Tarius that the Jethrik people were idiotic when it came to the simplest things. Yes, it was easier to make camp in the flats. But when it was raining and pooling up all around you, running your own shit out of the latrine trenches and up over your feet for you to walk in, it didn't make any sense. And it was raining again. It was the part of the country they were in—an almost subtropical region. The filthy water had pooled up making a breeding ground for the mosquitoes. It shouldn't have taken a genius to figure out that water didn't pool up on a hillside.

She immediately sent the sick and injured away in wagons bound for the nearest Jethrik village. Any able-bodied men would be sent back to their base camp. They moved and set camp, and the rain poured down.

"Sir Tarius!" She recognized the young soldier as Gudgin's page, Dustan. He held a shovel. "Master Gudgin sent me to ask where you want the latrines dug, Sir."

Tarius rubbed at her wet neck, then she looked at the river and smiled. It ran away from their camp towards the Amalites. There were no Jethrik villages downstream, because the river ran straight into Amalite lands. Tarius spotted a small gully that ran with rainwater; it met the river just past their camp.

"Tell Gudgin to put the latrines on that gully. No digging will be necessary. A nice little surprise for our enemies. Just make sure that everyone knows to get water from *above* the gully, not *below*."

The boy laughed and ran off to get Gudgin.

The portable latrines had been Tarius's idea. She had wanted them mostly because having them made her life easier, but had insisted that having privacy helped with morale. Holes were dug, a box with a hole was set over it, and a four-walled tent with a roof was placed over this. Twenty of them fulfilled the needs of their camp.

Gudgin had at first balked at the idea of being literally "Captain of the Latrine," but soon realized that he could delegate all the work, and that few things were as appreciated by the men as having a good clean place to take a crap. Gudgin followed Tarius's instructions to the letter, making sure that latrines that got full were quickly moved, the dirt piled on high, and a marker placed there.

The Kartiks and even the Katabull knew more about how disease spread than the Jethriks did. Tarius knew that disease could be spread through unchecked waste disposal. Of course, this was what she hoped to accomplish by feeding her enemies their shit.

Gudgin walked up to her then. He smiled. "Just to make sure..."

"Yes, I want them put on the gully."

Gudgin laughed out loud, slapped her on the back and walked away to direct his men.

Because of the rain, and because they were on the side of a hill, this time Tarius put the horses at the bottom of the camp. Thus ensuring that they wouldn't be walking through horse shit, either. There wasn't much fear of attack from above, since their camp spread to the top of the hill.

She was wet. She hated being rained on. Strange, she loved the water as all Katabulls did, but she hated being rained on. Maybe because she had no control over whether she got wet or not.

She made her way down towards the cooks' pavilion and saw that they had succeeded in starting a fire. Several of the Sword Masters, the king and Hellibolt stood under the pavilion out of the rain. They were laughing, and when Tarius joined them they laughed even louder. She looked at herself to see if she was anything but dripping wet.

"Tarius, did you really tell Gudgin to set the latrines on a gully that flows into the river?"

Tarius grinned sadistically. "Let the bastards eat shit."

They laughed still louder. They respected her now, but respecting her didn't mean they liked her, and she knew that many of them didn't and probably never would. She told herself she didn't care whether they liked her or not, but that wasn't exactly true.

At times like this when she felt not just their respect but their approval, she felt warm inside. Warm enough to almost—but not quite—forget that she was wet and cold. She moved closer to the struggling fire.

The head cook himself pushed a bowl of hot soup into her hands, and she took it gratefully.

"Thank you," she said. All the men just stared at her the way they always did when she thanked someone they considered to be an underling or worse yet a servant. She drank the soup down, marveling at the warmth it sent coursing through her body. She chewed the chunks and swallowed. Then she addressed a man named Yolen who had given her a downright scornful look when she had thanked the cook.

"Yolen, answer me this question. Can a hungry man fight as well as one who has eaten?"

"No, of course not."

"What happens to a man who has no food?" she asked.

"Eventually, he starves to death," Yolen said.

"And if some one saved your life in battle, wouldn't you thank him?" Tarius said.

"Why of course, but..."

"So why wouldn't I thank this man, who gives me strength to fight, and who saves my very life on a daily basis? No one in this camp is any more or less important to our effort than are the men who cook and serve our food. They are as heroic as any who take the field in battle. They endure the same hardships and dangers with none of the glory. The least we can do is let them know that they are appreciated." Tarius handed her empty mug back to the cook. "Thank you again." She walked away.

"Why, that insolent little Kartik bastard! I'll have his head!" Yolen muttered and started after Tarius.

Persius grabbed him by the arm. "Tarius has a good point. Let us all thank our cooks and servers."

Yolen looked as if he had been mortally cut, but joined along with the others as they repeated the king's words of thanks.

Tragon had been resting in his tent when Tarius walked in dripping water everywhere. She looked for and found her cloak, and Tragon knew before she looked at him with expecting eyes that he was going to have to go back out into the rain.

Tarius snuck into this Amalite camp more easily than she had the last one. She walked around the camp looking and listening. These men were in as low spirits as their own troop had been earlier today. Their camp was even filthier, and they seemed to have as many if not more sick and wounded. No doubt they had seen the reinforcements and knew they were up against more units.

Tarius went to where the horses were corralled, and she heard the guttural words of an Amalite at her neck. She turned, flinging back her hood and glaring at him. He froze in fear, and she grabbed his head between her hands and hit his head with her own, killing him instantly. She grabbed the logs of the makeshift corral, tore them out of their rope ties and threw them like they were firewood. Then she ran into the corral and chased the horses out. The horses, terrified by the Katabull in full hunting mode, ran kicking and screaming out of the corral. She herded them towards the encampment.

The terrified horses stampeded through the camp at an unstoppable pace, destroying everything as they trampled it. The men panicked, not knowing whether to run for their lives or try to catch their horses. They had barely had time to register the destruction caused by the stampede when the Katabull came ripping into their battered camp, swinging steel and killing everything it touched. When it left, they huddled together like men who had seen their own death.

The screams of terror from the Amalite camp were so loud that they were heard clearly across the killing grounds.

"What the hell is going on over there?" Yolen asked.

"Tarius and Tragon must have gone to scout out the enemy's camp," Persius said. "Tarius simply can't walk away without killing some of them."

Hellibolt stared at the king, but said nothing.

"What?" Persius asked harshly.

"Nothing that you have not forbidden me to say, Sire," Hellibolt said.

"Good, keep your madness to yourself," Persius said.

"Tarius is as black and tough on the inside as his armor is on the out," a Sword Master named Jerrad reflected.

"Exactly," Hellibolt said. Then when he got a glare from the king he added, "Of course, I only mean that in the very nicest way."

Persius smiled. "It suits him. Tarius the Black."

When they woke the next morning it was still pouring. Tarius placed her forces. Shield men first, pikes and spears next, and then the horsemen. They marched at a quick forced march, and by midday they descended on the battered Amalite camp.

The Amalites started to flee, and Tarius changed tactics quickly. "Shield men break!" she screamed, and the shield men broke away to leave openings for the horsemen. The horsemen went after those who were fleeing, and the shield, pike and spearmen got the others. The battle was over in moments.

After they had rested for two days they left the troop that had been there. They would follow just behind the king's army, and the base camp would follow them with pages running from them to the others and back, so that each troop knew exactly what was happening with the others.

They moved to the east as word had reached them that there was a huge Amalite contingent forming on their eastern border. The first week they met two troops of Amalites. Each time they easily cut them down. One day a page brought word that the base camp had run into a troop of Amalites some one hundred strong. They had taken a number of casualties, but had slaughtered the Amalites and were now—after having sent their wounded to the nearest village and picking up new recruits—on their way again.

Also they heard news that one village that had been attacked by marauding Amalites had beaten their attackers back and sent them running.

The trek was long and exhausting. They traveled close to the border, making sure it was clear of Amalites as they made their way east.

The journey tired Tragon. It was slow going, and they moved camp almost daily. It was as arduous on the days they didn't do battle as it was on the days that they did. He was ready to go home—a couple of months ago.

It was close to the end of the day, and as always this meant they were all exhausted and ready to do the work of making camp, get a meal and fall into their bedrolls. Not even Tarius heard or saw them until it was too late. The arrows rained down upon them from above. They were on a narrow section of road and had walked right into an ambush.

Persius was safe in his carriage, but wouldn't be for long if his men fell around him.

"Shields up!" Tarius ordered. "Dismount! Bowmen, take aim and fire on the archers."

For once, Tragon didn't argue. The men had been trained as to what to do in case of just such an attack, and they responded like the well-trained force they were. The horsemen dove off their horses and hid under their bellies while the shield men who marched alongside them put their shields over their heads and moved to help protect the horses and riders. The shutters on the king's carriage were slammed shut.

Tarius had to think quickly. Archers in the trees, and no doubt ground troops and horse men waiting in the tree line. She decided on the one course of action they probably wouldn't count on.

"Foot soldiers, attack!"

The commanders down the line echoed her orders, and the shield, spear, and pike men on each side ran into the trees, leaving the horsemen behind.

"Horsemen, mount up and attack!"

No doubt the Amalites had counted on the fact that they would immediately protect themselves only from the hail of arrows. Then with their bellies wide open, the Amalite sword and pike men could descend on them. Tarius hoped to throw them off by reacting in an entirely different way. With all the men—except those charged with protecting the king's carriage—running into the woods, the archers would have a harder time finding targets, and they would have the element of surprise.

Tarius left her horse behind and ran into the battle, sword in hand. The crossbow men dropped one archer, then another. Then the bodies of Amalite archers started to rain down from above. No Amalite archer could hold a candle to a Jethrikian crossbow. Since the Amalites had no crossbows, they had nowhere near the firepower or the accuracy.

She found Harris and Tragon engaged by three spearmen and a man with a great sword hiding safely behind four scoot-ems.

A spear gaffed deeply into Tragon's leg, and he lost his seat and fell from his horse, losing his sword in the process. The spearman stabbed at his fallen opponent, and Tragon knew that he had breathed his last. From out of nowhere Tarius appeared, and her blade came down on the spear shaft, severing the head from the pole. She slung back with her blade, all but decapitating one of the shield men with the backstroke. Harris jumped off his horse and joined her. Tarius jumped up and kicked at the top of one of the scoot-ems. She rode it and the fellow holding it to the ground, landing on the shield on top of his head. As he lay lifeless under her, she killed the greatswordsman and then, spinning, took out the last shieldman. Then Harris ran in and between them they killed the spear and pike men easily.

They stood there over Tragon, shielding him with their very bodies, fighting over the top of him. Tarius yelled commands, but she did not leave his side. Tragon tried to reach his own sword and could not. He was paralyzed by pain and fear. If they left him, he would be killed, and surely they would have to leave him.

But they did not. When the battle was over they had taken many casualties, but they had won. Tarius had not left his side, and because she hadn't, Harris had stayed with her and Tragon had survived. Tarius reached down and helped him to his feet.

Tarius and Harris had started taking Tragon back to the surgeon's wagon when a soldier ran over.

"Sir Tarius!" he shouted. There were tears streaming down his face. When Tarius saw that it was Dustan, Gudgin's page, a sick feeling washed over her. "Sir Tarius, come quick! It's Master Gudgin. He's hurt, and he asks to see you."

Tarius nodded. "Yolen, help Harris with Tragon."

When Yolen had taken her place, Tarius ran off after Dustan.

Gudgin was lying in the woods with a spear sticking out of his chest. His chain hadn't been able to stop it. His gambeson was stained red with his blood. She knelt beside him, and her tears started to flow. For a second she wondered if there was a way to remove the spear so that Gudgin could be saved. When she realized there was no chance for him, her tears flowed more freely. She took his hand, and it was unusually cold. She squeezed it tight.

"Gudgin, my brother." Her voice would hardly work for her. "I have failed you. I led us right into an attack."

"Don't be a fool," Gudgin coughed. "None of us saw them. We won the battle; what else matters?"

"You matter." Tarius wiped her face with her free hand, wiping blood across it.

"I feel honored..." Gudgin coughed. "...that Tarius the Black, the great Kartik bastard, would cry on my account." He coughed again.

"Don't talk," Tarius said gently.

Gudgin laughed painfully. "I won't get any other chance. Tarius... I didn't like you."

"I know that," Tarius cried.

"Now I count you my best friend. Never have I known such a man as you. I'm sorry that I taunted you." Gudgin coughed again.

"Don't worry about that now," Tarius said.

"I feel so stupid. I practically jumped on the spear. I never was very good, was I?"

"Gudgin... You are one of the best. Certainly, you are one of the bravest."

Gudgin smiled and then the light started to leave his eyes. He squeezed Tarius's hand one time, forcing his lifeforce back in him for one last moment. "Look after Dustan for me. He's a good lad."

"I will, my brother. I will," Tarius promised. The light left Gudgin's eyes, and he went limp. She pulled her hand from his and closed his eyes. Then she threw back her head and screamed one long angry cry that seemed to be dragged from the very depths of her soul. When it finally stopped, the silence was deafening, and the look in her eyes wasn't sane. Spying an Amalite body still moving, she sprang to her feet, drew her sword and started hacking at the body until it looked like it had been run through a grinder. When she finally stopped she stood back looking at what she had done and the wild look slowly faded. She took three deep, rattling breaths, and then sheathed the blood-covered sword. She looked quickly around at the crowd that had gathered around her, and they all quickly pretended to be doing something else. She walked over to Dustan, who was on his knees bending over the body of his fallen mentor. She helped him to his feet and embraced him, then she put her arm across his shoulders and led the sobbing boy away.

"You will travel with me now. Go find Harris and help him with whatever he's doing. I have to make a report to the king."

He nodded numbly and automatically went to do her bidding.

Tarius was surprised to find Persius in armor and holding a bloody sword. Apparently he had armed rather quickly from the looks of it and joined in the battle.

"I am sorry, Sire. I have failed us all. I didn't hear them; I didn't smell them," Tarius said. "My partner is badly wounded. Master Gudgin is dead. I don't know how many more have fallen or are dead."

"No one else heard, either," Persius said solemnly. "No one expects you to be the only one on lookout. You wouldn't allow it anyway, so don't take the blame upon yourself."

"It's no man's fault," Hellibolt said as he held out a fistful of some strange herb. "Some witch put a spell on this place so that we couldn't hear, see, or smell them as long as they were still. A camouflage spell is an easy spell that any competent witch could do."

"But the Amalites... magic is against their laws! They execute witches," Tarius said.

"Oh yes, but they're losing now. What do you want to bet that their gods told them it would be all right just this once? Their gods are always doing that, don't you know? Bending the laws to suit them. No doubt it would be evil if we used magic against them," Hellibolt said.

"But... They don't have any witches," Tarius said.

Hellibolt looked at both the king and Tarius as if they were idiots. "And what does that tell you?" Hellibolt asked.

The king shrugged.

Tarius looked puzzled for a minute and then smiled. "It means the witch is Jethrik," Tarius said. "Why would she help them then?"

"Perhaps they forced her. Perhaps they paid her, and she is without scruples. Either way the witch is not here now." He looked at Tarius. "You and I must find the witch and stop her from helping them again."

Tarius shook her head. "I have too much to do here, I..."

"What if she returns with more Amalites? What if this is just a simple spell for her?"

"My partner has been badly wounded. Take a group of men..."

Hellibolt stared deep within her eyes. "I need *you*."

Tarius looked at Persius, who shrugged his consent. So Tarius called her horse, and he ran over. Just gathering the horses was going to be a big job. She started to mount the horse and Hellibolt put a hand on her shoulder.

"We'll have to walk. Wizards never ride horses. They don't like us."

"Old man, I have much to do, and nightfall will come soon..."

"Don't you even want to know how the witch got past even you?" Hellibolt asked with thinly veiled meaning.

"What even makes you think she's close to this place?" Tarius asked.

"Because the nature of the spell is such that she must have been present to cast it. This way I think."

Hellibolt started walking with amazing speed considering his fragile appearance, and Tarius followed. When they could no longer hear the activity of the soldiers behind them, Hellibolt turned to Tarius. "We could have this done quicker if you would only change."

Tarius didn't miss a beat. She stopped and slowly turned to face him as the transformation became complete. "You mean like this?"

"Oh, yes! That's very good," Hellibolt clapped his hands together happily. "You really are an exquisite creature... Well, go on now, find the witch."

Tarius sniffed the air, gave Hellibolt a disgusted look, and then started off in the opposite direction from which he had them traveling.

"It wouldn't have happened if you had been like this," Hellibolt said.

Tarius turned and glared at him.

"Well, everyone knows that magic doesn't work on the Katabull."

"Everyone also knows that the Katabull can't belong to the Jethrik army," Tarius said.

"Not to mention your other little problem with gender," Hellibolt said looking at his nails as he followed her.

"So you know about that as well?" Tarius growled out. "Well, you must be very proud of yourself."

"Oh, I am," Hellibolt laughed. "You needn't worry, though. I've told Persius all about you, and he thinks me quite daft. He needs you. He can't afford to believe anything that means he might have to quit using you."

"People believe what they need to believe," Tarius said in agreement. She got down on the ground on all fours and sniffed the earth. After several seconds she stood up snarling and took off at a near run. "The witch is accompanied by two Amalites."

"Perhaps she was being coerced."

"Maybe so." Tarius was sure she was on the scent now, and she took off at a dead run, leaving Hellibolt far behind. Soon she saw the two Amalites dragging a woman between them. She stopped for a second and listened.

"You horrid witch! You purposely lifted your evil spell and got my men killed! You'll pay, bitch. Oh, yes, you'll pay, and it won't be pretty," one Amalite said in an ominous tone.

Tarius snarled, he spoke Jethrik, must be one of their damned missionaries.

"Please! I didn't lift the spell! I swear to you I didn't. I told you it would only last until the moment you attacked." She squirmed in their grip and tried to get away.

Tarius quickly closed the gap between them. She jumped on the bigger of the two, knocking both he and the witch to the ground. She rolled him to his back and cut his throat. She then descended on the second who had been in the process of drawing his blade. She grabbed hold of his wrist where it gripped the hilt and crushed it. He let out a blood-curdling scream just before she drew her own blade across his throat as well. The witch was running, but Tarius quickly caught her, dragging her to the ground. She was preparing to kill her, too, when someone tapped her on the shoulder. She swung quickly, blade at the ready, to see Hellibolt standing there. He took hold of the end of her sword between thumb and forefinger and carefully pointed it away from himself.

"Don't you even want to know why she did it?" Hellibolt asked.

"No," Tarius answered plainly. "I don't care. She is a danger to our war effort. She got my partner maimed and my dear friend killed. That is all I need to know. Now let me be."

The woman squirmed beneath her, obviously terrified.

"Please! I beg you! I didn't want to do it. They have my lady. Don't you see? They have her and they will kill her now. She is doomed, and what crime has she committed? Me... I admit I helped them, but she is blameless and without power. Only help me save her, and I will gladly let you kill me."

Tarius thought of her own love, of Jena, and her heart softened. She stood up. "I will help you save your woman, but then you must die, for you are a danger to the war effort."

"Fair enough." The woman led them down a well-worn path to a clearing where a small cottage with a large garden was nestled quietly in the trees. Six Amalite horses were hitched outside.

"What next?" the witch asked. "I have lots of spells."

"Oh, please. Allow me," Hellibolt said. "Rope of hemp, wood of tree, let these little horses free."

Both Tarius and the witch turned to stare at him.

"Hey! It works."

They watched as the rope fell away from the hitching post.

"Little horses by the house, go and play with the field mouse," Hellibolt intoned.

The horses started walking slowly and quietly away.

"I'm very impressed," the witch said.

"Why thank you," Hellibolt said. "Just a little trick I picked up from an old witch who only used it on weekends."

"How do you do it? I mean it's certainly not your incantations, which I have to tell you are just horrible," the witch said.

"Well, first you gather the energy of the forest into you, and then..."

"Quit it right now," Tarius hissed out. She glared at the witch. "You I'm going to kill, so you don't need to learn any more spells."

She turned to Hellibolt. "And you, I'm just plain annoyed with."

"Sorry," the witch said.

"Me, too," Hellibolt added.

"I don't want you to be sorry! I want you to shut up!" She glared at the witch. "If you hope to trick me..."

She gasped. "Oh! I wouldn't dare! You're the Katabull, and everyone knows that you can't use magic against the Katabull. Please, can't we just save Helen now?"

Tarius nodded and moved forward. She looked in the window. The girl was tied to a chair and there were four men in the house. She came back to the other two.

"What you say is true," Tarius said.

"Well, you don't have to sound so surprised," she said. "Is Helen all right?" she added with real worry.

"Seems to be. Can either one of you do a glamour?"

"Yes," they both said in unison. "But not on you."

"I know that; I'm not an idiot," Tarius spat back. "If Hellibolt goes in with a glamour on him, looking like one of the men that had hold of you back there, he can drag you back in there. He could say the enemy has followed him and that the other man has been killed. Then we can get them out of the house and away from your woman."

"Good. She hates it when the house gets dirty," the witch said.

Tarius stared at them expectantly. "Well, get on with it."

"Can I do it? I mean it's probably the last spell I'll get to cast, seeing as she's going to kill me in a little while," the witch said pointing her thumb at Tarius.

"Be my guest," Hellibolt said.

"Just get on with it," Tarius hissed.

"It's done," the witch said.

Tarius nodded. She couldn't tell, but she took their word for it.

"Go through the door and tell them your story. When they run out, shut the door behind them. I'll be waiting for them outside," Tarius said.

"Ooh, are you taken?" the witch asked with a wink.

"You can tell I'm a woman, too?" Tarius growled in disbelief.

"Well, it's pretty obvious," the witch said shrugging.

"No one else seems to notice," Hellibolt said. "She is taken by the way. Beautiful young girl. Has no idea she's married to a woman."

"Wow! That must be awkward," the witch said.

"Would you just get on with it? I have work to do back there," Tarius hissed, embarrassed as much as she was frustrated.

They started to walk away.

"It's so seldom I get to talk to one of my own kind," Hellibolt said. "It's so nice to be in the company of one that I don't have to explain the simplest of illusions to."

"Tell me about it! All the 'How did you do this, and how did you know that?' It gets tiresome after awhile," the witch said.

Tarius smacked herself in the head in total disgust. She watched as the door opened a crack and moved swiftly and stealthily into position. In a few moments the four men ran out the door bearing steel. Tarius ran at them, and they scattered in a panic. She killed the first two easily enough, but had to chase the other two down.

When she returned to the house they had already untied Helen and the two women were embracing.

"All right I have to kill you now," Tarius said coolly. She was in a hurry to get back to her men.

"No, please! Have mercy," Helen pleaded. Apparently they had already told her of the deal. "Jazel was blinded by her love for me..."

"She got a lot of my men wounded and killed. She helped the Amalites—the sworn enemy of all of our people," Tarius said, glaring at Jazel. "Now come on, we had a deal."

Jazel started forward, and Helen hung on her. "If you are to kill Jazel, then you might as well run us both through because I don't want to live without her."

"Don't you understand? She has helped the enemy once, what's to stop her doing it again? Good men's blood has been shed, better men are dead because of her," Tarius said. "It's really nothing personal."

"Please, I beg of you," Helen said, moving now to hang on Tarius's sword arm, as if that could stop Tarius killing her lover.

"Please, you're making this very difficult for me," Tarius said,

"Tell her, Jazel. Tell her you'd never do it again," Helen pleaded.

"But, darling, under the same circumstances I would," Jazel said truthfully.

"See?" Tarius said.

"But I wouldn't let her!" Helen pleaded.

"What if it were Jena who was held, Tarius?" Hellibolt asked.

"Ah, now, that's not fair," Tarius said. Then added, "Whose side are you on, anyway?"

"You can't tell me that there is anything you wouldn't do to save Jena," Hellibolt said. "Anyone you wouldn't betray to save her."

"Damn it, Hellibolt! She got men killed," Tarius said. "Is there to be no punishment for that? For treason!"

"What if we leave?" Helen asked. "Go to Kartik, where the enemy can never use Jazel again."

"Would you swear an oath?" Hellibolt said.

"I would. We'd leave tonight," Jazel promised.

Tarius shook Helen off her arm and sheathed her sword with a sigh. "Is a witch's oath any good?" Tarius asked Hellibolt, not looking at him.

"As good as the Katabull's," Hellibolt said, more than a little offended.

"And you'll leave tonight?" Tarius asked the witch suspiciously.

"Right away. Thank you. I won't forget your kindness," the witch promised.

"I know I'm going to regret this," Tarius mumbled and left.

"Well, it was certainly nice to meet you. Safe voyage," Hellibolt said.

They started the walk back to their troops. For all her talk of being in a hurry to get back, Tarius was walking at something less than a fast pace.

"What's wrong, Tarius?" Hellibolt asked.

"What isn't? I shouldn't have let her live. Gudgin's dead along with dozens of others. It's her fault. She'd do it again in a heartbeat. I let her go because you were right about what you said about Jena." Tarius walked with her head down. "I wish I'd never met her."

"Who?" Hellibolt asked.

"Jena, you old fool! She messes with my thinking."

"Because you love her."

"Yes," Tarius said. She took a deep breath. She had too much to do to waste time wallowing in self pity. She licked the blood off her hands and turned back into her human form. She gave her self a second to catch her breath after the transformation, and then took off running. When she got back to the road, Hellibolt was already there.

8

Tragon lay sick with fever, having the field stitches taken out to have the wound "repaired correctly," as the academy surgeon explained it, and she had not one question about him or his health.

Jena ran in and skidded to a stop just short of hitting the surgeon. "Is Tarius all right? Is he well?"

"Jena, I'm wounded. I've just spent a week in hell being bumped across the countryside on a horrible wagon." He screamed in pain. "Jena, they're taking my leg apart."

"I know all that, Tragon. Don't be such a baby. How is Tarius?"

Not even one word of concern about my condition. Not even a good to see you, Tragon. Only how is Tarius? Is he all right? Well, she's just fine, Jena, dear. I, on the other hand, am going to die. He screamed again as the sadistic bastard dug at another stitch.

"Just leave it be, man. It had almost stopped hurting until you started poking at it!" Tragon screamed.

"Tragon, please!" Jena pleaded.

"For the gods' sake! He was fine when last I saw him. There's a note from him in my saddle bags..." He hadn't even finished when Jena ran out the door to go look for his saddlebags, which she no doubt believed to be in the stable. "They're right there on the floor."

Darian chuckled. "Forgive her, Tragon. I'm sure you can understand what she's been going through having a husband on the front with little or no news."

"Oh gods!" Tragon screamed. He glared at the surgeon who shrugged, a hapless look on his face, and continued to dig. "The king's own surgeon sewed that, and yet you say it's not good enough. You awful hack! Why on earth did I listen to you? You wanted to cut Arvon's perfectly good leg off."

Darian laughed at the hurt look on the surgeon's face. Then he picked up Tragon's saddlebags and started digging through them till he found several pieces of parchment folded up bearing Jena's name in Tarius's own unique handwriting. There was dried blood on the parchment and Darian made a face.

"He wrote it right after the battle. Tarius won't allow the wounded to stay on the front even one single day. The regular soldiers are shipped off to the nearest villages for recovery, and after they recover they stay in that village. The protection of that village becomes their duty. We lucky Swordsmen get shipped back here, and when we recover we are to be sent right back up to the front as quickly as we can get there. The only ones who are any more abused than we are the poor heralds. They're on horseback constantly with little or no sleep, traveling from one camp to the other and bringing news of the war back here."

"Was he hurt?" Darian asked looking at the dried blood and trying to scrape it off where he could.

Tragon laughed. "Oh, it's not his blood; it's theirs. It's *never* his blood. The king has made Tarius chief warlord, you know."

Darian found a chair and sat down hard. "No, I didn't."

"Well, he has. The king doesn't piss without asking Tarius first."

"Evil boy!" the surgeon scolded.

"Watch your mouth, Tragon," Darian said.

"Well, it's true! The king takes the credit for it, but all the plans are made by Tarius. The men all know it, too," Tragon said.

Jena ran back in breathless. "They said you didn't have a horse..." Her father was holding up the letter and Jena ran over and grabbed it from him.

You would have thought he had given her gold. She held the folded hunk of parchment in her hand just looking at where Tarius had written her name. She would recognize his handwriting anywhere. Tears came to her eyes, and she just couldn't bring herself to open it. She was glad to have the letter, but at the same time it reminded her that he wasn't here.

Tragon didn't know what possessed him, maybe it was the fact that Tarius had just saved his life, or maybe it was just the medicine kicking in. "You know how I feel about you, Jena, it's never been a secret. How I envy Tarius because he has you, how I envy his skill and his bravery. I'd like very much to hate the lucky bastard, but now he has gone and saved me. He threw himself between the enemy and me and then stood over my wounded body protecting me. He and Harris stood by me throughout the battle shielding me from harm. For this reason, I have to tell you something I would rather not. I have to tell you how much he loves you and how he talks about you and misses you constantly. You know how hard it is for him to write, and at the time he was busy with the business of after-battle clean up and setting camp. Yet he sat there knowing that I would be coming back here and wrote you that letter."

"Thanks, Tragon," Jena said through choked-back tears, then turned and ran from the building.

She ran all the way to the clearing where Tarius had taught her to fight, where he had first made love to her. It was here that she felt closest to him. She sat for a minute just letting herself cry, and then she wiped her tears away and opened the letter carefully. There were three pages, but considering how big Tarius wrote, it wasn't as wordy as some might have thought.

Dear Jena,

First I must tell you how much I miss you. I have dreamt of doing battle against the Amalites my whole life. It is all I have worked for. All I ever cared about.

Now because of you, I only want to be home.

Gudgin died today with a spear in his chest. We hadn't gotten along when I was at academy, but on the battlefield we had grown to like and respect each other. He was a good man, my dear friend, and he will be sorely missed.

Tragon, as you now know by now, was badly injured in the battle. Many died; it was our highest death count yet. We lost eighty-five men as of the last count.

Harris is my best man and my trusted companion. I have also inherited Gudgin's page, Dustan, who seems a good lad.

I grow weary of sleeping with men, and I'm sure they grow wearier of having to peel me off of them by morning. It seems I grew too accustomed to sleeping with you too fast.

If all goes well, the war should be over soon. When it is, I want to go back to Kartik. I hope you will consider the move. I think it would be best for us.

All my love and devotion,

Tarius

Jena read the letter over and over again. She laughed at the thought of Tarius curled around poor Tragon or Harris. She wept over the death of Gudgin and all the others and for the pain Tarius must feel at their loss. She wished she could be there beside him to comfort him.

"They call him Tarius the Black you know."

Jena started at her father's voice and dried her eyes. "Father! I..."

"Oh, yes, I know all about this place, and I know about that heathen husband of yours teaching you to use a sword." Darian laughed at the startled look on his daughter's face.

"Why didn't you say anything?" Jena asked.

Darian shrugged and sat next to her on the log. "What good would it have done? Admittedly, daughter, I have to say that when I first saw you out here with your husband and young Harris I was appalled and wanted to strangle the lot of you. But as I watched you fight—when I saw that you were very good—well, I couldn't help but feel proud. In fact," he looked around, "...if you'd like, I could teach you a few tricks of my own."

"Oh, Father!" Jena hugged his neck. "I would love that... Did Tragon tell you any more about Tarius?"

"He is now the king's chief warlord. Seems Persius does not make a move without first asking Tarius. They call him 'the black' because he has gone back to wearing his old leather armor and has let his hair grow till it is almost to his shoulders. Before battle he paints his face with charcoal. Tragon says he is a fearsome sight."

"Please tell me," Jena held up the parchment. "… that the blood is not his."

"It isn't," Darian said. "It might have been nice if the barbarian washed his hands before he wrote to you, though."

"I don't care about the blood, Father, as long as it isn't his."

They talked for a long time about the war and the letter and what Tragon had said. But Jena didn't tell her father of Tarius's desire to leave the kingdom and move to the Kartik.

"I only hope that my letter gets to him," Jena said as she let her father help her to her feet. They started back to the house.

"Oh, it will. You couldn't have had a better messenger," Darian said.

The camp had to be laid out in perfect order and with careful preparation for the big battle ahead. The first aid tents had to be close enough to the camp to be accessible to the battlefield, but not so close that they would be hard to defend. Same with the cooks' wagons. Tarius made up maps of where she wanted things and handed them out to the warlords under her. There had to be enough room to accommodate the other units as they came in.

At first, as always, there was chaos, and then everyone seemed to realize their task and everything came together almost without a hitch.

Tarius had ridden out to the edge of the woods to look down at the valley below. The place was filthy with Amalites. They had been building up their presence here for weeks. Luckily the Jethrik army had also been building up their forces. They had already sent for the units following behind them and told them to come on in. In just five days' time they could be as large as the army they faced, and it would be no problem at all.

That is it would be no problem if the Amalite army chose not to ride against them for five days time. Which she truly doubted.

The Amalites hadn't counted on getting caught. They had been building their forces here in what they thought was secret in order to launch a full-scale assault against the Jethrik countryside and push on to the capital. Nothing brought down the morale of an opposing army quite like having a massive fighting force charge across the land killing every living thing, scorching the earth black with fire, and then destroying their seat of power.

Now they had been caught, and there was no way they could be ignorant of the fact that the Jethrik forces were there. They also had to suspect that at the moment they outnumbered the Jethrik forces.

The real trick was to not let any of them get close enough to scout

out the camp. To keep them in the dark about strengths and weaknesses. That's what Tarius was doing now. Riding the boundaries in case she might see something that the sentries didn't.

She had no idea how intimidating she was. She had patched her armor over and over, but still managed to keep it dyed jet black and the studs brightly polished. She wore metal-banded leather vambraces and metal elbow cops. Three-limbed pauldrons lay on her shoulders. She only wore her helmet when she knew there would be battle. Right now her black hair flowed out behind her. On either side of her head she wore tight braids that kept the hair out of her face. She cut her bangs, but that was all.

"You really are a stunning bitch," a familiar voice said.

"Arvon!" Tarius jumped from her horse and ran to greet him. She gave him a hearty hug, and he hugged her back. "Am I glad to see you!"

"I also am glad to see you. Although I'm not at all happy to see that," he said pointing down at the valley.

"I have sent orders for our other four units to come in. If we can keep them from over running us till all our forces arrive, we should be able to win this war and go home. Speaking of which, do you bring any news of my lady wife?"

"I happen to have a letter the dear lass wrote you right here in my pocket." He pulled out the letter and handed it to Tarius.

Tarius took it with trembling fingers, and a lump in her throat.

"You should tell her, Tarius. Her love for you is strong. I'm sure it would be a shock to her at first, but I think she would understand. I think she would love you anyway, given time to adjust."

"You don't know that," Tarius said. "What if Tragon is telling her even now?"

"Tragon is here... Isn't he?"

"No. He was wounded and he had to go home. You no doubt passed him on your way." Tarius seemed miserable. "I know how he feels about her. I'm not sure his loyalty to me will prevent him doing anything in his power to have her." She looked at the letter in her hands. "Whatever she has written here, it might have all changed by now."

"Don't think like that, Tarius. Read your letter and be happy to hear from her," Arvon said punching her in the shoulder.

Tarius nodded and she read the letter.

My Dear Husband,

I long for your touch. I only hope that the war will end soon that we will be victorious and that you will return to my side once again.

I hear that things on the front are horrible. They tell me that you ride out ahead of everyone else, charging head first into battle. Please don't do anything stupid. You don't have to prove anything to me or anyone else. Be more careful...

Sword Masters

The rest of the four pages were filled with flowery tributes of her love for Tarius. Some of it made Tarius blush, and much of it called for body parts Tarius simply did not have. When she had read it, she folded it carefully and tucked it into the top of her pants.

"Well?" Arvon asked. He really hadn't read the letter, which had been pure hell for him, and he very much wanted to hear what Jena had written. Vicarious romance maybe, but Arvon wanted to know anyway.

Tarius looked solemnly over the valley filled with Amalites.

"She wants a man, Arvon. She wants me to take her like a rutting pig..."

"You don't know that, Tarius."

Tarius pulled the folded parchment from her pants, unfolded and leafed through the pages. "*I long to feel your warm swollen form inside me,*" Tarius read in disgust, and once again folded the letter and put it away. "She wants me to be something that I can't be. She needs me to be something I can't be. What the hell have I done? I'm playing a game I can not win." She turned to face him then. "When I get home... How long can I hold her off?"

"Tell her, Tarius. Tell her and have it over with one way or the other. I think you're wrong about her. I look at you now, and I wonder how you have fooled anyone at all. To me, you are so obviously female. You are beautiful, and no normal man-loving woman would fall for you, my friend, because you simply don't look enough like a man."

"You thought me a man."

"Aye, but I thought you were a gay man and a fem at that," Arvon countered. "Jena could have had any man she wanted, so you have to ask why she pursued a woman instead."

"What are you saying?" Tarius asked.

"I'm saying that I think you and Jena are the same kind of women. She's just too ignorant to know it. She's young, and she's found a man who gives her what she needs. It's not so much that she wants a swollen cock inside her as it is that she wants to please you. You can't look at me and say that isn't exactly what you would like as well. Tell her. Yes, she'll be hurt at first. Of course she'll be confused. Eventually I believe she will come around, and then you can teach her to be the kind of lover you deserve."

Tarius laughed without humor. "I wish you were right, but you just don't understand. I only look like a woman to you now because you know that I am. Jena married a man; she wants a man."

"No. She *thinks* she wants a man. Any man would force her to be something that she isn't," Arvon said.

"Especially Tragon. He doesn't really love her at all. He lusts for her because she's beautiful. He wants her for a wife because she comes from a respected family. Mostly he wants her because she belongs to me," Tarius said. She was thoughtful for a moment. "When the war is over—if I can get her to Kartik. Then maybe there is a chance. If I can get her away from here, away from your strange rules..."

"You mean if you can move her away from her support base, across an ocean, so that she has no choice but to stay with you?" Arvon asked. "Do you really want to keep her under those terms?"

Tarius looked disturbed. She ran both her hands through her hair. "You said yourself that she loves me. You said Jena was like me. That she would still love me..."

"Yes I did, and I truly believe that she would. What you're talking about, though, is taking her choices away. Taking her to a place where she has no choice but to stay with you," Arvon said.

Tarius started to pace, throwing her hands around in huge circles as she talked and to Arvon's eyes looking more like a woman by the minute. "Maybe I don't care how I win as long as I win. The Nameless One knows that I have been accused of that enough lately." She motioned to the huge camp below her. "Do you think any of this matters to me now? It should, but it doesn't. All I care about is keeping Jena. Having Jena with me always. All I desire in this world is for her to love me for who I am. To be with her in every way. If I will break the unwritten rules to kill many men, why wouldn't I do the same to keep the only woman I have ever and will ever love? What? I shouldn't take her away and then reveal myself and make her stay with me because it's wrong? Everything I have done concerning her is wrong because I can't think straight when it comes to Jena. She restored my soul, Arvon, I can't live without her, I can't *breathe* without her love."

She stopped and turned away from him looking over the valley again. Arvon walked up behind her and put a hand on each of her shoulders. "I didn't mean to upset you, Tarius. I only want to help. I think you sell your lady short. Tell her the truth, tell her here, in Jethrik. If you spirit her away and try to force her to love you, you may make her hate you instead."

Tarius nodded silently. She tried to shake all thoughts of Jena from her head. The enemy lay before them. The Amalites outnumbered them ten to one. If the Amalites attacked tomorrow they would no doubt over-run them. They needed to hold the Amalites at bay for as long as possible, and there was only one way to do that.

She didn't have time to think about Jena or any of her personal problems. She had a war to fight.

"Arvon... I need you to do a favor for me."

They had tethered the horses, and Arvon had crawled through the brush along side Tarius.

"This is insane," Arvon said. "There are too many of them."

"I don't plan to plant a Jethrik flag in their midst. I simply go in, awaken all their Katabull fears, kill a few dozen of them and get out," Tarius said.

"I can do my eyes," Arvon started concentrating. After a few minutes the change occurred. "I can see better and my senses are more alert..."

"Don't be insane. No offense, but if I wasn't a fully formed Katabull I wouldn't even think of wading into that mess."

"You shouldn't anyway. They're waiting for you this time. All the guards are armed, not with swords but with spears," Arvon said. With the change he could now see as if it were daytime. "That's what I could do." Without another word Arvon crawled back to his horse. He reappeared several minutes later with his crossbow and a quiver of bolts. "I'll take out the guards outside the camp from a distance, clear a trail for you. Then you go in and do your worst. When you run out I cover your back, and we get out of here."

It was a good plan, and Tarius nodded. They crept slowly forward until the spearmen were in range. Then Arvon started firing, dropping one with each bolt he let fly. Tarius ran into the camp slashing, trashing and burning everything she came into contact with. She left a wide path of destruction through the Amalite camp, then she ran out under Arvon's covering fire. Together they ran back to their horses, mounted and rode away fast. When they were sure they hadn't been followed they slowed down. Then they looked at each other and laughed.

"I've... You know I've never really used it before," Arvon said conversationally. "I figured if I couldn't do a total transformation, why even bother? But I have to tell you there is an absolute plus to being able to see in the dark when your opponent can't. I was just picking them off and they had no idea where I was. They never even got close."

"Arvon... You mean... You never tried to change? You weren't trained?" Tarius said in shock.

"You can either change or you can't," Arvon said not understanding Tarius's questions.

"Who told you that?" Tarius asked.

"My father. My mother died before my tenth birthday while trying to have my brother."

"Arvon, don't you understand? It's like walking; you have to *learn* to do it. You have to *learn* to change. Your mother died before you were of changing age. Arvon... If you learned to change your eyes on your own, chances are you can shape-shift."

※

She led him to a stream far away from either camp. They both stripped naked and soaked in the stream's cold water.

"Why do we have to be naked?" Arvon asked in a whisper.

"Clothes might bind you in your changing. You bulk out as you change.

It's why I wear my armor looser, why I loosen the bindings on my chest before I shift," Tarius said, she made a face. "When I remember."

"OK. Now my second question. Why are we sitting in ice cold water?" Arvon asked.

"Because I needed a bath," Tarius said with a smile that shone through the night.

Arvon laughed and shook his head. "All right, what do I do?"

"Close your eyes and remember learning to walk..."

"I don't remember that."

"Well, pretend like you do," Tarius said in an agitated voice. "When you are learning to walk, you put a foot forward, hold it in the air a moment, then you lean into it, you fall forward and catch yourself. One step. It's the same. Picture in your mind your features. Reach into yourself and find a wild thing that wants free. Pick it up gently..."

"With what?" Arvon asked, opening one eye just a slit.

"In your mind. Gods! You're hopeless.... Pick the wild thing up, hold it and caress it. Can you feel it?"

"Yes," Arvon said as if more than a little surprised.

"Now let it go. Let it fall..."

"That doesn't seem right," Arvon interrupted.

"Just do it," Tarius said with a sigh. "You drop it. It hits the ground, it busts, and the beast is loose within you. Open yourself up to it. Let its blood mix with yours. It is you and you are it, there is no diffrence between the two."

Anything else she said was lost to him. Arvon felt dizzy, as if he'd had way too much wine. There was a sense of falling and then being snapped upright just short of hitting the ground. His skin seemed to be exploding, like the feeling you got when you put on a shirt that was way too small for you. When he opened his eyes, Tarius smiled at him approvingly, her canines glowing in the moonlight.

"Arvon, my brother. You are the Katabull."

The next morning their scouts reported that the Amalites seemed more than usually quiet. Still, Tarius made the men stay at the ready all through the day.

Tarius and Arvon sat with Dustan and Harris having a late lunch.

"Why do you suppose they wait?" Dustan asked. "They outnumber us ten to one. They could easily take us."

"Perhaps their gods told them not to attack yet," Tarius said jokingly. Then added seriously, "Perhaps they wait for still more reinforcements. The Amalite army is huge."

"Why wait then?" Harris asked. "It doesn't make sense. They could crush us with the men they have here now, and their fresh troops could ride against our reinforcements when they arrive."

"The Amalite scout we caught earlier today said, after a little coaxing, that there was a Katabull in their camp last night." It was Hellibolt who spoke as he neared the fire, and both Tarius and Arvon gave him heated looks. "See, boys, the Amalites believe that if you see the Katabull at night you'll die the next day." He smiled broadly at Tarius and Arvon. "Perhaps for them it's true, hey, Tarius?"

"Don't fill these young men's heads with your foolish chatter. Away with you, Hellibolt, go tell the future of some other soldier," Tarius commanded.

"Ah! But the spirits have commanded that I tell yours, dear Tarius. In three days time you will commit an act that will finish the cycle you started when you saved the life of your partner through extraordinary means. The coming act combined with that one will surely cause your downfall. Take care that you do not rob fate of its true prize, for if you do, you will become the prize instead." That said he tossed something into the fire and walked away.

"What a creepy old fool," Dustan mumbled. He immediately dismissed anything the old man had to say because Gudgin had despised him, and anyone Gudgin had hated, Dustan was going to hate on principle. It was his way of respecting Gudgin's memory.

Harris was a peasant by birth and highly superstitious. He did not dismiss the old wizard's words so quickly. "What did he mean, Tarius?"

Tarius shrugged as if she hadn't given his words a second thought. "Who can tell? He is an old fool who talks in riddles." However she did not for one minute dismiss his words.

"What did he throw into the fire?" Dustan asked, noticing it had a funny shape and stench. He pocked at it with his sword. When he saw what it was he jumped screaming. "Bloody hell!"

It was a human ear.

"Crazy old coot," Arvon hissed.

Tarius smiled. "I guess the Amalite didn't want to talk."

———•·•———

That night both Arvon and Tarius ransacked the enemy camp. First they sat safely outside the camp and carefully picked off the now far greater number of guards. When they had killed two dozen or more and the camp was running around in panicked circles, they had run in with their swords swinging. The Amalites scattered before them. Not even one man stood and fought. They killed, they burned, and then they took off before any of the Amalites changed their minds and decided to stand and fight.

Early the next morning Tarius stood with a looking glass at the top of the plateau watching the Amalites below. "Damn! There are more coming in even now. What in hell are they playing at? Do they hope to come at us with their entire army?"

"Why don't you tell me?" It was Persius and his entourage.

Tarius had heard them coming and wasn't startled by his presence. In fact she even took her own sweet time turning to face him.

"That's what it looks like to me," Tarius was thoughtful. "Stewart's troop came in last night under cover of darkness, and Jamison should arrive tonight, however..."

"What?" Persius asked.

Tarius took a map from her pocket and spread it on the ground. She pointed to different areas as she spoke. "This is us, and here are the Amalites. We have the advantage of high ground, but they have the river which gives them not only protection on that front, but a ready water supply. They could very easily cut off our water supply by deploying troops in this area. We have to fortify this area to secure our water supply. Then we have to split our forces, sending Jamison and Alexander along this route. They should lay in wait here and ambush any new troops that come to join the Amalites."

"But that will leave us badly out numbered here, and we can't expect them to hold off their attack forever," Persius said.

"Aye, but Thomas' unit will join us here in four days time. It's the only chance that I can see that we have of defeating the Amalites. Jamison and Alexander's units can stop not just Amalite reinforcements, but also cut their supply lines. An army of that size consumes a lot of food, and they are out of their country. Stop the supply lines, and they fight on empty stomachs."

Persius nodded. "So what do we do next? Wait for them to attack?"

Tarius looked thoughtful again. "No. We have to attack now so that they won't catch on. Make them think that we have sized them up and have decided to attack them now before they can get any more reinforcements. Hopefully their intelligence has found out less about our plans than we have about theirs. Our crossbows and longbows outdistance anything that they have, so I suggest we set a shield wall here with archers here. Pikes and spears here and here, and horse men here in the center of it all. Try to draw them out and make them go into the river. When enough of them have waded into the river the archers will retreat, the shield wall will open, and the horsemen will attack in the river. The shield, pike, and spearmen will then run up to the bank of the river and attack them before they can reach shore. Meanwhile, I will have taken my troop and gone to the west. There is a low spot in the river there and we can cross with ease and come in behind their camp."

"It's a good plan," Persius said. Once again he went to the center of the camp and laid out the plan to the men as if it were his own.

Tarius led her troop, with Arvon and Brakston taking control of the left flank, and Derek and his partner, Heath, taking the right. Derek had balked at being put under Tarius's command when he'd arrived with Stewart the night before. But when he got dirty looks and harsh words from everyone he complained to, he soon shut up. Now he was just worried about being in command. After all, by all rights he hadn't even finished his training yet. They needed good swordsmen on the front so badly that they were running boys through the academy as fast as they could. A lot of less than exemplary swordsmen would have their chance at a title because of the war.

Tarius heard the sounds of war in the distance and sped her troop up. Their horses pounded down on the north flank—the rear of the Amalite camp. The Amalites were totally unprepared for the attack on their flank. At first Tarius and her men mowed right through them. Then suddenly they ground to a near halt. Tarius jumped from her horse and stood on the ground, swinging her sword around her head, and shouting orders that her men only half heard. Without her hand signals, no one would have been able to carry out her orders. Harris and Dustan reined their horses in hard beside her and helped her fight off the Amalites, who seemed to be hitting her in waves.

"Ride on!" Tarius screamed, ordering Harris and Dustan to fall in behind Arvon and Brakston. Tarius ran into the battle on foot, hacking and slashing every Amalite she came across. Most of the Amalite horses were being used on the front line no doubt, and so most of the Amalites they encountered were on foot. However they were like lice. For every one you picked off, ten more seemed to appear in its place. Tarius continued running through them, hacking and slashing. An ugly red gash had been opened across her right cheek, and blood ran freely down her face.

They were being engulfed; there were too many of them. It was that same feeling you got when you dove too deeply. Those few awful seconds when you wonder if you can get back to the surface before you have to take a breath.

Tarius spoke a word she had never thought she would speak in battle. "Retreat! Retreat!" She whistled for her horse, and he came running. She jumped on, then watched as her men rode out first. Harris and Dustan waited for them, and they were the last to run out. They headed back for the river. Naturally, the Amalites followed.

"Harris, Dustan ride on. Send Arvon back to me."

Harris looked at the angry mob behind them in amazement. "But

Tarius, you'll be hacked to pieces..."

"Do it!" Tarius ordered.

Harris nodded and he and Dustan doubled their pace.

Tarius waited till she had reached the top of a little hill where the trail was narrow, and then she turned around. She jumped off the horse and called on the night. Within seconds she was the Katabull. There were no archers in the group that had chased them, and very few horsemen. Tarius ran at them, growling like a beast, and the Amalites froze for a second. Someone screamed a command, and they came at her again, although they did so with less than usual enthusiasm.

They were no match for the Katabull. When you threw a blow at her one place, she wound up several feet away in another. She ran over and on and up them. She kicked them in the face hard enough to force part of their nose out the back of their heads. Her sword decapitated or maimed with every swing. When a second Katabull, bigger than the first, arrived on the scene, they could no longer be ordered to fight. They turned and ran like frightened children.

Tarius licked the blood off her hand and changed back.

Arvon gave her a look of disgust. "That's human blood," he said.

"No. It's Amalite blood. We don't have time to hunt rabbits. I suggest you do the same. We have to go help Persius because there are even more of the bastards than we thought."

Arvon made a face and licked his hand. Then he smiled at Tarius as he changed. "Um, tastes like chicken."

"Just come on," Tarius ordered.

So far, Tarius's plan for the front line was working. But no matter how many of the bastards they killed, they just seemed to keep coming. Tarius ran in beside Persius and reined her horse in tight.

"We've got to retreat. We can't hold them in the open. Our only chance is to go back to the plateau. I've already positioned the archers. From there we can hold them off."

"For four days? Most of our troops have been sent west!" Persius was in a near panic.

"Only three more days—don't forget that most of today is gone," Tarius said with a half smile.

The Jethrik army retreated to the base of the plateau. The Amalites followed and arrows fell on them like rain.

Tarius dismounted, took a spear from a dead man and took his place behind the shield wall. "Press!" she ordered. The shield wall moved forward. The Amalites were falling, taking heavy casualties from the accurate rain of death. They started to retreat The Jethrik archers ceased fire, and the foot soldiers stopped their press.

"Who called a cease fire!" she screamed. She made a sign in the air with her spear. "Keep firing! Chase after them."

"But... Their backs are to us," Harris said from where he had been fighting at her shoulder.

She didn't have time to explain herself. "Push, damn it! I said push!"

Only about half of the archers continued to fire, and the foot soldiers were hesitant at best.

The Amalites were on the run.

"Halt!" Tarius screamed. She pushed through the shield wall to stand in front of them. "What the hell are you doing? When I give an order I expect it to be followed."

"You can't ask us to stab a man in the back!" someone screamed.

"Don't you understand? This is a holy war to them. They think their gods want them to do this to us. Do you think for one minute they would hesitate to stab *you* in the back? No they would not! They would go into your homes..." Tarius paced back and forth now. Even screaming, not all of them heard her, but it would filter through the ranks eventually till everyone knew what she said. "...they would rape your women and kill them, they would slit your children's throats and burn your homes to the ground. They would burn the fields so that anyone who did live through their attack would starve. And now because you didn't have the nerve to do what needed to be done, we did not get the edge we needed. Can you not see how badly out-numbered we are? If we fall here, those things will over-run your country and destroy it. They are like locusts. Kill one and three more will appear. Kill a dozen and a hundred will appear. This is war, haven't you learned by now that it isn't glorious? How many more of our men have to fall before you realize that this is not a game, and you can't play by any rules? We had the chance to even our odds, and you let them get away!"

The men all looked at their feet. Tarius just shook her head, walked back through the ranks and started up the plateau. Harris fell in behind her.

"I'm sorry, Tarius. I was as guilty as the rest. My heart also wasn't in it. I guess I didn't think..."

Tarius wasn't listening, she was mumbling to herself. "If I had ten Kartik soldiers, men or women, it wouldn't matter. If I had just *ten*, I could win this war. Stupid people, there are no ethics in war! There is only what works and what does not work." She started talking in a sissy voice. "I can't shoot people in the back; that's just wrong. We have to be on equal footing, too, and also have the same weapon. It has to be fair."

Tarius was funny, and Harris laughed in spite of himself. But when Tarius glared at him, he looked at his feet.

"They set a trap for us. A magic trick that got Gudgin and a lot of other good men killed. Was anyone thinking about that when they let the Amalites flee to re-group? What makes that any better or worse than killing them from behind?"

"Nothing, I suppose," Harris said. "For a moment I questioned your judgment, I'm very sorry..."

"Don't apologize. It's hard to get away from ideas that have been beaten into your head since your youth. Just don't let it happen again." She looked around suddenly. "Where's Dustan?"

"He stayed with Arvon and Brakston." Harris smiled. "I think he's sweet on Arvon."

"Is he?" Tarius asked in shock. She hadn't noticed. Of course she hadn't noticed a lot of things in the past few days. Something about narrow escapes from death, climbing over piles of dead bodies and being soaked in blood three to four times a day tended to wipe all other thought from Tarius's head. She certainly didn't understand how love could bloom in all this carnage. "Are you sure?"

Harris shrugged. "Admittedly I don't understand a man's attraction for another man, and I'm not very experienced when it comes to romance. However, when one person constantly asks questions about another person, when they find reasons to be around that person, when they purposely physically run into them, and when they ask if that person is taken... Well, I've seen all that with you and Jena, haven't I?" He grinned at the look on Tarius's face. "Oh, yes. I think even I now recognize when someone is stupid for someone else."

"I was never stupid for Jena," Tarius defended.

Harris laughed loudly and patted Tarius on the back. "Oh, yes, you were. You still are. All I have to do is say her name—Jena... and see? There is that stupid, far away look. Admittedly, she was more stupid..."

"Don't call Jena stupid!" Tarius growled out, glaring at Harris.

"Sorry. But that does sort of prove my point, doesn't it? I can call you stupid, and you merely protest. But if I suggest that Jena's stupid, you're ready to hit me." Harris smiled and looked smug. "I myself plan never to give my heart to any woman. I shall be now and forever a swordsman. Married to my sword and in the service of my knight."

It was Tarius's turn to laugh. "Oh, yes. I once sang that very song myself, and now look at me. By your own words, I am now stupid in love. It happens, and like a sword that finds its mark, it is too late to duck after you have been struck."

She stopped, whistled for her horse and waited for him to get there.

"You got your horse at the same time as I got mine. So why does yours act like a well-trained dog, and I have to hunt mine every time I dismount him and leave him untethered?" Harris asked, suddenly glad that he had a reason to change the subject. He didn't want to talk about it any more. Tarius was unique. He saw Harris as a whole man. He didn't understand that others didn't. Tarius didn't see the obvious; Harris would never have to worry about that particular "blow" hitting him, because no woman would ever chase him down the way Jena had chased down Tarius. No woman would ever want him. "So, what's your secret?" "Well, first I rarely let anyone else feed or water him. And second," Tarius reached into a pocket in her pants and pulled out a fist full of greens. She held them out to the horse and he greedily devoured them. "I watched him eating and found that he had a fondness for this particular clover. So now every time I see it I pick it and put it into my saddlebags. I keep enough in my pocket so that I always smell like the clover to him. Every time he obeys a command I give some to him." She patted the horse, and taking hold of his reins she started to pull him along.

Harris just smiled and followed. "You have a trick for everything." "The Kartik people live by their wits. The Kartik lands are never quiet. There are windstorms that will tear apart a house. Rain that falls in buckets or not at all. We live at the land's will. If we didn't have tricks, we would die out. We are clever only because we have to be. We aren't born clever, the Kartik land makes us that way," Tarius said.

"If it's so horrible, why would anyone live there at all?" Harris asked.

"Horrible! There is nothing horrible about it. It is the most beautiful of places. Plants grow there that you have never seen, and birds and animals of such magnitude and beauty that one never wants for sound or color. Nothing is dull on Kartik. There are few laws, but those are strictly upheld and enforced by the people themselves." As Tarius spoke, her voice took on a dream-like quality.

"If it's so wonderful, why did you ever leave?"

"The first time to find my father," Tarius said. "My throat had been cut by the Amalites when my mother was killed. Thinking that he had lost us both, he took off for Jethrik to help your people fight the Amalites. A young woman named Elise who had lost her children and her mate found me in a stack of bodies they were preparing to burn. I couldn't talk because I was very weak, and there were so many bodies on top of me that I could barely move. I had no way to let anyone know I was still alive except that I could move my hand. The burial squad thought the woman had gone mad with grief when she pulled me from the stack saying I was still alive. But when they saw that my main vein hadn't been cut and that I was still breathing, they sewed me up as best they could. The young woman claimed me as her own, vowing that she would one day take me to my father. She then hauled me half way across the island to the Springs of Montero. The springs have magical healing properties for my people, and they healed my wounds. I was even able to speak clearly." *Although it changed the way I spoke forever. Making it easier for me to pass myself off as a man.*

"When I was old enough to make such a trip, Elise took me across the sea to look for my father, for word of his greatness here had traveled even to Kartik. When we found him…" She stopped, smiling at the memory. "Ah! It was like we had never been parted. He realized Elise's attachment to me, and so he invited her to stay with us. We all lived together for years, traveling back and forth across the sea. My father trained me every day, whether at land or on sea, in the Kartik or in the Jethrik. When battle called him away, Elise continued my training. Every day, day in and day out, from the time I was old enough to hold a sword.

"When I was twenty, my father helped me to make my sword. Every day we heated and pounded the metal. Every day for two months, pounding and folding the metal, then grinding and sharpening it till it was perfect. Then I took it and cut my finger off with it."

Harris made a face, and Tarius laughed.

"The blade was so sharp that I hardly felt it till they put the hot metal to it," Tarius laughed again at the almost sick look that came over Harris's face. "When the handle was complete and the sword was whole, it was like nothing I had ever held before. I felt invincible. I felt I couldn't possibly lose. That no one could ever cause me to feel the pain I had felt when they had killed my pac… village, and my mother.

"I lived with this delusion for two years. I hated it when we would stay here, but my father insisted that we must hold the Amalites back. He told me that this war we fight now was coming. I wish now that we had never come here; that we had stayed always in the Kartik. I believe that being here at the time we were changed both of our fates forever and changed what was simple into something too complicated for words.

"One night I was hunting in the woods. I couldn't hear or see anything at the home site, because I was miles from home. Yet I knew something was wrong." The events started to run through her head as she spoke. "I was young and stupid. I thought that I could protect the people I loved. It never dawned on me that my father, who was three times the swordsman I was, hadn't been able to. I ran through the woods so fast… I covered so much ground so quickly… I have no idea how I did it even now. I knew I had been a damn fool. Somehow I knew the worst was happening. I came into the clearing and the house was in flames. I arrived just in time to see a sword go through Elise's midsection. I saw her sword drop from her hand and land on a body below her. A body I knew instinctively belonged to my father. There was a crossbow bolt sticking out of his chest. I guess I went berserk. I ran in hacking and slashing with no rhyme or reason to any move I made, and when I was done there were six dead Amalites. It didn't make me feel any better about my father or Elise. Hatred devoured me, and everything I did after that I did because of that burning hatred. Nothing mattered to me, nothing but killing the Amalites. Nothing, do you understand me, Harris? Nothing!"

There was such passion in Tarius's eyes that Harris dared not ignore him. "I think so." *I understand that we never really changed the subject of the conversation. I understand that this is why you don't feel bad about shooting the Amalites in the back or anywhere else, and I understand that from now on I will obey you without question.*

"Nothing at all mattered to me. My hatred made me blind to all the things I was doing. Because it just didn't matter what I did as long as it meant that I got to kill these bastards. Until I met Jena. Until Jena fell in love with me, and I felt once again the love of one who was connected to my soul. By then it was too late to change all that I had done. To undo it. I had to keep it all up. I *had* to."

Now Tarius had lost him. "What are you talking about, Tarius?" Harris asked in confusion.

Tarius looked as if he'd been caught napping on guard duty. "I... I have to..." She jumped quickly into her saddle. "I have to find Arvon." She rode off at a quick gallop.

Harris watched Tarius go. Finally he laughed, shook his head, and went off in search of his own horse. Being on horseback certainly gave him an edge in most battles, but there were times when you couldn't get to the actual fighting if you were on one unless you trampled your own men. He was going to try to train his horse the way Tarius had trained his.

Tarius hadn't found Arvon yet when she was summoned before the king. She rode up to the king's carriage and dismounted. The herald pointed her in the direction of the carriage, and she walked towards it. The door was opened for her, and she stepped inside. The king sat inside while his personal surgeon, Robert, cleaned a cut on the king's hand. Tarius looked at it and saw that it wasn't a sword blow but an armor cut. No doubt where the king's gauntlet had cut into him.

"Sit," Persius ordered, pointing at the seat across from him. "Tell me, for I believe wholly in your counsel concerning war, and all things pertaining to combat. You were in their camp. Is it really so bad that we must... kill men from behind?"

"If you insist on playing by gentleman's rules, we shall not win. Every one of us will die in the valley below. They easily out number us ten men to our every one. I was wrong to separate our forces..."

"No, you were right." Persius handed Tarius a piece of paper. "The herald delivered this into my hands only a few moments ago. They were getting reinforcements, and our units along their supply routes have stopped many shipments of food and medical supplies as well as hundreds of soldiers. They have done this easily and with few casualties. Meanwhile, the fifth division will be here in only two more days."

"That may not be soon enough." Tarius looked thoughtful for a few minutes and then nodded as if making up her mind. "Send one man to each of the surrounding villages that are less than a half day's ride away. Let him gather every able-bodied man with any weapon and a horse and bring him to the front. It will leave the villages unprotected, but I think all the Amalites are there below us anyway. It may give us enough men to push on till the fifth division gets here."

Persius wrote down what Tarius had said and then called for the herald, who appeared in the doorway. Persius handed the note to the herald. "See that these orders are carried out immediately."

Robert had been having a hell of a time trying to doctor the king's hand while he was moving all around talking to the Kartik bullyboy. Now the king pulled his hand away altogether. "That's good enough. Take care of Tarius's face. We don't want him to be so ugly that even his wife won't love him."

Tarius sat still as Robert roughly washed the dried blood from the wound and Tarius's face. No doubt dirt and dust had stopped the bleeding, and as the doctor cleaned it, it began to bleed again. It was a bad cut which ran from the corner of the right eye to almost the middle of the chin.

"Take this," Robert said offering some powders.

Tarius held her mouth shut tight and shook her head no. She remembered what his powders had done to her before. Knew that she couldn't become the Katabull if he gave them to her, and they were going to need the Katabull tonight whether they knew it or not.

"Take them, don't be a fool. I have to put stitches in that," Robert said.

"I can take a stitch without wincing," Tarius assured him.

Robert looked at Persius, and the king shrugged. The surgeon threaded his needle and started to stitch the wound. Tarius was as good as her word; she didn't move a muscle even though it felt like he was trying to tear her face off.

"That's a bad cut," Persius said conversationally. "He damn near had you."

Tarius was silent for obvious reasons, and Persius went on. "I called a cease fire on my line when they started to retreat. It goes against the Jethrik code of honor to shoot or stab a man in the back. You know that. Yet it didn't keep you from ordering the men to continue lobbing arrows into their backs. It didn't keep you from going after them. Because you understand the code in a way that none of the rest of us truly do. Because first and foremost, as a Sword Master you must defend the kingdom, and as king, I must protect the people. As you said, we can't do that if we are dead. We know as you do what the Amalites are capable of, and that they badly out number us. We know that we have been losing this war, and that we were losing earlier this day. Yet it was only you who remembered even under the pressure of battle what we are really fighting for. Not honor or glory, we fight for our lives and the lives of our people. How odd it is that you, a sword-wielding, out-country warlord should be teaching me how to be a better king!"

Robert had finished the stitching, and Tarius rejected his attempts to dress the wound. Anything sticking out would get in her line of sight. The swelling was bad enough. She looked at Persius, and smiled as if she'd heard none of his praise. "So, am I too ugly for Jena?" she asked.

Persius smiled back. "You always were, you ugly Kartik bastard... Why don't you go and get some rest?"

Tarius nodded and got up. She opened the door and stepped out of the carriage.

"Tarius!" Persius called after her. She turned to face him. "Be more careful; I need you."

"Thank you, Sire." She bowed to him and then walked off.

"Well, I'll be damned," Persius said in disbelief.

"What's that, Sire?" Robert asked.

"Nothing," Persius said. "Go on now. Attend to the real wounded. Make sure my best men get worked on first, then anyone who will be able to fight tomorrow. Anyone too badly wounded to fight tomorrow gets shipped back to the villages for treatment."

Persius watched the surgeon go, then leaned back in his chair and closed his eyes to rest. Tarius had never bowed to him before. "So, Tarius the Black finally respects me! And what did I do to deserve that respect?" Persius frowned. "I sanctioned stabbing men in the back." He rubbed his hands down his face. The world had gone mad. In war nothing was wrong but losing. No blacks and whites, only areas of gray. Whatever it took, whatever worked.

Robert walked towards the makeshift surgery. Just a big tent, really. The wounded were stacked up all around the outside of it. The medics were running around like chickens with their heads cut off, doing little but making the wounded more nervous than they already were. Robert waded in and got right to work. He tried to direct the medics, but they were all soldiers, and they didn't respect or listen to him because he wasn't.

It was ironic really. Not long ago he had been complaining about never seeing any serious injuries, and right now he'd give all he had to be able to treat a simple kitchen burn. The working conditions were impossible, and he needed help. Suddenly Tarius appeared by his side. Robert fully expected him to shout some orders at him, but instead he started to help him with the patient he was working on.

"This is a mess up in here," Tarius said, handing the surgeon some gauze. "You need more help, and the severely wounded need to be field dressed and shipped out."

Robert nodded and snapped. "I know that, but none of you military types will listen to a word I say."

"Oh, *yes*, they will." Tarius stood up. "Listen up!" Tarius screamed. He got almost instant silence. "We have lots of wounded here, and the men are still retrieving them from below. I need twenty more men to work as medics over here. I need wagons to haul the badly wounded to the nearest village, and I expect those wagons to come back loaded with able-bodied men. This man is the king's surgeon. He is very learned, and we are lucky to have him. He will run this surgery, and until further notice all medics will report to him and take orders directly from him. Anyone who does not listen to him and follow his orders will have to answer to me. Now where the hell are my volunteers?"

Robert watched in amazement as fifty men showed up. Tarius picked twenty and sent the rest out to the battlefield to bring in any wounded they found. Robert started giving orders, and the medics listened. Trained medics each took one of the volunteers to help them set up a triage, and soon they had things under control. The badly wounded were being field dressed and sent off, and the others were having their wounds treated. Seeing that things were working well, Tarius started to leave.

"Sir Tarius!" Robert called out.

Tarius turned to face him. "Yes?"

"Thank you."

Tarius smiled and nodded. "Thank you. For treating my men, and for sewing up my face. I should have thanked you then, but..." Tarius moved up close to him and whispered. "Between you and me, it hurt too damn much. I almost passed out. I would have taken the powders, because they helped me before, but could you see me handling all of this with those powders in my system?"

"I suppose not." Robert watched Tarius go. Kartik bullyboy he might be, but you had to respect him all the same.

Tarius made the crossbowmen take shifts in the trees, serving as both defense and watch. After she got the camp lined out and all of their wounded had been hauled in, she went to search for Arvon. She found him, not to surprisingly giving a sword lesson to young Dustan. She smiled and shook her head.

"Arvon!" She motioned with her head, and he came over to her. "It's almost dark."

"Are we going there again? Is that safe?"

"We are, and it's not, but we've got to cut the odds," Tarius said.

"Brakston's starting to ask questions," Arvon said. "And I can't seem to shake your newly-acquired page."

"Harris tells me he thinks the boy has a 'thing' for you," Tarius said, smiling at the look that came over her friend's face.

Arvon looked over at the youth who smiled back at him, and he sighed. "My mind was so far away from that, that it never even crossed my mind. He is kind of cute, though, isn't he?"

Tarius grabbed Arvon's chin and made him look at her. "Well, keep your mind off of it right now. We have work to do. Meet me by the big oak by the creek as soon as it's nightfall."

Arvon nodded.

He found Tarius asleep under the tree. She woke when one of his feet stepped on a twig and it snapped. She flipped her legs up, arched her back forward, and was on her feet with sword in hand in a flash.

"Wow!" Arvon said holding up his hands. He smiled at her. "Tarius, you're exhausted; I'm exhausted. They're going to be waiting for us, for anyone..."

"That's why we're going to sneak into their camp."

"And could it hurt to have a little help to do that?" Hellibolt had appeared from apparently nowhere, and they both turned on him with swords in hand.

"You old fool," Tarius said breathing heavily. She lowered her voice to a whisper and spoke to Arvon, "He's a friend... almost. So, what do you mean, old man? What sort of help?"

"Take back what you said, or I shan't help you at all," Hellibolt said crossing his arms across his chest and putting his nose in the air.

Tarius went over what she had said until she found the offensive item. "You are no fool, however it *is* stupid to sneak up on armed warriors."

"Point taken. I was thinking something in a nice stealth spell. Help you hide and keep you from being heard or scented."

"But magic doesn't work on the Katabull," Tarius said.

Hellibolt sighed disgusted with her ignorance. "The spell isn't against you. It's against them."

"Good, that would be great then," Tarius said. "Do a stealth spell."

"Little Katabull in the spring, they can do most anything. Let them go; let no one see what these two might really be," Hellibolt intoned.

Arvon made a face and looked at Tarius. She shrugged. "They're not very pretty, but they seem to work."

The Katabull sneaked into the Amalite camp where they killed men as they slept. They grabbed men from behind and slit their throats.

When they had killed a great many of them, they let their presence be known, sending the Amalites into a panic. Then they ran from the camp and into the night.

They went back to where their horses were tied and grazing by the creek. They changed back to human form, and Arvon started to throw up. Tarius patted him on the back, and Arvon pulled away. He sat on a rock and put his head in his hands. He was shaking. He looked over at Tarius, who seemed unmoved by what they had just done.

"Do you feel nothing?" Arvon asked, near tears. "I know what we did will help. I know it might very well mean the difference between winning and losing, but... I can't help but feel as if I left a piece of my soul back there with the first sleeping man's throat I cut."

"I feel, Arvon, but not for them. Never for them. See, they made me what I am today. They did it to me years ago, and now they have made you what you are right now. If that isn't reason enough in itself to hate them, then I don't know what is." She walked over and put a hand on his shoulder. "Do what I have done for years. Don't think about it; put it out of your mind, because to face it too fully is to go mad."

"How can I put something like that out of my mind? I snuck into their tents and cut their throats. They didn't have a chance," Arvon said. Now his tears did fall. "At the time I did it without thinking. It's the Katabull; it's the beast within. It doesn't care what it does; it is without conscience."

"*You* are the Katabull, Arvon, and the Katabull is you. Blaming it on the Katabull is the same as blaming it on yourself. It's like a drunk blaming the liquor for a crime he committed. He only did what he would have done sober if he wasn't too afraid," Tarius said.

"Are you saying I wanted to kill those men like that? That I enjoyed it?"

"No. I'm saying that you knew what had to be done, and being Katabull just gave you the courage to do it."

"It really doesn't bother you, does it?" Arvon asked, drying his eyes.

"It does. I'd rather not have to do it, but they won't leave us alone. They won't let people be. They won't be happy until they have killed every nonbeliever, and that's you and me and everyone and everything we love. It's funny, because you're older than me, but you know what your problem is, my brother? You haven't learned what it means to truly hate yet."

9

The word from the front wasn't good. Jena frowned and stared out at the courtyard from where she sat on a cut stone bench. She and Tarius had sat here for hours under this big tree, talking of everything and nothing, holding hands and just basically enjoying each other's company. It seemed like a lifetime had passed since he had held her in his arms and spoken soft words of love to her. She missed him in a way she had never dreamed it was possible to miss someone. Her body literally ached to hold him, to kiss him, to feel his lips on hers, to feel his hands on her bare skin...

She took a deep breath and let it out with a sigh. The day was lovely, sunny and bright. The air was fresh, and nothing here seemed to realize what was going on just on the other side of the kingdom. It was almost noon, and by now Tarius would doubtless be on the battlefield. Maybe hurt, maybe even... She shook her head; she wouldn't think it. Tarius would come home. The war would be over soon, and Tarius would come home. They would be together again, and all would be right with the world.

Suddenly someone was sitting beside her. She didn't have to look up to know who. Tragon limped around the courtyard and grounds, his leg seeming to be better one day and worse the next. She couldn't find a moment's peace from him anywhere save in the house. She knew what he was up to. He wanted her. He didn't care that she belonged to his friend and partner. He wanted her and hoped to win her while Tarius was away and she was vulnerable in her loneliness. What he didn't know was that every time he spoke to her she cared less for him. He was like a vulture waiting for hope to die in her so that he could rush in and devour her.

"It's a beautiful day," Tragon said. "As they say, a good day to die."

Jena glared at him through squinted eyes and hissed. "Is that supposed to be funny?"

"I was simply saying..."

"What! What were you saying? You know the war rages at the front. You know my own husband stands in the battle even as we speak. Why would you say such an awful thing?" Jena got to her feet, and she glared down at him waiting for his answer.

"It's just a saying, Jena. I'm sorry... I didn't think," Tragon said.

"And I think you did. I think you said it because you know that while you limp around here pretending to be hurt, my love fights for you both." She turned and started to walk away.

Tragon was suddenly angrier than he had ever been in his life. He didn't know why he was so mad. Maybe it was because in that moment he realized she'd never have anything more than contempt for him. Maybe it was just that she knew he was faking the severity of his injury so that he could stay here out of harm's way. Most likely he was so angry because he knew he shouldn't be going after Jena, not when he was only alive because Tarius had saved him.

He jumped from the bench and grabbed Jena's arm in one movement. "Foolish girl! You wait for Tarius," Tragon hissed with venom. "You delude yourself that he cares for you. All he cares about is his sword and cutting people in two with it. Do you know that they call him Tarius the Black? Not because of the armor he wears, but because that is the color of his soul. They call him the Kartik Bastard not because he was born out of wedlock but because he's such a hideous killer that no family would want to claim him. I am a man with a gentle soul, Jena. I am capable of love. I love you, Jena; I always have. Tarius doesn't love you. Tarius can't love you because his soul is consumed with hate. Answer me this... Has he ever made love to you?"

"Many times," Jena answered nervously.

Tragon laughed bitterly. "Have you, Jena, ever been allowed to so much as touch him?"

"What business is it of yours?" Jena hissed back and tried to pull out of his grasp.

Tragon held on tight. "He hasn't, has he? And do you know why, Jena? Do you know why?" Tragon screamed in her face.

"Let me go!" Jena demanded.

"Because he can't. Because Tarius is not a *man* at all!"

Jena's eyes burned into him like two blue coals of fire, and he started to tell her just exactly what she had married. Who she had let caress and touch her whole body, but then in her blue eyes he suddenly saw the cold black eyes of the Katabull, and terror gripped his heart. His voice calmed then, and his hold on her arm loosened. "Can't you see, Jena? Tarius is a monster; he lives only to kill. He could never love you the way that I do. Your life with him will always be what it is right now. Waiting for him to come home from battle; waiting to see if he is alive or dead."

Jena jerked her arm free of his hand. She glared at him. "I would rather wait for a lifetime for a brave man to return home from a battle, than live with a cowardly man with too little honor to fight." She walked away from him, and Tragon watched her go.

He *was* a coward, and the thing he feared most was Tarius. Yet he couldn't stay away from Jena, which was possibly the one thing Tarius would actually kill him for.

By midday their casualties were high, and they were losing ground fast. No matter how many Amalites they killed, there seemed to be just as many as before. It was as if they came from thin air. There were just too many of them. The men were losing hope, and their spirits were low. The king moved to the front of the ranks hoping to give his army courage, but they just had nothing left to give.

Tarius and Harris were running the right flank and barely holding their ground. Any hopes for advancement were gone. If they could only hold their ground till the reinforcements from the villages got there, they might be all right.

Tarius had a spear and from horseback was picking off men in the opposing shield wall. But more just moved in to take their place. The bodies were stacking up two and three deep in places. Their men, her men, under hoof and under foot. To fall to stumble in this battle was as deadly as taking a blow from sword, pike, arrow or spear.

Suddenly from the corner of her eye she saw an Amalite bowman on horse back taking careful aim. She looked quickly and saw his target. She broke rank and spurred her horse so that he jumped over the shield wall, trampling Amalites on the other side as he did so. Tarius spurred the horse on at full gallop. Without slowing the horse, she jumped into the saddle, standing on her feet, then she leapt into the air and grabbed the arrow as it raced towards its intended victim. She landed on the ground in front of the king's horse on her feet on their side of the shield wall and her horse followed. Immediately, she spun around to face the opposing army, held the arrow high in her left hand, grabbed her sword with her right and drew it. Then she let out a scream that was heard all over the battlefield. There was a moment of silence as people on all sides became aware of what she had done. Tarius screamed again, and then ran, sword in hand and screaming, straight into the fray. She ran over her own shield wall and then the opposing army's shield wall. Running up a shield, she decapitated the man holding it and started hacking and slashing everything in sight. The Jethrik army behind her all went as berserk as she had, and the tide of the battle changed even as the reinforcements arrived, racing down the hill to join them.

They soon had the Amalites on the run, and this time not one archer ceased fire. This time not one man stopped in his pursuit of the Amalites until they had crossed over the river and into their camp. On Tarius's instructions they canvassed the killing field, killing the Amalite wounded and picking them clean of weapons and armor. They hauled their own wounded back to camp and then they stacked all the dead bodies of the Amalites up as a barrier. In places it was three and four high. Their own dead they carried back to the tree line. They couldn't deal with them now, but they could keep the Amalites from defiling their dead the way that they were defiling the dead Amalites. It was demoralizing to see your dead abused by the enemy. Tarius knew this, and so she made them into a wall and used their bodies as a shield.

Twice the Amalites tried to stop them, and twice they drove them back into their camp.

Yesterday's bodies were already starting to stink. In the heat and the wet it was no wonder they were decaying quickly. At least in the shade of the trees it would take their dead a little longer to rot. Maybe they'd have a chance to bury them before they got too ripe.

Tarius was giving orders, setting up sentries and seeing to the wounded and the feeding of the men. All the things that were her duty. Hellibolt walked up to her and pulled her a little to the side.

"That was it," Hellibolt said shaking his head sadly. "I couldn't be sure what it would be, but now I know that was it."

"That was what?" Tarius asked curtly, not in the mood to deal with Hellibolt or his strangeness at that moment.

"It was Persius' fate to die on the shaft of that arrow. Now I am afraid you have sealed your own fate, and it won't be pleasant. You will be destroyed by the very men you have saved," Hellibolt assured her.

Tarius looked thoughtful. She did not all together dismiss the wizard's words. She knew he had great power, however... "I do not believe in prophecy, Hellibolt. Prophecy negates free will, and I believe all people have free will."

"True enough. But there are times in which the snapping of a twig may change the course of history itself. Some men are meant to die before they can do evil. Now you have saved a partner who loves your wife and knows who you are, and a proud king who'd rather die than take advice from a woman. It is a recipe for disaster. Tread carefully, Tarius. Tread very carefully, or the earth will pull away from your feet and suck you down into the abyss."

Tarius nodded and watched the old man walk away. Harris walked up to her. "What did the wizard want?"

"To warn me. Apparently the king was supposed to die in that battle, and now I have cursed myself," Tarius said, forcing a smile she did not feel.

Persius rode up to her and dismounted. He had been riding through the camp, assessing the damages and basically looking kingly. He had taken his helmet off, and he ran up to her and embraced her. Not at all a pleasant experience since he was wearing a full set of plate.

"What honor could I bestow on you which I haven't already?" He stood away from Tarius and put his hands on her shoulders. "You have saved my life. Not once but twice. Never before have I seen or heard of a warrior such as you who can pluck an arrow from the air as easily as one might pick an apple. Ask for anything, Tarius, and it shall be yours. Money, lands, jewels, servants."

"I have no need for any of those things," Tarius laughed.

"Then let me give you a title. Make you a Baron or better yet a Count, and..."

"The title of knight is enough of a burden for me to bear."

"Surely there is something..."

"Actually..." She grabbed Harris by the arm and dragged him over. "My squire, Harris is as good a fighter as any swordsman. He is loyal to country and to friends, and is by far the finest man I have ever known. He is my equal in every way. For this reason I want you to knight him this very day at this very time. That is what I ask."

Harris looked shocked.

The king smiled and nodded, obviously glad to have found something that Tarius wanted. He called his herald over and gave him commands.

"Hear ye! Hear ye! His royal Majesty the good King Persius wishes all to pay heed."

"Good men! On this day I give honor to one who deserves more than I can ever give him." He pulled his sword, and Harris knelt before the king. "I dub thee, Sir Harris the Nimble, and charge you serve the kingdom and the people well in times of peace as well as in times of war."

He put his sword away. "Rise, Sir Harris."

Harris rose and suddenly the crippled boy was gone. Harris was a man, a proud man. Tarius hugged him tightly.

"And you, Sir Tarius," Persius started. Tarius released Harris and turned to face the king. "You, my friend, are the greatest warrior who ever lived."

The men cheered loudly for a good ten minutes. Then Persius said, "Enough! Get back to work."

Harris watched the king go, then he turned to Tarius. "I... I'm not equal to you, Tarius! I never could be, I..."

"Deserve knighthood as much as I do. Maybe more so," Tarius smiled. "You should have been a Sword Master, but the stupid rules prevented you. The king picks who he knights, so the rules change with the king. Now, let's get back to work, Sir Harris."

"The nimble... Is that supposed to be some sort of joke?" Harris asked as he followed Tarius.

"When a crippled man moves the way you do, he is indeed the most nimble of men," Tarius said.

As the morning sun broke through, the fifth division arrived. They had sent word for their two units guarding the road into the Amalite camp to close in from behind. The battle went on all through the day and into the night, but now it was the Amalites who were getting slaughtered, and soon it was the Amalites who were badly out-numbered.

When on the very next morning their two divisions closed in behind the Amalites camp, the Jethrik army forded the river and entered into the Amalite camp. They cut a swath through the camp, and towards evening the Amalite leader appeared with a white flag. Persius called a cease-fire, and Tarius immediately rode up beside him.

"Persius," Tarius spoke, out of breath from the fighting. "We are winning. You can't make peace with the Amalites."

"We must at least hear them out."

"No! Send them away! They are our enemies, and we must kill them all," Tarius said. "They would not show us mercy."

"I will meet with them. Bring them to me."

They met in Persius' pavilion, which was erected for the purpose. There were five Amalites in all, only one of which spoke Jethrik. "Our leader wishes to retreat. To end the war."

"You are a liar. You are all liars," Tarius hissed.

"Tarius!" Persius said in a warning tone. "Go on. I'm afraid my warlord has even more reason to distrust your people than the rest of us do. You have attacked our country for the second time in less than twelve years. These were unprovoked attacks launched against us for the purpose of taking our country away from us. Make your plea ring with truth, or I shall turn my men lose on you to do as they please."

The leader spoke to the interpreter, and the interpreter spoke to them. "My leader says that we will leave you in peace. We wish to retreat in peace."

"Until they regroup, rearm, and prepare," Tarius insisted.

"Tarius, hold your tongue!" Persius warned.

"I can not, and I will not. Not while you harbor even one notion of listening to the words of these Amalite scum."

"Tarius," Persius whispered to her. "Do not make me have to ask you to leave. We all want an end to the war."

"Then let us end it," Tarius whispered back. "Let us go across their borders and hunt them down and kill out every fighting man and every priest in all of Amalite. Then and only then will there be lasting peace."

"Tarius... you are a warrior, but you do not understand everything about a war. While we fight farms go untended, crops don't get in, and people don't pay taxes. Our country doesn't run on the war machine. We need these men at home growing crops. Every day this war goes on, another field lies dormant and flocks go untended."

"And I tell you now that if you do not hunt them down to the last man, they will only rebuild their forces and come after you again. They are not like us. They don't care about fields getting plowed or flocks getting tended. All of that takes second place to serving their gods because they believe their gods will give them eternal life. So who cares if they starve to death or they die in battle? As long as they have served their gods, they will live on forever. And how do they serve their gods? By killing the unbelievers. And who would be the unbelievers? Well, that would be us. Ask them this one question, and if they answer it correctly, I will not question you again in this matter. Ask them to swear on their gods that they believe that we have the right to live here or anywhere else. Ask them to promise never to attack us or to send their filthy missionaries into our territories again."

Persius posed the questions. The interpreter told the leader what Persius asked, and then the leader answered.

"He says we will leave your lands now. That you may live as long as you like once you have seen the light. That we will take our missionaries with us," the interpreter said.

Tarius glared right into the eyes of the leader. "See how they dance around the truth? Swear an oath on your gods that you will leave us be, that you admit that we have a right to live."

"He's answered the question, Tarius," Persius said gently. "It's time to think about peace."

"There can never be peace as long as an Amalite breathes a breath on this world." Tarius glared at the Amalite leader again. "If you let them go now, we shall again be in this very same field fighting this very same war, and the next time we may not win."

"That's enough, Tarius," Persius said. "You're disrupting this meeting and making it impossible to negotiate with them."

Tarius didn't seem to care. She launched into a parable.

"There was a mother who had an infant child. One day she needed to go into town to get some milk for her child as she had gone dry. It was too long a walk to carry a baby, so she asked a wolf to watch the child for her. The wolf promised he would let no harm come to the child, and so the mother went into town to get the milk. When she arrived home the wolf had devoured the baby. The mother cried and said, 'How could you? You promised no harm would come to my baby!' She cried out to the Nameless One and asked for judgment against the wolf, but nothing happened to the wolf. For you see, it is the wolf's nature to kill and devour that which is weaker than him. The mother killed her own child," Tarius said. "Your fate will be the same if you make a deal with the Amalites. They will destroy your country, and you will have no one to blame but yourself." Having spoken, Tarius turned and left the tent without waiting to be ordered to do so.

The Amalite leader started to talk quickly, no doubt he wanted to know what Tarius had said, and the interpreter told him. The Amalite leader spat on the ground, then he glared at Persius. He spoke to him harshly.

"He wants to know if that was the one called Tarius the Black?"

Persius was curious. He knew men like Tarius gained reputations on both sides, but they knew him by name, which seemed odd.

"He is. What's it to you, and how is it that you know his name?" Persius asked.

The interpreter relayed the message to the leader, who spat something back quickly.

"He says that he heard his name on the wind. That it is him who your men cheer."

"He is a great and respected warrior," Persius said.

The Amalite leader spoke again, this time in a calmer tone.

"Our leader wishes to make a deal with you..."

Persius stood to his full height and glared at the leader. "Why would I make a deal with you? You have invaded my kingdom, killed my people, burned my land, and now when we are winning, you think that I should make a deal with you. The only deal I will make with you is that if you take your murdering scum back over my borders and stay out of my kingdom, I will let you leave with your lives, but not with your weapons."

The interpreter told the Amalite what Persius had said, and the Amalite frowned and made a long speech, all the while looking at Persius.

The interpreter looked at Persius. He obviously did not approve of what the leader had said. "We have many troops still in your lands, within your borders. He wants you to give them safe passage from your lands."

Persius thought about that. "No. I want you all gone, and I want you gone today. Any of your men within our borders who are alive shall be hunted down and killed to the last man. I know how you people work, and I won't allow it."

The interpreter relayed the message and the Amalite looked angry. He spoke angry words that the interpreter did not interpret.

"What did he say?" Persius demanded.

The interpreter looked at the leader and apparently told him that Persius wanted to know what he said. The leader nodded, giving Persius a look of utter contempt.

"He calls on the gods of light to smite you. He puts a curse on your house and your children, because you will not give our, 'missionaries' safe passage from your kingdom," the interpreter said.

Persius was mad now. Mad enough to seriously consider Tarius's proposal. But he had an idea, one that made him smile.

"All right, you want a deal? I'll give you a deal. You," he pointed at the leader. "Fight to the death with my champion. If you win, we will allow your 'soldiers' to leave unmolested. However, if you lose, you leave my country and we kill every single filthy Amalite we find in ours."

The interpreter told the leader, and he was just mad enough to take Persius' offer.

"We will prepare ourselves," the interpreter said, and he and the Amalite leader left.

"A barbaric practice my king?" Hellibolt said at his shoulder.

"Amalites aren't as good as Barbarians." He called his page over. "Go and get Tarius. Tell him to prepare himself for battle."

"At once, Sire." The page hurried out.

"You should take Tarius's counsel," Hellibolt said. "Kill the bastards to the last man. He hasn't steered you wrong yet."

"We have to have peace, Hellibolt!" Persius said in disbelief. "Too many good men have died already."

"But Tarius is right, Sire. If you do not kill them now, they will rebuild their army, grow stronger than ever, and come back after us," Hellibolt said.

"And we'll be ready for them if they do. For now, I want an end to the killing. I want to go back to my castle, my wives, and my children. I want to run the country, repair it after this conflict," Persius said.

"Then go home, by all means. Let your men push them back, hunt them down and destroy them," Hellibolt said.

"Do you see the future?" Persius asked a bit concerned. "Do you warn me because you see a future in which our armies will have to fight the Amalites again?"

"I don't see it, no. But I think Tarius does," Hellibolt said.

Persius slung a hand in the air dismissing the wizard. He grabbed his cloak from his throne and walked out of the tent. They had beaten the Amalites down. Now that they knew they could not win against the might of the Jethrik army, they wouldn't dare to try again. Tarius was a man filled with righteous hatred, and Hellibolt was an old fool who knew nothing more important than how to mix a few powders.

Outside the sun was still high in the sky. The Amalites were being stripped of their weapons and horses and forced to march on foot for the boarder. They deserved no more mercy than they were getting.

Tarius walked over to the king as soon as she saw him.

"Your page said you wanted to see me." Tarius was mad at Persius and made no attempt to hide the fact.

"Dear Tarius, please try to understand. Look on the bright side. After you have taken the first division and swept the country clean of the Amalites, you can go home to your bride," Persius said.

Tarius was not swayed. "What duty do you have for me?"

"A duel to the death with the Amalite leader. He's an insolent bastard who cursed my whole house, and I want him dead," Persius said.

This brought a smile to Tarius's lips. "Bring the bloated bastard on."

Tarius had sharpened her sword, and she stood poised and ready. The Amalite leader walked out with his retinue, cocky and self-assured until he got a look at the king's champion. His face seemed to fall a little, and his stride was cut in half for several steps. He carried a great sword, which was in Tarius's opinion one of the most worthless weapons one could have in single combat. She waited till he was almost too close before she drew her sword. Around her the men cheered her name over and over.

The Amalite slung his blade, and she easily jumped out of the way. It slammed into the ground, and she brought her blade up into the muscle of his left arm and slid the blade across it, opening the muscle. Before he could heave the sword from the ground, she planted a good hard blow with the flat of her blade to his kidneys.

She was playing with him, and everyone knew it.

He spun around quickly, slinging his blade wildly, and Tarius easily blocked the blow. She looked at him and smiled.

"That's right, you big dumb bastard, I can kill you any time I like," she said in a voice so low that he was the only one that could hear her. He couldn't understand her words, but he more than understood the tone in her voice. He knew that she was taunting him.

He screamed and ran at her again.

A knife appeared seemingly from nowhere. Tarius caught it by the handle in her left hand and threw it back at the would-be assassin, sticking it deep in his chest. At the same time, she sliced through the throat of his leader.

Tarius stepped back, blood dripping from her sword. She pointed her blade at the still tottering man with a knife sticking out of his chest. "See, Persius? What did I tell you? There is no honor among the Amalites. Kill them all and be done with it."

Persius called her over with a wave of his hand and did the same with the Amalite translator. "See this man?" Persius said to the interpreter pointing at Tarius. "He wants nothing more than to hunt you to the last man and kill you. I owe this man my life, not once but twice, and I would like nothing better than to let him have his way. However it is not in the best interest of my kingdom to continue this war, so I'm going to let you go. But tell your people this. If they so much as turn around on their way out of my country, I will not hesitate to kill them. Any Amalite who comes into the Jethrik for any reason will be killed on sight. We will not tolerate your missionaries or your traders. You stay on your side of the line, and we'll stay on ours. You cross over for any reason, and I'll let Tarius the Black do exactly what he wants to do to you and to your country. Now go... run."

By nightfall the Amalites were more than halfway to the border, being driven on by Jethrik soldiers on horseback. True to the king's word, any one of them who even looked over his shoulder was executed on the spot.

Tarius had been looking for Arvon with no luck, and had finally, to her horror, taken to the field and was searching among the dead. She found him kneeling over a body, and knew immediately what had happened. Tarius ran forward, dropping to her knees beside him. She looked down at Brakston, and her tears fell freely. She put an arm around Arvon's shoulders and braced him against his racking sobs.

"Oh, Arvon... I'm so sorry," Tarius said. The arrow had struck Brakston square in the chest. He hadn't had a chance. "We should kill every one of the bastards."

"It won't bring him back, Tarius. All the killing, it won't bring anyone back," Arvon cried. "You know what he said as he was dying, Tarius?"

Tarius knew that he didn't require an answer, so she waited silently.

"He said that he loved me. Why did he wait till now? What good does it do anyone *now*? We might have loved the greatest love ever known, but I didn't know! He never told me! And I loved him, Tarius. I loved him so much that it hurt, but he kept insisting he wasn't interested in me. Why did he lie, Tarius?"

Tarius was silent for a moment. "He was afraid of being rejected. Not by you, but by everyone else. This country is so stupid!" Tarius stood up suddenly and dried her eyes. "Rules upon rules, upon rules. Laws, within laws, within laws. All created to make sure that no one can be happy." She wasn't thinking about Brakston or even Arvon right then, she was thinking about herself. About her own problems. "As soon as I get home I'm packing up Jena and I'm leaving for Kartik. If you're smart you'll go with me." She put a hand down and helped Arvon to his feet. "Come, let's get a shovel and bury our dead."

A contingent of Sword Masters and swordsmen were left on the border to make sure the Amalites didn't attempt to cross over. The king and his retinue headed for the capital, and most of the soldiers headed for home.

Tarius, Harris and Arvon led a small company of Sword Masters on a mission. They would clean the country of the Amalite menace. They would make sure that not one Amalite stood on Jethrik held land. It was also their duty to see that every last man of their own who lay slain on the field was buried.

The Amalites were stripped naked and hauled off first. They were thrown into a nearby canyon for the buzzards to feast on their carcasses.

The flies were as thick as water by the time they finished the task, and the bodies were starting to slip. The stench was as vile as the job, and they had to fight the vultures to bury their own dead.

They buried them in shallow trenches, putting in as many bodies as possible. When they were done, the entire field was covered with mounds of dirt. It was only then, when they looked out on the field, that they realized all that had been lost in the war. How many wives had been widowed? How many children were now fatherless? How many parents were now childless?

By the time they had finished their despicable task, not one among them hated the Amalites any less than Tarius.

They moved out, a small unit only fifty men strong. They hauled with them five wagons, each overloaded with Amalite armor. This was to be distributed amongst the villages they came across. They would need every man and woman to be able to fight when next the Amalites decided to "cleanse" the earth of the unbelievers. When next the Amalites attacked, they would be ready for whatever Persius could throw at them. That was what Persius had failed to understand. He was saving a few lives now to get thousands killed later.

Tarius rode in front, and Arvon and Dustan brought up the rear. Harris rode just behind Tarius, watching him. The war had changed them all, but it had changed Tarius the most, although Harris doubted that Tarius realized it.

These days, Tarius was serious all the time. He never talked about home now. He never even talked about Jena. He was silent and brooding, and when he talked at all it was to give an order or damn the Amalites.

Arvon was not much better. He was as filled with hate as Tarius had ever been. Arvon was now prone to fits of emotion so violent that one never knew what to expect from him. He would be screaming in anger one minute and crying in grief the next. Tarius would take him aside and talk to him, and he would calm down. Then he would apologize to everyone in general and no one in particular. Harris had no idea what Tarius said to him, but it seemed to help.

The problem was that each time Tarius helped anyone these days, it seemed to take an incredible toll on him. No one else seemed to notice, perhaps because they all had problems that only Tarius could fix, but Tarius was having problems, too. Problems that no one was fixing.

Harris wanted to help Tarius, but he didn't know how to open a dialogue with him. Didn't know how to get Tarius to drop his guard long enough to unburden himself of some of what he was carrying.

Harris decided that as a friend it was his duty to at least try.

He rode up along side Tarius. "So, all's quiet so far."

"Aye," Tarius said.

"I was wondering if you could help me with a problem," Harris said.

He could almost see a dark cloud form around his mentor's head. One more problem. One more, and this one might be the one that was too much.

"Let's hear it," Tarius said, lacking his normal enthusiasm.

"Actually, it's not my problem. I have this friend with a big problem, and I don't know how to help him. He acts like the war doesn't bother him, although it is obvious to anyone with eyes that it does. Everyone comes whining to him with their problems all day long, and he never has time to catch a breath or think about his own problems. He's taking on too much responsibility; it's always work, work, working. He doesn't even joke any more, he's so serious. Everyone needs to smile every once in awhile, don't you think?"

Tarius smiled for the first time in a week. "Sounds a dreary fellow... Have I really gotten that bad?"

"You've gotten that good at leading the army," Harris said. "I'm just not sure it's good for you."

"I'm not sure anything is good for me anymore. We didn't kill the Amalites to the last man, and so all of this was a waste of time," Tarius said. "All the bloodshed was for nothing."

"You... You really believe that, Tarius?"

"Yes, I do. They'll go home. They'll regroup, rearm, and come back stronger than ever. Their country is three times the size of Jethrik. Do you know how it got that big? By gobbling up the countries on its borders. When your opponent is bigger than you, you can't beat him with might, you have to beat them with your wits. We had them beaten, and we shouldn't have stopped till we had gotten rid of them. Beaten them down, taken control of their country and outlawed their horrid religion."

"No wonder you've been in such a mood! You really believe that Gudgin and Brakston and all the others died for nothing?" Harris asked.

"Oh, they stopped the Amalites for this day. Maybe a year, maybe five, maybe ten, but a wound left unbound keeps bleeding until the body is dead. Their religion encourages them to have as many children as they can make. They breed like rabbits, and they'll just keep hitting us. We'll send our best out to die on their swords, and we'll beat them back and then let them regroup. Persius lacks vision. He sends farmers home now so that there will be plenty of food for this winter. Yet he can't see the death that he has ordered by pulling the army back before it has finished its work. That's why we must arm the common man. So that everyone can fight when next the Amalites rear their ugly heads. That's why we must make sure that not one Amalite takes a breath in all of the Jethrik."

"That's why you don't want to go home?"

"What makes you think I don't want to go home?" Tarius asked.

"Persius owes you his life. He respects you more than any man in this army—maybe on the planet. If you had said you wanted to go home, you would have been sent home. Obviously, you wanted to stay in the field," Harris said.

Tarius looked at him with a raised eyebrow. "Ah! Sir Knight, it seems that you have grown in more than just your fighting skills. No, I'm not ready to go home just yet. I feel I have let my wife and the country down. I have given them a temporary repair when they had hoped for a permanent cure."

Harris nodded. "When we first rode out, you talked of Jena every day. Now you hardly ever speak her name."

"How can one think of beauty and purity when one is gazing at death and flies and fighting buzzards over the bodies of your friends? Only at night when I lay down to sleep and all is silent do I gaze into the darkness and think of her." Tarius had a far away look. "I hope to convince her to leave this rock before the next war and go with me to Kartik. I had hoped to beat my father's enemies here. To stop them from destroying the earth. I now see that Persius means to feed his kingdom to the Amalites. The only hope for the world lies in the Kartik army. You should come as well."

"Leave Jethrik?"

"Yes. Join an army that knows how to fight and win. Go to a country not governed by so many stupid laws and rules." Tarius was excited now.

Harris laughed. "I don't know, Tarius. What of 'king and country?'"

"The king thought nothing of offering me up against the Amalite. He put me in a fight to the death without first asking how I felt about it, and he did it for no better reason than the Amalite made him angry."

"He knew you would win, Tarius."

"What if I hadn't?" Tarius asked. "He sends me to fight one of them for his pride, but he won't let us save the country by ridding ourselves of them forever. He cares neither for me nor for my opinion, so why should I care for him?"

Harris knew it was Tarius's philosophy that no one man was better than any other. Harris respected this above all other things about Tarius. Yet he personally couldn't get over the fact that Tarius was talking about "the king." He was silent.

Tarius took a deep breath and let it out. "I feel better having said all that. Thanks."

"You're welcome. Don't wait so long next time. I'll always listen to you, Tarius. You are my one true friend. I would do anything for you."

Tarius smiled. "I know you would, and it comforts me even at the darkest of times."

10

Jena had been watching the men ride by the academy all day. With each horseman that turned to enter, she held her breath hoping against hope that it was Tarius. Three days now the men had been arriving, and still no sign of Tarius. The war was over; they had won. The soldiers she spoke to told her that Tarius was fine, and that he was bringing up the rear.

Riders were more and more sparse, and Jena's hope was wearing thin. She saw the king's carriage come into view and she watched as it approached. Tarius had been working closely with the king, perhaps he was with the king now. But as the carriage drew closer, she did not recognize any of the horsemen surrounding the king as her husband.

The carriage stopped at the gates just feet from her. The door opened, and the king himself stepped out.

"You're the wife of my good friend, Sir Tarius the Black, warlord of all the Jethrik, are you not?"

She curtsied. "I am, Sire. If I may ask, do you have any news of my husband?"

"He stays in the field to wipe the Amalites from their hidden pockets all over our lands. I'm sorry that this has taken him away from you, but it is a job that he alone can do properly. He did send you this by my hand."

The king held out several pieces of paper folded together. Jena took them with a shaking hand, and tears dripped down her face. The king lifted her chin with his finger and wiped the tears from her cheek with another. "Dear lady, do not cry. If I know your man, he will have the job done and be home to you in due time. Be proud that you have such a husband. None like him has ever lived before, nor shall such a one ever live again. He plucked an arrow from the sky to save me, and only he would have the nerve and audacity to turn the king into a common messenger boy."

Jena nodded silently. She curtsied again, then turned and started back through the gates into the academy. She walked towards the clearing in the woods, clutching the note tightly to her. He didn't love her. He didn't love her enough to come home to her. Tragon was right. Tarius would rather stay in the field and fight.

She sat down in the middle of the clearing and slowly unfolded the letter. She couldn't stop crying, nor could she keep her hands from shaking.

She couldn't think such things. Tarius did love her, he did. He had a duty to perform, and he was doing it. It was that simple. No conspiracy to stay away from her at all. He wanted to be with her; he did! But he was busy making the country safe for her and for their future family. It was a noble thing that he did, and it still stank.

Jena was a young woman with a young woman's needs and desires. She wanted nothing more than to be with her husband. She would have gladly fought alongside him if such things were allowed, but they weren't, and his desire to fight kept them separated.

Jena dried her eyes and nose on her sleeve and finally looked at the letter.

My dearest love,

I know you may hate me, but I cannot come home now. Not while one Amalite bastard stands on Jethrik soil...

He went on to give her the events of the war in brief details. The letter ended in a very unexpected way.

Our king is a fool, and because of his foolery the Amalites shall swallow up the entire country. I do not want me or mine there when this happens. For this reason I once again beg you to consider moving with me to Kartik.

I miss you very much. All my love,

Tarius

Jena started to cry again. What did that mean, that he wanted her to consider moving with him to Kartik? Had he made up his mind that he was going, and she could go or stay if she liked? He had said he loved her, he had said he missed her, but most of the letter seemed cold and removed.

"I heard Tarius had decided to stay. I'm very sorry."

Jena's head snapped up at the sound of Tragon's voice, and she stood quickly not wanting to be sitting beneath him. "What are you doing here?" Jena asked hotly.

"Sorry, Jena, but you and Tarius's secret spot just isn't much of a secret," Tragon said harshly. "Didn't I tell you, Jena? Didn't I say he would choose war over you every time?"

"Did you come only to gloat at my misfortune then, Tragon?" Jena asked hotly.

"On the contrary. I have come to comfort you, Jena. You shouldn't be alone now," Tragon tried to smile sweetly, but it looked to Jena more like a snarl.

He had seen an opportunity to pounce, and he was pouncing. Problem was his prey was all too aware of his teeth.

"Comfort me!" Jena scoffed. "I don't need your kind of comforting, Tragon. I have a husband for that, and he will return home soon."

"That's why you're crying I suppose," Tragon said.

"I cry because I miss him, and his gentle words of love have touched my heart," Jena said quickly.

Tragon quickly grabbed the pieces of parchment from her fingers and easily held them out of her reach while he looked at them. "Oh, yes, this is a lovely sentiment," Tragon cleared his throat. "The dead were stacked up like cordwood. The flies were as thick as soup. So many of our men were dead it was hard to believe that we were the victors." Tragon slung the letter to the ground.

Jena wasn't stupid enough to reach over to pick it up. She didn't trust Tragon, and she wasn't about to put herself in that position. Something in his eyes right then told her that he wasn't quite sane.

"Some love letter you have there, Jena. Reads more like the log of a Warlord, and why shouldn't it? Tarius is after all the kingdom's only reigning Warlord. A killer tried and true..."

"The king himself told me that it was *his* decision to keep Tarius in the field," Jena countered.

Tragon laughed. "The king ows Tarius his life and his country. Do you really think that if Tarius had told the king he wanted to go home, that the king wouldn't have let him go? As I said, the king doesn't make any decisions concerning the war. Tarius does. If Tarius is in the field now, it is only because he wants to be."

Jena turned on her heel and started out of the field. She just wanted to get as much distance between her and Tragon as she could.

Tragon ran, caught her by the arm, and swung her around to face him. She kicked him in the knee, and he slung her into the ground and straddled her. He held one hand over her screaming mouth, and with his other gathered up her flailing arms. "Maybe I just need to show you what a real man could do for you, hey, Jena? Give you what Tarius hasn't, and isn't ever going to."

She bit his hand. Bit it hard, and he lost his grip on her hands. She drove the butt of her palm up into his solar plexus the way Tarius had taught her, and all the air was forced out of Tragon's lungs. Jena easily dug out from underneath him. While he was still gasping for breath she kicked him in his wounded leg, and he squealed in pain.

"Hear this and hear this well, Tragon. I will not tell a soul what happened here today, for I don't want to shame myself. My husband counts you among his friends, and I do not wish him to know what nature of man you really are. Let him believe he has saved a good man and not a wicked one. However, if you ever come near me again... If you even try to talk to me alone again, I will tell Tarius exactly what happened here today, and may the gods help you, because I think we both know what Tarius would do to you."

"I'm sorry Jena," Tragon called after her departing form. "Please forgive me." But she didn't turn around. He lay in the clearing clutching his leg in pain. "My gods what have I done, I have become an animal. A creature to be loathed."

Jena was right. If Tarius ever found out what had happened in this field, Tragon would be a dead man. The Katabull would shred him into pieces, and with the king as her ally, no one would dare to raise a hand or say a word against Tarius. In that moment Tragon wished that Tarius had let him die on the battlefield. Something had happened to him out there in combat. He wasn't the same man he had been, something had snapped in his brain, he knew that now. Jena had never liked him, so she'd never forgive him for this trespass.

Tragon knew his mind was completely bent because instead of hating himself for what he'd tried to do, he just hated Tarius all the more, because she was a better man than he was.

Tarius stood on a hill looking out over a small Amalite encampment. Soon they would sweep down and wipe them out, then they would be done. It had only taken them three months to hunt out and kill the Amalite "missionaries." The weather was turning cold, and it was time she got her troop back home.

Tarius walked over and got back on her horse. Arvon had the right flank this time, and he looked at her across the other men and shook his head. She was enough to scare a man to death. Her black armor, repaired a hundred times had gained some metal. Shiny metal pauldrons graced her shoulders, and seven limb tassets lay over her hips. She had cut the hair out of her eyes, but it now reached to the middle of her back, and she still wore two thick braids on either side of her face. She had smeared charred coals across her face in the lines of a skeletal design, so that she looked more beast than human. She took her helmet from her saddle horn and stuck it on her head, then she drew her sword. It wouldn't be long now.

The sword fell in a downward arc, and they started down the hill at a full gallop.

The Amalites had no idea what hit them. They weren't prepared for the attack, and they fell in a matter of minutes. When Arvon looked up from his last kill, he saw Tarius standing in the middle of the camp, sword in hand, desperately seeking another victim.

There was a crazed look in her eyes. Arvon quickly got off his horse and he walked carefully towards her. "Tarius, they're all dead. We can go home now."

She looked at him only a second and then wiped the blood from her blade with her fingers and flipped them in the air sending blood everywhere. She sheathed her sword, and only then did she look up at him.

"Home." She sighed and walked up to him. "We have to go home."

Arvon laughed. He looked around at all their happy comrades hugging each other and rejoicing that they could finally go home. "Have to? Tarius, it's over, and we *can* go home."

Tarius nodded silently.

"Tarius... Don't you *want* to go home? I know you miss Jena."

"Of course I want to be with Jena... It's just." Tarius shrugged and added in a whisper almost too low for him to hear. "She doesn't really want me, Arvon. I've tricked her, I'm the worst sort of heal and now I have to face that. It's worse than any Amalite."

"Tell her the truth. I think you'll be surprised."

The men all piled on Tarius, hugging her, and then carrying her around on their shoulders. Here she had acceptance. They completely bought her lies, but at home with Jena... How long could she fool Jena, especially when she didn't want to?

Harris rode up alongside Arvon. They had been on the road a week now, and they were almost home. Most of their fellows had left them to go to their own homes, and they were down to a mere ten men.

"What's with Tarius?" Harris asked quietly.

Arvon smiled. "Tarius is a warrior, Harris. Without an enemy to fight he feels sort of lost."

Harris slapped Arvon on the back. "I bet Jena can make him think about something besides fighting."

"Or at least give him a whole different fight," Arvon mumbled.

Harris rode up beside Tarius. "We're almost home, Tarius. Why don't we run the horses?"

Tarius laughed. "Since we are almost home, why not give our horses a well-deserved rest?"

"Aren't you excited to get home? To see Jena?"

"Yes," Tarius answered truthfully. She did long to see Jena, but she was scared, too. What if Tragon had told Jena? What if Jena now hated her? And even if she didn't, it was only a matter of time. What had Hellibolt said? *Her life was a recipe for disaster.* He was right.

However Harris's excitement was contagious, and the more she thought about how close she was to Jena, the more she wanted to see her. Finally, she looked over at Harris and smiled. "All right, I'll race you home. We'll be nice to our horses later." Tarius spurred her horse into a full gallop and Harris rode hard to try to keep up. The others did the same.

Jena was hanging out the laundry when she heard the sound of horses coming up fast. Her heart sunk in her chest; it could be bad news. She set the laundry basket down and ran towards the front gates. Suddenly a dark clad warrior rode hard through the front gates and jumped from his horse. The warrior landed mere feet away from Jena. She was startled, and it took her a second to realize that this grubby, soot covered warrior clad all in black leather and metal was her own dear husband… until their eyes met.

They met somewhere in the middle. Tarius lifted Jena in his arms and swung her around. Their lips met, and any fears Jena had were gone.

Harris rode in behind Tarius and got off his horse. He didn't look much less woolly than Tarius. He looked at Jena and Tarius and smiled. Nothing was going to peel them apart for a while.

Darian ran up and embraced Harris. "So, good Sir Harris, I see you have brought the heathen back to us in one piece."

"Aye, sir," Harris smiled.

"You smell a little ripe," Darian said, waving a hand in front of his face. "By the gods! It's good to see you lad."

Harris looked back over his shoulder. The others should have been there by now.

Darian smiled. "No doubt they've headed into town for some girls and some ale." He looked over to where Tarius and Jena stood just holding each other and smiled. "By the gods! He is a wild looking rascal."

"He paints his face when he goes into battle. Still has it all over his face," Harris said. "He is a fearsome sight to behold, at times he even scares me."

"Come on in the house. I'll have the servants draw you a bath, and we'll have an ale. Leave these two alone."

Harris nodded and followed Darian inside. "Ah! Chairs!" Harris said with a sigh looking at them. Darian laughed.

Tarius just held Jena for a long time, not moving and hardly breathing. The tears rolled freely down his cheeks, leaving streaks in the filth.

Jena moved back from him, looking into his face. She ran her finger over the unfamiliar scar on Tarius's face. "You do still love me?" Jena asked in a voice too small to be her own.

"How could I ever stop loving you?" Tarius said. He wiped the tears off Jena's face, leaving streaks of dirt, which he then tried to wipe off only making them worse. "Am I too ugly for you now?"

Jena laughed. "You are beautiful! A sight for my sore eyes. However, you are way too dirty even for me." She made a face at the stench coming off Tarius, he smelled worse than she could ever remember anything smelling.

"Then perhaps I'd better take a bath." Tarius released Jena and took her hand. He led her back towards his horse.

A young groom had run out upon hearing word that his hero, Sir Tarius, had just ridden onto the grounds. He had gathered the reins of both Tarius and Harris's horses and stood there happily waiting for an order from Tarius.

Tarius looked at the boy and smiled. He reached into his pocket and pulled out a ruby ring he had no doubt taken off one corpse or another. He tossed it to the lad who barely caught it and dropped the reins in the process. He quickly caught up the reins again, and looked at the ring then at Tarius

"For me, Sir?" he asked incredulously.

Tarius nodded. "Aye, you just take good care of my friend here. He has taken very good care of me."

"Thank you, Sir!" the excited boy said. "Thank you very much!"

Tarius grabbed something wrapped in several layers of leather off the horse, then grabbed his saddlebags. He nodded, and the boy started guiding the horses towards the stables.

"I have something for you," Tarius said. He handed the leather clad whatever to Jena.

It was much heavier than Jena thought it would be, and she almost dropped it. She started to open it, but Tarius grabbed her hands and stayed them looking quickly around.

"Not here." She took Jena's hand. "Come on." Tarius slung the saddlebags over his shoulder and started pulling Jena along.

Jena smiled at the familiar tug on her arm. Tarius hadn't changed. She squeezed his hand tight, and he turned to look at her and smiled, the kind of smile that lit up his whole face. This was no dark mindless killer who had returned home to her. This was the same warm and loving husband she had sent away to war, and his love for her was the same.

"I love you, Tarius," Jena said softly.

Tarius stopped tugging for a moment and turned to face her. He stepped closer to her, then bent down and kissed her gently on the mouth.

"I didn't realize till this moment how much I had missed hearing you say that to me, looking into your eyes, and knowing that it's true." He kissed her again, this time with more passion. He stopped abruptly, moved away and started pulling her along again. "Come on! I'm too filthy to be thinking about doing to you what I want to be doing to you."

Jena laughed and followed him. At the creek Tarius sat on a rock and dragged Jena down beside him. Tarius looked at Jena impatiently. "Well, open it."

It wasn't as easy as it sounded because it was wrapped in several layers of suede and had been tied with leather thong that had obviously been wet more than once by the tightness of the knots. It wasn't hard to tell what Tarius had brought her. Other husbands coming home from war would be bringing their wives rare jewelry, balms or soaps from far away villages. Tarius had brought her a sword.

She was happy with the gift before she had even seen it. When the last piece of leather fell away, she was looking at one of the finest blades she'd ever seen. She took in a deep breath, held the sword up and moved it carefully from one hand to the other. She stood up with it, walked a few feet away and started swinging it around. It appeared to be as perfectly balanced as her husband's sword, which was the only other real sword she had ever held. She slung it through the air faster and faster.

"Be careful now, Jena. That's a real blade," Tarius warned with a laugh.

Jena nodded, slowing down and watching carefully as the blade sliced the air.

"It's beautiful, Tarius! Thank you. Thank you so much."

Tarius just nodded, smiling. "It's a Kartik bastard sword. Don't ask me how a filthy Amalite got his hands on it. Makes me mad just to think of it. He didn't get to keep it, though. It was a woman's sword I'm guessing by the weight of it. I'm sure she'd be happy to know that her blade is out of the hands of the Amalites and in your hands."

"It seems to fit my hands. Almost like it was made for me," Jena said.

"You should have been with us," Tarius said. "You're as good as any man, better than most. Of course I have to admit that as much as I would have liked to have you with me, I would have been distracted with you on the field."

Jena stopped twirling the blade, resting it on her shoulder. She looked lustfully at Tarius, and the color rose in Tarius's cheeks. Jena carefully licked her lips, then laughed at the look on Tarius's face. "Find me a distraction, do you?"

"You'd be disappointed if I didn't. Besides, that's not what I meant. I meant I would be worried about you. I would have spent more time trying to make sure you didn't get hurt than I did fighting the Amalites," Tarius said swallowing hard.

"You don't think I could hold my own?" Jena asked with a wicked smile.

"That's not it. I just... I wouldn't want to live in a world without you in it, Jena. I never thought I could feel like this about anyone..."

Tarius looked Jena up and down. She was everything she had ever dreamed of. She wanted to be with Jena now more than ever before. Really be with her. Jena loved her, and she deserved to know the truth. She deserved to be able to make a choice. "I have something to tell you, and you had better sit back down."

The smile left Jena's face as she saw how serious Tarius was. "What's wrong?" she asked, sitting beside Tarius. She put the sword down and took Tarius's hand.

"Jena... Would you love me no matter what?" Tarius asked.

The color left Jena's face, and she slowly but carefully took her hand from Tarius's. "I realize you were gone a long time," Jena swallowed hard. "I realize a man has needs, but maybe if you had let me take care of them before you left..."

"Wow!" Tarius said waving her hands in the air. "I wasn't with another woman. I wouldn't do that to you. I love you, and only you. I don't have any desire left over for anyone else."

The color returned to Jena's face and she took Tarius's hand. She looked into Tarius's eyes. "I would love you no matter what you did, even if you had done that. I would have been furious. I would have tried to find some way to make you pay," she added with a wicked smile. "But I could never stop loving you. You're my husband. You're my man."

Tarius's confession died on her lips. *She doesn't love me. She loves the man that she thinks that I am. If I want to keep her, I will just have to go on being that man, and hope that I can keep her fooled till I can get her out of this gods-forsaken country.*

Jena squeezed Tarius's hand tighter. "You could tell me anything. You have to know that."

Tarius took a deep breath, and thought of yet another lie. "I was hurt in the war... My... Well... My thing doesn't work right now. I don't know when it will, or even if..." Tarius's heart broke at the look of disappointment Jena wasn't able to hide with her quick smile.

"Well, then I'll just have to find other ways to please you," she said and her smile broadened. "But first, you need a bath."

Tarius locked the door to the bathroom and then put a chair in front of it. She didn't usually bathe in the house. She went to a spot in the creek far away from observers and bathed there even in the coldest weather. She had even broken ice off the stream to get a bath. It was no way to live. Especially since the Jethriks had found the wonder of running water. They would go up stream and damn an area off, then use bamboo—no doubt imported from the Kartik as there was no bamboo in the Jethrik—with the petitions knocked out to pipe the water to their dwellings. Some of the water was directed into huge vats where fires were built under them and the water was heated for bathing. It was a wonderful luxury, and one Tarius could have thoroughly enjoyed if she wasn't scared to death of being caught.

Everything was such a mess! She had told so many lies she didn't know what the truth was any more. When she had asked for five yards of clean muslin, no one had even batted their eyes. Apparently they all knew of her "Kartik" practice of wrapping her chest for protection of body and spirit.

"What a crock!" Tarius said. "Now I'm telling her I was hurt in the war... Damnedest accident, honey, turned me right into a woman!" Tarius mumbled. She walked to the mirror and stood, appalled at her own reflection. "What the hell has happened to me?" She ran her finger down the new scar on her face. It was the first time she had seen it. There were other new scars all over her body. Most were small and would probably heal completely in time. Others, like the one on her face, would be there the rest of her life. She took another look. She had soot all over her face, and her hair was a ratted, tangled mess. She smiled, this was the way she saw herself, fearsome and battle ready. However if the hair was clean and combed, it was going to make her look too feminine, so it was going to have to go. She found some scissors and looked at her hair one last time. Except for the filth and mats it was just the way she liked it. Oh well, if she was going to keep up the act, she had to look the part.

She cut her hair short, and she didn't do a bad job.

Then she started stripping her armor off. She was dreading this part. She had only had it off all the way to the skin three times in the last few months. She was afraid of what she might find and for the moment glad that Jena wouldn't be seeing her without any clothes on. Because of course the Kartik people are such a modest people. So much so that they won't even undress in front of their own spouse. *Another big lie, and she'll know it if I can ever get her to Kartik. Of course, if I can get her to Kartik I will unmask all the lies. She'll be too far away to get home without my help, and I won't help her get home. I'll make her understand. I'll make her want me as much as I want her... If I can't, only then will I bring her home again.*

Her upper armor and pauldrons were no trouble, and she hadn't really expected them to be. Even the leather pants, which at least got pulled down and then up again when she had to relieve herself, weren't too bad. But her gambeson was soaked through with sweat and blood and never washed except when she was in it. It never came off; she even slept in it. Just as she slept in the wrappings. On the field there had been no time or place to remove either in privacy. No doubt the gambeson and wrappings were the bigger part of the great stench that they were talking about, and now that she was inside she could smell it, too.

She thought she knew more or less what to expect, so she pulled it off slowly. Sure enough, several layers of dead skin came with it. It smelled like death itself, and even she had trouble holding her stomach. She put it into the burlap sack she had them bring for just that purpose. Her skin looked raw, white and exposed. It would feel good to get a real bath. Good to wear normal clothes for a while. She started to unwrap the cloth that held her breasts flat against her chest. More flesh peeled away with the cloth, and the smell was if anything worse than her gambeson. She put the rags into the bag as well, then she looked at herself again in the mirror. The wrappings had left lines in her body, some of which looked deep enough to be permanent, and her breasts didn't immediately resume their true shape.

It was funny, when she had first started binding them, it had hurt. The discomfort had been almost unbearable. Now it almost hurt to have them unbound and in the open air. Her breasts, like the breasts of most Kartik women, were not very large. If they had been, she never could have pulled this off.

Her underwear was smelly, torn and threadbare. She threw them in the bag, too. The bag and its contents would be burned. She'd make a new gambeson, maybe Jena would even make it for her. Maybe they could work on it together—that would be nice.

They had warmed the bath water, and when Tarius stepped into the warm water and sank down in the bath up to her neck she sighed. After a few moments, she attacked the filth of her with luffa sponge and lye soap. Layers of dead skin were scraped off, leaving exposed delicate, new skin and more than a few scars. When she got out of the water, it was filthy. She drained it, ran cold water into the bath and got in again just to rinse the other off.

She was toweling herself dry when a knock came on the door and she jumped, automatically wrapping the towel around herself.

"Yes?" she said carefully.

"Are you all right, Tarius?" Jena's voice asked.

"Yes fine. Just very, very dirty," Tarius said. "I'm just now drying off. I'll be out in a minute."

She finished drying herself and dressed in the Sword Master's uniform Jena had left out for her. They were her clothes, but she noticed that the uniform was loose in some places and tight in others. The war had changed her body configuration. She pulled on clean new boots and sighed. She had forgotten how good it felt to be clean.

She walked out of the bathroom door, and Jena was waiting for her. She smiled brightly at Tarius and then hugged her neck, kissing her gently on the lips. "Dinner's ready."

"Ah! Food. Food that doesn't have bugs in it. Should be quite a treat." She held Jena tighter. "Of course, I can think of something I'd like better." She bent down and whispered something particularly wicked in Jena's ear, and Jena shook with desire.

"Oh! Now that sounds much better than anything I can think of. However, I believe my father would be a little disappointed if we were that late for dinner." Jena laughed and she pushed away from Tarius a little, although Tarius didn't loosen her grip. Jena seemed to be thinking, and then she frowned. "You know... I think I liked all the hair."

Tarius laughed. "Now isn't that ironic? I cut it off for you."

Tarius hadn't realized what a state of shock she was in until she was seated at the opposite end of her father-in-law's table. Sitting at a table about to be served a meal of several courses. Jena sat to the right of her, and Harris to the left. Tragon sat next to Harris, and Edmond sat next to him. Justin and his wife sat beside Jena.

It was to be a full-fledged feast. She motioned to Harris with a finger, and he bent to hear her whispered words.

"I know all you have thought of is eating, but heed my advice. We have been on warrior's harsh rations for months. Bad food and not enough of it. Don't eat too much of anything, or you'll get sicker than you have ever been," Tarius warned.

Harris nodded and frowned. "You just have to suck the fun out of everything, don't you, Tarius?"

"We were beginning to think we were going to be eating cold food, son-in-law," Darian said.

"I was very dirty," Tarius said. "Had to fill the tub twice."

Harris laughed. "Me, too, and my skin came off with my gambeson in layers. Smelt like dead bodies..."

"Harris! For the gods' sake," Tragon said making a face. "We are preparing to eat dinner."

Harris's spirits could not be dampened by the likes of Tragon. He just smiled and shrugged. "I guess we were at battle too long. It might take us awhile to get used to polite life again. Aye, Tarius?"

"Aye," Tarius said simply. Jena grabbed her hand under the table and squeezed. Tarius squeezed back, and they looked at each other and exchanged a smile.

Tragon was sickened by the obvious love these two exchanged in a glance. *But you don't know what I know, Jena. You don't know that you're great love is a dark demon hidden in human form. That your man is no man at all, but a woman just like yourself. You can't wait for Tarius to take you to bed and give you what you crave, but Tarius can't give it to you. You jilted me and your own frustration shall be your reward.*

Despite the warning, Harris ate too much and got sick just as his mentor had promised. They sent for the academy surgeon, who mixed some powders that were supposed to help, and they all retired to the drawing room. Tarius sat down in one of the over-stuffed chairs and delighted in the softness of it.

Jena sat on the floor at Tarius's feet, leaning against Tarius's legs. She kicked her shoes off and pretended not to notice her father's look of disapproval. The servant started to serve drinks, and Tarius waved him away.

"Tarius, have a little of the mint liqueur. It's really very good," Darian said.

"I don't drink alcohol," Tarius said plainly.

"As I live and breathe! I didn't know that," Darian said. "Why not?"

"To be quite frank, I become a raving beast when I drink. Impossible, quarrelsome and wanting to shed blood," Tarius said. "I fear I might do something I would later regret."

"Always a sensible man," Darian said.

"How is your leg, my brother?" Tarius asked Tragon, wanting to change the subject.

"It's better, though it still hurts and it doesn't work very well. I see you've picked up yet another scar, my brother," Tragon said a bit of sting in his words.

"I'm afraid it is one of many," Tarius said with a shrug.

"That's what happens when you stay for the whole war, Tragon," Harris said harshly. "But of course you wouldn't know about that."

Jena looked at Harris and smiled broadly. She was glad Harris had said it and not her. She didn't want Tarius to find out how she felt about Tragon.

"It's a good thing Tragon was here," Justin said, "or we would have had no instructors at all. As it was, we put many Sword Masters in the field who would not have made the cut in peace time."

Edmond nodded his head in agreement. "I barely had time to teach them the stripped-down basics."

"Enough of this. I have held my tongue as long as I can!" Darian rubbed his hands together. "Tarius, Harris, tell us about the war."

"I guess that's our cue, dear," Justin's wife said looking at Jena.

"I'll stay," Jena said.

Justin's wife made a face. "It's not seemingly for a young lady..."

Tarius glared up at the woman. "It's seemly for my wife, madam. If I can go and fight in the war, she can at least hear about it if she so wishes. I don't tell Jena what to do, and no offense meant, but I'll be damned if anyone else will."

Justin's wife gave Tarius a heated look, but held her tongue. She looked at Jena expectantly.

Jena smiled up at her sweetly. "I'm staying."

The woman left in a huff, and the war stories were told in detail and at length. Jena was neither sickened nor frightened as she listened intently to all that Harris and Tarius had to say. She was only glad that it was over and she had her husband back. In time he would heal, and then they could be truly together.

Arvon and Dustan had found a good tavern, had as good and hearty a meal as they could stand, and drank freely of the best ale in the house.

Some of the villagers had gathered around to hear the war stories.

"Then Sir Tarius the Black comes bounding on horseback over both shield walls. He runs through the Amalite forces hacking and slashing his way through. Then as if he'd had a vision, he jumped into his saddle, riding on his feet. He leapt from the horse, did a spin in the air and grabbed the arrow just inches from the king's face. Then he lands on his feet, looks at the Amalite horde, holds the arrow high above his head and screams like a million demons are being released. Then he just ran at them on foot, hacking and slashing, cutting a trail through the Amalites four warriors wide. Our troop's spirits were lifted, and we suddenly knew no force could stand against the might of the Jethrik army and the Kartik warlord that led them."

Arvon was drunk, and he simply nodded in approval. Dustan embellished a little, but he wasn't too far from the truth, and he told a good tale. Boy should have apprenticed to a bard instead of a Sword Master.

Suddenly Arvon didn't feel so good. Not really sick, just different and... *Oh my god! I'm changing! I have to get out of here before the transformation is complete and someone sees me.*

He jumped up and ran outside.

"Arvon, Arvon!" Dustan followed after him.

Outside Arvon headed for the wooded area behind the pub. If he could get to the woods, but he was drunk and was having trouble walking. The transformation seemed to make him even drunker than he would have normally been, and the liquor seemed to speed up the transformation.

"Arvon... Are you all right?" Dustan asked.

"Go away, boy!" Arvon snapped in a voice very different from his usual.

"Are you hurt? You don't sound right." Dustan took Arvon's arm and Arvon swung on him. Dustan let go of Arvon's arm and jumped back. "My gods! You're... You're."

"Yes I am," Arvon growled out. The transformation was complete, and his head was spinning. He looked around. No one else had seen him. He grabbed Dustan by the collar. "You shouldn't have followed me. Come on." He dragged Dustan into the woods, kicking but not screaming.

Dustan was in shock. He didn't know what to think or do. Only two things were clear in his mind. First, he didn't want Arvon to get into trouble, and second he didn't want to be in the hands of an angry Katabull.

When he realized he couldn't get away, he stopped squirming. Arvon ran like the wind, and it was all Dustan could do to keep up being half dragged, half carried. He tried to make his legs help him along when he could get his footing.

When they were far enough into the woods, Arvon let him go and started to pace around him in a circle, obviously thinking.

"So you were the Katabull the Amalites said visited their camp every night before a battle," Dustan said.

Still drunk, Arvon spoke without thinking. "A couple of times. Mostly it was Tarius." He stopped, raising his hands to cover his mouth. When he removed them he screeched, "Damn! Now she's going to kill me."

"She!" Dustan squealed.

Arvon covered his mouth again then started mumbling to himself. "He's a good man." He started circling Dustan again, and Dustan didn't dare to try and make a run for it. "I'd hate to kill him, but now not only does he know my secret, but he knows all of Tarius's as well, and I owe Tarius a debt I can never repay."

"Tarius is a woman?" Dustan asked in disbelief, seeming not at all concerned that Arvon or even the Katabull was going to kill him.

"Yes, and quite fetching, actually, if one likes that sort of thing," Arvon answered.

"But Tarius married... Darian's daughter, Jena!" Dustan said in confusion.

Arvon stopped and looked at Dustan as if he were an idiot. "Well, that's where all the trouble started, isn't it? I mean how long does she think she can fool the girl?"

"Jena doesn't know?"

"No... And she can't find out, at least not from us." Arvon sighed. "What the hell am I going to do with you?"

Dustan relaxed completely as he realized that the Katabull was still Arvon even in this state. He knew that no matter what Arvon might say, he was in no real danger.

"Actually, I can think of quite a few things," Dustan said with a smile.

"You're a wicked, wicked boy, Dustan," Arvon said in disbelief.

"I'm no boy, Arvon, and I've made no bones about the way I feel," Dustan said.

"But... But... I'm the Katabull!" Arvon protested and made a horrible face extending his hands like claws. It had quite the opposite effect Arvon had been hoping for. Dustan laughed. Arvon let his hands drop to his side. "Aren't you even a little afraid of me?"

Dustan shrugged. "Not really, you're still Arvon, and I am very, very fond of you. What better way to make me keep your secrets and those of your good friend Tarius than to make me your lover?"

11

Tarius had just finished making love to Jena as she had never made love to her before. Jena was completely sated, and she lay in Tarius's arms blissfully exhausted.

As long as I can keep this up, she's never going to want anything else. Tarius closed her eyes and was almost asleep.

"I can't wait till you're healed and I can please you as you please me," Jena said.

Tarius sighed deeply as her heart broke. "Jena... Can't you please believe me? You *do* please me. I'm happy with you. Just like this. I don't need any more."

Jena shifted in her arms to face her, although it was too dark for her to see Tarius's face. But Tarius could see hers by shifting only her eyes. There was such love there and such desperation as she spoke so softly Tarius could barely hear her.

"But I *want* to give you more, Tarius. I want to make you scream out with desire the way you do me. I want to be mother to your sons," Jena said.

Tarius held her tightly and choked on a ball of tears she fought to keep down. She couldn't keep this farce up. Eventually her house of cards was going to come tumbling down.

Tarius didn't rest long. A week after she got home she started to train the new group of recruits. They were the last of the quickly chosen, quickly trained, and they needed a lot of sword training.

Tragon had been the primary trainer, and it had made him feel important. With Tarius and Arvon back from the war, he was now forced to train the boys with even less skill than he'd had when he was in academy. They had just finished the lessons for the day, and Arvon and Tarius were sparing. Tragon watched them. Both Tarius and Arvon had gotten better in the war. Arvon had gotten much better, but of course Tarius could still whip him.

"You there, boy," Tarius called out to the young orphan they had found to replace Harris as the step-and-fetch'em boy. He was young, hardly twelve. "What's your name?"

"Frederick."

"Well, Frederick, run up to Sir Darian's house and fetch my wife and my good friend Harris and bring them back here."

"Aye, sir."

"When you get back I'll give you a copper," Tarius promised. The boy dropped the bucket he'd been carrying and ran out the door like he'd been shot from a crossbow.

Tarius and Arvon sat down on a bench to rest, and Tragon limped over to join them. "So, what are you two up to?"

"You might as well know, we've made a clearing in the woods and we go there to fight. Want to go with us?" Tarius asked.

Tragon shook his head. He didn't ever want to go back there, not to that place of great embarrassment for him. Besides, he tried to steer clear of Jena these days. She didn't want him around her, and if he made Jena unhappy or uncomfortable there was a very real possibility that she'd tell Tarius what he had done. Armed with that knowledge, Tarius would have all the excuses she needed to kill him. Tarius was not a person who liked lose ends, who liked to leave her fate in anyone else's hands, and Tragon imagined that she daily considered killing him just because it would be so much cleaner. He was only alive because of her code of honor, and if she knew what he'd tried to do to Jena... well, that same code would allow her to kill him without blinking an eye.

"Think I'll stick with sparing partners I can beat," Tragon said with a laugh.

Frederick ran in with Jena and Harris, and Tarius gave the boy a copper as promised. Tragon made a face. No doubt Tarius would get this water boy knighted like she had "his good friend Harris."

He looked at Jena, and she glared knives back at him. She was hardheaded like her father, and she had already made up her mind to never forgive him.

If Tragon had any honor or pride left, he'd pack up and head for home. But at home his father would view him as a worthless cripple. If Tragon dropped his masquerade, his father would see him for the coward that he was. So there was no winning, at least not until his father died.

Tragon couldn't help it. He had seen war up close and personal, and he just couldn't handle it. He couldn't. If he had gone back to the front, then more likely than not he would have gotten killed.

He'd had such plans for advancement. Now he'd be lucky if they kept him on here at the school as an instructor. Everything that he wanted Tarius had, including courage and skill.

He watched them go. It was like a club he had belonged to and didn't anymore. He had no one to blame but himself, but that didn't stop him from being resentful.

Tarius and Jena were sparring.

"That's the kind of woman I want," Harris said, speaking of Jena.
Arvon laughed and shook his head. "Think they broke the mold."

"Tarius says there are lots of Kartik women like Jena," Harris said. "When Tarius and Jena go to Kartik, I'm going with them."

"They're going to Kartik? I didn't know the decision had been made," Arvon said curiously.

Harris nodded vigorously. "Tarius has made up his mind." Harris smiled. "I'm not sure he's told Jena yet."

Arvon frowned. Tarius hadn't told him anything about it because she knew how he felt about the whole thing. Tarius called Harris in to fight Jena, and she went to join Arvon, wiping her face on her white shirtsleeve and leaving a long trail of dirt.

"So, young Harris tells me you two are hijacking Jena, taking her to Kartik whether she likes it or not," Arvon said in a disapproving voice.

Tarius glared at Harris. "The big mouth."

"It's true then?" Arvon said in disbelief.

"I've tried to tell Jena the truth a dozen times, but... well, something always happens. I tried to talk to her about going to Kartik, but she said all this stuff about me being kingdom warlord, and how disgraced Darian would be. I don't understand any of it, and I don't care. It's the only chance we have. When winter is over, we'll ride out for the coast, and..."

"Tell her now, Tarius. You aren't being fair to her, or to Darian for that matter..."

"And do what, Arvon? Even if she doesn't reject me outright. Even if she accepts and embraces me. What then? Pretend to be a man the rest of my life? Or tell everyone I'm a woman and be burned as a heretic? I want to go home. Back to Kartik where I can be who I am. Where women are treated as equals, and the Katabull are esteemed not shunned."

"Where you can trap Jena and make her accept your love," Arvon said. "It's not right."

"I don't care about right, Arvon. I love Jena, and I can't lose her. I won't," Tarius said.

"If you continue to lie to her, you *will* lose her," Arvon promised.

"I suppose you've told Dustan you're Katabull then," Tarius said accusingly.

"Not in so many words, but he knows. By the way, you might have told me that drinking can bring on the change."

"Can?" Tarius laughed. "If I drink even a drop I change. The Katabull have no resistance to alcohol. You must have some because you are half human. You were safe as long as you didn't know how to change... So he knows, and he doesn't care?"

"He knows, and he doesn't care," Arvon answered truthfully. "Neither would she. How can you love her so much, and yet trust her so little?"

"I'll trust her in Kartik," Tarius assured him.

"What if she won't go?" Arvon asked.

"Oh, she'll go, and if you're smart, you'll take your mate and go with us. You don't want to be here when the Amalites once again take hold of the land," Tarius said.

"And that's the argument you'll use to convince her?" Arvon shook his head disapprovingly.

"Especially when she is with child," Tarius said carefully.

Arvon started to laugh. "Well, you may be good, my friend, but we both know that's not going to happen."

Tarius looked up at him with appealing eyes. It only took Arvon a second to realize what she was suggesting. "Oh, nooo! Not me, my friend. I'll not help you in your farce. I'll not help you fool that naive young woman even if I could… and I'm not sure I could."

"Arvon, you said yourself you owe me a debt you can never pay…"

"But I don't owe you a child, Tarius. Any more than I owe you a wonderful lie when the truth hurts you too much. I won't do it. Guilt me all you want. Talk till you're blue in the face. If you'll tell her the truth and she still wants you, wants a child, then I'll see if I can do it. If you're smart, you won't carry out this fool's plan of yours. Love can't live with all these lies."

"Arvon, please! I beg you. She grows more and more impatient with me. Now she wants me to enlist the king's surgeon and Hellibolt to try and cure my problem," Tarius said.

"Tell the truth, Tarius."

"I can't, not here… She wants *it* Arvon, you said she would and she does. She needs it and I can't give it to her." Tarius looked away from him then watching Jena.

"And what of *your* needs, Tarius?" Arvon asked gently.

"I'm an adult, Arvon, a Kartik woman. I know how to satisfy my own needs."

"Aye, but you are an adult Kartik woman and one who's had many lovers I imagine. You and I both know touching yourself isn't the same as being touched, my sister."

"No," Tarius sighed, "but she doesn't want me."

"You don't know that. You haven't given her a chance to reject you, I don't think that she would. And if she really doesn't want you, do you really think that will change just because she's in a foreign land? Tell this woman you say you love the truth, the whole truth, before it's too late." Arvon got to his feet, pointing a finger at her. "Do not pursue this baby thing. It's wrong, and you know in your heart that it's wrong." He walked away.

Tarius sighed. "It's easy for him to make rational judgments. He's got nothing on the line." She watched Jena and Harris fight. Jena got better daily. *I want you to be with me always. I know what I am doing is wrong. I know you may hate me for it, but what can I do? I can't lose you, but Arvon was my only hope! What do I do now? What now?*

Tragon walked into the field then, and Tarius looked at him and smiled. Here might very well be the answer to her prayers. After all Tragon loved Jena, or at the very least thought that he did. He would treat her gently and with love, and she'd have no trouble whatsoever talking him into it.

"Tarius, the king's herald is at the gates. You're being summoned before the king on business," Tragon said.

"What business is that?" Tarius asked.

"Oh, I don't know. You are kingdom warlord. I would imagine it has something to do with defense," Tragon said making a face.

Tarius laughed. She walked over to Jena, who had stopped fighting, and kissed her gently on the lips. "I'll be back as soon as I can."

Jena nodded and kissed Tarius again just for good measure.

Tarius walked up alongside Tragon and slapped his shoulder. "Come along with me, my brother."

Tragon nodded eagerly.

They rode along at a slower than normal pace, considering Tarius had been summoned before the king.

"You want to tell me why I'm coming along?" Tragon asked.

"I have a favor to ask of you." Tarius explained her plan to Tragon.

Tragon saw only one problem with Tarius's plan.

"She'll know I'm not you. She'll know," Tragon said. God! How he wanted to hold her, to touch her, to make love to her.

"No she won't. Hellibolt is a friend of mine. I'll bet the old charlatan has a glamour spell he could use on you. She'd have no idea. You'd be happy, she'd be happy..."

"What about you?" Tragon asked.

"Truthfully? The thought of anyone but me touching her sickens me, but I can't make her happy. I've tried and I can't. I want her to be happy."

"I don't want you to think that I have dismissed what you said about the Amalites, Tarius," Persius said. "I want to know what you think we could do to thwart such an attempt if one is made. What would be most likely to make the Amalites afraid to try another attack in the first place?"

Tarius looked at the map. "Put fully-manned, fully-armed garrisons here, here, here and here, with a large one here at the field of the Battle of the Arrow. It won't stop them, but it will help. It will give you a better position from which to fight them. Also continue with the training of every man, and if I had my way woman, in this kingdom. So that the villages have their own defense. No man in this country should walk through the streets without a weapon at his side. Ever ready, ever vigilant."

"Women fighting is absurd, you Kartik bastard." The king patted

Tarius on the back in a fond manner. "The rest shall be done as you have spoken. Where will we get the men to run these garrisons?"

Tarius thought for only a moment. "Each village will give several men each month. Those men will serve at the garrison closest to his village for a full month. While they are there, a Sword Master will train the men in all manners of war. Then they will go home and more will come. In this way you will train all your men and keep your garrisons full of fresh men."

Persius shook his head. "Indeed, good Tarius, your wisdom never ceases to amaze me. Won't you reconsider a position as my personal body guard?"

"I prefer to teach and to stay with my wife," Tarius said.

Persius nodded.

"In fact, I need to get home now," Tarius said.

"Then go and thank you for your good council."

Tarius and Tragon left the king and went down a dark hall towards the old wizard's alchemy.

"So, what is it you want now?" Hellibolt asked from behind Tarius.

Tarius and Tragon jumped and turned around. "Damn it, Hellibolt," Tarius cursed. "One day you'll do that, and I'll cut you through before I get a chance to see it's you."

Hellibolt shrugged. "So what is it you need?"

"A glamour spell," Tarius said.

"Oh, now how did I know that was coming?" Hellibolt said. "So is it for you or him?"

"Would it work on me? Could you make me..."

"Look like it? Yes. Work like it? No," Hellibolt said.

"For him, then. So that he looks like me," Tarius said.

"You dig yourself in deeper, Tarius," Hellibolt said disapprovingly.

"What else can I do?" Tarius asked pleadingly. If Hellibolt could give her any other answers she wanted to hear them.

Hellibolt seemed to think about it a long time then shrugged. "Nothing comes to mind."

They followed him into his room. It was not nearly creepy enough to be a wizard's alchemy. Tarius was a bit disappointed. No creepy spiders or snakes or rats in cages. No cobwebs or shrunken heads in bottles. Hellibolt walked over and took a bottle down from a shelf on the wall. He handed the bottle to Tarius, but spoke to Tragon.

"It's a simple spell. Just take one swallow of the potion and repeat this magic incantation. 'Little bottle of brown goo, make me look like you know who.' Think of Tarius, and you'll look like her... At least your face will. However, it only lasts a half an hour, and if you take more you'll get very sick. Also when that bottle's gone, that's it. This shit is poison, and too much of it over a period of time can kill you. Besides, it tastes like crap."

Tragon looked at the potion and made a face. "What's in it?"

Hellibolt laughed. "Believe me, you don't want to know."

It was late, and Jena had gone to bed with a book to wait for Tarius. Tarius came in and took the book out of her hands. He turned the lights off, and then he took her clothes off. He started making love to her, and Jena groaned with delight.

When Tarius was sure Jena was satisfied she stood up and looked down at Jena. In the moonlight that streamed in the curtain she could see her without having to change her eyes. This was it, the ultimate betrayal. She was going to put a man into their bed with Jena. She was going to give Jena what Jena said she wanted. She hated herself for what she was about to do, and in that moment she hated Jena for making her do it.

"Give me a second," Tarius kissed Jena gently on the mouth, and then she walked into the next room. She stood there silently for a moment. They had three rooms of their own in the house. This one was a sitting room. Tarius walked over and opened the window and Tragon climbed in. He put the potion to his lips and drank, then he recited the incantation. In moments Tarius was looking at herself. He started to go into her bedroom, and Tarius grabbed him by the front of the shirt that was the same as hers.

"Don't hurt her."

"I won't," Tragon promised and he meant it. This wouldn't be like in the field. Jena would think she was with her great love. She would give him what he longed for. He walked in the door and Tarius went out the window.

She ran into the night with tears streaming down her face. She ran blind until she fell over something, and then she lay on the ground and sobbed. She had thought nothing could hurt her any more. She had thought she had felt all degrees of pain, but nothing had prepared her for this. She cried as long as she dared indulge herself, and then she got up and wandered back towards the house. Tragon crawled out the window.

"Is she all right?" Tarius demanded.

"She seems more than all right," Tragon said. Tarius fought the urge to slap the stupid grin off his face. After all, he was doing her a favor.

Tarius paced the sitting room before walking into the bedroom. She hesitated, then crawled into bed with Jena. Jena was silent. Tarius kissed her gently on the cheek.

"Are you all right?" Tarius asked gently. "I didn't hurt you, did I?"

Jena turned to face her and she smiled. "Not at all, you were very gentle." She smiled a reassuring smile. "What about you? I thought you were going to scream your lungs out!" She laughed.

Tarius was seared through with the pain of it. "I love you, Jena," she said softly. "You'll never know how much."

———•◆•———

Jena rolled back over. She was confused. She had begged for it, fantasized for so long about what it was like, and... well she'd hated it. She felt bad about lying to Tarius, but how could she tell her dear, sweet husband that she hadn't liked it? That it had felt invasive to her and made her uncomfortable with herself and with him.

She'd get used to it. It just took time, that was all, and he had been so careful with her. He had fulfilled her desires hundreds of times, and if that's what it took to fulfill his, then she would work on liking it.

———•◆•———

There were only four doses in the bottle, and to make sure they had the best chance at pregnancy, they spaced the doses a week apart.

Tragon knew this was the last time he was ever going to be with her, and he couldn't stand the idea. He had to make it count, so he unleashed his passion on her. He wanted to make her scream and groan the way he heard her do when he was waiting outside the window for Tarius to change places with him. He almost waited too long, he was just changing back into himself as he stepped out the window.

He looked at Tarius, smiled and said. "If that doesn't do it, I'll take my chances with that potion again."

"Get out of my face," Tarius hissed and she shoved him hard. She watched him walk away then she crawled in the window, shut and locked it.

She walked slowly to the door. It was over. Hopefully Jena was pregnant, but even if she wasn't, Tarius decided she could not do this to herself again. Either way she'd made up her mind, Jena would just have to do without *it*. She would move Jena to the Kartik, and in time Jena would learn to love her, if she could ever forgive her. She walked in the room closing the door behind her and went and crawled into bed. She wrapped herself around Jena, and Jena cringed. She realized Jena was crying, and not just a little.

"Honey... What's wrong?" Tarius asked.

"Tarius... You hurt me."

"I what?" Tarius exclaimed.

"You hurt me," Jena said again.

Tarius's first instinct was to get out of bed find Tragon and kill him, but she realized that wouldn't help Jena now. Right now Jena was hurt and scared and she thought Tarius had done this to her.

"I'm so sorry," Tarius said. "I won't do it again. See? That's why I didn't want to do it. Men are like animals when they get aroused. I don't need it, Jena, and I'll never do it again." In fact, if Jena wasn't so upset Tarius might have celebrated the fact that Jena didn't want *it*.

"I'm sorry, Tarius," Jena cried.

"What are you sorry for? I'm the worst sort of brute, and you would be right to hate me. I hate myself. I never wanted to make you cry." Tarius started to cry herself. "I told you, Jena, remember in the beginning? I told you I had secrets. Secrets I couldn't tell you. That I'm dark and awful."

Jena turned and held Tarius close. "No you're not. It's me. There's something wrong with me. I tried, but I just don't like it."

Tarius kissed the tears away from Jena's cheeks. "There is nothing wrong with you, my love. Only me, only me. I'm what's wrong. Now sleep."

Tragon was still riding high from the night before. He was setting up the arena for the day's exercises. He was early today. He hadn't slept much. He had laid awake most of the night wondering just how toxic the potion was and whether Hellibolt would give it to him without Tarius.

Tarius ran into the arena, screamed and threw herself on him. She tackled him to the ground and started to beat his face in with her fists. "I ought to kill you! You bastard!"

When Tragon looked at his attacker, the Katabull's eyes looked back at him. Tragon tried to fight back, but finally wound up just holding up his arms to protect his head. "What... What did I do?"

"You hurt her!" Tarius stood up and pulled Tragon to his feet. She punched him hard in the stomach, and then slammed a fist into his face so that he landed on the ground in a pile. She looked down at him with utter contempt. "You hurt her, and she thinks that I did it."

"I'm... I'm sorry, Tarius. I didn't mean to. Please believe me, Tarius, my passion for her got the better of me," Tragon said gulping for air.

"Is that supposed to make me feel better?" Tarius moved forward to attack him again but stopped as if he just wasn't worth the trouble. "You rutting pig. I saved your worthless life, I asked you to do a favor for me, and you just couldn't control yourself. I wish I'd run off and let you die that day. I'm only going to let you live because of our former partnership, what we once meant to each other, and the fact that you tried to help me. But if you ever go near her, or even *look* at her again, I will rip your belly open and suck your guts out with my teeth. Do I make myself clear?"

"Very," Tragon said. He watched Tarius go, feeling lucky to be alive and wanting very much to find a way to get rid of the beast girl once and for all.

"Want to tell me what that was all about, or need I ask?" Arvon asked as he fell in behind Tarius who was walking at a fast clip across the courtyard. Tarius glared at him. "So you got Tragon to do the deed and then beat him for his troubles."

"He hurt her," Tarius said in a whisper.

"*You* hurt her, Tarius. You did it with your lies."

"I know that! Don't you think I know that!" Tarius cried. "I hate myself. I hate what I have become. She hated it! But of course she was afraid to tell me because she didn't want to make me mad. I swear if I live to be a hundred, I will never understand your country women and their subjectivity to men."

"Did it ever dawn on you that maybe Jena didn't like it because she doesn't like boys?" Arvon asked.

"She said she wanted *it*, Arvon. She kept begging me for *it*," Tarius said. "I couldn't do it, so I found someone who could—which practically killed me!—and she hated it! I don't know what I think anymore."

"Jena's naive about sex. She doesn't know what she wants. She wants to please you because she loves you," Arvon said.

"Or she knew. Part of her knew that she was being tricked. That something wasn't right," Tarius said. "I just hope she's pregnant."

"Oh, don't even tell me that you are still bent on your insane plan to rip your wife from her homeland by making her believe the country is unsafe for children!" Arvon gasped in disbelief.

"The land is not safe. You know that as well as I do," Tarius said. "Whether she's pregnant or not I will not stay in this accursed country another year, and I will not leave without Jena."

Arvon shook his head. He stopped and made her stop as well by putting a hand on her shoulder. "My dear friend. I tell you this from the love that I have for you. You are destroying no one as fast as you are destroying yourself. Tell this woman who you are, then she'll understand why you want so badly to go away. If she loves you as much as I think she does, she will forgive you even for putting a man in her bed... eventually. You are heading for a disaster that no one can stop."

"Now you sound like Hellibolt," Tarius said.

"Perhaps you had better heed his words."

12

Jena had waited till she was absolutely sure. She was sure now. Tarius crawled in beside her and took her in his arms. He kissed her gently.

"Tarius... I have good news," Jena started. She could feel Tarius stiffen. "I'm with child."

"Does it make you happy?" Tarius asked carefully.

Jena laughed and slapped him playfully in the shoulder. "Of course it makes me happy." *If for no other reason than it means we don't have to do that again until we want another baby.* "Doesn't it make you happy, Tarius? I mean you didn't just do it because I wanted a baby, did you?"

"No, I want a child. You will be a good mother."

"And you, Tarius, will be a great father." She lay down with her head on his chest and looked up at the ceiling. Tarius wrapped his arms around her and held her tight. "Guess I'll have to stop fighting for awhile."

"I guess so," Tarius said. "Jena, with the baby coming I think we seriously need to consider our move to Kartik...."

And so it all began.

Tragon did not take the news of the pregnancy well. At first he ignored it and pretended it wasn't happening, but as Jena started to show, he became obsessed with the idea of having her and the child for his own.

One night three months into her pregnancy, he rode into town and got falling down drunk. He fell off his horse three times on the way back to the academy. He stopped in front of Darian's house and fell off the horse again. He finally stumbled to his feet.

"Tarius!" he screamed. "Tarius you fake! You great phony! Come out here. You have something that belongs to me. In fact, everything you have belongs to me!"

Tarius ran from the house barefooted, but her sword was on her back. She grabbed him by the collar and pushed him back fifteen feet, pushing and dragging him till she popped him against the wall of the academy.

Jena stood in the doorway. "Go back inside," Tarius ordered her. She started to protest, but Darian came and took her elbow gently and brought her back inside closing the door.

"What the hell are you doing, fool?" Tarius asked with venom.

"I've come to take what is mine. The woman and the child; both mine. You took her, but I'm damned if you'll take the child."

She banged his head against the rock wall hard. "Listen to me, you drunken idiot. I saved your worthless life. All I'm asking you to do is keep my secrets. You know—a secret—like the one you've been keeping about your leg. Don't look so shocked. Harris walks with a limp. A real limp doesn't come and go. Perhaps you'd like to explain that to your father the great war hero."

"I'll tell them all what you are, Tarius. You think she'll love you then? She'll be glad to have me when she finds out the truth about you," Tragon said.

"Do you think I won't kill you, Tragon? Because you are dead wrong. Hear me! Dead wrong!" Tarius said. "I warn you, Tragon, and I beg you for all of our sakes... Do not play out this game, it can only end in disaster for us all. We had a friendship once, Tragon, we were like brothers, and we were partners. Please... Let this go."

Tragon cried in his drunkenness. "How can I let it go when I see her? When I see the child within her?"

"By leaving. Leave in the morning. The first garrison is finished. I'll put you up for commission there. The king will listen to my plea. It's a safe position. Mostly training, no fighting there."

"Don't do me any favors," Tragon said.

"Ride towards the garrison in the morning, Tragon. I will take care of you there, make sure you have everything you could want. If you are not gone by morning, then it will be the last sunrise you will see. I will kill you without guilt, and secure myself and my secrets," Tarius said.

Tragon nodded and started stumbling towards his quarters in the academy building. Along the way he saw the window he had climbed in to be with Jena. He smiled, Tarius only thought that she had won.

In the morning Tragon was gone, and Tarius started to write up a letter to the king.

"You never did say what was wrong with Tragon last night," Jena said rubbing her belly and looking at the light streaming in the window.

"You mean besides being filthy drunk? I'm sending him to work at the new garrison, and he's not happy," Tarius said simply.

Darian walked in holding a cup of steaming hot tea. "Tragon's left already. Must have gotten up with the first cock's crow."

"I'm afraid I was a little rough on him last night. He's changed... He isn't the same person that he was," Tarius said, putting the finishing touches on the letter.

Jena was glad to see the end of Tragon. He made her uncomfortable, and she had enough to worry about with her husband insisting on whisking her and their unborn child off to a different country. Tarius was obsessed with the idea that the Amalites were going to come back and that they wouldn't be able to stop them from taking over the country this time.

Jena didn't want to move from her homeland. She didn't want to leave her father, but Tarius's feelings on this matter were strong, too. He didn't want to live in a foreign country anymore. He didn't care about the title and prestige he had earned here. He wanted to take her to a place where he thought they would all be safe, and who could blame him for that?

He wanted to move now. Now before the baby was born. He wanted the baby to be born in Kartik.

Jena was torn, and she was glad with all the decisions she had to make she wouldn't have to deal with Tragon's prying eyes every time she walked out of the house.

———⋅•⋅———

"Tarius is what!" Persius screamed.

"I know. I couldn't believe it myself at first, but had to believe the witness of my own eyes," Tragon said.

"Tell me again how you came to learn this?" Persius said in disbelief. The story the man told was absurd.

"Tarius said he was hurt after the war... You know, that he couldn't... Well, you know take care of business, and his wife of course badly wanted a child. Tarius, having no brothers, asked me to stand in for him, which is our custom. The only thing Tarius asked that was strange was that I should pretend to be him so that she wouldn't know."

"And, Sire, I must again remind you that poor Jena has no idea what Tarius is. The poor girl has been duped along with the rest of us," Tragon said. "Anyway, I snuck in a window as Tarius snuck out. It was dark, and Jena never knew it was I that took her husband's place. I felt I owed Tarius this as he—*It*—saved my life. Last night as I came home quite late, I saw Tarius crawling out the window. I thought this odd, so I stopped and watched. He undressed before my eyes, and I saw that Tarius is not a man at all, but a woman. Then to my amazement, he... she... It... *changed* into the Katabull."

Persius seemed pensive. It sounded an outrageous lie, but what could this man gain by telling such a hateful untruth? If he was lying, he would easily be found out.

"Where is Hellibolt?" Persius asked.

"Gone to visit his sister for the day, Sire," the herald said. "Should I fetch his apprentice?"

"Yes, do so at once. I want to get to the bottom of this, this very day," Persius said. He glared at Tragon. "If you are lying, I shall see you hanged, drawn and quartered myself."

———⋅•⋅———

The night was shattered by the sound of Jena's screams as two big men grabbed a sleeping Tarius from the bed. The lights were quickly lit. Tarius was still. Her hands had been slapped in metal cuffs, and she was being held between two huge guards. She knew immediately that she should have killed Tragon last night. She realized from the fog in her head that someone had put a spell on her to make sure she didn't wake before they had their hands on her.

"What is all this?" Jena asked fumbling with her robe to get it tied.

The king walked in then, closely followed by Tragon. Tarius looked at Tragon with utter contempt. "What the hell have you done?" Tarius demanded.

"I'm sorry," Tragon said looking at his feet. He might fool everyone else, but he didn't fool Tarius.

"No you're not," Tarius looked at Persius. "This man is angry. Angry because he has been faking an injury he doesn't have, and he doesn't want to be sent to the garrison. Walk away from this, Persius. Walk away, because the truth you seek will only hurt everyone. The truth will serve none of us well."

Darian walked in, started to scream a protest, then saw the king and bowed low.

"Is it true then, Tarius? Is what he says true?" Persius asked in a hurt tone.

"Please give me a few moments alone with Jena, and then you can do with me whatever you wish," Tarius said. "She has done nothing wrong, she knows nothing of what I am. I beg you, please, let me explain myself to her. Then I'll go with you... stand by whatever judgement you see fit."

Suddenly Persius was filled with rage. He took a dagger and walked forward.

"No!" Jena started to rush forward, and Darian stopped her.

"What is this?" Darian asked. "As a servant of the kingdom, I demand to know what it is you think my son-in-law has done."

Persius closed in on Tarius, and she glared at him. "Persius, do not do this to me. I have saved your life not once but twice. For those deeds I beg you give me this one consideration, let me tell Jena myself. Is that too much to ask?" Jena was crying loudly. Darian tried to comfort her and prepare for whatever Tarius had done. He couldn't believe Tarius capable of treason. None of it made any sense.

Persius cut Tarius's shirt down the front with the knife, then he inserted the dagger in the top of the wrappings.

"I beg you, Persius..."

"No!" Persius screamed in her face. "You have made an utter fool of me."

"How so? By helping you win a war you were destined to lose? By saving your life? Give me, I beg you, this one thing."

"Tarius! My gods!" Jena cried. "What is it?"

"Jena, I never meant to hurt you."

Persius cut down the length of cloth, exposing Tarius's chest. A few trickles of blood ran down her front, between her breasts where the knife had cut her.

"He's a woman," Persius said. "My warlord and your husband, is a woman."

Jena fainted dead away, and Darian caught her and quickly carried her from the room. He didn't know what Persius would do to Tarius, but he was sure Tarius would fight back, and he had to get Jena to safety.

Tarius looked at Persius and started to change. "If you know that, then you know what else I am, and you should not have done that, Persius. You should not have done that at all." Tarius busted the chains behind her back and slung an ironclad fist into the king's head. He stumbled back but didn't fall.

"Get it!" Persius screamed, putting a hand to his dazed head. The world was spinning, and it was all he could do to stay on his feet.

Harris had finally been awakened. He ran into the room, surveyed the situation quickly, and knew where his loyalty must lay. He dove on the floor underneath the combat overhead and grabbed Tarius's sword from under the bed where he knew she kept it.

"Tarius!" Harris screamed. When she looked at him, he tossed her the sword. She nodded at him and fought her way to the window. She dove through and Harris followed, landing on the ground beside her. She ripped what was left of the shirt off, as at this point it was only getting in her way. She looked at Harris and shook her head.

"Do you have any idea how much trouble you just bought yourself?" Tarius asked.

"You... whatever you may be, are my one true friend," Harris said. "Come on, let's get the hell out of here."

They started to run and ran right into a group of infantry. Tarius looked at Harris. "Get to the stables and grab our horses get one for Jena, I'll not leave here without her. I'll hold them off."

Tarius dove into the fray as Harris ran in the direction of the stables. Tarius jumped up on top of a table in the courtyard, then leapt over the men to land behind them. "Listen to me. Most of you have fought beside me, and I don't want to kill anyone, but I won't let anyone kill me, either. I have committed no crime. Leave me be and I will take what is mine and go."

They didn't listen to her speech, and if they did they didn't care, so she didn't hold back. There were too many of them to play with, so she started killing them.

Persius watched out the window. Tarius was too good. Man or woman, human or Katabull, there was no one who could stand against Tarius with a sword. Persius looked at the apprentice wizard.

"Does it love the girl, or is she just part of her disguise?" Persius asked.

"She loves her. There's nothing she wouldn't do for her," the apprentice answered. "She would kill for her, and she'd die for her."

"You and you," Persius ordered. "Bring me the girl."

He followed them. They found Jena with her father in the drawing room. She was just coming to. "Get her," Persius ordered.

"Sire, I must protest!" Darian said.

"Tarius is mowing my men down out there, and when he's... *she's* done, she'll very likely come after me. Now the wizard says that Tarius loves your daughter. I won't harm her, this I promise, but if Tarius thinks I will harm her, she'll give herself up without a fight."

"Why not let her go?" Jena said weakly.

"How can you say that after what that thing did to you?" Darian asked.

"Who has she hurt more than me? Please... Let her go," Jena pleaded.

"Get her," Persius ordered. Two guards took hold of Jena and drug her outside.

"Tarius!" Persius screamed into the night. "I have your woman, Tarius. I have to have my revenge. If you won't let me take it on you, what better revenge than that I kill the one you love?"

Tarius seemed to appear out of nowhere then. She ran up, sword in hand stopping some ten feet in front of him. No one was behind her. She was covered in blood and very much the Katabull. "Get your hands off her," Tarius ordered in a hiss.

"I will not release her till you are securely cuffed, chained, and in my dungeon," Persius said.

"You've got no quarrel with Jena," Tarius said. "She's committed no crime, nor has she broken any of your stupid rules. Let me have her. We will go away, and no one will ever know what I am."

"*I* will know!" Persius screamed. "Give yourself up, or I will kill your woman." He pulled his sword and put it to Jena's throat.

"Jena... I'm so sorry. For everything," Tarius said. She threw her sword as far as she could. It rolled through the air, the moonlight gleaming off the blade till it was out of sight. She put her hands above her head and dropped to her knees. "There now, Persius, you have beaten me."

Harris watched from a distance on horseback. He saw Tarius throw her sword, and saw where it had landed, so when everyone had left he rushed in and got it. He also picked up her armor.

He would find a way to save his friend. He didn't know how, though. He wasn't the plan man; that was Tarius.

Arvon... Arvon would know what to do, and surely he would help

Tarius no matter what she was. So he rode off fast taking the back trails to Arvon's house.

Tarius's hands were cuffed in much stouter metal this time, and her hands were chained to cuffs that also cuffed her feet together. They weren't taking any chances.

She looked at the thick metal bars in front of her and wished she had killed Tragon a dozen times over. Better yet, she could just have let him die on the battlefield.

They wouldn't give her a shirt, and it was cold. However she had sucked the blood off one arm, and she was human again. She was stronger and warmer as Katabull, but if Jena should happen to make it down to see her, she didn't want to be the creature as well.

"My great crime! I have tits instead of a dick," Tarius mumbled. "I'm Katabull instead of a human."

"Your great crime was that you fooled *all* of them," Hellibolt said from inside the cell with her. "My, her skin is awfully bare, give her something warm to wear."

It was a red shirt, and Tarius nodded approvingly. "How appropriate, won't show the blood when they shoot me through with arrows. How about a spell to get me the hell out of here?"

"You don't really want that, though, do you?"

"Not without Jena," Tarius said shaking her head. "I deserve whatever happens to me because of what I did to Jena. I ruined her life."

"Ah, my friend that's not true. You gave her true love, and some people never have that. Besides, she still has lots of life left. It's a minor setback at best."

"Aren't you even going to say I told you so?" Tarius asked.

"What would be the point now? You've taken all the fun out of it," Hellibolt said with a sad smile. "To tell the truth, sometimes I hate being right all the time."

"I just wish I could make sure that Jena was going to be all right. Then I could die happy," Tarius said.

"You'll not die for a very long time, Tarius, and she'll be fine just as soon as you are together again."

Before Tarius had time to ask the old charlatan what he meant, he was gone.

Tarius paced the cell like a caged animal.

Arvon appeared outside the door of her cell. He looked as miserable as she felt.

"How you doing?" he asked.

"Oh, fine! Never better. How is Jena?" Tarius asked.

"You had better start worrying about yourself, Tarius," Arvon said.

"The king is talking about executing you in the morning, thanks to Darian's insistence. He really hates your guts. Harris is holed up at our house awaiting your further instructions, apparently not upset at all that you are a woman and the Katabull. He expects me to find a way to get you out of here, but I don't have a clue. What about you?"

"I can't do anything. He's threatened to kill Jena if I do. Besides, I'm not leaving here without her. I'd sooner die," Tarius said.

"All right. I didn't want to tell you this, but *she* hates you, too. She doesn't give a damn what happens to you. Apparently at first she didn't want you hurt, but now that she's calmed down and had a chance to think about it, she really hates you. She demanded to know who the father of her baby is, and when she found out it was Tragon, she started to scream that she hated you and him, too. Your father-in-law was demanding a death sentence, and let me tell you she didn't try to dissuade him."

"I'm having a bad day," Tarius said with a forced smile.

"Quit feeling sorry for yourself and figure a way out of this one, because otherwise you'll be dead by morning. I'll do whatever you ask me to, and so will Harris, but you have to think of something, because everything I've thought of is guaranteed to get us all killed."

"This is my plan," Tarius said carefully. "Tell Harris to get his butt to Kartik. He won't be safe here now, that's for sure. As for you, you take care of Jena for me. Make sure she and her baby are safe when the Amalites come."

Arvon started to cry. He reached through the bars and took her hand. "I can't bear to just let you go, Tarius."

"You must. Save yourself; you have much to live for. Without Jena, without her love, I'm better off dead, and it will be easier for her, too."

Arvon squeezed her hand. "Good bye, my sister."

"Good bye, my brother," Tarius said. "I know you're mad at Jena right now, but remember you're the one who told me what I was doing to her was wrong. How can we expect her to react? Promise me you'll take care of her."

"I will guard her with my very life." He left crying so loudly that she could hear him several minutes after he had left.

She walked over and sat on a plank bench. She secretly hoped she didn't have to go to the bathroom. She'd hate to die with wet pants.

"Tarius."

Tarius's head snapped up, and she jumped up and went to the bars. Jena jumped back.

Tarius ignored the pain in her heart. "Are you all right? Have they hurt you?"

"What a stupid question, Tarius! How could I be all right?" Jena screamed. "You know, when you didn't want to have sex with me, I thought of a million reasons why, but it never dawned on me even once that it might be because you were a *woman*."

"I'm very sorry, Jena." Tarius said.

"Sorry... What do you think that is? A magic word that makes all the pain and the lies go away? Was it funny to you? Did you get a good laugh because I was so stupid?" Jena's angry tears fell like rain. "And you love me, don't you? You must because you could have gotten away, and you gave yourself up because you thought they might hurt me. Do you have any idea how confusing that is? You love me, so you did all these terrible things to me."

"I never wanted to hurt you. I certainly never wanted you to find out like this. I wanted us to go away someplace where the love I have for you is commonplace. Where you might have loved me, too," Tarius said miserably.

"But that's the problem... I do... did love you. My mind and my life are a mess now, because I loved you. You want to hear the real kicker? I've been going over and over this in my head, and what's weird is that if you had told me you were Katabull, it wouldn't have bothered me at all. I could even forgive all the lies and the deceit and the fact that you didn't trust in my love enough to tell me the truth. I might even have been able to forgive the fact that you're a woman, but what I can never forget... what I can never forgive, is that you put him in our bed with me. That you would do something like that without my consent or knowledge."

Tarius didn't try to stop her tears now. "Jena... There is no excuse for what I did. I thought it was what you wanted. You said it was what you wanted."

"I wanted it with *you*!" Jena screamed back. "Except I was too stupid to know you couldn't give it to me."

"You're not stupid. I didn't just fool you, Jena, I fooled an entire country. Them I fooled because they wouldn't let me do what I wanted to do, and you I fooled because I couldn't stop myself from loving you." Tarius tried to raise her hand to dry her eyes and couldn't, so she wiped her face on her shoulder instead. "I know it doesn't matter now, but I tried to stay away from you. I tried not to love you, but you awoke within me something that I thought was long dead. You made me love again, gave me some reason for living other than revenge and killing. I'm sorry that my love hurt you. I'm sorry that it will continue to hurt you for a long time to come, but I'm not sorry for loving you. I don't regret having been with you, it was worth anything I will have to endure. If I die, then I die, and even at the moment of my death I will not regret one moment I spent with you. In fact, I would rather die. Better that I should have never been born than I should have had to live my life never knowing your love."

Jena cried louder and buried her face in her hands. After a moment she looked up at Tarius. "What's wrong with me? I should hate you! I want to hate you! But... I don't know what to feel, Tarius. I trusted you.

I trusted you completely, and look what you have done to me. You have disgraced me and my house. I'm carrying the child of a man I hate..."

"I thought you *liked* Tragon," Tarius said.

"Like that would somehow make it all right." Jena laughed bitterly and shook her head. "See now—this just gets worse and worse—because that was because of *my* deceit. Had I told you how I truly felt about him. When you were away, Tarius... While you were at war he tried to rape me. I didn't tell you because he was your friend. I didn't want to make trouble. Now you've helped him to violate me."

"I'll kill him!" Tarius cursed. She started to change, as the Katabull there was a good chance she could get free. Jena was right there. She could grab her, get to Harris and Arvon and they could get away.

But Darian walked in then.

Tarius stopped the transformation. Darian glared at her with such hate she inwardly cringed.

"You won't be doing anything. The king has ordered your execution at dawn," Darian spat. "As for Tragon, he has offered to marry Jena and clean up the mess you have made."

"I'll never marry him!" Jena cried. "Never!"

"You will," Darian ordered. "The king is ordering a silence on the matter." He glared at Tarius again. "In the morning you'll be killed. They will say you died in a riding accident. No one will know that you have violated my daughter and made fools of us all. Tragon will marry Jena and wipe away the filth you have put upon her."

"I won't marry him. I hate him," Jena said.

"You will marry him. He's your child's father, and the only one that would have you after this." Darian looked at his daughter with almost as much contempt as he had for Tarius.

"You want to punish me, Darian?" Tarius screamed savagely. "Fine, then you punish me, but why are you punishing Jena? She did nothing wrong."

"Go!" Darian ordered Jena. "Get some sleep."

Jena cried harder and took hold of her father's arm. "Father, please. Who has he... she hurt more than me? I don't want her dead. Please, talk to the king, he'll listen to you. Send her away, but don't kill her."

"The king *has* listened to me, that's why she's being executed. Now come on," Darian dragged her up the stairs and out of the dungeon.

Tarius hung on the bars watching her go. At the top of the stairs Jena turned and looked at her, then she was gone.

13

The crowd assembled was small. Persius had Tarius's head and hands placed in wooden stocks. There was a small crowd gathered on the edge of the woods on the outskirts of town. Persius, Hellibolt, five of the king's personal guards, Tragon and Darian who had forced his daughter to come, thinking it would do her good to see Tarius punished for her crimes against her.

"Don't do this thing," Hellibolt whispered to the king. "Had Tarius not saved Tragon, had she not saved you, she would have lived a long life. Why make her regret these acts of selflessness?"

Persius wasn't listening. "Tie her to the horse," he ordered.

The guards tied Tarius to ropes already connected to an unbroken stallion.

Persius took the bow and an arrow from one of the men.

"No!" Jena cried. "Exile him, but don't hurt him!"

"Darian, quiet your daughter," Persius ordered.

Darian pulled Jena to him and put a hand over her mouth.

"So, Tarius, have you any last words?"

Tarius didn't hesitate. "Tragon, your own treachery shall bring about your death. You are a liar and a coward. I hope you die a slow and painful death at the hands of one you trust as much as I trusted in you. Jena. I'm sorry, Jena, for everything. I love you and only hope that someday you will find it in your heart to forgive me. That one day you will think of me without hate."

Persius waited to make sure she was done and then he knocked the arrow. "Heed my warning, Persius," Tarius said with venom as her eyes met his. "I am not afraid to die, but if you mean to kill me, make it quick and clean. You have returned evil for good, and your punishment for that will come at the end of days. But if you shoot me with that arrow, make sure you kill me outright. Shoot me in the head or in the heart, because if you do not I will find a way to live. And if I live, I will make you pay for my pain a thousand times over. You will not get a decent night's sleep, nor shall you have even one moment's peace. Believe me, Persius, I shall see to it."

Persius smiled and let the arrow fly into Tarius's stomach. Jena screamed and hid her face in her father's chest.

"You mean like that, Tarius?" Persius laughed.

Tarius looked up at him with pain in her eyes. "Yes, precisely like that," Tarius said.

Persius nodded his head, and the man holding the horse released it as another beat a whip against the horse's rump. The horse took off at a high speed, dragging Tarius behind him.

"She'll only become the Katabull," Tragon protested with fear. "She'll get loose, and she'll come back for us."

"Interesting thing about the Katabull. If you pierce them with any wooden weapon they can't change form," Persius said. "Wood is toxic to their systems."

Tragon smiled.

Hellibolt watched the horse go and muttered an incantation under his breath. "Little horse thin and mean, make tracks that can not be seen." It was the best he could do on short notice.

Hellibolt walked over to Darian slowly and he held out his arms. "Let me see the girl, she's had quite a shock. I'll bring her to the surgeon."

Darian nodded and Hellibolt took Jena from him. She was like a lifeless doll. He helped her towards the castle. "They didn't kill her, you know."

"They want her to suffer," Jena cried.

"Yes, and because of their cruelty, Tarius will live," Hellibolt said. "I have foreseen it." It wasn't exactly true, but who cared about the truth when a lie might help the girl cope? Besides, with Tarius there was a very real chance that the desire to get even would give her the will to live.

"Tarius has told me that you are very wise. What should I do?"

"You should follow your heart, Jena," Hellibolt said quietly. "Go were it begs you to go, and do what it begs you to do. That was Tarius's only real crime."

Jena nodded. "I said terrible things to her. Terrible!" Jena said.

"Yes, well, that's the great thing about love. It allows one to forgive anything."

"Not anything," Jena said sadly.

"Yes, anything," Hellibolt insisted. "You'll see what I mean in time. Ah! Here we go."

Robert looked Jena over in silence. He suggested she lie down to rest for a while.

Hellibolt pulled him aside. "How is she?"

"In shock. The baby seems fine. I gave her some powders to calm her nerves... Is Tarius..."

"The king shot her through the stomach with an arrow, and is currently having her dragged around the countryside by an enthusiastic young stallion. If she lives, it will be a miracle," Hellibolt said quietly. "Of course, as we both know, miracles are Tarius's strong suit."

The surgeon nodded. "May I say something in the strictest of confidence?"

"Yes, you may."

"The king is an idiot," Robert said. "Man or woman, Tarius is a good person, wise beyond his... her years."

Hellibolt had a thought. "I put a spell on the horse so that it left no tracks. However, I could put another spell on a certain surgeon so that he could follow Tarius's exact route. With medical help, she just might have a chance."

Robert thought about it only a moment. "If you can make up an excuse for my absence from the castle for a few days, I will go. If I find her still alive, I will do all I can."

Harris had followed the activities at the castle carefully, always keeping himself and the horses in the shadows. He would obey Tarius's wishes to a point, however if he got a chance to save her he would take it. When he saw the horse run off with Tarius he took his cue and went after her.

He followed as closely as he could without being seen, but never losing sight of Tarius. When he was sure the others could no longer see either of them, he closed in. He rode up hard and fast drawing his sword, and after several tries he was able to cut Tarius loose. She rolled for several feet and landed against a tree. The horse took off in the other direction.

Harris immediately jumped from his mount and went to his friend's side. He rolled her over, took the stocks off her head and arms and cradled her head and shoulders against his chest. She was almost unconscious and so badly beaten and dirty that she was hardly recognizable. The arrow had been shorn off on both sides and only a splinter of it stuck out. Her breathing was raspy, but she was alive. He quickly got to his feet and picked her up. Reluctantly, he lay her over her horse's saddle and tied her on. It was the best he could do for now. The king's men would come hunting the body soon, and he had to get her out of there before they came. He rode on as quickly as he dared guiding her horse behind him.

At midday he decided he had put enough space between him and the king's men. He smiled when he thought how surprised they'd be to find the horse but not the king's prize. Gently, he took Tarius from the saddle. She was still alive, but barely, and the blood was dripping from her saddle. He carried her over and lay her on a stack of leaves. Then he carefully dribbled some water into her mouth. Just when he thought he'd failed, she swallowed it and then coughed. Harris tried to wash the wound, hoping to find the arrow shaft, but as soon as he was sure he had seen it the blood covered it again. At one point he got hold of it, but it slipped from his fingers.

"Why?" Tarius choked out.

Harris looked at her and smiled glad to see she was conscious. "Why what?" he asked.

"Why didn't you desert me?" she asked.

"Why would I desert you? Man or woman, you are my kin. You believed in me when no one else did. You showed me a kindness I had never known, and made me all that I am. So you're a woman. Does that make everything you did for me nothing? So you're the Katabull. Does that mean everything you have taught me is wrong? You are the best person I have ever known, Tarius. I know what it's like to be cast out because you are different, and if I could have hidden my difference, I would have, just as you did," Harris said.

"My one true friend," Tarius choked out. "I don't deserve your loyalty."

"You have many true friends, Tarius. And do you know why? Because you have helped everyone you ever touched. Even Jena. She'll see that in time. You taught her to be all that she wanted to be. You let her be herself when no one else would. Now be quiet. You're wasting your strength, and I'm having trouble getting hold of the shaft."

"Perhaps I could be of some help."

Harris swung around quickly, sword in hand. He looked up at the king's surgeon. "You... But how?"

"Hellibolt helped me," the surgeon said. "As you said, Tarius has many true friends. Now let's see what I can do. Why don't you go ahead and set up camp? We'll need a good fire and a tent for sure."

Harris nodded and went to work.

"Robert?" Tarius asked in disbelief.

"Yes." He knelt and started tending to her wound. "The king is a proud fool, Tarius. However, he is my king, and before I work on you I must ask you to make a promise."

Tarius nodded.

"Leave the kingdom; go back to the Kartik."

Tarius nodded. "There is nothing for me here now."

Robert had Harris lay out a blanket in the sun where he had the best light. He stripped Tarius of her clothes and covered her lower body with a blanket. He wondered fleetingly how much different Katabull anatomy was from that of humans. *A bit late to worry about that now.* He pursed his lips in determination and went to work. With a scalpel he cut the skin over the arrow shaft to give him enough room to work in, and then he gently took hold of the shaft with some pullers and teased it out. There was a nick in the bowel, which he cauterized. He'd never had much luck with the procedure before, but this time it seemed to work. He sewed up the entrance and exit wounds, then made a poultice and wrapped it to her body with gauze. Finally, he attended to the multitude of scratches and bumps she had all over her body, fortunately he found no broken bones, just deep bruises and shallow scratches. At some point in the procedure she'd passed out, and she was still out cold. Together, Harris and Robert picked up the corners of the blanket and carried her into the tent. Then they walked back outside and Harris handed Robert a cup of tea.

"Will she be all right?" Harris asked solemnly.

Robert shrugged. "I don't know. If she makes it through the night, that will be a good sign. I'll stay with you for a couple of days, and then I'll have to get back. Problem is that Hellibolt says that wood is almost like poison to the Katabull. No telling what effects it's going to have on her."

Harris nodded. "How long before she can travel?"

"She shouldn't travel for weeks, but that's not very logical. You'd better leave when I do. Persius isn't going to rest until he finds her body, and it will be obvious that someone cut her loose when they find the horse and the stocks," Robert said.

Harris nodded silently.

Robert laughed. "Really chaps their butts that a woman is a better fighter than all of them. That's really what this is all about, you know. That a woman outsmarted them. That she could out-think them. If she had just been Katabull, I think they would have seen that as forgivable, might even have just ignored it. It's the fact that she's a woman that pushed Persius and the others to do this to her. They want to establish that they can beat her. If she lives, I for one will be happy to have helped to prove them wrong."

Jena glared at Tragon where he sat at their dinner table—in Tarius's seat. They had been legally married, and he seemed to think that gave him a license to touch her whenever he liked. She made sure he knew it didn't.

"Jena, you're awfully quiet," Darian said.

How very bright of you, Father. It's only taken you three days to realize that I'm not talking to either of you. You could make me marry him, but you can't make me love him. You can't even make me like him.

"Are you all right, Jena?" Tragon asked with a cultivated sound of concern in his voice.

"No, I'm not all right!" Jena screamed back. She looked at Tragon accusingly. "I've been thinking about the things you have said to me all along, and one thing becomes quite obvious. You knew from the very beginning what Tarius was. You knew and said nothing. Why would you do that? What were you getting from her, or maybe it's something you *weren't* getting—like killed."

She glared at her father then. "This man you insisted I marry is no less a liar to us than Tarius—and with less cause. At least her reasons were noble. Not so him. He wants to own and conquer me. He held his tongue only because he couldn't think of a way to get rid of her. When he did, he spoke. But he knew all along."

"How dare you speak like that of your husband!" Darian said. "He told you how he came to find out."

"He is a liar!" Jena screamed. "A liar and a coward just like Tarius said."

"You sound as if you'd rather be with that beast, that woman..."

"I'd rather be with *anyone* but him," Jena said.

"Hold your tongue, daughter! Chose your words carefully..."

"Or what? You'll have me tied to the back of a horse and dragged to death? Oh... But it's too bad they never found the body, isn't it, Father? Oh, yes. I've overheard the king's herald reporting to you."

"Harris is gone without a trace, Tragon. Where do you suppose he has gone?" Jena asked turning her attention to Tragon. "If Tarius is alive, and there is a good chance she is, she will come back and kill you. You know her, she is very much a believer in revenge. If she is alive, she'll come back and kill you, and I hope to the gods she does. If she doesn't, I just might do it myself."

"Jena!" Darian screamed. "We'll hear no more of that talk. Tragon is the father of your unborn child. A little respect isn't too much to ask for. A little caring."

"He is not the father I choose for my child," Jena said. "Yes, it was dark, but I saw Tarius's face that night. It was some sort of glamour."

"You talk nonsense, daughter," Darian said. "Where would Tragon get such a thing?"

Tragon couldn't, but Tarius has a friend in the wizard. She could have easily acquired it. No sense in implicating Hellibolt. No sense in this conversation at all. I'm stuck here with no way out. Tarius ruined my life, and I should hate her. Instead I hate Tragon even more than before. I blame him because I was happy in my ignorance, and he wouldn't let me remain ignorant.

She pushed away from the table and went to her room, locking the door behind her to make sure Tragon couldn't join her. She lay down on the bed and cried. If it weren't for the baby she'd kill herself. But the child gave her hope. It was someone she could love who would love her back.

I had that with Tarius, but it's gone now. It was all a lie anyway. All a lie, except her love. That was real. But could I love her? Would I have loved her had I known she was a woman?

She was confused and lonely and filled with hurt. In a few short weeks her life had gone from a dream to a nightmare.

It took them three weeks to reach the coastline. Tarius could barely walk or ride, and she didn't seem to be getting any better. She ran high fevers almost every day and woke with night terrors every night.

He helped her walk along the docks. They were looking for a Kartik vessel, any Kartik vessel headed for home. They finally found one at the end of the dock. Harris had seen ships in pictures, but nothing he had seen had done them justice. They were huge beasts of wood and rope, cloth and metal. And the ocean! It was so big! He had never seen such a huge body of water.

"Sister," a sailor said in the Kartik tongue, holding his hand up in the traditional Kartik greeting. Tarius grasped his hand in the air and brought their elbows together.

"Brother," Tarius answered in Kartik.

"What can I do for you?" the sailor asked.

"I wish to talk to your captain about booking passage for myself, my young friend here, and two horses," Tarius said.

The man nodded and led them on board the ship and to the captain's quarters. The captain wasn't a big man, in fact none of the Kartik people Harris saw on the boat seemed to be carrying even one extra pound. They were tall—on average over six foot—but they were thin and well-muscled. The captain wore bright colors of red, orange and yellow, reminding Harris of Tarius's old gambeson.

The women Harris had seen on deck were beautiful—dark, and sultry and all wearing swords. Doing what in his country would have been considered men's work. Both the men and women were dressed in minimum clothing all just as bright as their captain's.

"What can I do for you, sister?" the man asked in Kartik.

Tarius had started teaching Harris Kartik as soon as they had decided to move. The last three weeks she had made him crazy refusing to speak to him in anything but Kartik. Now he was glad she had. It would be too weird to have people around you talking and not know what they were saying.

"I wish to book passage for myself, my friend, and two horses back to the Kartik," Tarius said.

"I'm afraid we are full up this trip," the captain reported. "You're hurt. Accident? Or are you in some sort of trouble?"

"I'm in trouble. I was fighting in the Jethrik army against our enemy the Amalites."

To Harris's shock and amusement, both the captain and Tarius stopped to spit on the floor before Tarius continued. "The King of the Jethriks found me out, and now he wants me dead. It was he who put the arrow in my side. My need is most urgent. I must get to the Springs of Montero, or I will die."

"Are you the Katabull?" the captain asked with a raised eyebrow.

"Aye," Tarius said.

"Then say no more. We'll make room for you," he said. He took her hand and shook it.

"I can't pay much, but I swear to you that if you will give us safe passage I will pay you the remainder of the fare after I find sword work," Tarius promised.

"Your word is good with me. Collect your horses and your gear; we sail with the tide."

As they left the ship to retrieve their belongings Harris asked, "What was all that about?"

"The Hot Springs of Montero have healing properties for everyone, but especially for the Katabull," Tarius said.

"I know that. You have told me about a hundred times. I mean why did he change his mind when you told him you were Katabull?"

Tarius smiled. "Because while the Amalites think we are bad luck, and the Jethrik barely tolerate us, the Kartik believe that the Katabull are blessed by the One Who Has No Name. They believe we bring them luck. Sometimes superstision can work in your favor."

Jena looked out the window just in time to see Arvon arrive. He hadn't been coming to help with the training of the recruits since Tarius had been found out. She ran through the house and to the door, hoping to catch him before he entered the academy. She flung the door open in his face, and they both jumped.

Jena shook her head. "I'm sorry, Arvon. I saw you ride up and wanted to talk to you before you went into the academy."

Arvon frowned hard and shook his head. "I have no business there. I came to see you. To talk to you. Are we alone?"

Jena shook her head no. "These days the servants make daily reports of my actions to my father. We could walk down to the creek."

Arvon was silent as they walked along. Finally, Jena could stand it no longer. "Is Tarius... Is he... she. Is she..."

"Dead?" Arvon asked, his voice filled with contempt. "Why do you assume I would know, and would you even care?"

"Yes, of course I would. I didn't want her hurt," Jena said.

Arvon stopped, deciding they were far enough away from the house and the academy. "This has been very hard for me, Jena, because the last words Tarius spoke to me were of you and your safety. She made me promise to keep you and your baby safe from harm, and to take care of you. I gave my word that I would. But the last time I spoke to you, you had only words of contempt for her. Such hate and such loathing that I don't really want to help you. Still I find myself in a position where I must."

"Then you knew all along, what he... she was?"

"Not all along but I've known for a long time."

Jena nodded then looked confused. "I was very angry and hurt, Arvon. How could I not be? In all truth I still am, but now my hatred has turned to Tragon and even to my father and the king." Jena walked on a little further down to the creek and sat down on a rock. She heard Arvon walk up behind her. "My mind wanders from chaos to madness and back again, it's as if I can't hold on to even the simplest thought. Every night I dream of her, Arvon. Of how gentle was her touch. Sometimes I dream that I make love to her as well. I dream that we are together. May the gods help me, Arvon, it is only those dreams and thoughts of my baby that keep me going these days. I miss her, I know I shouldn't, but I do. Tell me, Arvon, you're queer. Do you think that I am? Could I be?"

"Frankly, Jena, I always thought that you were. Tarius didn't look like a man. Ask yourself this; why did you choose Tarius? You're a beautiful woman. You could have had your pick of a hundred different gorgeous fighting men, and yet you chose Tarius. Why? Not only does she not look like a man, but she doesn't act like one, either. You may not have known it, but all of the things you found in Tarius that were missing from the men you knew were female traits. You fell in love with Tarius because she was a woman," Arvon said. "I couldn't convince her of this, and now she may be dead. She was afraid that you would react in exactly the way that you did."

"And, how else did you expect me to react, Arvon? I thought I had married a man and I was married to a woman, and not just any woman but a *Katabull*. She even put that bastard into our bed to impregnate me so that she could continue to hide her secret." She started to cry then. "Gods won't someone please tell me what I'm supposed to feel? She's not dead; I know she's not, she couldn't be… Oh Arvon… Please don't hate me; I'm so alone." She turned a tear-streaked face to look at him. "Tarius asked you to take care of me. Well, please do, Arvon, because I need someone to talk to. I need to figure out where my heart is. The wizard told me that Tarius wouldn't die. He told me to follow my heart, but I just don't know where it is anymore."

Arvon nodded and took her into his arms. He couldn't see her like this and stay mad at her. She couldn't be held accountable for what she had said that night. She needed him, and he had made a promise.

When they had first set sail, Harris had been filled with excitement. Then they had sailed out of the harbor and he realized there was still more to the ocean. He stood and gazed at it in astonishment—there was nothing but blue as far as the eye could see.

"How… how do we know which way to go?" Harris asked Tarius.

"It's that way," she said pointing. She was sitting on a barrel covered with a blanket fighting yet another fever. She wasn't really in the mood to talk.

"But how will they know when we're in the middle of it?" Harris asked, too excited to be concerned for the moment with his sick friend.

"Charts and stars," Tarius answered.

"Huh?" Harris said.

Tarius realized she wasn't going to get off the hook that easily, so she started a lengthy explanation about how star maps and charts and compasses worked. She was almost glad when he got seasick, because it meant he left her alone. The Kartik sailors all laughed at him, but when he had been good and sick for several hours they finally brought him their world famous hangover/seasickness remedy. It didn't work right away, and Harris asked one of the sailors to take care of Tarius.

The woman bathed Tarius's face with a wet rag. "Your fever is very high," she told Tarius.

Tarius was almost delirious. "I know."

"Can I look at the wound? I know a little about healing."

Tarius nodded silently. She didn't remember when they had last changed the dressing. The girl pulled the dressing off and made a face, so Tarius decided it had probably been awhile. She hadn't been coherent enough for long enough to mess with it, and it was only now that she realized she had been remiss in not teaching Harris anything about first aid.

The woman began cleaning the wound. "Well, there's part of your problem. You didn't take the stitches out and a couple are infected." She took her dagger and gently and skillfully cut the stitches and pulled them.

"You're pretty good at that," Tarius said.

"Thanks," she said. "A salt water poultice might be a good idea."

"There are stitches in the back, too." Tarius leaned forward and the woman removed the stitches and cleaned the wound. Then she put a saltwater poultice on it, wrapping it to Tarius's body.

"It burns," Tarius said.

"That's good, means it working. Here..." She handed Tarius a canteen. "Drink this."

Tarius took a long drink. "So, what's your name?"

"Elise," she said.

Tarius smiled a sickly smile. "My foster mother's name was Elise. Thank you very much." She handed the canteen back to the woman.

"What's your name?" Elise asked.

"Tarius," she answered.

The girl looked startled. "Tarius, like Tarius the Black?"

"Aye... One and the same," Tarius said.

"You're a woman? In town we heard stories about you, but they said you were a man," Ellis said. "You are a very great warrior."

"Thank you," Tarius said.

Elise stood and yelled out. "Hey everyone! This is Tarius the Black! The savior of the Jethrik is a Kartik woman."

They all laughed and whooped and hollered, apparently very happy to be in the presence of such a warrior, and thrilled with the irony that a country that didn't allow women to fight in their army had been saved by a woman warrior. They gathered around her and wanted to know which stories they had heard were true.

She was tired and fevered and the saltwater burned, but as she started to tell the battle stories she forgot even the pain in her chest. In battle none could equal her. She knew it. The only battle she had lost was the battle for her heart. She would become what she was meant to be, a warrior and nothing but a warrior. She would live by the blade and for the blade and think of love no more.

She would truly become Tarius the Black.

———•◆•———

Jena lay in bed and looked at the ceiling. She couldn't sleep. Who was she? What did she really want? Did she still love Tarius? Had part of her known all along that Tarius was a woman? No, but she couldn't convince herself that she hadn't chosen Tarius because "he" looked and acted like a woman. In fact, the more she thought about it, the more she was sure that was exactly why she had found Tarius so attractive.

She'd never known her mother's love, maybe she craved a woman's love because of that. Somehow she didn't think that was the answer either though.

She allowed herself to do something she had consciously blocked from her mind since she had learned that Tarius was a woman. She thought back to the first time that Tarius had made love to her in the open field. She remembered all the times that Tarius had made love to her, trying to recall if she had ever felt repulsed the way she had when Tragon had posed as Tarius. There was no such time. With Tarius she had felt special, cherished, loved. Nothing Tarius had done to her had made her feel anything but pleasure.

On the other hand, what Tragon had done to her had left her feeling violated. When she'd first learned the truth she had told herself that it was because she knew somewhere in her heart that it wasn't Tarius, but that simply wasn't true. If she'd any idea it wasn't Tarius, she never would have allowed it.

What does it all mean? That I am queer? That I like girls? Or just that I love Tarius so much that it doesn't matter if she's a woman or not? I don't know! I just don't know if I could make love to her... knowing. If I could do to her the things she has done to me.

If she's even alive. And what if she is? She can't come back here; I would have to go to Kartik and find her, and I can't go anywhere now. I'm getting bigger by the day. Do I pack up an infant and carry him off in the night? Run with him to a foreign land to find a lover I don't even know if I want? All I do know is that I don't want this. I don't want this life with Tragon and my father telling me what to do and who to be.

A knock on the door brought her out of her thoughts. She didn't answer the knock; she would pretend to be asleep. The knock came again.

"Damn it, Jena, let me in!" It was Tragon, and from the sound of his voice he was drunk.

"Go away and leave me be!" Jena hollered back.

"No! You're my wife. Mine!" He hit the door hard with his shoulder, and it opened.

Jena jumped out of bed, grabbed her robe and threw it on. "I demand you leave at once," Jena ordered.

Tragon laughed. "Jena, Tarius let you get away with that sort of shit because she was a woman. I'm not a woman; I'm a man. I'll take what is mine."

"I don't belong to you!" Jena screamed. If her father heard the fight, he was ignoring it. Jena silently wished that he would pick now to be on her side.

Tragon walked up to her, and she backed away.

"It's time we consummate this marriage. Time that you had a real man," Tragon said.

Jena snarled back. "I've had you, remember? It wasn't pleasant for me."

"That's because it was too quick. I didn't have enough time. I could make you feel pleasure like you have never felt before," Tragon said.

"Did it seem to you, Tragon, that I wasn't sated when you came to me?" Jena asked with venom. "You could never give to me what Tarius gave to me."

"You bitch!" he hissed.

He punched her hard in the jaw, then grabbed her by the shoulders and threw her so hard that she landed not on the bed but went over it. She landed on the floor stomach first, and knew before she felt the blood flow between her legs what had happened. She lay there for a second in pain and fear. There was an immediate sense of loss like she had never felt before. Then she looked under the bed and saw the hilt of her sword.

"Oh my gods! Jena! My gods, the baby! I'll run get the surgeon. I'm sorry! I'm so sorry," Tragon said.

Jena stood up from the floor, sword in hand. "You bastard!" she hissed. "First you destroyed my world, and now you have killed my child."

"No!" Tragon screamed.

Jena didn't stop to think. She plunged the sword into Tragon's chest under his solar plexus up at an angle and twisted it, just as Tarius had taught her to do. She drew the sword out and waited for him to fall. As he fell, Jena saw her father standing in the doorway.

"Jena, what have you done?" Darian asked in disbelief.

"You... Where the hell were you when this bastard was taking the last thing I had that mattered to me?" Jena cried. She swung the sword in front of her. "Get the hell out of my way, or I'll kill you, too."

She ran past him then turned. "Don't come after me. If you ever loved me, give me enough time to get away."

"Jena," Darian cried. "Let me help you."

"It's a little late for that *now*, Father."

Jena ran out of the house and towards the stable. She was in incredible pain. The cramps in her abdomen were three times as strong as any she'd had with even her worst period. She was still losing blood, and now she was having trouble keeping her feet. She didn't have time to pick and choose, so she grabbed the first horse she found that was saddled and bridled—probably one that was kept ready for a king's herald—and added horse theft to the list of her crimes.

She raced out of the academy grounds, feeling like all her innards would fall out if she allowed her seat to leave the saddle just a little bit. She knew what it was. It was the baby; it was being born. It was being born dead.

Arvon opened the door and Jena fell on him her, sword clattering to the floor.

"What the hell!" Dustan asked walking in from the other room.

"Jena," Arvon carried her over and sat her in a chair. It was then that he saw all the blood. "My gods! What happened?"

"Tragon killed my baby," Jena cried. "That bastard killed my baby."

Dustan picked up Jena's sword and showed it to Arvon.

Arvon looked at the blood on the blade. "Jena, what did you do?"

"He killed my baby, so I killed him," Jena said, her eyes bright.

"Oh my gods, she's killed her husband," Arvon said. In Jethrik, the penalty for a woman killing her husband was death. According to Jethrik law, there was no just cause for such an act. "Dustan, get the horses ready and pack some gear. We have to leave tonight."

Dustan nodded and ran outside.

Arvon knew Jena needed help. She needed a mid-wife, but all she had was Arvon, and the only thing Arvon had ever helped deliver was a lamb.

It wasn't as hard as he thought. Still, when he'd held that tiny dead thing, it had broken his heart.

"Do you want to see him?" Arvon asked.

Jena closed her eyes and shook her head no. "I have enough nightmares in my life now."

"I'll be back." Arvon took the child and the placenta outside and buried them quickly. Then he went back inside and cleaned Jena up. Finally, he helped her dress in some of Dustan's clothes. Dustan was busy tearing any clothing they wouldn't need into changing rags. Jena was going to need them.

Slightly more than an hour after Jena's arrival they rode out. Arvon held Jena on the saddle in front of him, trying to ease the jarring. They rode all through the night with Arvon enlisting the help of his Katabull eyes to see. He led Dustan's horse by a rope, and Jena fell asleep against his chest. By morning they were completely exhausted, so they stopped and made camp. They only had one tent, and Arvon put Jena between he and Dustan to help keep her warm.

"Arvon?" Jena said.

"Yes, Jena," Arvon answered.

"I feel so empty inside." Her voice was choked with tears.

Arvon held her to him and Dustan patted her back.

"What now?" Dustan asked.

Arvon shrugged.

"We go to Kartik," Jena said wiping her face. "If Tarius is still alive, we'll find her."

"Is that what you want?" Arvon asked.

"Yes. I have to know once and for all. Besides, where else can we go? I just killed my husband, remember?"

"I've always wanted to go to Kartik. They say it's beautiful there and always warm," Dustan said.

Arvon smiled at Dustan over Jena. He could not have asked for a better partner. Dustan had made no promise to Tarius, yet he was willing to pull up his whole life and run off to a foreign country because Arvon was bound to do so.

"I love you, Dustan," he said.

Dustan sighed but not without a smile on his face. "I love you, too, Arvon. You know, you might have picked some time when there wasn't a woman between us to tell me."

14

Tarius was still weak and sick, but feeling better than she had since she'd been shot. The saltwater poultices and having the stitches out had helped. The fact that she hadn't even thought about removing them said just how sick she really was. Tarius was an old hand when it came to wounds. She knew how to dress and take care of them. She'd just been too sick to think straight.

She stood at the head of the boat looking out at the ocean. It was good to be at sea again. She had been on and off ships all her life. She hadn't realized how much she'd missed just seeing and being close to the ocean until right this second when she was actually well enough to enjoy it.

Harris had been sick most of the first two days they had been at sea. After that either the Kartik seasickness potion started to kick in, or more likely than not, he was just getting his sea legs.

At sea there wasn't much to do, so they repaired nets and took turns at watch in the crow's-nest. After that Kartik sailors passed the time wrestling, drinking too much, and having sex.

They were on the main deck now, wrestling, and Harris had joined them. They had thought they would be able to trick him with Kartik moves he wouldn't know, but he was her protégé, and he knew them all.

He was wrestling with Elise right now. Tarius smiled. If he were smart, he'd let her win. Tarius had feared at first that Elise had some sort of crush on her because of the way she cared for her, but when Tarius's head had cleared she realized that Elise was just one of those very compassionate people who liked to care for the sick. If she had any interest in Tarius at all it was for what Tarius could teach her about the sword. In fact, with each new day it became more and more obvious that she had taken a shine to young Harris. When he let the girl beat him wrestling, Tarius knew that he had taken a shine to her as well.

Suddenly she saw something off the port bow. She took a second look.

"Captain!" she hollered, but her voice was lost in the waves. She limped forward finding the captain at the helm. "Captain, I think I see a ship off the port bow."

"Jasper! Into the crow's-nest," the captain called out seeing that it was unmanned.

The young lad scurried up the ropes to the crow's-nest. He took the eyeglass and looked out. "Amalites!" he screamed. "Amalite raiders!"

For a second there was not a sound. Then the captain started screaming orders. The sailors started rushing around gathering their weapons and loading crossbows.

The captain looked through his own eyeglass at the ship that was coming on quick. "Damn! There must be fifty of them on a ship that size. I have a crew of fifteen, seventeen men in all counting you and your friend. You are the great warlord. Tell me. How do we stay alive?"

"Can our ship outrun them?"

"We're at full sail now," he said.

Tarius couldn't lie to him. She didn't have the strength to do much more than hold her sword. Harris could take out a bunch of them, and the sailors were all good fighters she was sure. But it wouldn't be nearly enough against a fully manned, fully armed Amalite raiding party.

"See if their captain or look out has a glass," she said.

He looked. "Aye... both have them."

"Then I'll change," Tarius said.

The captain smiled. The sight of the Katabull might just send the Amalites fleeing in the other direction.

Tarius reached down within herself and tried to call on the night. But she couldn't stay focused, and she couldn't make the change. "Damn this wound! I can't do it on my own. Quick! Bring me a bottle of rum."

The captain yelled the order, and in moments there was a bottle of rum in Tarius's hand. She downed half of it quickly, and before she removed the bottle from her lips the change had taken place. She stood up, pulled her sword and standing on the helm she looked at the Amalite ship, beat her chest and swung her sword above her head.

In seconds the Amalite ship had changed course and was running in the other direction. The sailors all cheered.

Harris walked up to Tarius as she put away her sword. "What the hell was that?"

"That was only one of the reasons that the Kartiks think the Katabull are lucky." Tarius stumbled and fell, and Harris caught her.

"Are you all right, Tarius?" Harris asked.

"No, I'm quite drunk," Tarius slurred out.

Harris helped her to the hold and set her down in a chair.

"It's a good thing they didn't know how sick you are," Harris said speaking of the Amalites.

"Very good. Do you know what else is good, Harris?" Tarius asked.

Harris had never seen her drunk before. She was funny. "No, what else is good?"

"Sex... Sex is good. You should bed Elise immediately."

"Shush," Harris laughed, covering her mouth with his hand. When he thought it was safe, he took his hand off her mouth.

In a voice she obviously thought was a whisper, Tarius said, "Don't let a prime piece of tail pass you by. Why when I was single, if I smelt it, I had to have it."

"Now see, Tarius," Harris said making a face, "that was something I didn't need to know."

Suddenly she became maudlin. "Get it now while you can, because once you fall in love, you'll only want her. Then when she doesn't want you, you won't get it any more. I don't even care about it now. If I can't have Jena, I might as well sew it up like a big wound."

"All right... Now, Tarius, you're drunk, and you're just getting weird," Harris said gently. He tried to sound scolding, but lost the effect because he was laughing.

"I can't believe you are laughing at my pain!" Tarius said hotly.

"I'm very sorry, Tarius," Harris said, and made himself stop smiling by biting his bottom lip.

Elise walked in then. She knelt beside Tarius and looked into her eyes. "Is she all right?" Elise asked Harris.

"She's very drunk, but I don't think she's hurt any worse than she was," Harris said.

"The Katabull have no tolerance for alcohol. They are the world's cheapest drunks."

Tarius grabbed Elise by the collar and dragged her close. "I had a woman, you know. A beautiful woman."

"I'm sure you've had many," Elise said. She looked at Harris and rolled her eyes. Harris smiled.

"Yes I did. But I only cared for one, and now she hates me." Tarius started to cry, the way only a drunk can.

"You should not drink," Harris said as he cradled her in his arms.

"My life was a farce... My whole life was a farce, and now I have been found out. My life is worth nothing to me or anyone else. I can't go on without her. I can't. I won't. Toss me into the sea and let me drown."

"You were doing just fine until you got drunk," Harris reminded her.

Elise handed Harris a canteen. Harris held it to Tarius's lips and she drank. "Would it help if she changed back?" he asked Elise.

"I don't think she can change back until the alcohol wears off."

Tarius suddenly pushed Harris away and jumped to her feet. "I feel good now. I must be well." She took three steps, stumbled and fell.

Harris ran to her side and helped her back up. He started half-carrying, half-dragging her back to her bunk. She was singing some sailing song that made no sense at all. It was a stupid song, and to his dismay Elise started to sing it with her. At least Elise could sing, which was more than you could say for Tarius.

"Oh! And up went her pantaloons, right up the mast. Down came the captain, fell flat on his ass! Dancing on the kegs of ale without any pants!"

Harris poured her into her bed where she promptly passed out. Then he looked at Elise and laughed. "So now I know two things that Tarius isn't good at. Drinking and singing."

"I'm assuming since she was talking about a woman that you and she aren't lovers?" Elise asked.

Harris laughed. "Hell, till a few weeks ago I thought she was a man, too. I love Tarius, but not like that. She's my family, my brother, ah I mean sister."

Elise moved closer to him, then she jumped on him, wrestled him to the ground and started kissing him. Before he knew what was happening, she had most of his clothes off.

Harris decided he could love this girl.

Persius looked down from his throne at Darian. He had sent for Darian upon hearing the news, but still didn't want to hear what he knew the man was going to say.

"So Darian... tell me what happened."

"I can't be certain, Sire," Darian started.

"Then tell me what you think happened!" Persius demanded impatiently.

"When I got up this morning I found Tragon dead, lying in a pool of his own blood, and my daughter was gone. A horse was stolen from the stable, and there was a trail of blood leading from my house to the stables. No doubt where the sword had dripped. Have they... have they found Tarius's body yet?"

"No, why do you ask?" Persius didn't really want to hear the answer. No doubt Darian had come to the same conclusion he had.

"Sire... Tragon was killed with Tarius's signature cut—a plunge up at an angle under the rib cage into the heart and a twist for good measure. Now it's true that she has taught that move to Harris, who's still missing, and to Tragon, who now lies dead... I think, Sire, that Harris somehow found Tarius and nursed her back to health. And then Tarius came back, killed Tragon, and took my daughter."

Persius nodded. It did seem to be the obvious piece to complete the puzzle. He took a deep breath. "So. It must be true. Who beside Tarius would have reason to both kill Tragon and take your daughter?" Persius lowered his voice. He leaned closer to Darian, and it was then that Darian noticed the king's haggard appearance. He hadn't had much sleep if any in days, and it was obvious. "She'll come for me. She said she'd get Tragon, and she did. She'll come for me as well. I will double my guards... No, triple them."

"Not a bad idea, Sire."

"If it's any consolation, Darian, she won't hurt your daughter," the king said.

Darian nodded. He knew that. He also knew the truth. It pained him to lie to his king, but this way Jena could come home if she wanted to... someday.

They had stayed camped where they were for a week, and Jena was improving daily. At least she was getting better physically; emotionally she was a wreck. Nothing seemed clear to her. Her thoughts were cluttered and made little if any sense.

One minute she'd be gloating over having killed her enemy, Tragon. The next she'd be crying over having taken the life of her child's father. One instant she was absolving Tragon for his misdeeds because he hadn't meant to kill the baby, saying his only real crime had been loving her. The very next she was damning him to some eternal anguish for having destroyed her world, and for having killed her child.

Her thoughts about Tarius were just as jumbled. She'd sit and very carefully make excuses for everything Tarius had done. Then just as quickly she'd argue away all the excuses.

It had all happened too fast, and it was too hard to comprehend. Tragon had loved her, or at least he'd loved her by his definition of the word, and yet she had hated him. Tarius loved her, and she loved Tarius, but Tarius was a woman and a Katabull, and she had put into Jena's bed the one man on earth that Jena had truly hated.

One minute she was sure that Tarius was all she wanted in the world, and that all she wanted was to go and find her, to be with her and to see if they could make a life together. The next she wanted nothing to do with Tarius. Tarius was a beast, a woman, and a liar who had used her only to further her position in the kingdom. She was the ultimate disguise that helped Tarius masquerade as a man.

She cried openly several times a day. There was a hollow spot in her womb where her baby had been and a hollow spot in her heart where Tarius had been. She wanted to turn back the clock. Turn it back to a time somewhere before she had started practically demanding that Tarius give her something that Tarius could not. Then maybe she'd have never known. Ignorance had truly been bliss.

Yet try as she might she couldn't wish Tarius completely away, return to a time before she knew Tarius, and she supposed that fact told her as much as she needed to know.

Arvon walked up and sat on the rock beside her. "Copper for your thoughts."

Jena tried to smile, but didn't quite make it. "Why does everything have to be so complicated, Arvon?" she asked in a quiet voice.

Arvon managed a smile just for her. "Because that's the nature of life, Jena."

"My life didn't used to be complicated at all," Jena said.

"Ah! But you had never been in love. Love changes everything."

"It should make things better, not worse," Jena said in confusion.

Arvon laughed. "Now who told you that? Love rarely makes one's life better."

"But it's not supposed to be like this! Not like what it's done to me, to my life."

"True." Arvon put an arm around her shoulders. "But try to imagine what it was like for Tarius, Jena. To love someone as desperately as she loved you and to know that in order to keep that person you have to lie about what you are. Do you really believe that she didn't want you to make love to her? She couldn't give into her desires for fear of rejection. What must it be like to know in your heart that the person you love doesn't actually love you, but rather the person you are pretending to be? I won't condone what she did to you, but she never meant to cause you any pain. Because she loved you, loved you for exactly who you are, she lost everything. Had she not been with you, she never would have been found out. So as much as this love has cost you, it has cost her even more. For all we know Tarius is dead. By all rights she should be... "

"Don't say that, Arvon. Don't ever say Tarius is dead," Jena said.

"Then you've definitely decided to go to Kartik—to look for her?" Arvon asked. Over the last week her thoughts on this issue had changed a hundred times.

"We have to go to Kartik. There is nowhere else for me to run," Jena said thoughtfully. "After that... I don't know, Arvon. I just don't know right now. If she is... dead... then there is no sense in looking for her. If she's not, she may never want to see me again. Even if she does, I'm not sure I ever want to see her again. It's too soon for me to make a decision."

Arvon nodded. "I understand, but maybe this will help you. Tarius could have gotten out of that cell at any time. She could have escaped that night before the king tried to execute her. She didn't leave because of the king's threat against you."

"How could she have escaped? I know that the Katabull are very strong, but surely not strong enough to break chains of the caliber that held her that night. Then there were the bars, and..."

"She could have gotten away, because I offered to help her," Arvon said.

"Arvon, what could one man do against the palace guard?" Jena asked.

"One *man*, nothing," Arvon said. "But I'm not a man, I am the Katabull."

Jena was a little taken aback, but didn't seem frightened by his revelation.

Arvon continued. "Once Harris, Dustan and I had freed Tarius, the four of us could have very easily escaped, but Tarius wouldn't even consider escape because of you. It may not be what you wanted, Jena, but remember this. No one will ever love you like that again. No one else will ever love you the way Tarius did."

Jena nodded. "I know that, Arvon. And I don't truly believe that I will ever love anyone the way I loved her. That's what confuses the crap out of me."

Arvon stood and took her hand, helping her to her feet. "Come on, we need to get on the road. I saw signs of people not far from camp. Might be a farmer or trapper, but we can't risk any chance that it might be the king's men."

Jena nodded and followed him. When they got back to the camp, the fire had been doused, everything was packed, and Dustan was waiting holding the saddled horses. Arvon helped Jena onto the smaller horse. Then he mounted the larger and helped Dustan up behind him. Dustan held on tightly and smiled at Jena, obviously happy with the arrangement.

Jena smiled back. It was the first real smile she'd managed in days, and she realized that simply making a decision was lifting the dark cloud from her mind, and the physical action of traveling was only going to help more. Life wasn't stalled any more. It went on, and now that they were moving, her mind began to fill with all that could happen ahead. Even the worst thing she could imagine wasn't as bad as anything that had already happened. Suddenly she was filled with relief. The worst had happened, and she had lived through it.

Everything from now on should be easy in comparison.

15

When they pulled into port, Tarius was once again running a high fever and seemed to have taken a turn for the worse. Changing into the Katabull had made the effects of the wound worse. The crew helped Harris make a litter to pull behind Tarius's horse, because it was pretty obvious that she couldn't ride. The quicker he could get her to the Springs of Montero, the better. Thank the gods it was only a day's ride away.

Harris looked back at Elise standing on the bow of the ship. He hated to leave her, but she was a sailor, and he had to get Tarius some help or she was going to die. Still, he hoped he would be able to link up with her again some day. He waved to her and then turned to go.

Tarius's horse was pulling the litter, and Harris had it on a lead that was loosely wrapped around the pommel of his saddle, thus freeing his hands for battle. He arranged this automatically, and when he thought about it he grinned wryly at how much the timid little crippled boy had changed. He patted the parchment in his belt to be sure it was still there. The captain had drawn him a map through town and to the springs, and he was going to need it because the country he faced was like nothing in his experience.

Harris took a good look at the city before him; he saw no end to it, and yet there was nothing ugly or sterile about it. Kartik was everything that Tarius had said it would be. The buildings, streets and walls of the city were made of bricks and rocks instead of wood like most Jethrik villages. The people wore little clothing, but what they wore was bright and cheerful. It looked like everyone carried a weapon of some kind, and they all seemed to be smiling. People stared at him openly, they weren't even trying to hide their interest. He knew exactly why, and it had nothing to do with his crippled foot. There simply wasn't another blond-headed, fair-skinned person in sight.

As he rode, Harris saw that there were beautiful plants and flowers everywhere, and the air was heavy with the scent of them. Harris decided at once that he much preferred this perfume to the stench of horse shit, human waste, and garbage that hung over most Jethrik cities. The streets were amazingly clean, as were the shops he passed. He saw one shopkeeper cleaning up a pile of horseshit in front of his store. So, this must be how they kept the streets clean. No doubt some ordinance forcing shop keepers and house owners to clean the streets in front of their dwellings.

Suddenly there was a tug on his pants leg. Startled, he reined his horse in with one hand, drew his sword with the other and stopped. When he looked down, he saw Elise looking up at him, out of breath.

She had a bag on her shoulder.

"I want to go with you," she said eagerly.

"Elise... We don't even have any money... We couldn't even pay all our passage fare, so when we do make money it won't be ours. We have no food or supplies, and Tarius is very sick," Harris said.

"Do all your people talk so much? I paid the rest of your fare with my earnings from this shipment. I bought enough food for a few days, and I want to go with you. There is much I can learn from Tarius, and I think I love you."

"But... I want you to go, too, but I can't promise you anything. It's crazy..."

"Harris!" It was Tarius who spoke, and her voice was so weak he had to lean over precariously to hear her. "We aren't Jethrik women; we don't expect men to take care of us. She wants to be your partner, not your possession. Shut up and help her onto your horse. I'm not getting any better down here eating dust and horse shit."

Harris looked at Elise and smiled. "Are you sure?"

For answer she held up her hand. He took it, and she practically jumped on the horse behind him.

Arvon counted the money that lay on the inn table between them for the fourth time. "The only way we can manage our passage is if we sell the horses. That way we'll have that money to add to this, and we won't have to pay for the horses' passage, which is more than our own." He looked at Dustan when he said it. Arvon wasn't really attached to the horse he was riding. Since his own horse had been killed in the war by an arrow, he hadn't bothered to get attached to this one. Dustan, however, was very attached to his.

"Can we afford to keep Jackson?" Dustan asked. "If we stretch it, can we?"

"I'm sorry, Dustan. I've counted and recounted, and even if we get the lowest fares imaginable, we won't have enough. We have to sell both horses. I'm very sorry," Arvon said taking his hand.

Dustan nodded, resolved. There was a tear in his eye when he said, "Can we at least try to sell him to someone who will appreciate him?"

Arvon nodded.

"I'm so sorry, Dustan," Jena said putting a hand on his shoulder. "This is all my fault."

Dustan looked at her. "Jena, you lost your mate and your child, and you have lived. It's just a horse. I will try to find a good buyer for both horses."

Arvon nodded. He knew Dustan needed to do this on his own.

Dustan got up and started to question people around the inn. Soon he started talking to an older man at the end of the bar. They talked for a good long time, then they got up and started out of the inn. He nodded his head at Arvon and Jena as he walked outside with the man. Half an hour passed, and Arvon was about to go check on him when Dustan walked in carrying the saddles and tack. He set it by the door and headed towards them. He'd obviously been crying, but he forced a smile and sat down at the table. He dropped a bag of coins in front of Arvon.

"It took some talking, but he finally gave me what I asked for. Seventy-five silvers," Dustan said.

"Very good." Arvon leaned across the table and kissed Dustan on the cheek. Seventy-five silvers was a damn good price for two war-trained horses; there hadn't been any haggling. Dustan had spent the time in some alley crying about his horse so that he could present a brave face. Arvon knew this, and loved him all the more for it.

They got up and started to leave when two big, dirty, toothless men moved to block the exit. "Look at these three, Gordo," the bigger, dirtier one said. "They look like Jethriks, but they act like Kartiks. Men kissing men in public, a woman with a sword."

"We don't want any trouble," Arvon said.

"Well, that will cost them now, won't it, Gordo?"

"Yup, yup, shur will." The other one was obviously a *total* idiot.

Before Arvon had a chance to try to reason with them, Jena had pulled her sword.

"You want trouble?" Jena asked in a very quiet, very ugly tone. "We'll give you trouble, but you'll get none of our money."

Arvon slapped his palm to his forehead and drew his sword. Dustan drew his steel as well. The two men that barred their way drew there swords, and the other customers moved to a safe distance and turned to watch. It was pretty obvious that no one was going to try and stop them.

"Like I said," Arvon said coolly. "We don't want any trouble."

"Then hand over the money," the big greasy one demanded.

Arvon kept hoping that management would step in to deal with this injustice, but of course this was a seaport town, where Kartiks, barbarians, and every other people except Amalites were allowed to trade. The law meant nothing here.

"No more crap!" Jena screamed. She lunged forward, throwing a slicing cut that ripped through the man's throat. She swept sideways and blocked the blow the other man threw at her while Dustan ran him through from the side. Five other men ran up from behind them. Arvon, not yet engaged, turned quickly and kicked out at one, taking out his knee as he sliced through another's arm.

Jena only saw blood, and realized that blood was all she wanted to see. At that moment, each attacker was Tragon. She realized as she sliced through a man's stomach and watched as his entrails fell to the floor that she would never be done killing Tragon.

Arvon laid his blade into the head of one man, slicing all the way into the man's brain, and the two men left uninjured stood back and dropped their swords.

The bartender started to cheer.

"Blood thirsty bastard," Dustan said as he wiped his blade between his fingers to clear it.

"Which one?" Arvon asked, looking meaningfully at Jena.

Arvon moved forward and put a careful hand on Jena's shoulder. "Jena, put your blade away."

"No more crap, Arvon," she whispered in a hiss, surveying the men in front of her blade. "No more crap from anyone."

Arvon looked at the men and smiled. "You heard the woman. No more crap."

The men nodded.

"Jena, honey... Put your blade away," Arvon said again.

Jena shook her head, and she didn't take her eyes off the men in the bar.

Arvon grabbed her by her scabbard and started dragging her towards the door. Dustan picked up the saddles and the tack and went out first. Arvon continued dragging Jena out. At the door, she spun around to make sure no one was behind her.

"OK, killer can you put your sword up now?" Arvon asked.

Jena wiped her fingers down her blade and flipped her fingers in the air, slinging blood all over her and Arvon.

"Damn it, Jena," Arvon said, wiping the blood out of his eye. Then he took one of the saddles and one of the packs from Dustan. "What the hell were you thinking back there?"

Jena thought about that only a moment. "That I've had enough crap to last me a lifetime. That I don't want any more crap. They were giving us crap."

"You can't just kill everybody who gives you crap!" Dustan said in disbelief.

"Why not?" Jena asked.

"Because dead bodies tend to get people to asking questions," Arvon answered. "Come on, we'd better get to the ship, and hope that no local magistrate stops us before we can board."

They started walking fast. He cringed when he realized how blood-covered they were. They'd be damned lucky to get to the ship without getting stopped, and luckier still if any ship would take them the way they looked. Three desperate, blood-covered people carrying the bare necessities with packs, saddles, and no horses. They looked like what they were—fugitives on the run.

At the pier they went down to the water and washed the blood from themselves. They couldn't find a translator who would work for anything near what they could afford, and none of them knew the first word of Kartik. The only thing that was clear from talking to the different captains was that none of them wanted to take them as passengers for the amount of money they had.

It was the last ship at the pier. Old and run down, it looked like it was as likely to sink as it was to sail. However, the captain was Jethrik.

"Hail, brothers!" he called from the helm. They went up to meet him eagerly, thinking they had finally found someone who would sell them passage.

"Am I ever glad to see you!" Arvon said.

"How can I help you?" the captain asked, giving Jena the once over and obviously liking what he saw.

"We need to book passage to Kartik," Arvon said. "We have..."

"Don't even bother. I'm sorry brother, but we're over-loaded right now, and there is no amount of money that would be worth leaving anything behind."

"But you're our last hope. We have a hundred silvers..." Arvon started.

"And one crate will bring me two hundred. Sorry, mate."

The three turned to go. "Only way I'd give anyone passage right now is if they were the Katabull."

Arvon smiled and turned slowly around, changing as he did so. "I am the Katabull."

The captain clapped his hands together happily. "Crew!" he hollered down the deck. "We've got the Katabull! Unload a crate!"

The cheer that answered his shout was heartening.

It took them one and a half days to get to Montero. Harris was all the more glad to have Elise along, because Tarius got worse. Elise seemed to know how to help Tarius while he had no idea what to do.

When they got to Montero there were no open springs. Spas had been built on top of every one of them, and they charged huge fees to enter. More money than Harris had, and they didn't extend credit.

"Tarius... I'm going to have to sell the horses."

"No," Tarius said, coughing up blood.

"Don't be such a hard head... Horses will do us no good if you're dead."

"The springs are free," Tarius said.

"Not anymore," Elise said.

"Don't sell my horse," Tarius said.

"Tarius... Don't be ridiculous!" Harris screamed, totally frustrated and out of patience.

"Excuse me," a woman said approaching them. She was the owner of one of the spas that had turned them away earlier, so Harris was short with her.

"What do you want?" Harris asked. "To rob us? To trade our horses for a bath? What?"

The woman ignored him. "Did you say Tarius?"

"Yes."

"Is that then Tarius the Black? The Kartik Bastard? The scourge of the Amalites?" the woman asked as she walked closer to the litter.

Harris moved to block her way.

"Well, is it?" she asked, clearly impatient.

"What's it to you?" Harris asked.

"I owe Tarius the Black. See, once she didn't kill me," the woman said.

Tarius's head fell limply into the bubbling pool in front of her.

"Oh, no you don't, my friend." Jazel grabbed Tarius by the hair at the back of her head and dragged her face out of the water. The wound in Tarius side bubbled freely in the water. Jazel looked up at Harris who stood watching over the whole procedure with Elise by his side. "So, I'm guessing they found out what she was."

Harris nodded.

"And her woman?" Jazel asked.

"In Jethrik," Harris said simply.

"Guess she couldn't handle it, either."

"No," Harris said simply.

Helen ran in then carrying a large stack of towels. "How is she?" Helen asked, not even bothering to pretend like she wasn't checking out Tarius's nude body in the water.

"Damn near dead," Jazel asked. "Passed out and went limp as a rag as soon as I put her into the water."

"I could get in and hold her up. That always helps," Helen said.

"Well, go ahead," Jazel said with a shrug.

Helen quickly stripped and got into the water, splashing Harris and Elise. She went over to Tarius and held her up. Jazel let go of Tarius's head as Helen leaned Tarius back against her chest and held her head on her shoulder.

Jazel stood up rubbing her hands on a towel. "Damnedest thing, fate. About a year and a half ago this woman," she said, pointing at Tarius. "...decides against her better judgment to let me live. See, I put a silence spell on the Amalites so they could attack your troops. I didn't want to at all. I hate the Amalites as much as you do, but they had Helen. Anyway, it's a long story, the gist of which is that Tarius—in full animal form—tracks me down, kills all the Amalites, and is about to kill me when Helen begs for my life and Tarius lets me live. But only after making me promise to move to Kartik. So we come here, buy this spa, and now I hold Tarius's life in my hands."

"It's very neat," Helen said from her place in the hot spring.

"Helen has been fantasizing about Tarius ever since. Are you having fun, dear?" Jazel asked in a grating tone.

"Actually, yes I am. She seems to be coming around, but the wound is bad," Helen said.

"I mean, she's all right, I suppose," Jazel addressed Elise. "If you like the big, well-muscled, butch type. But you would think she crapped gold the way Helen goes on and on, and she only saw her that one time. Who wouldn't look good in Katabull form? I've tried every spell I can think of, and she still... just on and on and on. She makes up stories about her."

"That's not true, Jazel, " Helen said blushing.

"Oh, it is too... Well, there she is in all her splendor. Can't even hold her head up, and twenty pounds underweight. Tell me, do you think she looks any better than I do?" Jazel asked Elise.

"Well, no," Elise said quickly. Last thing she wanted to do was piss off a witch.

"Jazel," Helen giggled. "You're being ridiculous again. You know I love you."

"Yes, but you *lust* after her," Jazel said.

"Well, I can't help that, now can I?" Helen giggled out.

Tarius's eyes flew open, and she suddenly jerked in the water. "Jena!" she screamed.

Harris knelt by the side of the pool and caught Tarius's eyes. "Tarius... You're OK. You're in one of the Springs of Montero."

"The witch," Tarius said, remembering. She turned in the water, jerking away from Helen and looking for Jazel. When she found her, she moved over to the side of the pool where she was. "I had a dream... I dreamt that Jena was hurt. What does it mean?"

"What was the nature of the dream?" Jazel asked.

"We were together; we were making love..."

"Oh, this should be good," Helen said. Jazel glared at her.

"Everything was fine, but then she started screaming. She jumped out of bed. Her sword was in her hand, and there was blood on the blade. It wasn't her blood, but she was in pain. She cried out for me, but I couldn't reach her."

"That's very interesting," Jazel said.

"What does it mean?" Tarius asked.

Jazel shrugged. "Damned if I know. I'm a witch, not a dream interpreter."

Tarius made an angry sound and dunked her head under the water. When she came up she realized she was seeing clearly for the first time in days.

She looked at Harris and smiled. "I'm going to live," she said with conviction.

Harris smiled back. "I never doubted it for a minute."

The king woke screaming, and his favorite wife put her arms around him to comfort him.

Two guards ran in the door. The king looked at the one on the right. "Go and get Hellibolt at once," he ordered.

A few minutes later a bedraggled, half awake Hellibolt stumbled into the room. "What do you want now?" he asked.

"A little respect; I am your king," Persius said angrily as he got out of bed.

"I'm wearing clothes," Hellibolt said flippantly. "What else do you want? Now, what's the problem?"

"I dreamt it was here... the Katabull. I dreamt that Tarius was here in my bedchamber. That she killed me by cutting me into little pieces, leaving my head for last," Persius said. "What does it mean?"

"Why did you wake me for this, Sire? You know what it is as well as I do, as does anyone who was there that hateful day. It's the curse which Tarius the Black laid on you."

"Don't tell me of curses, old man! No intelligent person believes is such nonsense! Tell what it is. It's a spell, isn't it? Counter it, I command you!"

Hellibolt shook his head and continued quietly. "No, Sire, it is no spell, and there is no counterspell for what ails you. Did she not say that if you did not kill her quickly she would find a way to live? Have we not had word of a Kartik sailor who was overheard saying that Tarius made passage to Kartik? We have never found a body, so I for one believe that this is more than mere gossip. For one thing, when questioned the sailor knew that Tarius was a woman and Katabull, and was damned proud of both facts. So, she has indeed found a way to live. She said further that she would make you die a thousand times, and that you would have neither a decent night's rest nor any peace of mind."

Persius started to interrupt, but Hellibolt held up a silencing hand, drew himself up to an impressive stance and continued. "Sire, all of these things have come to pass. You forget who you are dealing with. This Kartik woman, this female Katabull, is the one who single-handedly brought you victory in the war. She did it because she is cunning, and because she knows people. She knows you, too, Persius. She knows you better than you know yourself. You acted in the heat of the moment. You allowed your anger and your injured pride to cloud your judgment and you therefore attempted to execute a friend simply because her gender had made you look foolish. Which, by the way, was never her intent.

"The Katabull's curse haunts you with your deeds, and your guilt at what you have done drives you from your bed and robs you of rest and peace. You know you deserve to die at her hands. You know she is capable of doing it. And you know that she has managed to live in spite of you. The power behind that curse was that she knew you wouldn't be able to live with what you had done. She knew you would punish yourself a hundred times better than she ever could.

"Persius... the Katabull will never come after your physical person. Don't you understand? Killing you would be too easy. This..." he gestured toward the king, drawing attention to his haggard, sleepless condition. "*This* is what she wants. For you to have to live with her blood on your hands. To live in fear of her vengeance till the day you die. She has won, Persius. She has won, and she isn't even here."

The voyage was horrible. Jena managed to make it with the help of some Kartik tonic, but poor Dustan seemed to throw up all through the entire four-day passage.

The captain helped them learn a little Kartik, but the price of the lessons was that he kept chasing Jena around like a bull in rut. He shipped out with a full Kartik crew, and he kept a home in the Kartik. This was as close as he had been to any Jethrik woman in years, and certainly he hadn't seen any as beautiful as Jena. At least he didn't press the issue. Every one of the hundred times she said no he backed down immediately, shrugged and said, "You can't blame a man for trying."

Arvon walked up beside her. Way in the distance they could see land.

"Soon," Jena said to him.

"Not soon enough for poor Dustan," Arvon said.

"The captain's looking at me again, isn't he?" Jena asked.

Arvon nodded.

"I swear, I can feel his eyes on me."

"He's a nice fellow," Arvon said. "Not a brutish sort of man at all. He really seems to like you. You do well at sea, he makes a decent living, he owns his own ship, and he's very handsome."

"What are you getting at?" Jena asked suspiciously.

"Only that any normal woman would be happy to have him as a suitor."

"I prefer the dark Kartik men like that one over there," Jena said pointing.

Arvon laughed heartily.

"What's so damn funny?"

"Jena... That's a woman," Arvon said.

Jena looked closely. "Oh! So it is." She laughed at herself then. "They're Kartik. There just really isn't all that much difference," she said with a shrug.

"So you still haven't decided?" Arvon said.

"It's not really a decision, is it, Arvon? I mean, I know what I want. I want Tarius. But I don't know if I can live with the kind of crap you and Dustan live with."

"Oh that's right. Your new motto. No more crap!" Arvon said with a smile.

"That's right. Anyway, it's all immaterial if Tarius is dead... I must be getting better; I can say it now—even think it without crying."

16

Two weeks had passed, and Tarius was starting to feel like her old self. Helen and Jazel had treated her well, given her the right herbs and powders and diet, and the baths had soaked all the poison out of her system.

"Just do it!" Jazel pleaded.

Tarius laughed, splashing Jazel with water. "No, I will not. It's insane."

"Come on! My life's a living hell, and it's only going to get worse now that she's actually spent time with you. Just do her, and do a really horrible job. Then she won't lust after you anymore," Jazel pleaded.

"You're sick, Jazel," Tarius said. "It's just a game she plays with you to make you jealous. She doesn't want anyone but you."

"See now, big, worldly, sword-wielding woman, that is where you would be wrong. She loves me, and I love her, but that doesn't mean that we don't occasionally lust after other people. I would just as soon she bed you and get it over with, but if you're better than me, then it will only make things worse. So all I'm asking is that you do a really rotten job."

"Sorry," Tarius said with a shrug.

"What the hell am I supposed to do?" Jazel asked.

"Work harder at it, I guess." Tarius stepped out of the pool and started to dry herself.

"Can't get her out of your mind, can you?" Jazel asked carefully.

Tarius shook her head sadly.

"And I know just the thing to take your mind off of it..."

Tarius gave her a look that burned into her.

"Or not."

Tarius put a robe on and walked out of the building the hot spring was in and into the courtyard that was between the bath and the main house. Jazel and Helen's spa was no more than a fenced in area with a shack built over the top of the hot spring and a house that had grown as they needed the rooms. They had five people staying at the spa, which meant all their rooms were full. Tarius, Harris and Elise had been sleeping on pallets on the floor in the dining room.

Some people came in just to bathe. Some people also came in for potions, herbs, powders, spells or readings.

The courtyard was usually filled with people going to or coming out of the baths, but it was early morning, and the courtyard was empty. It was filled with the heady scents of flowers, reminding Tarius of her childhood. She had spent days out here in the sun, relaxing, healing, and sewing a new cloth over the Jethrik kingdom colors on her gambeson.

She covered the blue and white with Kartik colors of the brightest reds, greens, blues and yellows she could find. Her hair had grown almost to her collar, and she would let it go. She would be a woman again. She would be Katabull again. She would be Kartik again. She would embrace all that she was, immerse herself in her purpose, and forget about Jena.

She sat on one of the benches and just took it all in.

"You're leaving, aren't you?" Jazel asked.

"Yes. You heard what that man said at lunch yesterday. The queen is paying for Amalite scalps. For me, getting paid for killing Amalites is like getting paid to eat my dinner. It's something I want to do any way," Tarius said. "I'm well and my body is healed. It's time for me to get back to work."

"I understand," Jazel said.

"When next I come here, I will pay for your services," Tarius said.

"Good, because I consider us even now. Of course, if you could see fit to do my mate... badly, I would let you stay again for free."

"I'll pay, thank you," Tarius said with a laugh. She stood up. "Time to ride."

"Good luck... with everything, Tarius."

Tarius, Harris, and Elise started for the coast. Since they had lost the war with the Jethriks the Amalites had once again focused their attention on the Kartik. They had been raiding Kartik ships at sea and then using the ships to sneak into the country. They were trying to build up strongholds along the seacoast. Tarius hoped to stop them there before they got a chance to get inland. Before their numbers could grow.

The Amalite presence in the Kartik now fueled Tarius's hatred for the Jethrikian king. It was his fault that their were still Amalites in the world.

When they camped at night, Harris and Tarius took turns training Elise with sword, spear and staff. Tarius was happy for Harris, he seemed to have found his perfect match in Elise. However it left her odd man out, and she found herself getting more and more attached to her horse.

It was warm, and there was no threat of rain, so they slept in the open. Harris and Elise were having sex, which was what they usually did as soon as they were sure she was asleep. As if their noisy love-making wouldn't have awakened the dead.

As the sound of their ecstatic groans filled the night, she felt more alone than ever. She looked up at the sky through the trees and smiled at the stars. It was good to see her own night sky again. Good to be back in Kartik with all the familiar sights and sounds. She caught a scent on the wind—one that did not belong. She got up and carefully snuck out of camp, although she doubted Harris and Elise would notice if a horse went galloping past them at that moment.

She called on the night as she walked. Her senses became keener, and the scent became stronger. She ran through the brush making hardly a sound. Now she smelled smoke, too, and in a few minutes she saw them through the trees. She stopped abruptly and looked down on the camp.

Amalites. From the size of their encampment, there must have been at least twenty of them. They appeared to be armed to the teeth, and they had at least ten horses.

They slept in six tents with two guards. From the looks of the camp and the manner of those she observed, these men were accomplished at war, but they were no match for her and Harris. Not with the element of surprise on their side.

She went hunting, and then she went back to camp.

They had a hell of a time breaking the language barrier. They just didn't know nearly enough Kartik. They wound up with a job waiting tables and washing dishes in a pub for room and board. They had finished with the dinner rush and had just sat down for a meal.

"Well, how did you do?" Arvon asked Jena as she sat across from him and Dustan.

"I made twenty coppers in tips," she said. "I only messed up five orders, so I think my Kartik's getting better."

"I just made fifteen coppers," Dustan said, "and I only messed up two orders, so that hardly seems fair."

"Well, I only got a whole *two* coppers in tips, and I didn't mess up *any* orders, so I think this stinks," Arvon said making a face.

"At this rate we'll be here the rest of our lives," Dustan said pulling a face. "We'll never make enough to buy horses, and I'm getting tired of the three of us living in the same tiny little room."

"I don't know what you're bitching about. You have the bed. I'm sleeping on a bedroll on the floor," Jena said.

"Where you listen to us," Dustan said.

"I'd have to be deaf not to hear you!" Jena protested.

"You could pretend not to," Dustan said hotly. "At the very least you could contain your urge to laugh."

Jena laughed. "All right, I'll try."

"Any word about Tarius?" Arvon asked.

"I still don't even know if I'm asking the right questions," Dustan said, "and I can only understand about half of what they say."

"Same here," Jena said.

Fact was, Arvon was picking Kartik up quicker than either of the others. "Everyone I ask says they have neither heard of nor seen a Katabull fitting Tarius's description. Nor has anyone seen Harris, and Harris would be more likely to stick out in their minds. I think the three of us are the only Jethriks I've seen since we've been here. But catch this, there are about fifty ports where boats dock. She and Harris could be anywhere."

"Or nowhere," Jena said with a sigh.

"When we get a little better with the language, we'll be able to understand more, and when we get a little more money, we'll buy horses and go looking for her," Arvon said. "Shouldn't be to hard to find a Katabull woman in Jethrik colors and a tall, thick, blond-headed Jethrik lad."

"Unless they don't want to be found," Jena said. "We're talking Tarius. She doesn't have to come into a town unless she wants to."

"But what's to keep her in the field? She'll have to find work teaching at an academy or in the king's army..."

A man sitting at the next table laughed. When they looked at him he stopped. "Sorry. Couldn't help over-hearing you. I'm a sea-faring man myself. Work the shipping lines, own my own ship. Comes in handy if you can speak the language where you trade. First thing you need to know..." He moved over to their table. "We don't have a king right now; we have a queen. Queen Hestia. Second. The queen is paying five silvers apiece for Amalite scalps, so if your friend's a fighter, she could be anywhere."

"Have you heard of anyone by the name of Tarius the Black?" Arvon asked.

"Aye. What sailing man hasn't? One of our people who saved your people from the hand of the Amalites and was shot through with an arrow by your own king for her troubles," he said matter-of-factly.

"If they know that, then Tarius must be alive!" Jena said excitedly.

Arvon looked at her, not following Jena's logic. "It was a *secret*, Arvon. No one was supposed to know that Tarius was a woman or that the king had her shot. She's the only one who could have told that story."

"She or Harris," Arvon reminded her gently.

"But he didn't tell. Was the Katabull what told the story," the sailor said. "A friend of mine gave safe passage to your friends. She was in a bad way. Katabull don't do well when they are pierced with wood. They headed for the Springs of Montero."

"Thank you! Thank you so much!" Jena ran over and kissed him. He blushed and harrumphed in discomfort.

She looked at Arvon. "Come on! Let's go!"

"How far away is it?" Arvon asked.

"Five day's ride inland to the west," he said.

"Then let's go," Jena said.

"On what?" Arvon asked. "A five day's ride is a twenty day hike. We don't have enough money to buy even one horse."

"Sorry I can't help you more," the sailor got up. "If you needed a lift out to sea..."

"Thank you," they all said to him at once.

He nodded, turned and walked away.

"We're so close," Jena said resting her head in her hands.

"At least we know she's alive, Jena," Arvon said. "If only we could get even one horse. I could ride over to see if Tarius is there."

"We don't even have enough to get a decent meal away from the pub," Dustan said with a sigh.

There was a commotion at the bar, and the owner called out for Arvon. Arvon got up and ran over.

"Arvon, throw this man from the pub."

Arvon grabbed the man by the collar and belt, hauled him to the front door and threw him out.

"And don't come back, you bum!" the owner screamed over Arvon's shoulder. "I wouldn't give you credit if you were the Katabull!" He walked over to the bar and started wiping glasses again and Arvon followed him.

"Excuse me for my ignorance, Henry. But what did you mean, if he were the Katabull.?" Arvon asked.

"The Katabull bring good luck. They are notorious for generosity towards those that help them, so if you give one credit you will be rewarded ten fold," he said.

Arvon smiled. That was the reason behind Tarius's strong ethics. Not Kartik, but Katabull ethics. Ethics he hadn't learned because he hadn't been raised Katabull. However, he *was* Katabull, and he would give back better than he got if that was what was expected of him.

Arvon brought on the change and looked across the bar at Henry. "I need to borrow a horse, and I need a few days off."

The owner smiled. "I've got a stallion out back. Rides like the wind. Take as many days as you need."

The dawn was just starting to break, and below them the camp was silent. Tarius called on the night then she ran into the camp. She slit the throat of one guard, and he never even knew she was there. Then she sneaked across camp to the other guard. He almost had time to yell before she separated his head from his body.

Next she slipped into the biggest of the tents, and had killed five men before they even woke up. Two more never made it to their feet.

Elise and Harris came riding into the camp, and the men ran out of their tents, armor-less and unprepared for the ferocity of the force that faced them. Twenty-three men were dead before Tarius was even winded. They took the scalps and any money, armor, weapons and gear that was worthy. Then they stacked the bodies on one of the fires, stacked the tattered tents and broken poles and some deadfall on the bodies, dowsed the pile with coal oil and set it ablaze. It wouldn't reduce the bodies to ash, but it would keep the flies down until the animals could pick the bones clean.

They loaded everything else on the Amalite horses and started for the nearest town where they turned in the scalps for money and sold everything that they didn't need. Now Elise had good armor and a horse, plus they had a packhorse, good gear and supplies, so they started back into the field to look for their next target. They were already rich by Kartik standards.

Arvon hated to even walk into the pub, but he finally walked in with his head hung low.

Jena hit him first, even before Dustan. "Well...well?"

"Tarius is well healed. But she left Montero long ago to hunt Amalite raiders along the coast, and no one seemed to know in which direction she went."

Arvon hugged Dustan tightly and reveled in the fact that when they kissed after being parted for ten days, not one person had even a single snide remark for them. Arvon was tired, and he pulled Dustan along with him to a seat.

"I've taken care of your horse already!" Arvon hollered at Henry who just nodded. "Thanks a lot."

"I'm sorry you didn't find your friend," Henry said.

"Thanks," Arvon said.

Jena sat down across from Arvon. "But you said she is well?" Jena asked. She couldn't hide either her relief or her disappointment.

"Well enough to ride out after Amalites. Get this—Harris has a girl friend! A Kartik swordswoman who's traveling with them now. They might be headed this way, or they could be headed the other. Listen, it seems like I can get just about anything on credit just because I am the Katabull. I could get horses for Dustan and I, and we could head out—go hunting Amalites. We may just run into Tarius and Harris, and we can probably make enough money to pay back our debts here..."

"I want to go, too, Arvon. I can fight. Better than I can wait tables!"

Yes, just what I need! I should take Tarius The Black's woman out and get her killed or injured. "Jena... we may run in circles all around her. If one of us stays put here... Well, the odds are very good that she'll eventually come through here. Especially since everywhere I went I told people that if they saw her to send her here to this pub. Someone has to stay here in case she shows up. And, frankly, for very selfish reasons, I would prefer to have Dustan with me."

Jena nodded, resigned.

So she continued to work at the pub while Arvon and Dustan ran off to fight the Amalites. They were gone a month the first time, and when they returned they had not seen Tarius. However they heard tales of how she was single-handedly wiping the Amalites from their shores. They hadn't done too badly, either. They came back with three horses, enough money to pay off all their debts, and to leave her with quite a chunk of change before they took off again.

They told her about their adventures in detail. They were careful not to pick on groups of more than ten Amalites, and they used the guerrilla tactics they had learned from Tarius.

Jena didn't tell them how restless or lonely she was. She had learned Kartik well by now, and heard the same stories that they had heard about Tarius. With each person she talked to she sent on the word that if they should see Tarius to tell her that Jena was waiting in Pasco. She knew she had to stay here, but she hated it. There was nothing to do but work and think. She talked the boys into staying a couple of days and was glad of the company. When they left, she had a horse of her own, and he gave her some company as well as a way to get out of town a little bit and explore the countryside.

Kartik was beautiful. Every bit as breathtaking as Tarius had said it would be. Jena loved the bright costumes, and the wrap-around dresses that barely covered enough for modesty. Men usually wore brightly colored loincloths and nothing else but a sword and a smile. Yet another lie Tarius had told. It was far too hot here to bother with modesty. If you were going to be comfortable, you were going to have to wear as little as possible.

When Arvon and Dustan left, she took some of the money they gave her and bought some new clothes. She indulged in a couple of the colorful wrap-around dresses, although she went with a more modest cut than the local girls wore. She bought a pair of black pants and a couple of bright, multicolored shirts to go with them. She also bought a dagger, as it was easier to handle than the sword when she was waiting tables. Everyone everywhere was armed. No one walked anywhere without steel in sight, and amazingly no one really bothered anyone. Oh, she'd had more than one man try to manhandle her, but as soon as she let them know she'd just as soon kill them as look at them, they backed off. That was another weird thing about Kartik. Here in Kartik, if you so much as threatened a person, they had the right to kill you and there would be no questions asked. Even so, she hadn't seen a single altercation that ended with anyone having more than a black eye or a fat lip.

Best of all, everyone was treated as an equal here. No one said anything derogatory to her because she was from out-country. In fact, the phrase "out-country" didn't appear to be part of their language. Same-sex couples walked down the street, openly holding hands or kissing. The Katabull were revered, and women were considered every bit as capable as men.

Yes, Jena liked Kartik; she liked it a lot. However after five months in the pub with still no sight of Tarius, and the boys only making it home about once a month, she was bored to tears.

Harris and Elise's more or less constant love fest was wearing on Tarius's nerves. It was hard to pretend she didn't see them necking or hear their insipid, love-filled whispering. It was annoying in the extreme, mostly because it reminded her of her own loss. So she had asked them to go on into town without her saying she wanted some time on her own to bond with the jungle. It was an out and out lie. She wanted to eat real food and sleep in a real bed. She watched them ride away telling them she'd meet them in town in a couple of days. As soon as she was sure they were gone she'd packed camp, jumped on her horse, and headed in the other direction for the nearest town. She didn't feel bad about her lie. Though they'd never say it, they were probably just as glad to be on their own for a change.

She stopped on the outskirts of the small seaport town and took a long refreshing bath in a creek. Then she put on clean clothes, saddled up and headed on into town. She could feel the energy of the town before she entered it. People were running every which way and the sounds of the street were like music to her ears. She needed some diversion besides killing men. There was life here, she hoped to take vicarious pleasure from watching other people who actually enjoyed their lives, as long as it didn't include Harris and Elise making baby talk with each other. The mere thought sent a chill up her spine.

A man and a woman were chasing each other around the posts of a porch awning laughing as they grabbed at each other.

Was I ever that silly? Tarius thought as she watched the couple. *It seems like a lifetime since I held her in my arms, yet the pain in my heart is as new as if it were only yesterday. I should try to make a new life for myself. Harris keeps telling me that I should try to find someone new, someone who will love me for who I am. I know he's right, but I don't think I will ever be over Jena, and how fair is it to make someone else sleep with my memories of her?*

Tarius tried to chase the thoughts from her mind. She was here to indulge herself, eat too much, and sleep too late, and maybe if the mood struck her she would have a woman, too, someone who wouldn't mind that it was just for a night.

She found a pub that looked friendly and smelled good. Then she dismounted and tied her horse to the rail. As she started inside she became all too aware that people were watching her, and heard her name whispered amongst them. She had become a creature of legend among her people. This should have warmed her, as a child it was what she had dreamed of, now it meant less than nothing to her because age and experience had changed her desires.

If only she had killed Tragon any of the dozens of times she had wanted to. If she had let him die, let Persius die. Her whole life would have been different. Maybe she'd be here with Jena now. *And maybe she'd still hate me. I can't build a future trying to rethink the past.*

She walked through the doors of the pub just in time to see a drunken man accost a Jethrikian woman, and she reacted without thought.

It was the end of a busy day, Jena was tired and hot, and not in the mood to put up with any crap. A drunk grabbed her arm and tried to pull her into his lap.

"Let me go," Jena ordered.

"Ah, come on, be nice to Fred. You're so pretty," he slurred out.

"I said, let me go," she said again.

"I'll let you go... To my room," he laughed drunkenly.

"Let the woman go, or I'll split you!" a voice boomed behind Jena.

Jena had been holding a mug in her right hand, getting ready to slam it into this man's head. She dropped the mug and it hit the floor, shattering into a hundred different pieces.

The man let go of her, and she turned to face her savior.

Tarius stood with her sword held out in front of her in her right hand, her head tilted back and to one side. It was a stance that Jena instantly recognized, but it was a Tarius that Jena had never seen. Her long black hair was braided on either side of her face. She wore a brightly colored gambeson with metal pauldrons tied on the shoulders. The gambeson only came to her waist, and it didn't quite lace closed across her chest. The only other thing she wore besides boots was a black leather loincloth. Tarius was definitely a woman, and surprisingly, that didn't bother Jena at all.

The whole bar was suddenly silent followed by murmurs of, "Tarius the Black."

If possible, Tarius looked even more stunned than Jena was. The proof being that she almost dropped her sword. Tarius caught it quickly and then sheathed it almost in one movement.

"Jena..." Tarius rubbed her eyes as if not trusting them. She looked again, but still seemed unsure. "Jena?"

For answer, Jena ran to Tarius and threw herself into Tarius's arms. Tarius picked Jena up and swung her around. Then, as if suddenly remembering how they had parted, she let Jena go and pushed her away from her.

"Jena... What the hell are you doing here?" Tarius asked.

"It's a long story," Jena said. She wouldn't let go of Tarius; she just hung on to any part of her she could reach. There was no part of her that was willing to let go. "I have been looking for you. I had begun to believe that I'd never see you again. I have missed you so much."

"After everything I did?" Tarius shook her head trying to comprehend.

"Maybe *because* of everything you did," Jena said softly. She got on tiptoes and kissed Tarius's lips gently, and Tarius—no doubt still in shock—didn't respond.

"How did you get here?" Tarius asked, still afraid to trust her eyes and ears.

"Arvon and Dustan brought me."

Jena looked over at Henry appealingly. He just smiled and nodded. Jena took Tarius's hand and started pulling her towards the stairs. Tarius stopped when she reached the man who had accosted Jena, and she glared down at him. She put a finger in his face only an inch from his nose and said in a hiss. "If you ever touch *my* woman again, I'll kill you."

He gulped and nodded his head in understanding.

"Jena!" Tarius protested as she continued to follow. "Where are you taking me?"

"To my room," Jena said with a wicked smile that made Tarius blush.

The patrons in the bar cheered, and Tarius allowed herself to be led up to Jena's room, where Jena pulled her in, closed and locked the door.

Tarius looked around the room nervously.

"Jena, what about the baby?"

"I lost it," Jena said. "I don't want to talk about it right now." She undid the buckle on Tarius's scabbard, and sword and sheath fell unceremoniously to the floor with a *clunk!*

"Jena, I'm so sorry for everything," Tarius started.

Jena kissed her lips again gently, and this time Tarius kissed her back. "Oh, gods! You smell good," Jena said, breathing in deep of her scent.

"I stopped and took a bath... I feel like there's so much that I should say. So much I should at least try to explain."

"Yes. Well, all I want right now is for you to get naked." She started to undo the laces on Tarius's gambeson. She saw the beaded necklace she had given Tarius the day they married still hanging around Tarius's neck, and she smiled as she touched it. She pulled the chain with the coin from the top of her dress.

"I still wear mine, too. I never took it off. Even when I was so mad at you I could have killed you myself, I still couldn't bring myself to remove it." She intentionally ran her hand across Tarius's breasts, and felt Tarius shake.

"Are you sure, Jena?" Tarius asked, her voice thick with repressed passion.

Jena looked at Tarius. "Do I look like I'm just kidding, Tarius? Do I act like I'm unsure? Arvon and Dustan have been looking for you for months, and I have been waiting, and waiting here. I'm tired of waiting. I've had lots of time to decide what I want. I don't want a man—any man. Nor do I want any other woman. I only want you. I want you, and I want *all* of you. I want to be the one to make you cry out. I want to see you, to feel you. Be with you completely, in every way, and..."

Tarius grabbed Jena up, carried her to the bed, and put her down. She finished unlacing her gambeson and slung it aside, then she lay down next to Jena.

Jena smiled. "You're still not naked."

"Oh, gods, if I'm dreaming, don't let me wake up this time," Tarius mumbled. She took a deep breath. "I might change, you know."

"Into the Katabull?"

Tarius nodded. "It's happened to me before."

"I've seen you that way before, Tarius, and I've seen lots of them in the bar. They have one drink, and they're all teeth and hair and bulk. I can handle it. It doesn't scare me. You don't scare me." Jena started to undo the strings holding up the loincloth. Jena wasn't too surprised to find that Tarius knew the quickest and easiest way to get the wraparound dress off her.

When bare flesh met bare flesh for the first time, it was like lightning striking, and Jena knew she'd made the right decision.

Jena didn't know how long they made love, but they didn't stop till they were both exhausted. She lay with her back to Tarius, loving the feel of Tarius's bare flesh against hers. She was wrapped up in Tarius's arms, and she finally felt whole again.

Tarius kissed the top of her head. "I love you, Jena. I always have, and I always will."

"And I love you, Tarius. You. Not the person you were pretending to be. I loved you all along," Jena said. "I..." she laughed nervously, "well I thought I could do it—you know make love to you—because I just wanted to make you feel the way you make me feel, because I do love you so much. I never imagined that... well, that I'd *enjoy* it so much."

Tarius smiled and pulled Jena close. "Did I not tell you that making love to you was enough for me? That wasn't a lie, Jena. Not that I didn't long for your touch."

"Did I... Did I do all right?" Jena asked shyly.

Tarius laughed. "All right? Far more than just 'all right'." Tarius held Jena tighter. "You were amazing.. How did you know?"

"I know what I like when you do it to me," Jena answered.

She turned in Tarius's arms and ran a finger over the scar the arrow had left. It was a bad scar, a deep one. "He almost killed you, didn't he?"

"Almost." Tarius kissed Jena gently on the lips. "But worse than all of that was losing you. Knowing that I'd hurt you. Even as I struggled for life I wished I would die and even long after I was well I found myself wishing I had died. My life had no meaning, I could take no pleasure in it without you. I will spend the rest of my life trying to make it all up to you. Jena, I am so sorry..."

"Shush," Jena held a finger over Tarius's lips. "There is nothing to be sorry for. I love you more than ever, Tarius. Everything that happened is as much my fault as it is yours. I've had a lot of time to think and I realized that you must have tried to tell me a dozen times, and every single time I said something stupid that made it impossible for you to tell me."

"I was afraid, I don't know that there is ever an excuse for cowardice. Jena... What happened to the baby?" Tarius asked gently.

Jena told Tarius everything, and they cried and held each other until they were spent.

"I wish you didn't have to go through any of those horrible things, and you wouldn't have if it hadn't been for me," Tarius said.

"I don't want to dwell on the past, Tarius. You warned me about you and your secrets. Still I wouldn't leave you alone. I had to have you, and we both know why now. Yes, we went through hell, you and I. And none of the crap you went through would have happened to you if it hadn't been for me. So, we could blame ourselves and each other for an eternity, but the fact is that we loved each other, and it took all that for us to be able to be together now. I didn't know who I was, and the old Jena never would have accepted you as a lover if she had known. Let's leave the past in the past. I'll forgive you, and you forgive me. And no more lies."

"No more lies," Tarius promised. "There's nothing to lie about now."

"I am tired of walking," Dustan complained. His horse had stepped on a rock and come up lame, nothing that wouldn't heal in time, but he couldn't be ridden. Dustan had been walking the better part of the day. "Couldn't we make camp for the night?"

"It's midday," Arvon said. "We can make it home if we don't stop."

"What's one more night out?" Dustan said. His feet were killing him, and he just wanted to lie down.

Arvon stopped. "You ride for awhile, and I'll walk."

Dustan shook his head. As much as he was tired of walking, he didn't want Arvon to have to walk. Arvon's leg still bothered him, and long walks caused him great pain. "No. I'm fine. I'm sorry I was whining. I'm all right, really."

"I just..." Arvon stopped. "Tie your horse to mine, and we'll ride double. He'll be all right; it's only a few more miles." Kartik horses were not as large as Jethrik horses, and carrying two men was really too much, but it wouldn't hurt for a short way. Dustan tied his horse to Arvon's saddle and got on behind him.

"Why are you in such a hurry to get home? We haven't found Tarius and Harris, and I hate to have to face Jena empty-handed once again," Dustan said.

"I just have a feeling... I don't know how to explain it, except to say that I just feel like there's something happening with Jena," Arvon said.

"Something bad?" Dustan asked, suddenly worried.

"I don't know," Arvon said. "But something."

By the time they got to the pub they had worked themselves into such a lather that they didn't even care for their horses, they just tied them at the hitching post and ran in. Jena was nowhere in sight, and a new girl was working the tables. Panic welled up inside them. Terrified, Arvon grabbed Henry, making him spill a pitcher of beer.

"Damn it all, boy! What did you do that for?" Henry demanded, wiping beer off his apron with his hand.

"Where is Jena?" Arvon demanded.

"Oh that," Henry smiled. "She's gone off to Montero with Tarius the Black. They're waiting for you there."

Arvon and Dustan just stared at each other. It took a second to soak in, but then they both let out a whoop of joy that startled Henry into nearly spilling another pitcher. They embraced each other and danced around the bar for several minutes. They spent that night at the pub hardly sleeping at all and took off early the very next morning. They bought a new horse and led Dustan's along behind them as they rode.

They had rented three of the rooms at Jazel's, reserving one for when Arvon and Dustan got there. Tarius and Jena got up early and went to the spring before anyone else, so they had it to themselves. Jena had never seen anything like it. The hot spring had carved a perfect circle in the red rock. It bubbled up from the bottom and ran over the top on one side. The water had a greenish-blue tint to it, no doubt from the heavy mineral content, and it was almost, but not quite, too hot. It felt soft, like being wrapped in silk.

Tarius soaked in the water, enjoying having Jena rub her back and comb out her hair with her fingers.

"You know what?" Tarius asked.

"No, tell me," Jena said kissing the side of Tarius's throat.

"I think... No, I know. This is the first time that I have ever really truly relaxed. The first time in my life that I'm not wondering where I am going to be tomorrow or the next day. I'm not sitting around worrying about things way in the future. I'm not even thinking about what I'm going to do in the next few minutes. I'm just happy to be right where I am, here with you. For the very first time, everything is right," Tarius said.

"We will have a lifetime like this, Tarius," Jena said in a hoarse whisper. "You and me, here in Kartik. With no one to point fingers or click tongues."

Tarius turned in the water to face Jena, and they started kissing. Tarius pushed Jena gently against the edge of the pool and started running her hands over Jena's body. Soon they were consumed with each other.

"Ah... Now that's the way it should be."

Tarius pried herself away from Jena, looked up at the intruder and smiled. "Arvon!" She jumped out of the pool, seemingly oblivious to her nakedness, and embraced Arvon, getting him almost as wet as she was. "I was beginning to think that some Amalite had taken you out of the game."

Arvon held her tightly. He realized that tears were running down his face, and he didn't even try to check them. "I thought... I had begun to believe that I would never see you again."

"No such luck," Tarius said.

Jena snuck from the pool and grabbed a robe. She still wasn't used to the Kartik people's complete lack of modesty, and wasn't quite ready to run around unclothed in front of anyone who wasn't Tarius. Not even Arvon, who had delivered her poor, dead baby.

She walked over to Arvon, and when he finally released Tarius, Jena hugged him. "Biggest lie she ever told was about the Kartik's modesty. *She* certainly has none."

"Never did." Arvon hugged Jena tightly then released her, and Jena walked over and grabbed a robe for Tarius. She brought it over and helped Tarius into it. Then Jena wrapped her arms around Tarius, putting her hands into the pockets of Tarius's robe. Pockets were another great Kartik invention.

Jena leaned her head on Tarius's chest, and Tarius wrapped her arms around her.

Arvon looked at them together and smiled. "So I'm guessing, Jena, that you didn't have any trouble with Tarius's gender."

Jena moved her head just enough so that she could see him. "None at all."

"You should get in the spring. It will do your leg good," Tarius said.

"Of course you'll have to bathe first."

Arvon nodded. He'd wanted to try it when he'd been here before looking for Tarius, but he hadn't had the money. Besides, Jena and Dustan had been waiting back at Henry's pub.

"So, where's Dustan?" Tarius asked carefully. When people lived by the sword, if you didn't see them immediately where you thought they should be, you tended to think the worst.

"He was detained by Harris. I didn't realize how close they had become when they were riding with you. They're catching up. I like Harris's young woman, very nice. She hugged me like I was a long-lost relative."

"It's a Kartik thing, she did the same thing to me," Jena explained.

"So what now, Tarius?" Arvon asked. "When do we ride out?"

Tarius thought about it only a minute. "For now we stay in Montero, enjoy the spring, the atmosphere and each other. I don't know when we ride out again. I refuse to even think about it right now."

17

They were prosperous and successful in their slaying of Amalites, and so they soon collected a small army of Kartik and Katabull followers. They swept the seashore until the pickings were slim. No force could stand against them, and word of the might of Tarius's the Black's mercenary army spread throughout the kingdom. The word also spread by way of trade ships into the land of the Jethriks.

The king stood at the window looking out at the city below as the herald read off the latest reports.

"Tarius the Black has assembled a small army. The Kartiks call them the Marching Night. They have swept practically every Amalite from the kingdom of Kartik. They say no man can stand against Tarius the Black, and that no army can stand against the Marching Night. The Amalites are beginning to retreat from their attempts to infiltrate the Kartik and are starting to once again push through our borders. Two towns close to the border have already been taken in spite of their best efforts."

"Had you followed through with Tarius's plans to strengthen the borders, had you not halted the construction of the garrisons, the training of the peasants... You know, your stupid pride will be the death of us all," Hellibolt said in a whisper at Persius' back.

Persius turned, his face a mask of rage. "Shut your mouth!" he hissed at Hellibolt. "Your words tell me only what I have done wrong. They give me no way to fix it."

"Try to put it right now, Persius, before it's too late. Restart the work effort on the garrisons. Start training the peasants," Hellibolt begged. "It's not too late if you go to work now."

"Go!" Persius screamed at the herald, who left at a dead run. Persius looked at Hellibolt. "The whole kingdom knows now. After three years there is not a peon in even the most remote village that doesn't know that I put Tarius the Black, a woman, at the head of the Jethrik armies. Not one that doesn't know that I tried to kill her for her betrayal, and not one that doesn't know that she cheated death. What will they say? What will they think if I start up again with plans that they know she made?"

Hellibolt put a gentle hand on Persius' shoulder and met his eyes. "Perhaps they will say that Tarius the Black is the greatest warrior that our world has ever known. That she drove the Amalites from our land, and now she is driving them from the Kartik. Perhaps they will say that you care more for the welfare of your people than you do for your pride.

Do it, Persius. When you went to Tarius's bed in the night and exposed her without even giving her a chance to explain herself to the naïve woman that married her, that was wrong. When you threatened Jena, when you incarcerated Taruis, when you decided to execute her, when you decided she should die a slow and painful death, all of these things were wrong, and everything you have done since has been wrong. Can't you see that, Persius? The first sin led you to commit all the others. If you do not stop the madness now, it will consume you.

"If Tarius knows nothing else, she knows warfare. Did she not say that if you didn't follow the Amalites in and kill them all, that they would attack us again? Well, you didn't, and they are. Build the garrisons where she said to build them. Train and arm the people as she told you to train and arm them. Think like Tarius, and you just might save the country as Tarius did."

Persius looked into the old wizard's eyes. "You know, old man, that I once thought you nothing but a dead weight. A charlatan."

Hellibolt nodded his head.

"I couldn't understand why my father had so trusted in your counsel, and now I know why. You never tell me what I want to hear; you only tell me the truth as you see it. You are right. I will give the commands at once."

⁂

They were fifty fighters strong now, and roughly half of those Katabull. Just now they were resting between raids in the Valley of the Katabull. The Katabull had carved out a new homeland in the west on a fresh water lake less than four miles from the sea.

Tarius remembered the first time she had come here. She had been amazed at the numbers. She had thought her people almost dead, but they were thriving. Even making a comeback. The packs spread out in all directions around the lake. They even had a meeting lodge and a leader.

People had taken to calling Tarius and her mercenary army the Pack of the Marching Night. Tarius felt like they were, too. Although a very different pack, since roughly half of them were human. But whatever its composition, it was good to be part of a pack again.

Her new pack had built small round huts of small logs covered with clay mud and topped with thatched roofs that matched the other Katabull dwellings. Having done this, the Marching Night was firmly established as part of the Katabull nation.

They would rest here, enjoy the quiet life for a while, and then ride out again.

Today Tarius lay by one of the fire pits, her head in Jena's lap, just relaxing and taking in some sun.

"It's a beautiful day," Jena said conversationally.

"Aye... that it is," Tarius said.

"What are you thinking?" Jena asked.

"I'd rather not say," Tarius said with a laugh.

Jena slapped at her playfully. "Well, I'd rather you did."

"All right, but remember you asked," Tarius said. "I was just remembering your father's house. You know, the big house with the running water and the servants? I was wondering if you ever missed that. If you ever missed your father."

"I miss the person I thought my father was," Jena said in a far-away tone. "I think it's like you miss your parents. Like he's dead instead of across the sea. I don't miss anything else. I love our life, Tarius. Every day is a new adventure. I love fighting beside you, loving you. Sleeping out under the stars when the weather's clear. Or in our little hut when we're here. I love being part of this pack. Each one of these men and women who ride with us are like brothers and sisters to me. Each one hand picked not just because of their fighting skill, but because of their personalities, their ethics. I love the Katabull and the Kartik people—so accepting of everything except that which is unquestionably wrong. They are a people who abhor thievery, murder and injustice. I love all the flowers, and the way the people keep their streets and cities clean. There are no venomous snakes, and it's never cold enough to need more than a long-sleeved shirt. No, I don't miss the Jethrik at all."

"Good," Tarius said flatly and seemed to relax again. "I think, however, that we will bring running water to our camp. After all, we have the bamboo, and admittedly I do miss the running water. I wonder how they make those big pots..."

Suddenly a Katabull in full beast-mode ran into the middle of their pack. Tarius jumped up in a single motion. "Can I help you, brother?"

"Tarius..." He was out of breath. "It's the leader, he's been in an accident. We know that you have good medics."

Of course they had good medics. They needed them, they were mercenaries, and they were always getting hurt. Even Jena now had a sword scar across the upper part of her left arm.

"Elise, Edson, Jesop!" Tarius screamed. The screams echoed through the camp as everyone that heard the order shouted it out. These were trained fighting people, and in minutes the three had joined them. They ran to the place not far away where they had taken the leader, but Tarius knew when she saw him that there was nothing the medics could do. The man had been more or less gutted, and the strong smell of bowel meant something that shouldn't be cut had been.

"What the hell happened?" Tarius demanded. It looked like a sword wound to her. No accident. The Katabull who had come for her answered quickly as the medics tried desperately to save the injured leader.

"We don't know... he went riding this morning alone. He rode towards the ocean, and we assumed he fell from his horse onto something sharp," he answered.

"You're wrong. Any fool can see that this is a sword wound." Tarius's eyes burned with rage. "He must have run into an advance party." Tarius's mind raced back to the time when the Amalites had fallen upon her pack. The Amalites were always either running in fear from the Katabull or falling upon them like locusts. No one likes to live in fear, and the Amalites feared the Katabull, so they wanted them dead. When they got up enough courage and enough men, their "gods" ordered an attack and they went looking for the Katabull. When they found them in their homes where they would be more concerned with protecting their young than with warfare, they attacked.

"Jesop, see what you can do for Tarak." Jesop was a Katabull and understood Katabull anatomy better than the others. "Elise, Edson, Jena. Come with me. We'll assemble the Marching Night and try to find the advance party. You," Tarius shouted to the Katabull who had come after her. "Sound the alarm, and scream it through the camp. Get the children to a place of safety and prepare to do battle. The Amalites have once again decided to attack the Katabull. We must show them once and for all that to attack us is folly. Assemble our forces outside the village towards the ocean. That is the direction they will come from."

The man nodded quickly and ran off to sound the alarm. The others ran to gather their weapons and horses and to start the word through camp. Tarius called on the night and beat the others to the Pack of the Marching Night. She called out her orders, and in mere minutes all were armored, armed, and on horseback.

Arvon took the left flank, Harris the right, and Tarius the center. Tarius found and then followed the trail of Tarak's blood. It led them right to the Amalite advance party. They must have been terrified to face the wall of Katabull and Kartik that thundered down upon them, but they stood their ground.

"They will be hard to beat!" Tarius screamed out. "Their priests must have promised them victory." She thought about it only a second. Seconds were all they had. "Attack!"

They thundered down upon the less than twenty Amalites, totally annihilating them in mere minutes. Tarius spit on one of the bodies. "Tell this to your gods. When I am done, no Amalite will ever darken the shores of the Kartik again." She looked at the trail the advance party had made.

"Jessy!" she called out. In seconds a Katabull lad rode up beside her. "Yes?"

"Go ahead and scout the trail. I want to come in behind the main assault and squeeze the bastards between two walls of Katabull," Tarius said. The lad took off at a hard gallop. They followed several minutes later at a slower pace. Jessy was a good scout, the best she'd ever known. He'd come back in a few minutes with the exact location of their enemy.

Jena rode up alongside her. "Tarius... What are they doing here? I don't understand. I thought we had almost erased them from the island. I thought they had given up. That they were afraid of the Katabull."

"They can't give up, Jena. Their gods have commanded them to take over the world. They are here now because they have decided to make a full-scale attack on the Katabull. They think that if they can kill us, kill us all, they can be free of our curse and can march across the Kartik unmolested. They are ignorant savages who believe their power-hungry priests really talk to their gods. They're ignorant. That's why they're so dangerous."

Jessy came riding back, his horse blowing and lathered in sweat. "Six ships off the coast. Three hundred men, maybe more. They are headed up through the pass."

"Come on!" Tarius ordered, and they doubled their speed.

Like Tarius had been, the Amalites were surprised by the vast number of Katabulls. They had assumed that the actual number of fighting Katabull would be small. By the time they realized the size of the fully-prepared army they had come up against, it was too late to retreat. Besides, their priests had promised them victory. Their gods would help them to strike down the evil Katabull and bring the Kartik people to their knees, thus bringing peace to the world.

They had no idea as they engaged the line of Katabull that they faced that the infamous Marching Night was falling on them from behind. It had been so long since there had been an actual full-scale battle between the Katabull and the Amalites that they had forgotten how much stronger, faster, and more resilient the Katabull were.

Katabull flung themselves over their own shield wall, coming down on the Amalites behind the wall and slicing them in two with one blow. They dodged sword blows, spear thrusts, and even arrows with the grace and agility of cats.

Then *she* was there. Behind them, within them, through them. The she-beast herself. The woman who had posed as a man, and who had at the Battle of the Arrow so utterly destroyed them and sent them running home with their tails between their legs. Several of these men had been there that day. They had barely escaped her wrath then. Today she was the Katabull leading the Katabull army, and they knew they would never go home again. As they died they began to doubt their gods, but it was a little late for that.

Tarius stopped, suddenly realizing there was no one left to kill. The Katabull cheered.

"Wait... wait!" Tarius screamed. "It's not over yet. We have to get back to the ships, kill the crews and seize the ships. Quickly... Undress their dead and put on their armor. We will masquerade as Amalites, get onto their ships and take them. I only need fifty people in addition to the Marching Night."

No one asked why, they just did as ordered.

Tarius, dressed in an Amalite's uniform, grabbed Jena's arm as she prepared to strip the body of an Amalite. "Jena... you stay behind with Elise and help with the wounded."

"But... I want to go with you!" Jena said.

"We need you here more. You have done enough killing for one day." Tarius kissed her cheek.

Then she turned and jumped on her horse. "Ride on!" she ordered.

Jena watched the more than a hundred warriors ride off. Then she went to find Elise and help her with the wounded, only to find that Elise was one of them. She had taken an arrow in her shoulder. She looked up at Jena weakly as Jena knelt beside her.

"You'll be all right, Elise," Jena said.

"Easy for you to say," Elise groaned out.

Jena looked at the wound. The arrow was in, but unfortunately not through.

"Where is Harris?" Elise asked.

"He went with Tarius. I'm sorry, Elise, if he had known..." Jena was glad she hadn't gone now.

"No. I'm glad he went. Last thing I need is his screaming and crying. I'd be sure I was dying, and it's just not that bad, is it, Jena?"

She needed reassuring, and Jena nodded. "It's not bad at all."

Jena got up and helped Elise to her feet. She half carried her to the medics gathered around the fire pit.

A Katabull medic in full beast mood ran over, took one look at the wound, and without warning reached down and forced the arrow through.

Elise passed out cold.

Jena helped hold her up as he snapped the shaft on the arrow and pulled it out.

"Is she Katabull?" he asked as he irrigated the wound.

"No," Jena said.

"Then she'll heal quickly," he said. He grabbed a fresh iron from the fire and cauterized the wound on both sides. "Can you dress it?"

Jena nodded, and he handed her the equipment. He started to walk away and then turned. "Tarak is dead," he told her.

"I'm very sorry. He was a very great leader," Jena said.

"Your mate, Tarius, she will be my choice to succeed him." He walked away and got back to work.

Jena only then recognized him as the leader of one of the other packs.

She tended to Elise's wounds, then tried to make her as comfortable as one could be when wounded and lying on a blanket on the ground. She covered Elise then went off to help with the other wounded. Katabull wounded and casualties were low, however several injuries were from spear or arrow, and the wounded were treated as best as they could be, loaded into wagons and shipped off to Montero which was only a half day's ride away.

The Katabull were not a stupid people. The springs helped their healing, so they picked a homeland close to the springs. The Amalites had picked them off when they lived in small packs across the countryside, so they had gathered in one place, making a huge army that the Amalites could not hope to conquer. Jena was sure that if the Amalites had attacked an unprepared Katabull encampment as they intended, the Katabull would have suffered only a few more casualties.

The Katabull were born warriors. In full beast mode, each one was as mighty as ten humans. Even when not catted out—she never *did* understand why the Jethriks called it that, they looked nothing like cats—they surpassed humans in every way. This was why she didn't worry about Tarius now. If Tarius could live through what Persius did to her, nothing a boat full of unsuspecting Amalites could do was going to even so much as scratch her.

"Keep your heads down," Tarius ordered the Katabull. "We don't want them to know what we are. "The humans will watch for us. Now row, row!"

"How did they get their horses ashore?" Harris asked.

"It was low tide," Tarius said in an exasperated tone. "They let the horses out, and they rode them to shore. They didn't have that many to begin with. The rest of the men came ashore in boats, then they pulled the boats above the high tide line."

"Guess maybe they're not so sure of their gods as they would have us think," one of the Katabull said.

"Why do you say that?" Harris asked.

"Because they left their boats above the high water mark in case they had to retreat at high tide. Are you all right, Harris?" Tarius asked.

He nodded, although his mind was obviously otherwise occupied.

They rowed up alongside the ships, and the Amalites helped the first couple of invaders aboard, wanting to know what had gone wrong before they realized that they were under attack. The Katabull and the Marching Night swarmed the ships, and in minutes the Amalites had been utterly annihilated.

Tarius and her boat had taken the biggest ship. She stood at the helm looking smug. She turned to Harris and smiled. "And now the Katabull have a fleet," she announced.

Harris grinned back.

When they arrived back at the camp they were met with cheers and hugs. Jena ran through them till she found Harris.

"Harris, Elise has been hit. She's OK, but she's in a lot of pain..." She didn't get to say more. Harris was gone, running past he and in the direction of... nothing.

He stopped and turned suddenly in mid-stride. "Where is she?" he yelled back at Jena.

"The wounded are in the main hall!" Jena yelled back.

"Is she really all right?" Tarius asked, putting an arm around Jena.

"She took an arrow in the shoulder. It's bad, but she'll definitely live, and it will probably heal well," Jena said. "So, tell me about the ships."

"We killed all the Amalites, and we now have six ships. We cut down the sails and the flags so the Kartik wouldn't see them and think we were under siege. I will have a report made out about what happened and have it sent to Queen Hestia. She must be made aware of what the Amalites are up to," Tarius said. "I have a plan to rid the Kartik of the Amalites forever, and it has to do with those six ships we just captured."

Suddenly, the cheers and yelling became so loud she could no longer hear herself think. It took her a second to realize that they were screaming her name. She blushed a little and waved to them all to be silent.

"The victory belongs to us all," Tarius said. They just started chanting her name again. She looked at Jena and shrugged. She was tired, and she wanted out of the stinking Amalite armor and into the lake. She told Jena as much, and together they walked out of the crowd and towards the water.

Harris fell on his knees beside Elise. "Oh, Elise! Can you ever forgive me? It was only after I had boarded that boat, and we were rowing out to the ship that I realized I hadn't seen you after the battle. That I hadn't even *looked* for you! I am a worm who doesn't deserve you. I am..."

"Long winded," Elise said, mustering a smile. "I appreciate the sentiment, my love. But we are warriors, and this is what we do. Had the tables been turned and Tarius had called for me to go with her, I would have gone. I wouldn't have noticed whether you were wounded or not. In battle if you hesitate you lose. It's our way of life; a way we have both chosen."

"If I had lost you, I don't know what I'd do without you, Elise! I feel like you are part of me. The best part. Your love has made me whole," Harris said.

"In that case, stop talking all that mushy stuff and take me home. I want my own bed," Elise said.

Harris smiled, gathered her in his arms and headed back for their house.

Following the death of Tarak and the defeat of the Amalites, the leaders of the forty-six packs gathered outside the main hall. Outside, not inside, because the wounded needed the shelter.

"Jerrad is Tarak's son; he should be leader in his place," one of the Katabull pack leaders threw out.

Tarius was bored by the whole procedure and was only here because they made her come. She was lying on the ground thinking of nothing more important than making love to Jena. Battle always made her feel randy, and she wanted to get this whole thing over with and go home.

"What think you, Tarius?" Herek asked.

"Yeah, fine," Tarius said with a shrug.

"I think Tarius should be leader in Tarak's place," Herek said.

Tarius's head snapped up. "Oh, now I *don't* think that's such a great idea."

"Why not?" Farel asked. "There is no greater leader among the Katabull."

"Because I'm a warrior, a mercenary, my pack is not even pure, my own wife is of a different race. Because I don't understand anything but battle, and you definitely don't want someone like me to lead the Katabull people."

"It's precisely for those reasons that we need you," Sharel a female pack leader commented. "The Marching Night is the tightest pack in our nation. Only your pack among all the others never goes to the council to settle disputes, and yet your pack should have more trouble than all the others because you *aren't* all the same."

"Besides, if there is to be a time of war, who better to lead the Katabull than a proven warlord? One who has beaten the Amalites before. The one who brought us this great victory today." This time it was Jerrad that spoke.

"Your father was a great leader, Jerrad. You, too, will be a good leader, after all, he set you an excellent example," Tarius said.

"But I don't *want* to lead. I am happy to lead my own pack at my father's death. I am unworthy of such an honor," Jerrad said.

"You're unworthy? Then what am I? I am a killer of men. A single-minded warrior. Just now when the meeting started I was not thinking of the people or of who would best fill the position. I was thinking of having sex with my mate. Is that the sort of person you want to lead the Katabull people? I certainly don't want the position. It will take up too much of my time."

"We have two worthy candidates," Sharel said. "For who is more worthy to lead than the person that doesn't want the power?"

"I'm telling you," Tarius started in disbelief. "I would rather be having sex right now than wasting time in this meeting."

"So would we all," Herek said with a grin. "I say we put it to the vote. All in favor of Jerrad..."

"There has not been enough discussion," Tarius interrupted.

He ignored her. "All in favor of Jerrad."

"Me," Tarius said holding her hand high. Only two other people voted for Jerrad. Tarius glared at Jerrad, who just smiled back. "You might have at least voted for yourself," she mumbled to him.

"As I'm sure you would vote for yourself," he mumbled back.

"I've changed my mind," Tarius said quickly. "There is nothing I want more than to be Great Leader. Power—give me *power!*"

They looked at her as if she'd gone crazy.

"And for Tarius?"

Jerrad was the first to hold his hand up, followed swiftly by all but three hands of the pack leaders. "Long live Tarius, great leader of the Katabull!" Jerrad screamed.

"You'll all be sorry," Tarius said standing up and addressing the group with a glare. "You'll see I'll do a horrible job. Now since I'm leader I'm closing this meeting so I can go have sex." She stomped away from them, and they all looked at each other and smiled.

"Oh, she really hates the position," Farel said rubbing his hands together.

"Far more than I would have hated it," Jerrad said. "We couldn't have made a better choice."

Tarius hit the front door of the hut mumbling and flopped down in a chair. Jena handed her a cup of hot soup she had just finished making. Tarius took it from her still mumbling.

"What's wrong?" Jena asked with a smile.

"Oh, nothing. They've just gone and made me leader!" Tarius said hotly. "I should have *demanded* they choose me from the beginning and I would have been safe. As it was they knew just exactly what I was doing and they all laughed at me. I spent too much time away from my own people, I forgot how the Katabull mind works. Stupid! Stupid! Stupid!"

"You'll be a good leader, Tarius," Jena said gently, sitting down across from Tarius.

"You're supposed to be on my side," Tarius grumbled. She sipped at the soup. "It's good."

There was a knock on the door.

Jena opened it and two men walked in carrying the throne of the Katabull.

Tarius sighed and slapped a hand to her head.

"The leader must always sit on the throne," one announced.

"Oh, for craps sake!" Tarius said standing up. "I don't want that in my house. I don't want to be leader. I don't want that throne." They took her chair and carried it outside, and then put the throne in its place. It was a plain wooden chair that was way too big for any one person, and it was draped in rare animal skins. She looked at it and sighed. It took up too much room.

"Thanks a lot," Tarius said facetiously.

"The council wishes to know what to do with the bodies of the Amalites," one man asked, and Tarius realized with a pain in her stomach that he was the equivalent of a king's herald.

"Tell them I said they can stick them up their..."

"Tarius," Jena scolded with a laugh.

"I don't want to lead," Tarius told her, "and it's not fair for them to make me do it."

"No one would be as good at it as you will." Jena said. "It's a done deal, so you might as well make the best of it."

"Oh, all right. In the morning we will strip the bodies of anything of use. Then we will haul them up to the ridge where the hurricane took out all those trees a season ago. There should be enough deadfall there to burn the bodies and keep the stench from bringing in flies and disease," Tarius said.

"Very good plan, Great Leader," the herald said grinning.

"Don't rub it in, just go away," Tarius said.

They had taken her chair away, so she moved to sit in the throne. It was actually quite comfortable, and she found that she liked sitting in it. She looked up at Jena, smiled, scooted over and patted the chair beside her. There was plenty of room, so Jena came and sat beside her on the throne. Tarius finished her soup and set the cup on the arm of the throne.

"So, you know what I've been thinking all evening?" Tarius asked with a wicked grin.

Jena smiled back and moved to crawl into Tarius's lap. "If I didn't, I wouldn't know you at all."

They found a new use for the Katabull throne.

18

Hestia looked from the report the Katabull had sent to the report she had just received from the tradesmen's guild.

"The Amalites have become too aggressive," Hestia said. "We must put an end to them now before it is too late. Bring me Tarius the Black, the leader of the Marching Night and the Katabull Nation."

"At once, my Queen," the chancellor said. "But what if the Katabull should decline your invitation?"

"It's not an invitation, Colin, it's an order. The Katabull still come under Kartik rule," Hestia said.

"My Queen... The Katabull are celebrated among our people and no Katabull more so than Tarius the Black. Do not, I implore you, *order* the Katabull or their leader to do anything. Instead, prepare a feast in honor of this woman who has killed so many of the queen's enemies, and who is now leader of the queen's mightiest subjects," Colin said.

Hestia nodded with a sigh. "You are right, of course. I'm sorry to be so ill-tempered. I was just hoping that the Amalites would not so darken our shores during my reign. My father did not see the signs, Colin. The Amalites swept down on his shores, falling first on the Katabull and then on us. He waited till it was almost too late to drive them away. I do not want to wait that long. I want to stop them now, and I need this Tarius the Black and the Katabull people to drive the Amalites away. Therefore I should approach her with friendship, not orders."

Tarius sat in her throne surveying the workers below, having taken a break from her own work. Jena brought her a mug of water and sat in her lap as she gave it to her.

"The work goes well," Jena said.

"In a week it should be done," Tarius said.

The Katabull were building docks for their newly acquired ships. It was a huge undertaking, but all took turns with the work. Since Tarius and the Marching Night worked alongside them, they didn't feel inclined to complain about mistreatment. The docks and the boats would serve the entire Katabull nation. First as a means of defense, and second as an obvious boon to fishing. They had the perfect harbor for the docks and more than enough trees.

Her herald, Rami, came running up to her out of breath.

"Great Leader..."

"What did I tell you about that?" Tarius asked sternly.

"Tarius... the queen's herald has come with word from Queen Hestia herself," he said excitedly.

"Well don't just stand there, bring him on," Tarius said.

A few minutes later, the queen's herald stood before Tarius. He seemed only a little surprised to see Jena in the Katabull leader's lap, and Jena smiled.

"Great Leader," the Herald said. "My Sovereign, Queen Hestia, Ruler of all the Kartik, Herald of the Dawn, and Daughter of the Moon, requests the presence of you, your mate and the Marching Night at a great feast to be held in honor of your great service to our kingdom."

Tarius smiled broadly at Jena. "What did I tell you?"

"You told me," Jena said with a smile.

"When is this feast to take place?" Tarius asked.

"The queen leaves the time to you."

"Then make it three weeks from today. We are engulfed in this project, and I must not leave it unattended. Tell the queen we will be happy to dine with her."

The herald stood there for a moment just looking at Tarius.

"Is there something else?" Tarius asked.

"I'm sorry, Great Leader. It's just... you're bigger in the stories."

Tarius laughed. "Am I really, now? Go boy, tell the queen we'll be happy to meet with her." The boy started to go and Tarius reached out quickly and grabbed his arm. Startled, he turned to look at her. "Tell Hestia that I have the answer to her problem and will explain it upon my arrival. Can you remember that?"

He nodded and repeated. "You have the answer to the queen's problem and will explain it upon your arrival."

"Good man, now go."

"What was all that about?" Jena asked.

"Hestia needs help with the Amalites," Tarius said. "When we are finished here we can give her the help she needs."

Hestia waited with baited breath. Her heralds had just informed her that the Marching Night could be seen from the castle garrison. She had word sent to the kitchen staff, and she dressed and prepared to meet her guests. Her consort rubbed at her shoulders.

"Everything will be fine, Hestia. Did she not send word saying she has a solution to your problem?" he said gently.

"Which problem, Dirk?" Hestia asked. "The Katabull talk in riddles; it's their way. The gods alone know what she meant. What if I say the wrong thing? This woman is a mighty warrior. I run an army, but I know nothing about warfare. I only do what has been tried and true. I do know that it would be a grave mistake to ignore what the Amalites are doing to our shipping lines, and I need her help to find a solution. I need the help of the Katabull Nation. If I make a mistake, the entire kingdom will pay for it."

"Then you won't make a mistake, my love." Dirk gently kissed her neck.

The queen stood in her throne room with her champion standing on her right hand side and her consort on the left. Her retinue stood all around her. The trumpet sounded, the door opened, and her herald strode in.

"My Queen, Tarius the Black, the Leader of the Katabull Nation, her consort, Jena of the Jethrik, and the Marching Night."

She had tried to prepare herself for any kind of entrance, but still wasn't prepared for what she saw. Tarius the Black was tall and dark, her long hair braided in small braids all over her head. Her armor was leather as black as the darkest night and studded with metal that shone even in the darkened castle hall. Her pauldrons and knee cops were pounded into the shape of skulls. Her arms were bare except for studded black leather vambraces. She wore black leather breaches with a loincloth and a cloak of a dozen brilliant hues. She bore the scars of a hundred battles. Little scars ran up and down both her arms, there was a scar across her throat and one down her face. She looked every bit as powerful as her legends proclaimed.

Yet she gave Hestia a smile that put her instantly at ease.

The woman at the warlord's side was definitely of the Jethrik and an unquestionable beauty. She wore a colorful wrap-around dress, not unlike the one the queen was wearing, but she also carried a sword on her back that wasn't much smaller than the one her mate carried.

The Marching Night was a mixed batch who had obviously cleaned up for the occasion, re-dyeing their leather armor and shining the metal parts. And they didn't bow to her. That meant that at least their leader was a follower of the Nameless God. Must be hard to wield such power and yet harbor the belief that no person was any better than another.

"My Queen," Tarius said.

"Great Leader." Hestia remained standing to show that she, too, thought herself no better than anyone else. She knew that any show of fear would lose her the respect of this woman and her followers, so she walked right up to her. "Sister," she said holding up her hand.

"Sister," Tarius said, taking her hand and bringing their elbows together. "We have much to discuss concerning the Amalite menace."

"Yes. But first we shall feast."

The queen watched as the Katabull throne was placed at the table next to her own.

"Some stupid custom of my people. The leader always has to sit on the throne. You should see the way they fall apart if I go to sit on a rock. Not that it stops me anyway," Tarius explained to Hestia.

Hestia nodded graciously.

They sat on their thrones at the same time. Tarius on the queen's right hand side in the place of honor. Everyone else sat only after Hestia nodded and Tarius waved her hand wildly in obvious and utter impatience with the whole procedure. Jena sat to Tarius's right, followed by Harris, Elise, Arvon and Dustan.

The queen's retinue consisted of her consort, her councilors and their respective mates. They were not nearly as colorful or as good looking as Tarius's people. Nor were her subjects as entertaining as the Marching Night. They all started to reach for the food in the middle of the table, and their leader looked at them and growled. They snapped their hands back to their laps like scolded children.

The hall steward filled the queen's glass, and then the servers around the room filled all the glasses of the waiting guests.

Tarius coughed, looking at the Marching Night and moved her head closer to the queen. "Queen Hestia... You are aware that I myself and a good half of my troop are Katabull and that we therefore have no tolerance to alcohol."

"Well aware," Hestia said with a smile. "And as I have no desire to have my hall filled to the brim with drunk Katabull, this toast will be made with grape juice. Then we will bring out the wine, and if your people choose to get drunk, then so be it. I will hold no grudge."

Tarius nodded, looked at her people and nodded again.

The queen raised her glass and stood, motioning with her hand that they should remain seated. "I raise a glass to our honored guests. Tarius the Black, Great Leader of the Katabull Nation, to her lovely and capable consort Jena, and to the Marching Night. May your people forever prosper and have power over your enemies."

They all drank, and the queen sat down.

Tarius stood up raising her glass. "May the queen and her consort live long, healthy lives, and may all our enemies be as the dust beneath our feet."

They all drank, and Tarius sat down.

Then the servers started bringing the food in. First to the queen and the others seated at the head table, and then to everyone else.

"So, I'm assuming that you are a follower of the Nameless God," Hestia said conversationally.

"I am, as are most of the Katabull," Tarius said.

"Yet you have leaders?"

"Yes, it does seem contradictory, but only to those who don't understand our philosophy. See, all are equal, from the monarch to the man who cleans the public privy. Both serve important functions, and both are needed. I am leader; it's a job. If I abuse the power of that job, if I treat people as if they are underlings, then I am breaking the code. A good leader is not the master of the people, but the servant," Tarius said.

She's eloquent, not at all the barbarian I was expecting, Hestia thought.

"Well put," she said.

"Thank you. The leader does not make laws, nor does the leader pass judgment on the people except when problems cannot be solved within the pack. My main job is to defend my people, to make sure we have a strong defense, and that's what I will do. I personally believe that a strong *offense* is the only real *defense*. What say you, Hestia?"

Tarius didn't blink an eye; she seemed to look right into Hestia's soul. She dispensed with any formalities, either real or implied, and called Hestia by her name not her title. Hestia found herself so off balance that she felt obliged to tell the woman the plain and simple truth.

"I know nothing of warfare except what is in books, and what I have learned in a training ring," Hestia answered in a whisper.

Tarius smiled. "Well, then we truly are the same. Because I know nothing else."

Riddles... why must the Katabull always talk in riddles? Never a straight answer. It puts me off my guard.

Jena stuck her head around Tarius to address Hestia. "She means that you are missing the skills she has, and that she is missing the skills you have."

Jena slapped Tarius on the shoulder playfully. "Say what you mean, dunderhead."

Then she again addressed Hestia. "The food is good." Jena went back to her plate.

Hestia watched the way Tarius's whole face seemed to light up when the woman spoke to her. She wasn't offended, and Hestia realized she had to relax. This woman knew nothing of a gentle life. She was a mercenary—a killing machine who had lived by her wits, but she was also filled with good humor.

"I need your advice, but it can wait till after dinner," Hestia said.

"The last time I gave council to a monarch I was shot through with an arrow and left to be dragged to death behind a horse for my efforts. As for dinner, I do my best thinking while I am eating," Tarius said.

"I am not Persius. I am Kartik. I would never reward good with evil," Hestia assured her. "The Amalites are raiding about one in five of our trading ships, killing the crews, and slowing down trade with the Jethrik and the barbarian nations. Worse still, as many as we kill, there are always more coming in on our own ships—the ships they steal from us. Despite our best efforts, the attacks are not lessening, they are becoming more severe. Case in point, the recent attack on your own people. What should we do?"

"I have six ships and a port from which to sail. Even as we speak my people are fixing the boats with Kartik sails and flags. We need supplies. As you know the Katabull people are primarily an agricultural, hunting and gathering culture. We have no wealth with which to outfit our ships. We need supplies from you. I also need a hundred of your best men. I myself will man one ship and put a mixture of humans and Katabull on all of them. We will sail in the areas where the ships are being raided. Then, when the Amalites come to raid us, the Katabull will call the night, and we will attack them. We will kill all on board and take their ships for our own. We will bring the ships back to the closest port where your people will outfit them for the coming war..."

"The coming war?" Hestia asked.

"The Amalites will never stop coming after us until we destroy them utterly. At the very least, we must destroy all their ships. Burn them and their ports. Make sure there is not even one fishing boat left. Take away their ability to sail, and you take away their ability to torment us. Send ships periodically to make sure that they never have the chance to rebuild their ships and their ports, and we get rid of the Amalite menace."

"I will get you everything you want," Hestia said. "Whatever you need, you have but to ask and I will seal it. I will not make the same mistake that my father made; we will crush the Amalite horde now and forever."

Hestia realized just then that about a half a dozen drunken Katabulls were dancing around the hall.

Tarius smiled at her. "You did say you didn't care," Tarius reminded her.

Hestia nodded, clapped her hands, and musicians started to play. Music filled the air, and then Hestia clapped her hands again and six scantily clad Kartik women came out dancing. "For your entertainment," Hestia said to the reigning Katabull leader. Tarius nodded in appreciation. The Marching Night went crazy with wolf whistles and yells. Jena noticed Tarius paying particular attention to one of the dancers and slapped her.

"Ow!" Tarius said rubbing her shoulder as if wounded.

"You keep your eyes over here," Jena said pointing at herself.

Tarius smiled at her. "But my dear love, you're not dancing... I'd of course much rather see you dance."

"All right then, I will." Jena had downed just enough wine to think it was a good idea. She had learned all of the Kartik dancing moves, and could dance as well if not better than any of these girls, and she showed them all she could. When she started to dance, the Marching

Night got still louder. Soon all of them were dancing around, including Tarius who was dancing with Jena in a manner that was almost—but not quite—sex.

Hestia looked at Dirk and shrugged. "Oh, well then..." She got up, took his hand, and they too started to dance.

A good time was had by all.

Hestia was walking through the courtyard early the next morning, just looking at her garden and thinking. As luck would have it, Tarius's consort was doing the same thing, and again wearing almost the same dress. It was starting to become embarrassing.

"Good morning," Jena said curtsying.

"Good morning," the queen nodded back. The girl still had court manners. "So, how does someone like you wind up with someone like Tarius the Black?"

Jena laughed. "I'm assuming you don't mean that in a hateful way." She stopped to smell a rose and smiled.

"Not at all. But you are Jethrik. Definitely a lady..."

"Oh, you should only talk to my father if you think I was ever a lady. I was sort of a tomboy, actually. But yes, I was of the gentry," Jena said.

"*She's* not. She's Katabull, Kartik, and a trained killer."

"So am I. Not Katabull or Kartik, but a trained killer," Jena said.

"Ah! But you weren't always. Jethrik women aren't allowed to fight. You have a kind face, a gentleness about you that while it may be somewhat deceptive, is there none-the-less. Your mate has neither quality about her," Hestia said.

Jena laughed again. "See, now? You don't know her the way I do. Yes, she is relentless, even ruthless when it comes to her enemies. But there is nothing she wouldn't do for a friend. True, she is vindictive, but she will show mercy if you can prove you acted against your will or have repented. The Katabull say you can see the merit of a person by their true friends. When the king tried to execute Tarius, the king's own wizard and surgeon conspired to save her. Harris, Arvon, Dustan, myself—we all changed our lives forever to be with her. She is very kind, but only to those who deserve it. As for her gentleness," Jena smiled wickedly. "As I said, you don't know her like I do."

Hestia laughed. "I'm still curious. How did the two of you get together?"

"It's a very long story," Jena said.

Hestia sat down on a bench in the garden and patted the seat beside her. "I've got time."

Jena sat down next to the queen. "All right, then, but I did warn you.

You see, in the beginning I didn't even know she was a woman, much less the Katabull..."

When Jena had finished, Hestia knew all about the true nature of her new ally, and had no doubts about either Tarius's integrity or her abilities.

"Well, it certainly was a long story, but not at all a boring one. You are very lucky to have kept each other through it all," Hestia said.

"Yes we are," Jena said with a smile. "I'd better go. If she wakes up and I'm not there, she runs around looking for people to kill. Life with her does have a few drawbacks."

Hestia watched Jena go almost with envy. Jena had passion, and she had adventure. Hestia had neither; she had only duty. Her father had died when she was only sixteen, and she assumed the throne. Before that, her life had been filled with school and sword training. After that, her life had been filled with decisions and responsibilities. Even her relationship with Dirk was not so much a love match as it was a convenience. Oh, she cared for him, and he for her, but there was nothing close to the depth of feeling these two fighters held for each other. There was nothing to bring them that close; nothing had tried to rip them apart. Neither of them had ever come close to death. They didn't rely on each other to watch their backs except in a political way.

Hestia decided to make the time to find some passion and adventure and add it to her life. The problem with living a safe life was that it kept you from really living at all.

She decided there would be more dancing.

The ships were loaded, and they were preparing to take to sea.

Arvon had already told Tarius that he and Dustan would not be going. Dustan couldn't handle the sea even with Kartik seasickness potions, and Arvon wouldn't leave him behind. Tarius not only understood, but she had anticipated their decision and had come up with a plan that would benefit everyone. While the Marching Night was at sea, Arvon and Dustan would take a troop of fifty men and Katabull and comb the shores, cleaning them of any Amalites they found and assuring that no new Amalite beachheads could be established.

Both fronts, land and sea, were being funded directly by the queen.

Tarius divided her people and the queen's people evenly among the ships. To ensure that all pre-sailing problems were addressed, Tarius's ship would leave last.

Before embarking, Tarius stood at the main lodge and addressed all the Katabull. "We will return frequently with more ships. I will handle what I can when I am at port, but in my absence any urgent decisions shall be settled by Jerrad. When we return we will leave some of you, and others will go back out with us. We will do this until every Amalite has been driven from the sea, and their homeports are utterly and completely destroyed. No longer shall they blight our land or threaten our future."

The crowd cheered. Tarius nodded to those assembled, and she and the Marching Night headed for their ship. This was their ship, manned almost entirely from their pack. They would take the most dangerous waters. There were ten Kartik soldiers with them whose duty it was to sail back any captured prize. When they had captured a second, they would bring both ships back and take a short break.

Harris followed directly behind Tarius; he had been trying to talk to her all day. "Tarius... Tarius!" he said.

"What is it Harris?" Tarius asked a bit annoyed. She was busy checking the last minute details with her herald.

"I'm... I'm not going."

Tarius stopped dead in her tracks and turned to face him. "Excuse me? What did you say?"

"I'm not going," Harris said.

"What about Elise? What does she say about this?" Tarius looked around and realized Elise was nowhere in sight. "Where's Elise?"

"She's not going, either," Harris said. "In fact, her not going is why I'm not going."

"Why not? Did I do something to hurt her feelings? Yours?" Tarius asked. "Have I done anything to either of you? If I have, I apologize. I know I've been busy, but..."

"You have done nothing, Tarius," Harris said with a smile. He took her shoulder in his hand and gave it a reassuring squeeze.

"She's pregnant isn't she?" Jena asked.

Tarius looked at her then back at Harris who was nodding. "She just told me. She thought if I couldn't give you advance notice that I would go with you, but I *can't*, Tarius. I can't, and I won't. When she was shot I left her to bleed on the field and followed you into battle. I won't leave her behind again, not now. What if something should go wrong? What if we get stuck out at sea, and I don't get home in time..."

"You need not explain," Tarius kissed him on the check. "This is where you need to be. I will do without you for the time being, though it won't be easy."

Harris had tears in his eyes, as did Tarius. Jena suddenly realized that they hadn't been separated for more than a few days since Tarius had come to the academy all those years ago.

They hugged for a long time, then Tarius pushed away and straightened. "I need two volunteers!" Tarius screamed out.

Fifty ran forward, and she chose two. "Quickly go and get your gear and say your good- byes. We sail with the tide."

Tarius hugged Harris again. "I love you, Harris."

"I love you, too. Come back whole," Harris cried openly now.

Tarius nodded silently and started back towards the docks and her ship. She cried as soon as Harris was out of sight, and Jena put an arm around her.

"I'm happy for them," Tarius cried.

"I know," Jena said.

"It's just..." Her sentence died on a sob.

"I know that, too," Jena said.

The sea was rough, and even the most steadfast seamen where throwing up their lunch. Jena was right along with them. Tarius barked out orders, and they brought down all but the storm sail, secured all cargo, and tied off the masts.

Tarius walked over to where Jena stood against the railings. "Jena! Get below," she screamed over the roar of the waves.

"No. Please, Tarius; I'm so sick," Jena said.

"Find a bucket and get below. It's only going to get worse, and I'm sending all the sick below. The last thing I need is you going overboard into that," she said pointing at the churning sea. Jena looked where Tarius was pointing and threw up again. Tarius let her finish, then grabbed her by the back of her shirt and forcibly hauled her below.

The storm raged all through the night, and it was only close sailing and Tarius's cool head that kept them from foundering as the storm drove them further and further off course and towards the Jethrik coast.

Dawn brought calm seas and enough light to see how much damage they'd taken. They were taking on water, and needed to put in for repairs as soon as possible.

With the calmer seas, Jena felt better. She found Tarius in the captain's quarters going over charts and maps with the ship's helmsman. Tarius looked haggard and frustrated. Jena walked over, wrapped her arms around Tarius's waist and lay her head on her back. Tarius clasped her arm with a free hand and squeezed it reassuringly.

"Feeling better?" Tarius asked.

"Yes, thank you. You look like you could use some sleep, my love," Jena said.

"Not just yet. The ship's taken a lot of damage, and we need to dock her," Tarius said. "I just hope the rest of our ships missed the worst of it."

"If it's any consolation, Leader, I think we bore the brunt of the storm, and the others probably missed most of it as they left earlier," the helmsman said.

"You did a damned fine job keeping us afloat," Tarius said.

"So we're going home." Jena shrugged. "I mean it's maddening that we didn't even get to fight one boatload of Amalites, but surely nothing to look so glum about."

Tarius gently removed Jena's hands and turned to face her. "The ship won't make it home. The storm blew us way off course, and the closest port of call is Wolf Harbor..."

"But that's in the Jethrik! Not a day's ride from... home," Jena said. "Tarius, we can't go there. If you are seen, the king will have you killed!"

"He's tried that before," Tarius said with a smile. "He won't have any better luck now. I will stay on the ship. Our people know how to keep their mouths shut, and hopefully none will be the wiser."

"Isn't there any other way? Even a Jethrik port further away from the capital?"

"We might make it, but why take the chance? Jena, the ship is taking on water, and we can't pump the water out fast enough. There's a breach in the hull that a temporary patch won't seal. We'll be lucky if it can be fixed without dry-dock and full-scale repairs," Tarius said.

Jena nodded reluctantly.

———•◆•———

They docked, and the helmsman set out in search of a shipwright to fix the battered vessel. It was taking on water fast now, and it was obvious that the ship *would* have to be dry-docked for repair. During high tide they guided it into the log stocks that would hold it, and when the tide ebbed, the ship could be worked on.

Tarius and Jena stayed on the ship while the others ventured out under strict orders not to speak of who they were traveling with, who they were, or what they were doing. If anyone asked, they were tradesmen blown into the wrong port by the storm after having to dump their cargo at sea.

Jena looked out at the land she had once called home. She would never tell Tarius, but she longed to go ashore and revisit those familiar sights and sounds, but she dare not leave the ship for fear of being recognized. They were like sitting ducks here—out of the water with no horses. The day was warm and sunny, showing no signs of the horrible storm that had driven them here. She stood on the bow of the ship looking out at the town with more than a little longing. If nothing else, she was tired of being on the ship. They had been here a whole week, and she was beginning to believe the ship would never float again. The rest of the crew were running around the town spending their money on all sorts of fun things while she and Tarius were stuck here alone most of the time. Which wasn't necessarily a bad thing, except that Jena was just sick to death of being trapped on the ship. She admitted to herself that if she could have left the ship, she probably wouldn't have wanted to.

But since she couldn't leave the ship, the land seemed to call out to her, compelling her.

Tarius walked up behind Jena and wrapped her arms around her. She rested her head on Jena's right shoulder. "Bored?"

"Ah no... Not at all... OK. Yes, yes incredibly bored," Jena said with a sigh.

Tarius held her tighter. "I have a cure for boredom."

"Yes, you certainly do. But, you know what, honey? We can't just do that all day every day," Jena said.

"We could try," Tarius said.

"You know how they say you can't wear it out? Well, I think you're trying," Jena laughed.

"All right... So, do you have any better ideas?" Tarius said.

"Actually, no... Race you to our quarters," Jena said, wrestling out of Tarius's arms and running for the cabin. Tarius chased after her. The shipwright and the workmen just laughed and shook their heads.

Three days later the repairs were finished, and they were tied to the docks, properly afloat.

"This is it! Go out have a good time, but come in early. We leave with the tide before dawn. May the Nameless One be merciful to the swine I have to go find before we can leave—because I won't be. If you're hung over in the morning then you'll punish yourself," Tarius said addressing the crew. The bulk of the Marching Night left in spite of Tarius's warning. Enough stayed to leave adequate protection for the ship and their leader.

It was still light when they left, and Tarius stood at the end of the gangplank and watched them go. Jena walked up beside her. "Half the bastards will come in drunk," Tarius said with a sigh.

"At least the Katabull haven't been drinking."

Tarius nodded. After a moment, she looked down the side of the boat across the deck in the direction of the capital. "The bastard is less than half a day's ride away, Jena. It would be so easy to get in, kill him, and leave him bleeding on the floor of his own throne room. We could be gone before anyone was the wiser, but I promised Robert I wouldn't kill him."

"No. You promised Robert you'd go to Kartik, and you did," Jena said. Personally, she wanted to see Persius drawn and quartered, and knew the Marching Night could easily get in, do the deed and get out again before the palace guard even knew what had happened.

Tarius laughed. "Those were his words, but I knew his meaning, Jena. He risked a great deal by helping me, and who knows if I would have lived at all if it hadn't been for him? I can't... I *won't* break my word to him. Not only the letter of my promise, but the intent must be safe with me. So Persius will continue to live. But how much joy does he get from his life when he knows that I am alive, and that I possess both the motive and the means to kill him?"

"He deserves to die." Jena rubbed the spot on Tarius's side where the arrow had done its damage. "Nice and slow."

"And that's precisely what he's doing," Tarius said with a satisfied smile.

Darian rode alone into Wolf Harbor. Most of his life he had lived a stone's throw from the port but had steered clear of it, having no desire to mingle with the riff-raff and foreigners who lived and traded in and around the docks.

Now he came here twice a month trying to learn anything he could about Jena. Stories of Tarius and her deeds flowed like wine in the pubs, and tales of the Marching Night were commonplace. He even occasionally heard stories about Harris and Arvon, but there was little news about Tarius's woman except that she was of the Jethrik and beautiful. And that didn't, necessarily, mean that she was Jena.

He had learned much about the Kartik on his trips here. He'd even picked up a bit of their language. Although he hadn't learned enough to carry on a conversation, he could usually get the gist of theirs.

Darian tethered his horse at a pub he liked to frequent and went inside. It was usually a quiet pub with few customers, where he could listen to others gossip. He was a little startled when he first walked in because tonight it was packed to bulging with Kartiks. A second look told him they weren't sailors, either, although they were dressed the part. Under their brightly colored shirts and puffy pants he could make out the outlines of armor, and their swords were too finely made and too well cared for to belong to mere fishing men or the crew of a trader. They were also too well muscled in the arms and upper torso to be anything but fighters. But why so many, and why here?

Darian carefully made his way to the bar where he ordered an ale and grabbed the bartender gently by the arm when he brought it. He leaned in close. "What's all this then?" he asked indicating the crowd in the pub.

"Ah, don't mind them any, Master Darian. It's just a Kartik trader's crew doing a little celebrating. Their ship came up lame in the storm and they had to dump their payload. Their ship's been in dry dock a little over a week and it just came to the docks today. They'll ship out tomorrow, so they're getting in the last of their partying. Of course, between you and me, they've been in here like this most every night they've been here, and they've been spending money left and right."

"Now that's funny, isn't it? You wouldn't expect them to be free spending considering they lost their payload. Are they taking anything back to Kartik with them?"

"No, apparently the lost shipment and the cost of repairs has left the captain with no money to bring anything back with him to Kartik," the barkeep said.

"Yet the sailors have money to throw away," Darian said thoughtfully.

The bartender shrugged. "It'd be the captain's loss, not the crew's. It's a mighty fine ship. Huge. Three masts it has!"

The bartender ran off then to take care of one of the Kartiks, and Darian saw that the man had a sword scar on his chin. He looked back at Darian, glaring at him, and Darian looked quickly away. Then one of the Kartiks came up and touched Darian's sword making some derogatory remark about the workmanship.

His fellows apparently said something about not causing trouble, but he was too drunk to listen. He tried to pull Darian's sword from its scabbard, and Darian turned, quickly drawing steel. The young man started to draw steel as well, and immediately three of his fellows were on him, dragging him away and mumbling an apology to Darian. Darian nodded and returned his steel to its sheath; he realized he was sweating.

Thank the gods! I haven't done anything but practice in ten years. I'll drink my beer, and I'll go. I wouldn't want to strike steel with one of these women much less the men.

Just then a drunken Jethrik wandered into the bar.

"What the hell is all this crap then, Amos? You only serve Kartik sea swine now?" he slurred.

He grabbed hold of one of the young women's arms. "Out of my way, you Kartik whore!"

The young woman threw the man into the bar, breaking a stool that happened to be in the way. The drunk just lay there groaning as the Kartik woman yelled things at him that Darian only partially understood.

One of the older ones shouted at all the others. Darian could only make out part of what he said, but apparently he was threatening them with return to the ship if they didn't show a little restraint.

The man sitting at the bar beside Darian turned to his fellow and whispered something that was lost to Darian in the noise of the bar, all that is except the name Tarius. All the color drained from Darian's face. *Could it be? Could they be the Marching Night? If so, what could Tarius and her people want here except to storm the castle and kill Persius? And it's like Tarius to pretend to have a crippled ship; to wait for the right time to strike. But the barkeep said they were leaving in the morning.*

Of course this is all speculation. It's probably not Tarius at all, and these people are not the Marching Night. I'm a foolish old man who has let my imagination run away with me. A foolish old man who wants to see his daughter just once more before he dies.

He paid for his ale without finishing it and left. Then he walked down to the docks just to see the ship. The barkeep hadn't lied; it was huge.

Darian was a little taken aback. The ship was Amalite in design, but clearly had Kartik sails and flags. Then he saw her; a Jethrik woman standing on the bow of the ship looking out at the town, and he didn't have to get any closer to know it was his Jena. He ducked into some shadows and watched her until she went into the cabin.

———•◆•———

It was late, and most of the crew had come in. Jena was asleep, and Tarius sat in the log room going over the charts and calculating how long it would take them to get back where they needed to be in order to get raided.

Damn! We don't have enough supplies to stay out to do more than one ship! Besides if we're not back in port when we are supposed to be, everyone will assume we have been captured or killed.

She sighed and leaned back in her throne rubbing her brow. The night was hot, and even with the cabin window open she was sweating. She sat at the table wearing only a pair of brightly striped puffy pants and her sword on her back.

A sharp knock came on the door, and she jumped. She looked at the charts again before she answered.

"What is it?" Tarius asked impatiently.

"Great Leader..."

"Rimmy, what did I tell you?" she asked hotly.

"Sorry, Tarius," he said.

"Don't just stand there! Come in."

Rimmy and Tweed came in and dumped the load they carried on the ground in front of Tarius's table.

Tarius looked up at Tweed expectantly.

"We found this old man trying to get on the ship," Tweed said.

"Well, lift him up here so I can see him," Tarius said.

They lifted the man up off the floor.

"Did he put up a fight, or were you just in the mood to kick some ass?" Tarius asked angrely.

"He put up one hell of a fight for an old man. Took three of us to get his sword out of his hand," Rimmy said.

Tarius nodded. "I have many enemies in the Jethrik. You have done right to capture him." She thought for a moment, and then spoke in the Jethrik tongue. "So, old man, what business do you have with me, my ship or my crew?"

Darian looked up then right into the face of Tarius the Black. She was wilder than he remembered and harder, but there was no mistaking her. She sat there in a huge fur covered chair wearing nothing on her torso but the sword across her back. She had a gold ring in one of her nipples, one in her eyebrow, and three in her left ear. He had learned that multiple piercings were a sign of power and wealth among the Kartiks. Tarius had apparently acquired both. She was bronze and dark and hauntingly beautiful. Finally he saw the scar where the arrow had pierced her.

"I asked you a question, old man. I believe in giving everyone a fair chance. However if you do not answer me, I shall have my men kill you, and in the morning we will dump you somewhere between here and the Kartik for fish bait. What business have you with me, my ship or my crew?"

"I only have business with you." Darian looked into and caught Tarius's eyes. "Do you not recognize me, Tarius? I took you into my home, and I loved you like a son. I gave you my daughter, and you betrayed me."

Tarius was instantly on her feet. "You! How dare you!" Tarius started to breathe so hard that he could hear her every breath. "Who betrayed who? You took me into your home to bring you honor, and I did. I loved you as a father. Your daughter was never yours to give, she gave herself. What the hell did you hope to gain by coming to this ship?"

She switched to Kartik without a pause. "Quick, Rimmy, sound the alarm, and have the ship searched. Get our people back on board as soon as possible. This is some sort of trap."

Rimmy nodded and ran off.

Darian got the gist of Tarius's orders if not the particulars.

"I came alone. No one knows I am here," Darian said.

"Why would I believe you, old man?" Tarius spat out with venom. "After all you have done to me, after all you did to Jena..."

"I am the injured party here."

"After all this time, you still think that?" Tarius laughed. "Are you really that big a fool?"

"I want to see my daughter. After that, do to me whatever you want," Darian said. "Will you allow her to see me, or is she your prisoner, too?" he asked holding up his tied hands where she could see them.

"Jena has never been *my* prisoner, Darian," Tarius hissed. "Only you and Tragon ever tried to keep Jena prisoner. You should know better than anyone else that Jena could never be caged."

Tarius walked over and grabbed a black shirt from a chair, slung it on and tied it. "Tweed, go and get Jena."

"Yes, Great Leader," he said and left the cabin.

A few minutes later Jena ran in. She was wearing a blue and red silk robe that came to just above her knees and her sword was in her hand.

Tweed took up a position at the door.

"What in hell is going on?" Jena asked running to Tarius's side.

For answer Tarius nodded her head towards Darian.

Jena looked at him, not recognizing him with a beard and in the dim light. The recent beating didn't help, either. "A stow away? What?"

"It's your father, Jena," Tarius said in the Kartik tongue.

Jena took a second look, and she moved still closer to Tarius. "The bastard! Has he brought the kingdom upon us?"

"I don't think so. I have the crew looking to make sure, but I think he just wants to see you."

"Well, I don't wish to see him," Jena shot him a hateful look.

Darian got the gist of their conversation.

"Why don't you want to speak to me? Is there no room in your heart for forgiveness?" Darian asked. "What I did to you... With Tarius, encouraging you... Pushing you towards him... her. Then making you marry Tragon... It was wrong. All wrong, and I'm sorry."

It took Jena a second to remember her Jethrik. "Where did you learn Kartik?"

"I know just a little. I learned it hanging out on the docks here hoping to hear some news of you," Darian said.

Jena looked at Tarius and spoke. "See why I don't want to talk to him? He still thinks what he did to you was all right. He thinks you and I together is a mistake. Throw him off the ship."

"I can't; he knows too much," Tarius said. "And we both know he can't be trusted."

"We could kill him," Jena said angrily.

Tarius made a face. "We will not kill your father, Jena."

"Then what?" Jena asked.

Rimmy ran in then. "Great Leader..."

Tarius sighed. "What is it Rimmy?"

"Great Leader. All are on board and accounted for. No army or forces found. We are awaiting your orders."

"Weigh anchor and hoist the sails. We head out tonight," Tarius said. She glared at Darian. "Why take any chances?"

"Aye, aye." Rimmy ran off.

Darian finally figured out what had been said. "Leave? You're going to leave port? You're going to kidnap me the way you did my daughter?"

Tarius had started for the door, but she turned in the doorway. "I was in the Kartik when your daughter came looking for me there. Jena *wants* to be with me, and that is the crime I have committed for which you cannot forgive me. I have to go to the helm." She glared at Darian and turned again to leave.

"Rimmy, keep an eye on him."

Jena glared at her father, and he glared back. Except for her coloring, he might as well have been looking at a Kartik. Jena had six gold rings in her right ear and three in her left. Her hands were callused and covered with sword cut scars.

She moved to sit in the big chair Tarius had been sitting in, and she set her sword on the table in front of her as if daring him to try and grab it.

"Can I sit down? I'm not as young as I used to be."

"Rimmy, get him a chair, please," Jena said.

Rimmy nodded and did as he was asked. Darian sat down slowly, favoring his right side.

"You know I never told them that it was you who killed Tragon. I blamed it on Tarius, and they believed me. You could have come home at any time," Darian said.

"Don't you get it, Father? I *wanted* everyone to know I killed Tragon. I'm *glad* I killed him. Because of him Tarius was very nearly killed, my whole world was turned upside down. The bastard killed my child. Do you know what it's like to have something alive in you one minute, and then have it painfully thrown from your body? To have to put that tiny dead thing into the earth, burying the dreams you had for a child in a grave?" Jena asked. She choked back her tears.

"If you are not a prisoner, then leave with me now. Let Tarius go where the wind blows her, but you stay here in the Jethrik with me," Darian pleaded.

Jena got up and started pacing the room. "Haven't you listened to a word I've said? I don't *want* to be here. I love the Kartik. The Marching Night is my pack. Tarius is my mate, my lover, the only one I have ever wanted or will ever want. I love Tarius. I love her because she is a woman. I love her because she is the Katabull. I love her because she is Tarius the Black. And do you know what, Father? *She* loves *me*. That wonderful, damn-near goddess-like person loves *me*. She worships the ground I walk on, and what is so damn awful about that?" Jena grabbed her sword up and started to leave the room, but she turned in the doorway. "What the hell are we going to do with you?"

She turned to Rimmy. "Take him to the hold and lock him up. You're needed on deck."

Darian felt the ship pull away from the docks even as he was being locked in a cell in the hold. They didn't leave a guard, but one look at the lock and bars told Darian he wasn't likely to get out.

Where the hell would I go if I did get out? I'm out at sea surrounded by the most fearsome group of fighters ever assembled. Hell, most of them are probably Katabull.

Jena appeared at the door to his cell with a cup. "Ever been at sea before?"

"Not since I was a lad," Darian answered.

"Better drink this then. It's a Kartik tonic. It tastes vile, but it beats the hell out of sea sickness." She handed it through the bars to him, and their hands touched. She quickly drew hers away.

"Thank you," Darian took the cup. His hands were still tied, and he had trouble getting it to his mouth. When he had finished it he handed the cup back.

Jena sighed. "Here, let me untie your hands."

He held them out, and she untied them. As soon as they were loose, he grabbed her hand without warning, and she moved swiftly, banging his head into the bars. Darian stumbled back rubbing his head.

"I wasn't going to hurt you!" Darian protested.

"Then I'm sorry," Jena said.

Darian looked sad. "You've seen a lot of action, haven't you?"

"I've seen my share," Jena said noncommittally.

"Is Harris..."

"He's fine. Married to a Kartik swordswoman, part of the pack of the Marching Night. They're expecting their first child, so they are at home with the Katabull Nation," Jena said. In spite of herself, she was enjoying talking to her father.

"And Arvon?" Darian asked.

"Arvon and Dustan stayed to continue to clean the coast of the Amalite scum," Jena said.

"They're still alive and together then... that's good," Darian said in a far away tone.

"All right, Father, explain this one to me. Why are Arvon and Dustan a good thing, and Tarius and I aren't?"

"Because neither of them ever pretended to be anything different. Because neither of them are my only child," Darian said.

"Fine," Jena started to go.

"Wait, Jena... I'm sorry," Darian looked at the floor. "Tell me what you and Tarius and the Marching Night are doing at sea in an Amalite vessel? You've fixed it up to look like a Kartik freighter, but it was originally Amalite."

Jena was silent.

"Who can I tell?" Darian asked.

"We are working with Queen Hestia and the Kartik army. We have five such ships, which the Katabull captured from the Amalites. The Amalites have been raiding Kartik ships. When they raid our ships, they will get a surprise," Jena said.

"I'll give her this; she's clever," Darian said with a laugh.

"You'd better decide she's more than that, or this will be a very long trip for you, and when we get to the Kartik I'll have Hestia throw you into the darkest dungeon in her castle," Jena promised.

"You have that kind of pull with the queen, do you?" Darian scoffed.

Jena smiled wickedly. "Haven't you heard what the crew are calling her, father? My mate, Tarius, is the queen's most powerful ally, because she is the chosen leader of the Katabull Nation. Hestia will do anything I ask her to do just to keep Tarius happy."

Jena went to bed and went to sleep. When she woke up Tarius was with her, but Jena didn't remember her coming in. She got up as carefully as possible so as not to wake Tarius. She dressed in puffy pants and a wrap around shirt, slung her sword on her back and went barefooted up on the deck, only to find her father standing on the bow looking out to sea. Jena ran up to him. "How did you get out?" Jena demanded. She was about to call for someone to come and get him and lock him up when her father answered her, not bothering to turn around.

"Tarius released me. Said she saw no sense in keeping me in lock up since I couldn't go anywhere," Darian said.

"Tarius... What in the gods' names was she thinking? Why, you'd kill her in her sleep if given half a chance," Jena said.

Darian turned then. "How dare you accuse me of such a thing."

"Oh, I don't know, maybe because you condoned... No, *demanded* that she be executed for the great crime of loving me. Or maybe it's because you held me still with your hand over my mouth while you gleefully watched your precious ruler stick an arrow through her body while she was stocked and tied to the back of a wild horse. Maybe because you watched as that horse dragged her off through the underbrush and did nothing but cheer. She may trust you, but I most certainly do not. In my eyes, you're no better than an Amalite. Worse, because Tarius never turned a stone to hurt you." Jena stomped back down the deck towards the hold. Halfway there she stopped, and without turning around said with venom, "You so much as look at her the wrong way, old man, and I'll kill you myself."

Darian watched as she disappeared from sight. He didn't know what he had expected when he tried to sneak on the ship to steal Jena last night, but it certainly wasn't this. Jena hated him. She was not being held captive by Tarius or the Marching Night. She was here only because she wanted to be here. She loved the man, woman, beast, human—whatever. Truly *loved* her, so much so that she would renounce her kin and her country.

That being the case, what real crime had Tarius committed against him? He had lost face, and he had lost his daughter. But how much of that was Tarius's fault, and how much of it was his own?

He was stuck with them now, because they would never let him go back to the Jethrik. Darian wondered who would run the school. What would they think had happened to him when they found his horse at the dockside with him nowhere in sight? His whole life had changed, and only one thing was really clear. If he didn't want to spend the remainder of his life in a dungeon in Kartik, he had better find a way to forgive Tarius the Black and get Jena to forgive him.

"But why? Why did you do that?" Jena demanded, nearly screaming.

"Because... he's your father, Jena."

"Exactly my point. My father, the man who helped Persius try to kill you. The man who made me marry that awful Tragon!" She was screaming now.

"If you could forgive me, you can forgive him," Tarius said looking up at Jena from where she was sitting on the deck working on her armor.

"It's not the same, Tarius," Jena said, breaking Tarius's gaze. She started pacing back and forth in front of Tarius, waving her hands wildly in the air. She had all of Tarius's attention now, her armor repair temporarily forgotten.

"It *is* the same," Tarius insisted. "I'm sure that in his eyes what I did was much worse than what he has done."

"You didn't order him killed," Jena said. "You didn't stand by and ignore the fact that Tragon was going to rape me. Didn't stand ideally by and do nothing while he killed my baby, and you never would have."

"But I wasn't there for you, Jena," Tarius said in a low voice.

"But that wasn't your fault, Tarius. It was at least in part his fault that you weren't there with me. You weren't there—you don't know how he pleaded with the king for your death." She started pacing again. "Why the hell did he have to come on our ship? Another few hours and we would have been gone. Now we're stuck with him, and it just makes me want to scream."

Tarius let out a growl and jumped up. She ran to Jena, grabbing her and throwing her over her shoulder.

"Tarius," Jena laughed. "What the hell are you doing?"

Tarius just growled and continued carrying Jena towards the cabin as the crew whistled and yelled.

Jena laughed and shook her head. "But it's the middle of the day! What about your armor?"

"You do something to me when the fire's in your eyes," Tarius said in a low voice.

"Well, in that case," Jena started playing at getting away.

Seeing Jena struggling against Tarius as Tarius started to carry her off below, Darian made a move to go "rescue" his daughter.

"You'll only embarrass yourself, old man," a woman said in Jethrik as she grabbed hold of his arm. "She's not hurting Jena, and she's certainly not forcing her. They're just playing a little game."

"How can you be so sure?" he asked.

"Because I've been riding with them for three years now. I know you'd like to believe different, but Jena is with Tarius because she wants to be. Tarius doesn't have to force her," she said.

"I'm beginning to understand that, but... a game?"

"We Kartik like our sex," she said with a smile. "My name's Radkin, and you are?"

"Darian," he said simply. "At home I have much wealth. Help me get back to my homeland with my daughter, and I will make sure the deed does not go unrewarded."

Radkin laughed. "First off, I have no idea how one would go about doing that. Trying to get Jena away from The Great leader, I mean. If Jena didn't kill you, Tarius most surely would. Second, I don't think you understand the nature of the pack of the Marching Night. None of us would betray Tarius, not for any amount of money. Not for anything. Every one of us would give our life for her—or for Jena for that matter. As they would for us. Riding with her, to be part of the Marching Night, is to know that you are the best. That you are a part of the greatest fighting force ever assembled, and no one I know would give that up. Third, if you are going to ask one of the Marching Night to betray Tarius, at least have the good sense not to ask the Katabull." Radkin smiled at the look of shock on Darian's face.

"She is queen of the Katabull?" Darian asked.

"She is our Great Leader," Radkin answered.

"Is she a good leader then?" Darian asked curiously. "I know in battle she is one of the best."

"In battle she is the best. And as leader she is the best. Understand this, Tarius was not set upon the throne without much thought. She didn't beg for the position, she pleaded against it. What better leader could you ask for than one who doesn't want the power?" she said.

Katabull logic he presumed. "Where did you learn to speak Jethrik?" Darian asked.

"Working the docks in Kartik," Radkin said.

"Do all of the women there do men's work then?" he asked.

Radkin stared at him. "Men's work? What does that mean? Work doesn't belong to men or to women, but to both. What a strange culture you must live in! Men's work indeed! Next you'll be telling me they have women's work as well." She laughed.

"Is that," Darian pointed in the direction Tarius and Jena had gone. "Is that common, too, where you come from?"

"Game play? Why sure! As I said, we Kartik like our sex, and you have to keep it fresh, don't you?" Radkin said.

"I meant women with women and men with men," Darian said.

"Oh, aye... Very common. Especially among the Katabull. Roughly two thirds of the Katabull are queer, myself included," she said.

"How do you propagate?" Darian asked curiously.

"Cross mating," Radkin said with a shrug.

"What's that?" Darian asked, ashamed to show his ignorance.

"One couple is female, one couple is male, and they cross mate with each other. We have the children together, and all four raise them. Cross mating. It makes the cubs strong, and makes sure they get lots of attention."

Darian kept asking questions about the island and their culture and Radkin happily answered him.

Truly it was a different world his daughter had been living in. No wonder she was so changed. No wonder she wasn't embarrassed about her relationship with Tarius. It was normal on the island. According to Radkin, Jena was the envy of every queer woman in the Kartik, and there were apparently plenty of them.

Rimmy ran up to them. "Radkin, Jasper thinks he sees something from the crow's nest."

Radkin nodded and ran off. Darian watched as she scurried up the ropes into the crow's nest. She took the glass from the man, looked a second and then screamed out, "Amalites off the starboard bow and closing fast!"

Both Radkin and Jasper slipped down the ropes to the deck. Everyone everywhere seemed to change places as the Kartik soldiers moved to look like a typical Kartik sailing crew, and the Marching Night ran below.

"You'd better come with me." Radkin took Darian by the arm and dragged him below. He watched as the hand on his arm changed, became thicker, hairier. When he turned he was looking into the face of the Katabull.

"Rimmy! Go get Tarius and Jena."

Rimmy had changed as well.

"Do I have to? You know they're going to be..."

"Just go get them," Radkin ordered.

Rimmy turned to go after them just as Tarius arrived pulling on her armor. Jena was right behind her doing the same.

"Did anyone get my knee cop off the deck?" Tarius asked.

"Here Great Leader," Tweed said handing it to her. Tweed also was the Katabull.

"Thank you." Tarius nodded as she took it from him.

They were armored faster than any army Darian had ever seen.

"Give me my sword, and I will help you," Darian said. "The Amalites are my enemy as well."

"No," Jena said. "You'd as likely kill Tarius as one of them."

Tarius was busy giving orders, and slowly the fighters started to sneak back out on deck. They went on hands and knees crawling up against the edge of the ship's rails, out of sight of the Amalite raiding ship.

Tarius seemed to look down at her feet, and as she raised her head she was the Katabull as well. She looked at Darian and smiled. "Wait till you see me sling steel as the Katabull."

She kissed Jena on the cheek, and then together they crawled onto the deck.

Faced with only a token resistance, the Amalites got their grappling hooks into their prize and pulled the ships together. The Kartik soldiers did their part by running around and looking mortified and panicked. When the first Amalite foot touched their ship, Tarius gave the call, and the Marching Night attacked. Darian watched from the cabin as long as he could stand it, then he grabbed a mop, broke the head off it and ran into the fray.

Nothing, absolutely nothing moved like the Katabull. Up sails, up ropes, over rails and barrels and each other. And no Katabull moved like Tarius the Black. Tarius leapt over the rail and into the enemy ship, slicing the first man she fell on almost in half. Punching the second in the face with the hilt of her sword so hard that she drove part of his face into his brain, killing him instantaneously. Then she was everywhere, and so, he noticed was Jena. The oddest thing was that Tarius seemed to always be aware of exactly where Jena was and just what was happening to her. At one point in the battle Jena was easily holding her own against not one but two men. Tarius appeared swinging in on a rope and killed them both before moving on. For his part, Darian helped to keep the Amalites from coming onto the Kartik ship. He slapped one man in the head with enough force to daze him and pushed another back into the boat.

In minutes the battle was over. The Katabull took no prisoners. The Amalite bodies were tied together, weighted with one of the anchors and dropped into the ocean. They off loaded enough supplies from the Amalite ship to keep them at sea for a while, hopefully long enough to capture another Amalite ship. Half the Kartik soldiers and all the badly wounded boarded their prize. They changed the flags to Kartik banners and then they pointed the ship towards the Kartik. They would tell the others that Tarius and the Marching Night were delayed but well, so that they could stay at sea until they took out another raiding ship. Then they, too, would head for home.

Tarius looked at the bloody stick in Darian's hand and smiled. "Kill any?" she asked him.

"I think maybe one," Darian said, and he smiled back. "It's been a long time since I was in an actual battle."

Tarius nodded and went off to check her troops. She made sure that every minor injury was being cared for. The girl was right. Tarius *was* a good leader.

"Give me that," Jena grabbed the stick from his hand. "Leave it to you to wield a Katabull killing weapon."

"It was all I had," Darian defended. "Damn it, daughter! I am trying to understand. I'm trying; can't you give in just a little?"

"She's too much like you, Darian," Tarius said in his ear. She was still the Katabull. In fact, none of them seemed like they were in any hurry to change back.

"What a horrible thing to say, Tarius!" Jena turned on her heel and stomped off.

"See what I mean?" Tarius asked Darian in a whisper.

"You aren't mad at me any more, are you?" Darian asked more than a little confused.

"I have thought about what we said to each other the other night. I hurt Jena a great deal. If anyone else had hurt her that badly, I would have wanted them dead. I understand that. I could be mad at you for making her marry Tragon, but at least you didn't actually put him in her bed, and I did. Understand this, though. I was trying to give her what she said she wanted. It was never my intention to hurt her. I love her. I can't help myself; she's magnificent. We have both hurt and been hurt," Tarius said. "I never meant to fall in love with Jena, and I certainly didn't want her to fall in love with me. Surely you can see that it was only my love for Jena that was my great undoing."

Darian thought about that a moment and then nodded in reluctant agreement.

"I know it's not what you're used to. I know that our relationship, like the Katabull, is something that is tolerated by your people but never really accepted. But you have to realize that where I come from—in the Kartik—I could have been all that I am. But the Kartik were not at war with the Amalites, and the Jethrik was. My pain over my father's death still raged, and so I left my home to fight your war as my father had done before me, breaking your rules as he, too, had done. I love Jena with all my heart and soul, and I know that she loves me the same. I can give her everything a man could give her. In fact, I can give her more, because I let her be whoever and whatever she wants to be. When the war is over and the land is safe we will even have children if that's what she wants." Tarius stopped for a moment looking out at sea. "So the real question is not whether I'm mad at you, but rather are you still mad at me? Can you try to put aside your hatred of me long enough to see what I really am, instead of what you have decided I am? And then there is the second problem."

"Which is?" Darian asked.

"Can you convince Jena that you are truly sorry for what you did to her?" Tarius said. She turned and walked away. Darian watched her go.

For the next three days, Jena would not even deign to talk to him. She acted as if he did not exist in her space at all. It was driving Darian mad.

Tarius was on the deck looking out to sea. She had hoped to run into another Amalite raiding party before this. Darian stomped up to her. "Tarius, you were once a Sword Master. You are a fighter, so you know what I must be going through being separated from my weapon, knowing that if we go into battle my only defense will be whatever I can grab hold of on the ship. Give me my sword."

Tarius turned to look at him, but before she could speak Jena ran between him and Tarius. "You will never hold a sword on this ship while I still take a breath," Jena said.

"Tarius... are you the leader or is she?" Darian asked.

"You still don't understand old man. As I have told you once before, Jena's a woman, not a toad. As I am a woman as well why would her will be any greater or smaller than mine in my eyes?" Tarius smiled and clasped her hand on Jena's shoulder. "In matters both great and small I always take Jena's counsel. In matters concerning you, since you are her kin and not mine, I'm afraid the decision is simply not mine to make."

"The Marching Night—are they better than the Sword Masters?"

"There is no comparison whatsoever. The least of the Marching Night could destroy utterly the best of the Jethrik Sword Masters," Tarius said boastfully.

"Then put it to the test. I have seen you playing with practice weapons on the ship. Let me pick my opponent. If I can beat them, then give me my sword," Darian said.

Tarius looked at Jena appealingly. It was a sucker bet. One she could not lose.

"You're on," Jena said and went herself to grab two practice swords from their storage place on the deck. "So, chose your opponent," Jena said.

Darian looked around at the Marching Night. He even looked at Tarius for a second, which made them all grow very quiet. "You, Jena. I pick you."

"Ridiculous!" Tarius screamed. "Preposterous! No! I say no! Pick another opponent."

"Why? Can Jena not hold her own? Is she not part of the Marching Night?" Darian asked.

"Because it's twisted and..."

"I'll fight you, old man," Jena threw him the practice blade, "and you will lose."

"Jena, I don't think..." Tarius started.

Jena looked at her. "I want this."

Tarius shrugged and stepped back, prepared to watch the old man trounced by his own daughter.

Jena was relentless in her first attack, and Darian was glad they used the hollow bamboo sticks instead of the wooden swords they practiced with at home. Her first blow to his head would have likely driven him head first into the deck if they had. He landed one blow to her stomach, she flinched, and out of the corner of his eye he saw Tarius start forward and then stop when Jena glared at her.

Jena caught him in the head, in the leg, in the stomach and in the head in a combination so fast he had no time to block, and he hit the deck. Jena turned to walk away as the Marching Night cheered.

Darian stumbled to his feet, his nose bleeding. "I'm not done yet."

Jena turned on him, the anger shooting from her eyes reminding Darian of her mother when she was mad. He smiled smugly at her, and she landed on him with a sound blow to his head. Then she sent a flying kick to his stomach. He fell again, and again she walked away.

Darian again crawled to his feet. "I'm still not finished."

Jena spun on him again, this time in a red rage. She battered him in the ribs with a series of blows that again knocked him off his feet, and scalded all the air from his lungs.

This time she stood glaring at him. "Damn you! Stay down."

"Sorry, can't oblige." Darian again crawled to his feet. He threw a blow at her, which she easily blocked, and again she battered him till he fell.

"Stay down!" Jena cried, looking into his bruised and battered face.

But he stood up again, tottering now and unable to stand straight. "So, are you still mad, Jena? Or have you had enough?"

Jena started to swing the sword again, but Tarius was behind her in an instant. She grabbed Jena's arm and took the sword from it. She threw it onto the deck, and Jena collapsed in her arms crying. Tarius held her tight. "Shush, shush! It's all right," Tarius said gently.

"Sosha! Take him below, clean him up and doctor his wounds."

"Rimmy!"

"Yes, Tarius."

"Get this man his sword and some clean clothes. Kartik clothes."

Darian lay on the deck in the sun in clean if somewhat gaudy clothes. His sword lay by his side on the deck and he hurt everywhere.

Someone strode up to his feet. He shielded the sun out of his eyes and looked up at Jena. It was obvious that she had been crying a good long time. She'd washed her face, but her eyes were red and puffy.

"Why did you do that?" Jena hissed at him. "Did you hope to beat me in front of the Marching Night? Make me look a fool?"

"If I did, then I failed miserably, didn't I Jena?" Darian forced a smile. "You kicked my ass good, and I have to tell you, although I'd rather lie, that I didn't hold back on you. You just really out-class me. In fact, I'd venture to say that you are better than I have ever been, even in my youth."

"You... Why would you pick me, then?" Jena asked. "The Katabull all outclass me, but only a few of the Kartik fighters do."

"I knew that. The Katabull woman Radkin told me."

"Then why?" Jena asked.

"Because I need you to forgive me, Jena, and you aren't even trying." Darian moved painfully into a sitting position. "I'm trying to understand about you... and Tarius. It's not easy, Jena. This was never what I wanted for you. I thought maybe if you could beat the crap out of me, we could get past the rage."

"You begged Persius to kill Tarius," Jena accused.

"At first you my dear girl didn't argue about her fate. Still, I'm sorry."

"You knew I hated him, and yet you made me marry Tragon."

"And I'm sorry, my only defense is that I thought I was doing the only thing that could be done to repair your good name."

"You didn't protect me from him, you didn't..."

"And there is no excuse for that Jena. None at all except that I had no idea he was actually being phisacaly violent until it was too late." He sighed. "If your mother had lived, things... you would have been so different. I wanted so much for you and I failed you in every way."

Jena sat on the deck next to him. "What about what I wanted, Father? What about what I wanted for myself? I never wanted the frilly dresses or any of the stuff that went with them. The idea that I might wind up washing clothes and taking care of a man the rest of my life terrified me. Arvon had a good point; he asked me why I thought I was attracted to Tarius in the first place when I had never been attracted to any other man. He told me he thought I fell in love with Tarius not because I thought she was a man, but because she wasn't like a man at all. When I realized he was right, I knew I had to find Tarius and be with her no matter what, and that's what I have done."

Darian sat up and nodded. "Truthfully, Jena, I don't know that I will ever truly understand it. However I have missed you, and I can't lie, I have missed Tarius as well. I can accept the two of you together as long as she continues to make you happy." He looked at her and held out his hand as if to shake. "So, can we call a truce?"

Jena hugged her father. He cringed a little at the pain, but said nothing.

Across the deck Tarius saw them and smiled.

"This is a good thing?" Radkin asked at her shoulder.

"Aye... very good. A woman should never hate her father," Tarius said.

"Just because you put him in Kartik clothes does not make him a Kartik, my sister," Radkin said.

Tarius smiled at Radkin and playfully slapped the side of her face. "Ah, my friend, but it is the first step."

19

Darian ran up to Tarius, covered in Amalite blood. "I had forgotten the thrill of battle," Darian said. "How alive it makes you feel to kill other people."

"It damn near made you dead, old man," Eldred laughed.

"Yeah! Thanks for catching that blow," Darian said.

Eldred smiled. "We non-Katabull have to stick together."

Tarius patted Darian on the back and went to supervise the tying of the dead Amalites to the anchor. She helped hoist them over the side.

They split the Marching Night into two crews and headed back for the Kartik with Tarius's ship sailing just behind the other. They had just finished a meal of hard tack and stale biscuits, and Darian was walking the deck just enjoying the cool sweet sea breeze. He saw Eldred sitting on a bench and joined him there.

"I wanted to thank you again for saving my life," Darian said. Being forced into using it, he found that he was picking up the Kartik much faster now. Although they still laughed at him over his pronunciations, they at least understood what he was saying most of the time.

"That's what we do in the Marching Night. We watch ourselves and each other. If one man falls it makes a hole in our defense, and we all lose a friend, a brother or sister. I saved you today, and maybe tomorrow you will save me, and if you weren't there then I would die as well," Eldred said.

Darian nodded silently.

Eldred had a bottle he was drinking from, and he handed it to Darian. Darian took a sip and coughed. Whatever it was, it was sweet and hot and strong.

Eldred smiled at the look on Darian's face.

From the cabins below loud groaning wafted up into the night. Darian made a curious face. "What's that?"

Eldred looked somewhat embarrassed. "We just had a battle. Tarius and Jena always make love after a battle. That would be Jena."

"Oh," Darian said and took another drink of the liquor.

A louder, more gravely sound came from below, and Eldred smiled, "And that would be Tarius."

"Well good. Good for them," Darian said, nodding his head as he took another drink quickly.

The Island of Kartik loomed before them, and all hands were on deck preparing to dock. The other ship had just put in ahead of them. Tarius was standing at the helm looking through her glass at the dock. Suddenly she started jumping around excitedly. She waved and screamed out, "Harris! Arvon!"

Darian could just make out two blond-headed figures in the crowd waving wildly at the approaching ship. He had been told that the actual docking could knock you off your feet if you weren't prepared, so Darian had been hanging on for longer than necessary when the boat struck dock. Tarius was the first one off. Not even waiting for the gangplank to be set, she bounded over the side and onto the dock. Then she ran over and embraced first Harris and then Arvon, and then she hugged Harris again, before hugging a very obviously pregnant woman. Darian guessed correctly that this was Harris's wife.

The minute the gangplank was set the rest of the crew boiled off the ship to greet waiting friends and loved ones.

Jena came up and took hold of his arm at the elbow. "Come on, Father."

He nodded and walked with her down the gangplank. It took his legs a second to get used to stationary footing again, but then he looked around him in awe and wonder. It was like being on a different world. The plants, the trees, the people, the structures were all so different from the Jethrik. It truly was a beautiful and enchanting land.

"Jena!" Arvon screamed and snatched Jena's arm away from him with the force of his embrace.

Jena held him tight, glad to see him again, too. In many ways her bond to Arvon was as strong as Tarius's to Harris. For much the same reason, Harris had saved Tarius, and Arvon had saved her.

"Where is Dustan?" Jena asked looking around.

"Hurt," Arvon said briefly. Then answering the look of worry on Jena's face added, "Not badly, but he doesn't feel much like walking."

"What happened?" Jena asked.

Arvon smiled a little. "He got drunk and fell off his horse. Twisted his ankle."

He looked at the man that stood beside Jena recognizing him as a fellow countryman. Then he looked again and his eyes widened. "Darian?"

Darian smiled. "Yes, you traitor, it's me."

Arvon hugged him, and Darian hugged him back, glad to see his old pupil. "But... how?" Arvon wanted to know.

"Now that is a long story," Darian said.

Four Katabull men went onto the ship, and minutes later came back carrying the throne. They set it behind Tarius and looked at her expectantly.

Tarius sighed, made a face and sat down. Then the four men picked it up and started carrying it back to the village.

Harris staggered through the crowd, dragging Elise behind him, obviously looking for someone.

"Over here!" Jena screamed waving her hand in the air. Harris and Elise walked over and they exchanged hugs.

"How was the fighting?" Elise asked.

"It was good," Jena said. "The Amalite flat cannot fight the Katabull. There is too much inborn fear."

"I can't wait to get a sword in my hand again," Elise said.

Darian looked at the girl in disbelief. It simply was not the sort of thing one expected a pregnant woman to say.

"You! What the hell are you doing here!" Harris screamed, drawing steel. He was glaring at Darian, and if Darian moved forward even an inch, Harris's blade would be in his stomach.

"Harris, calm down," Arvon said patting him on the shoulder. "It's Darian."

"I know who it is! He had the power to sway the king in his dealings with Tarius, and he as much as ordered her killed," Harris said looking at Jena accusingly.

The racket on the dock suddenly ceased, and every eye turned on Darian.

"I'm... I'm sorry, Harris. I was wrong. I know that now," Darian said.

Jena gently took Harris's sword hand and pushed it down. Then she looked into his eyes. "If Tarius can forgive him, and I can forgive him, surely you can as well."

Reluctantly, Harris sheathed his weapon, and he looked Darian straight in the eyes. "It is in Tarius's nature to forgive you because she believes she wronged you, and you, Jena, did not see how she suffered, how she clung to life. I did. I won't kill you, old man, but I won't forgive you, either. Nor will I trust you." Harris took Elise's arm and walked away, hurrying to catch up to Tarius.

"He's very loyal to her," Darian said thoughtfully.

"Of course he is," Arvon said. "Until Tarius, who loved Harris? Until Tarius, who even talked to him like a human?" He quickly looked at Jena. "Except for you of course Jena."

"I treated him well, gave him food to eat, a warm bed, clothed him..." Darian said.

"In return he gave you his youth, and did all the crappy chores that no one else would do. Do you know how many times he cleaned out the academy privies? Because he knows the exact number. Did you know that on several occasions Tarius helped him with this task just so that Harris could have more time to train with her? Without Tarius, Harris would still be mucking out shit at the Academy, and he knows it. This, as much as anything else, is why he reacted to you the way he did," Arvon said.

Jena took her father's arm and together they started to walk off the deck. "But... according to our laws and traditions... I did well by the lad!" Darian said.

"There is a big difference between good and well," Jena said gently. "Tarius treats, and has always treated Harris as if he were no different from anyone else. No better and no worse. It is because of this that Harris has become the man that he is. Even when he knew what Tarius was he didn't hesitate to help her. He will never understand why any of us hesitated."

As they walked, the people reached out and touched Jena. It seemed everyone wanted to touch her. Darian thought this strange, but Jena seemed to take it in stride, so it must be some strange Katabull custom.

They caught up with Tarius at the great meeting hall. It was then that Darian noticed that not just Jena but Tarius and all of the Marching Night were being touched by the Katabull.

Jena released him and went to stand on Tarius's right hand side while Harris moved to stand on her left. Jena put a hand on Tarius's shoulder, and Tarius looked up at her and smiled. She covered Jena's hand with her own and seemed to be waiting for the crowd to quiet down on their own.

Arvon was standing next to him, so Darian took the opportunity to ask, "Arvon... why are the Katabull touching the Marching Night like that?"

"The Katabull believe that by touching someone who has recently had the blood of their enemies on their hands, they will be victorious when next they go into battle. The more people they believe you have killed, the more desirable it is to touch you. That's why Tarius, Radkin, Jena, Tweed and Rimmy get more attention than the others. People know of their legend, and know that they kill many Amalites in battle."

"Jena really is that good, isn't she?" Darian didn't know whether it was pride he felt or guilt. Perhaps if he had raised her right she would be home nursing babies now instead of paired with a woman, content to spend her days killing Amalites.

"Jena's very good, but to tell the truth at least half of the Marching Night are better. Jena is, however, the beautiful, exotic wife of their leader, and they just happen to like her," Arvon said with a smile.

"She's so different," Darian said. "So changed."

"It's true she's not the same person she was before Tarius made her a part of her life. No, she's not the same person she was, Darian. Not a naïve little girl. She has lived. Some of it has been very bad and some good. She's grown into a beautiful and powerful woman. Tarius, 'The Great Leader,' does very little without first talking it over with Jena. People trust Jean's council because she has become very wise in a very short period of time. Hardship has a way of doing that for a person. It also has a way of binding a relationship together."

"She seems so hard," Darian said. "So unforgiving. She had to beat me damn near senseless before she would even think to forgive me."

"She's not harder, Darian, just smarter. Less forgiving because she knows more about the world. Jena is a passionate woman. She loves passionately and hates in equal measure. Yes, Darian, Jena's different," Arvon smiled. "She's better."

Tarius didn't order the crowd to quiet down even when Jerrad came to fill her in on all that had happened.

"Yours was the only ship damaged in the storm," he reported.

"Well, that figures," Tarius said with a sigh.

With her spoken words the crowd quieted.

"As you can see by the number of vessels in the harbor, all of our ships were successful in bringing in at least one ship. The Orion, like your crew, has brought in two. All crews are currently at sea except yours. The crew of the Orion suffered the highest casualties, losing ten fighters in all." He went on with his report for several minutes, finishing with... "Queen Hestia has asked to be kept informed of your progress at all times, and I have sent heralds every three days at her request."

Tarius nodded. "You have done very well, Jerrad." She smiled at him. "OK, so if everything's fine, I'll just get back on my ship and..."

"Don't you dare," Jerrad said with a laugh. "There are several disputes which call for your attention."

Darian watched as the packs brought their disputes before Tarius. Nothing seemed very serious to Darian. Most were claims of petty thievery and disputes over who had the right to fish or hunt where.

"Why do they waste her time over such trivial matters? What of murder and rape, such crimes as those? Are they saving those for last when she will be too tired to decide?" Darian asked.

Arvon laughed. "Ah! Enter the world of the Katabull, my friend. We are a very ethical people, for whom such issues as petty thievery are anything but trivial. Where rights of hunting and fishing are all important. The Katabull are warriors who never fight amongst ourselves, and our original language didn't even have words for murder or rape. When the Katabull get mad enough to fight, we wrestle. The loser admits defeat, and we go on with life. In all the long history of the Katabull, no Katabull has ever murdered another, and no Katabull has ever raped another."

"But they are beasts! They turn into wild beasts!" Darian protested.

"Who hunt and fight our enemies but not each other. I think it's *because* of the Katabull that we do not commit violent crimes against each other—that link to the primitive, the knowledge that you are a power to be reckoned with. Perhaps it is because we have always had enemies from without that we have never fought among ourselves. I used to wonder why they called even a single Katabull, 'the Katabull,' and now I know. It is because every Katabull is connected. Every Katabull represents the whole people. It is for this reason that we never slay one another, because if you kill even one of us, it is as if you killed the whole nation."

"We..." Darian laughed. "You have lived among the natives too long, my boy. You are one of us, a Jethrik."

"Well actually, no I'm not. Tarius wasn't the only one who broke the academy rules," Arvon said with a broad smile. "I, too, am the Katabull."

Darian stood shaking his head in disbelief. "But how?" He looked around at the dark headed, dark skinned Kartik-looking Katabull all around him.

"The Katabull are everywhere, Darian. In the Kartik mix breeding has made them dark, and in the Jethrik mixed breeding has made them fair like me. Who knows? Perhaps there are as many Katabull in the Jethrik as there are here, and you don't know it because there we are treated like second class citizens, while here we are treated like gods," Arvon said. "Believe it or not, Darian, when you are here for awhile you will never want to go back to the Jethrik. Ever."

Suddenly the dispute behind them got heated.

"He stole my chickens," one man accused.

"Is that true?" Tarius asked.

"Yes... But he slept with my daughter," the other countered.

"Is that true?" Tarius asked the first man.

"Well, yes, but she is of age," he said.

"Where is the woman?"

"Here, Great Leader." The girl stepped forward.

"Did he make you a promise he didn't keep?" Tarius asked her.

"He made her no promises at all! That's my point," the father said.

"I asked her," Tarius said.

"He made no promises," she said.

"Did you want to make love with him, or did he coerce you?" Tarius asked.

"I wanted to."

"Was any commitment made because of it?" she asked.

"No."

"You! Give the man his chickens back. He has committed no crime against your family and should not be forced to pay restitution," Tarius said. Then turning to both the young man and the young woman said, "Both of you, either be more responsible with your couplings or do not involve your families. There is no crime against sex with consenting parties, however remember that we as a people do not condone promiscuity."

Darian nodded approvingly and said in a surprised voice. "She's very good at this!"

"Don't sound so surprised. Running a village isn't a whole lot different than running a war camp, and she did a damn fine job of that didn't she? I mean for a girl, of course."

Darian made a face when he realized Arvon was making fun of him, and Arvon laughed.

"She's very fair," Darian said.

Arvon's features turned dark. "Tarius was always fair. It was everyone else who treated her unfairly. Admit it, Darian. Tarius is as good as any man at everything, including being a mate to your daughter."

———•◆•———

The Amalites were never a very bright people. If they had been, they wouldn't have bought into a religion that promised so many things it could only deliver after a person was dead. They proved their stupidity now. They didn't know what was happening to their raiding ships, so they kept sending out more raiding ships to find out what had happened to the others—only to have them disappear as well.

The Katabull/Kartik navy was rapidly becoming a force to be reckoned with, and it didn't hurt that the Amalites were completely clueless. They could not conceive of an alliance with the Katabull, so they assumed all other humans were just as narrowsminded. Soon the new naval force had captured twenty-five Amalite ships. The next step was to re-work all the captured ships and turn them into a Kartik armada that no force on the planet would be able to stand against.

Six ships scoured the ocean, tricking and capturing yet more Amalite ships while some of the others were being refitted. Those that were ready simply stood down, waiting for the time that would soon be at hand.

Hestia summoned Tarius and the Marching Night to the castle. A great feast was laid before them, and as had become their custom they discussed business during the festivities.

Tarius leaned towards Hestia. "The time has come to strike their harbors and strike them hard." Tarius had made a rough map of the known world with gravy and bowls on the tablecloth. She pointed to the bowls on her "map." "They have ports here, here, here, here and here. We split our armada into five fleets, the largest one hitting Armond here, because it is the biggest port and well-fortified against attack. This is where myself and the Marching Night will strike. I will put ten Katabull onto each of the other ships in the Armada. We will strike them all at an agreed upon time on the same day. Most of their troops are busy fighting on the Jethrik front here, so the harbor towns will be under-manned, and there will be no chance of reinforcements. We must utterly destroy their ability to go to sea. But, Hestia, we must not stop there."

"What do you mean?" Hestia asked, curiously.

"Hestia, I do not believe you to be as short-sighted as Persius," Tarius said. She pointed to a spot on the "map". "See this spot? This is the spot on which the Jethrik almost lost the war. The Valley of the Arrow, so called because it was there that I caught an arrow in my hand that was fated to kill Persius, King of the Jethrik."

"Every one knows that, honey," Jena said, looking around her at

Hestia and making a face. Hestia smiled, and Tarius turned to see what Jena was doing. Naturally, Jena was doing nothing when Tarius looked, so Jena looked at Tarius innocently and shrugged.

Tarius turned back to Hestia, for the moment ignoring Jena. "It was here that I warned Persius about the Amalites, and he did not listen. Listen to me now, Hestia, if you have never heard my council before. Do not have us stop at the Amalite coast. The Amalites will never stop. They will never learn. They believe their gods command them to smite the unbelievers and they will never rest till everyone in the world worships as they do or we are all dead. So if we only pound them back, they will regroup, rebuild, grow and come after us again."

"So we will keep an armed armada in the harbors and make sure that they do not," Hestia said.

"We can't watch every inch of shore, nor can we keep them from buying or taking ships from others. They are obsessed with killing us, and will do whatever their priests tell them their gods ordered them to do. You haven't fought them face-to-face; I have, many times. When you see the hate and fear in their eyes, you know how evil are their beliefs and how relentless. Look at the Jethriks if you don't believe me. Twice they have had to push the Amalites back behind their borders, and now they have to do it again. Not once have the Jethriks moved to attack the Amalites. For that matter, neither have we. Yet despite the fact that they have over twice the land that the Jethrik has, and over five times what we possess, they will not stop attacking. I tell you they never will unless we utterly obliterate every fighting man and priest in their country. Let their civilian population live. Perhaps there is hope that without their leaders they will turn from this evil religion. But I implore you, Hestia, let us not stop at the shore. Let us press inward. Let each group of us leave waste the harbor towns and then run along the coast, meeting up here. Then let us crush the remaining Amalite army between our forces and that of Persius, King of the Jethrik."

"You would help Persius and his people after all that they have done to you?" Hestia asked in disbelief.

"I would use them to help us crush our only real enemies—the Amalites," Tarius said. "The Jethrik people have stupid, short-sighted rules and traditions, especially where it concerns women and the Katabull, but they are not an evil people. If we do not help them, the Amalites will over-run them, and then the barbarian kings and their countries will also fall. Then there will be no way that the Kartik can keep them at bay. Only if we help the Jethriks crush the Amalites shall we be utterly rid of them."

Hestia was thoughtful for a moment. When she spoke again it was with purpose. "And when we have crushed them utterly, then let the Jethriks take half of their land, and we will take the other half. We will both agree not to allow the Amalite religion to exist. We will destroy every temple, every sacred vessel, every religious text, and we will kill every priest. Then they will never be able to rise up and smite the world again," Hestia said.

Tarius looked at Hestia in delight. "You are brilliant, Hestia! Such a course could rid us of the Amalite menece forever!"

"We will give our people incentives to inhabit the land..." Hestia was on a roll.

By the end of the feast every one of their followers was drunk and in a festive mood, and Hestia and Tarius had conceived and carefully planned out the fall and total destruction of the Amalite Empire.

Hestia looked at Tarius. "So, will you let me ride with the Marching Night and help you command the army, or would you rather I took one of the other units in?"

"You will ride with us, and together we will make history," Tarius said.

It took time to load the boats, to prepare for the battle, and to gather enough supplies to feed, arm and care for an army of this size for an unknown length of time. They used the time to prepare themselves mentally and physically for the war ahead. They also used it to relax and be with their loved ones. Everyone knew there was a good chance that many of them would never see the Kartik again. They would all go, and they would all fight, and none doubted that they would crush the Amalites. However they knew that many of them would die in a foreign country without ever again seeing their mates, their children, or the land they were fighting for.

Tarius and Jena sat together on the Katabull throne watching Radkin play with two of her four children. She had borne two, and her mate had borne two. Rimmy was Radkin's children's father, and Radkin's mate, Irvana, had her children with Tweed, Rimmy's mate. Of the children's four parents, only Irvana was not going with them. These children could lose three parents in this war. These thoughts and more of the same were running through Tarius's head as she watched them play.

I ask people to go with me. To take up swords and go and fight a war that could conceivably get us all killed. Many of them will die. Children will lose parents, lovers will lose partners, parents will lose children, and there will be no homes among the Katabull where there will not be mourning. As a people we are just now starting to recover from the last slaughter. There are fewer of us than there are of any other people in the world. Yet a bigger part of our population is going than that of the Kartiks, or even the Jethriks. I will either lead my people to extinction, or at last make sure that we will be safe in the world. I have made the decision already; it is too late to pull back now. All I can do now is pray I've made the right decision for us all.

"What are you thinking?" Jena asked, leaning her head on Tarius's shoulder.

"That many of us will die," Tarius said morosely.

"Well that's very cheerful. Don't think like that, Tarius," Jena said.

"I must," Tarius said. "I must realize what I am asking my people to do, and I must realize that because they follow me many of them will die. I will lead all of them into battle, but some of them I will lead to their deaths."

"They go willingly, Tarius. You have forced no one to go, and you can't hold yourself responsible for every person who dies in this war. In war people die, you told me that, and everyone knows that. We do what has to be done," Jena said.

"I want you to stay here," Tarius said. "I don't want you with us at the front."

Jena laughed. "In other words, you're feeling guilty because everyone else is sending their loved ones into war, and you want to leave yours here where it's safe. Well, you can quit worrying, my love, because I *am* going. I wouldn't think of asking you to stay; you shouldn't think of asking me."

"Jena a battle—a skirmish—is not like a war," Tarius said. "You have never seen what happens when war is waged in the middle of a civilian population. We will be forced to attack whole villages in our first wave, and there will be civilian casualties. Men, women and children who had nothing to do with the Amalite war effort will be just as dead as the men carrying pikes and spears. Some of them, through no fault of their own, will catch stray arrows or run between two swordsmen while trying to flee. Others will decide to help defend their country, they'll grab sticks, pitchforks, or kitchen knives, and they can kill you as dead as any fighter. You don't have time to see whether they mean you harm or not; if they get close, you have to kill them. You may realize when you are pulling your sword free that you have just killed a man doing nothing more dangerous than trying to carry a child to safety. There will be rivers of blood and more bodies than you have ever seen. You will trample the bodies of your comrades beneath your horse's hooves or be as dead as they are. There is a stench to war. Rotting flesh, shit, vomit, entrails, and flies so thick you breathe them up your nose if you're not careful," Tarius told her. "That is my life, but it doesn't have to be yours. I don't want it to be yours."

Jena jumped up and stood in front of Tarius, glaring down at her. "Your life *is* my life. I will not say goodbye to you on the docks and wave as you sail off to war like I did when I was a good little Jethrik wife to Sir Tarius who wasn't yet The Black. I will go with you! I will never again be separated from you, left behind to wonder whether you are alive or dead. I will stab children by mistake, and have my horse trample my friends into the ground and breathe the stench of death and flies up my nose. It's my privilege as your mate to be as miserable as you are, and you'll not take it from me!"

Tarius laughed, then grabbed Jena by the wrists and pulled her down on her lap. She wrapped her arms tightly around her, resting her chin on Jena's shoulder. "Please, Jena..." She kissed the side of Jena's neck, and Jena tried to squirm away from her.

"Quit it! I'm trying to be mad at you," Jena said, but laughed in spite of herself. She slapped at Tarius's hands. "You really are awful. I swear, you are as bad as a Jethrik man sometimes the way you think you can boss me around."

The ball rolled into Tarius's legs, and then so did the young boy. He picked up the ball then looked up and realized who he had just run into. He bowed his forehead low, almost touching the ground. "I am sorry, Great Leader."

"Laz!" Tarius said, clicking her tongue and shaking her head. "What did I tell you?"

The boy looked confused; he was young—only six—and really didn't remember. He shrugged.

"I'm still Tarius, Laz," Tarius said with a sigh. "Don't bow to me. I'm no better than you are. Don't bow to anyone. No one is any better than anyone else. 'Leader' is my job, just a job. Part of my job says I have to sit in a big stupid chair and have people call me Great Leader, but you are part of my pack, and I am just Tarius to you."

"Yes, Great Leader," Laz said.

Tarius popped herself in the forehead with her hand. "Just... go play."

Jena laughed. "You should let them call you Great Leader if they want. It makes people feel better to think that someone else is in control of the big decisions. Especially the children. They want to look up to you."

"Let them look up to their own parents. I am a better fighter, but I'm no braver than any of them. Radkin or Rimmy, either one, would make just as good a 'Great Leader' as I do," Tarius said.

As if he'd heard his name, Rimmy came running up, stopping just short of running into them. Jena was up, expecting trouble, and Tarius was on her feet as soon as Jena was up.

"What's wrong?" Tarius asked.

"It's Elise, the baby's coming," he said out of breath.

Jena looked at Tarius. "It's too soon."

"Where are they?" Tarius asked.

"At the birthing hut," Rimmy said.

"Send for the witch Jazel. Tell her what is happening. Go at once," Tarius ordered. Rimmy took off running again, and Tarius took off in the direction of the birthing hut, changing into the Katabull as she went, her speed increasing with the change.

Radkin ran up to Jena. "Jena... what's going on?" she asked.

"Harris and Elise's baby is coming," Jena said.

"It's too soon," Radkin said. Jena nodded and ran in the same direction Tarius had gone.

Tarius burst through the door of the hut and was glad to see that besides the head birth attendant there were two others in attendance.

Tarius walked up and put a hand on Harris's shoulder, and Harris looked up at her with a terror in his eyes that he had never known in battle.

Elise was obviously in pain.

"Can you stop the pains?" Tarius asked the head birth attendant. "Keep her from having it yet?"

"We tried," he said, "but her water broke a few minutes ago, and the baby is coming."

Elise just cried. Tarius looked at her. "Nothing will happen to your baby, Elise. I won't allow it." Tarius sounded ridiculous, and she knew it, but Elise seemed to calm down immediately.

Tarius let go of Harris and pulled the attendant to the side. "Is it too early? Can the child live?"

"It is rare, Great Leader, but not unheard of. If the baby is breathing when it is born, it may live."

"I sent for the witch Jazel, but it will take her most of a day to get here," Tarius said.

"We will do everything we can," he said. Tarius nodded.

"It's my fault!" Harris screamed suddenly. "The child is deformed like me. He's dying because of me!"

To everyone's shock and surprise, Tarius walked over, took Harris by the collar, jerked him to his feet and dragged him from the hut. Outside she looked him straight in the eyes and slapped him hard. "Calm down! The child should be so lucky to be deformed like you. This is *not* your fault, and it's not Elise's fault. This sort of thing happens, that's all. You have to hold it together for her." Tarius hugged him quickly. "We will do everything we can do, Harris, and what you have to do is be calm and strong."

Harris nodded, and together they walked back inside.

Jena got there out of breath. She went to the other side of Elise's bed and took hold of the hand Harris wasn't holding. She said nothing, there was nothing to say. This whole thing reminded her a little too much of her own loss, yet she felt she had to be there for her friends.

About an hour later the baby was born, blue and not breathing. "I'm sorry," the attendant said with sadness.

"You give up too easily," Tarius said. With tears streaming down her face she pushed Harris out of the way and took the baby from the attendant. It was still attached to its mother by the throbbing umbilical cord. Tarius scooped the goo from the baby's mouth and nostrils, covered both with her mouth and breathed into him slowly. They all just watched her in awe, thinking her mad. "Get me a blanket." The attendant handed her one. Tarius wrapped the tiny baby in it and continued to do what she had been doing. Except now she also started rubbing the baby's chest with her thumb.

Elise was screaming and crying in grief, and Harris was trying to comfort her.

Jena put a gentle hand on Tarius's shoulder. Her tears rolled down her cheeks unchecked. "Tarius... the baby is gone. Let it go..."

"I am not crazy!" Tarius screamed. "I have seen Robert do this to wounded men on the front to bring them back." She continued what she was doing.

The baby made a tiny cry, so low it could hardly be heard, yet everyone in the room was suddenly quiet. Tarius held the baby upside down and slapped his butt. More mucus came from the baby's nose and mouth, and she quickly wiped it away with the blanket. The baby's color was changing from blue to pink as she watched. He was breathing, labored yes, but he was alive. Tarius carefully handed the baby to Elise, who looked at him and smiled through her tears. She still cried, but this time they were tears of relief and joy.

The birth attendant undid the blankets just enough to tie a string around the umbilical. "Do you want to cut the cord?" he asked Harris.

Harris looked from his son to Tarius. "I want Tarius to do it with her blade."

"I would be honored." Tarius pulled her blade and cut the cord where the birth attendant instructed.

"You must show me what you did, Great Leader," he said with admiration.

Tarius nodded silently and sheathed her sword. She wiped the baby goo and blood from her mouth with a towel one of the lesser attendants handed her.

Harris undid the baby's blankets and looked at his feet. "He's all right!" Harris cried. "He's tiny, but he's not deformed." Harris looked at Tarius. "How can I ever thank you, Tarius? You saved our son."

"Harris, you saved my life, remember?" Tarius said. "You owe me no debt; it is I who will owe you. Always."

"We shall name our son Tarius," Elise said. "It was you who brought Harris and I together, and you who breathed your very breath into him to give him life."

Harris nodded in an approving way. "If it's all right with you and Jena, Tarius."

"It is," Tarius said.

Jena nodded silently.

"I... I have to go now." Tarius stepped quickly from the hut.

Jena looked at Harris. "I better go check on Tarius. I am so happy for you all." She left to go after her mate. She found her a few feet away leaning against a tree with her hands on her knees and crying like Jena had never seen her cry before. Jena went to her and put an arm around her waist. "Tarius what's wrong? You saved him. He'll live now. I just know it."

"I don't know why I'm crying," Tarius cried. "Yes, I do. Your child—*our* child died because of me. Who was there to save *him*? Not me."

"Tragon killed our child, Tarius. You are no more to blame than I am. All I had to do was ask Arvon to take me to you, and he would have done so. But I was afraid, so I waited till it was too late. It was not to be, love," Jena said gently.

"I had just told them I wouldn't allow their child to die, but when I was standing there breathing into him and rubbing his chest I was just guessing. I had seen Robert do it, but that was on full-grown men. Not a tiny baby. And even with all Robert's skill, most of the grown men didn't live long. For a minute I was as sure as everyone else that the baby was dead, and that I had failed Harris. Harris, to whom I owe my life. It was just luck, and the will of the Nameless One that the baby started to breathe. Then Harris and Elise heap these honors upon me. There was only one other time in my life that I have felt as helpless and as truly frightened as when I was holding that tiny baby in my arms trying to breathe life into it. That was when I realized that Persius was going to expose me in front of you." She dried her face on the back of her hands. "He named his son after me. Me! And I owe *everything* to him."

"And he owes everything to you. So the two cancel each other out, and there is no debt between you. He knows how you feel about him, and you know how he feels about you." Jena smiled then and kissed the top of Tarius's head. "If it makes you feel any better, you can name our first son Harris."

Tarius smiled and stood up; she hugged Jena tight. "And I was just thinking how confusing it was going to be to have two of me running around."

The baby struggled that first night, but by noon the next day Jazel was there with her powders and her potions. Within hours the baby's breathing became more regular, his appetite increased, and his color improved.

Tarius invited Jazel to eat with them. She sat across the table from Tarius. "All right, so what is it you want now?" Jazel asked after they had finished their meal.

Jena laughed and started to clear away the plates.

"I want you to go to Amalite with us. To help us annihilate the Amalites," Tarius said. "Run a few stealth and silence spells, do a little medicine."

"I'll do it on one condition," Jazel said.

Jena didn't let her finish. "Tarius is not sleeping with Helen."

"Now damn it, Jena," Jazel said. "Put yourself in my position. How would you like to have a woman who was always lusting after another? If Tarius would just do her once and do a really bad job of it, slobber and fart maybe start talking about a beheading—Helen has this fear of being beheaded—my life could get back to what it once was."

"Sorry," Jena said.

"Then I'm not going," Jazel said crossing her arms across her chest.

"All right then," Tarius said.

"Over my dead body!" Jena screamed out angrily.

"Jena, we have to do what's right for our people. We all have to sacrifice. Of course I can't promise to do a bad job, because I am after all the Katabull." She looked at Jena with meaning, and Jena smiled.

"Yes, you are the Katabull," Jena said.

"What the hell has that got to do with anything?" Jazel asked.

"Sometimes when I'm... Well, you know doing it. I become the Katabull."

Jena looked starry eyed. "Does she ever!"

"After that, I really have no control over what I do sexually."

"It's amazing!" Jena moaned out.

"Wait a minute," Jazel said suspiciously. "Are you trying to scam me?"

"It's a little-known fact about the Katabull," Tarius said. "But I wouldn't worry, Jazel. I mean after all it's a one-time thing, and Helen does love you, doesn't she?"

"The last thing I need is you doing her so good I can never compete!" Jazel fumed. "OK, then here's my compromise. Whenever you are around Helen, you have to wear this special potion which will make you unappealing to her."

"Will it affect me as well?" Jena asked.

"No... All right, so it's not really a potion, it's just a fragrance Helen hates, but maybe it will do the trick anyway," Jazel said. She shrugged. "So, I guess I'm going to go fight your war with you."

20

Three weeks later, the Kartik armada set sail for the coast of Amalite. Hestia, Dirk and the royal retinue rode on the Silver Eagle with Tarius, Jena and the Marching Night.

Hestia was taking a sword lesson from Tarius on the deck. She had thought herself a fair swordswoman, but after four minutes of sparring with Tarius the Black, she felt inadequate and wondered why she hadn't stayed home in her castle where she was safe.

"She's very good," Darian said to Dirk.

"Tarius is trouncing her, so how can you tell?" Dirk asked with a laugh.

"By how long it's taking for Tarius to trounce her. There is no shame in losing a sword fight to Tarius. She's the best swordsman who ever lived," Darian said.

"You're her woman's father, aren't you?" Dirk asked.

"Yes," Darian said. "I once tried to have Tarius killed, did you know?"

"No, I didn't," Dirk replied.

"Well, I did. I was filled with a red rage and couldn't see past my own hurt and embarrassment. I thought I'd never get used to the two of them together. Now I can't imagine them being apart. They just seem to belong together."

"After the war, will you remain in the Jethrik?" Dirk asked curiously.

"No. If I live, I will go back to Kartik. Jena is there, and she tells me they'll start their family when they get back. I hope I live to tell my grandchildren stories about sitting on the deck of this ship heading for war with the Amalites, talking to the queen's consort."

Dirk laughed and nodded. "I hope we all get to tell stories to our grandkids."

Hestia held up her hand. "I must rest."

Tarius nodded. Hestia sat on a chair, and Tarius sat on the deck getting glares from every Katabull that saw her. She waved a flippant hand in the air, dismissing their disapproval.

"So, have I got time to learn everything about combat and strategy before we land and start fighting?" Hestia asked.

"I thought that's why you were riding with us," Tarius said with a smile. "The truth is you can only learn technique from practice. You learn warfare by fighting in it. You wanted to be Hestia the Warrior

Queen, so prepare yourself."

Hestia nodded. "I'd rather die being Hestia the Warrior Queen than live being Hestia the Dull," she said. "I was trained for battle all my life, yet I have never really crossed swords with anyone. I have never drawn my enemy's blood or had mine drawn. I have never watched my opponent's life drain from his body or wondered whether I was about to die. Look at you, Tarius. Your body is a map of scars telling where you've been and what you've done. Minstrels write songs about you and your adventures, and bards weave tales. There is no one in all the world who doesn't know who Tarius the Black is. I doubt the average Kartik in the street even knows my name let alone anything about me. I'm a good ruler, but a highly forgettable one. I don't want to be. I want passion; I want this." She flung her arms wide. "The sea wind blowing through my hair on a ship with the best fighting force the world has ever known going to do battle against our enemies with no idea of the outcome."

"War isn't romantic, Hestia..."

"Jena has already told me the little speech you gave her, so spare me, Tarius," Hestia said. "I know all the cons of going off to war. The gods know, my advisors have pointed them all out to me. Leaving my younger and dumber brother in charge while we're away, the very real possibility I'll be killed, and all the rest. I just don't care anymore. I know it's a terribly selfish thing for a monarch to say, but I want to have an adventure, to truly taste life. I want to do something that I want to do. This is something I want to do."

Tarius nodded. "Like me you were born to the sword."

"How can you say that after you just trounced me?" Hestia said in disbelief.

"Because I beat everyone," Tarius said smugly and jumped to her feet without using her hands. "I'm also the Katabull." She took off for the helm where Jena was standing looking out to sea.

Hestia watched her go.

"She's amazing isn't she?" Dirk said at Hestia's shoulder.

"She's like no one I've ever met," Hestia said. "She taught me more about fighting in a few minutes than I learned from all my instructors in twenty years."

"There is no one I have talked to that doesn't adore her. Yet she is blunt and uncultured and quite frankly a little scary if you ask me," Dirk said.

"Well, the Amalites don't like her, and neither does the Jethrik king," Hestia said. "At some point I will have to meet with Persius, and I haven't quite figured out how to handle that as far as Tarius is concerned. I mean Tarius is my ally; she's running the war, really. I'm just here for show. How do I force Tarius into a meeting with the man who betrayed and tried to kill her?"

"Could be a sticky situation," Dirk said.

Hestia nodded. "Surprising enough, I don't think Tarius would be the problem. Don't get me wrong, I don't think she'll ever forgive him, but she's obviously willing to overlook her personal feelings to go after the Amalites. Of course that only proves that she hates the Amalites more than she hates Persius. No. Tarius won't be the problem; Persius will be. I mean after all if I were him, I'd be scared to death of Tarius the Black."

The garrisons hadn't been finished when the Amalites started to attack in force. Thank the gods the villages had been armed and trained and were able to slow down the Amalite horde. The garrisons, even half-finished were better than nothing at all, but they were losing ground daily.

"By the gods!" Persius screamed. "Must this accursed woman haunt me all the days of my life with her curses?" He literally pulled at his hair. Then he glared at Hellibolt, who shrugged.

"Don't look at me. I told you she was right about the Amalites, but you wouldn't listen to me, either," Hellibolt said.

"What can we do now?" Persius walked over to the map and looked down at it. "They are everywhere like locusts, and we are spread ever thinner to cover their attacks."

Hellibolt looked at the map, then he sighed and took a deep breath. Admittedly, it didn't look good. "Tarius used to go into the camps as the Katabull the night before an attack. It gave us an edge."

"You knew! You knew all along that she was the Katabull!" Persius screamed accusingly.

"Excuse me," Hellibolt said raising a hand in an elaborate gesture. "The moment I first laid eyes on her I told you she was neither male or human. You ordered me not to ever say it again. Remember?"

"So I did," Persius sighed. "Perhaps we could call for the Katabull in our country to come forward to help us in our war effort. Perhaps..."

Hellibolt was shaking his head violently. "After what you did to Tarius, the Katabull have become more secretive than ever before. As for helping us, why would they?"

"Because they don't want the Amalites to win the war," Persius said. "The same reason that Tarius joined us in the first place."

"Won our war for us and was ordered killed by our king for her efforts. You won't get the Katabull to help you, Persius," Hellibolt said. "I wouldn't help you if I were them. They can always go to the Kartik. It's a wonder to me that any of them have stayed here at all."

"What then? We're running out of forces, and I'm running out of ideas," Persius said.

Hellibolt looked thoughtful. Suddenly he snapped his fingers together. "I've got it! We don't have to have the Katabull, we just have to make the Amalites *think* we do. We can use the same underhanded tactics Tarius did." He started pacing then and mumbling to himself. "Yes, it just might work."

"What might work?" Persius asked.

"We put a glamour on some of our better fighters to make them look like the Katabull. We send them in under cover of night. I will put a stealth spell on them, and they shall travel silently through the camp, slitting the throats of the Amalites in their beds. When they are detected they will run around like mad men killing anything that moves and then retreat," Hellibolt said. "This is what Tarius did that gave us an edge in battle."

"She slit the throats of sleeping men?" Persius asked in disbelief.

"If you mean to kill a man, why does it matter how you kill them? The only ethics that can be applied is whether you choose to kill them slowly and with pain, or quickly. We both know what you choose when given a choice, so who are you to be judgmental?" Hellibolt said.

"Our men will never agree to this," Persius said.

"They will. They know how badly we are losing. They know the cost if we lose this war to the Amalites—death or slavery to the priests of the Amalite—no one wants that. They will do what has to be done," Hellibolt said. "I also suggest you get in touch with the barbarian kings and beg for their support. They are good fighters, and they no doubt realize the stakes if we fail," Hellibolt said.

Persius nodded. "We will put your plan into action, but I'm afraid our best efforts will only mean we will not be defeated as quickly. I have doomed my country and my people to death and tyranny, just as Tarius said I would."

Hellibolt was silent.

"You know what I have said is true," Persius said, correctly reading the wizard's silence. He laughed almost hysterically. "You want to know the thing that haunts me most, Hellibolt?"

"What's that, Persius?"

"I never loved any woman as I loved Tarius. When I thought her a man, I thought my feelings for her sick, perverse, and I locked them away. I thought I was going mad. When I knew she was a woman, I knew I loved her. But because she was queer, I knew she would never love me. It was the worst of everything. She had fooled me into believing she was a man, but as a woman she would never return my feelings. That's the real reason I wanted her dead, Hellibolt. The real reason I wanted her to suffer. I was a blind fool, not once, not twice, but over and over again. Every day is for me a private hell, and the thing that makes it unbearable is that I know I have done it to myself. I know I deserve it."

"She's not dead yet, Persius," Hellibolt said, moving to put a hand on Persius' shoulder. "While you are both still living, there is yet a chance that you might redeem yourself. Not just in her eyes, but in your own as well."

Persius pulled away from him and walked to the window. "There are some crimes for which one dare not ask forgiveness. Such are the crimes I have committed against Tarius the Black."

―・◆・―

The ships attacked the docks at Armond. At approximately the same time their ships hit every other harbor in Amalite. Tarius's army poured out of their ships, some before the gangplanks were dropped. The fighters on horseback boiled up out of the belly of the ship over the gangplanks and into the unsuspecting harbor towns. Meeting little resistance, the Katabull and Kartik armies laid waste to the Amalite seaports.

Hestia and Dirk followed directly behind Tarius, Jena, and Harris, who rode behind a line of walking shield men. Behind Hestia were the rest of the Marching Night and the queen's guards with Arvon in command.

Hestia had tried to prepare herself, but Tarius was right. There was no way to prepare. Their crossbowmen quickly took out the bowmen in the watchtowers, stopping the hail of arrows falling on them from above, but not before three arrows had landed in the small shield Hestia had strapped to her arm. Not before several of their men were wounded.

Tarius called a charge, and their shieldwall opened for them to charge through. They were engaged immediately. The men tried to make a wall around her, to protect her, but the Amalites boiled in on them. She had killed her third man before she realized she had killed her first. All around her the Katabull were changing. They didn't do so before because they didn't want the bowmen to target the Katabull. The Amalites turned and fled in terror before the might of the Kartik/Katabull army that had landed in six ships on their shores. Not one escaped. Terrified civilians ran in every direction, and some—as Tarius had foretold—were mowed down, mistaken for fighters or in the way of a blow meant for one.

Hestia saw Dirk to her right, but couldn't keep up with where everyone was or what they were doing. Tarius was screaming orders that were echoed through the ranks, and it was all she could do to try and do what she thought Tarius was commanding her to do. It was every bit as brutal, every bit as bloody, and every bit as frightening as Tarius had said it would be.

And Hestia felt really alive for the first time in her life.

―・◆・―

Darian was working hard at keeping up with the rest of the ranks. It wasn't easy because he'd taken an arrow in his left arm early in the battle. Eldred stayed back fighting with him, helping him. In front of him he saw Radkin come off her horse at the end of a spear point. She stumbled, grabbed the spear shaft and dragged the Amalite from his horse. She then pulled the spear out and spun it around, killing the man with his own weapon. But she was hurt and afoot, and the Amalites were all around her. Darian forced his horse through them, slinging his sword wildly without really thinking about what he was doing. When he reached Radkin, he leaned down and grabbed her with his wounded arm. With her help he dragged her onto his horse behind him. Then he took off as quickly as possible to get back to help Eldred.

"Thanks," Radkin said in his ear.

"Are you hurt?" Darian asked.

"Didn't pierce my armor. Might have cracked my ribs, but I'll be fine." She slung her blade into a Amalite who was running towards them with his sword raised and hit him so hard she separated his head from his shoulders. "I feel better already."

"Darian! Eldred!" Arvon screamed from somewhere out of sight. "Go right!"

They did, and were soon joined by the queen's guard's shield wall.

"This is where I get off," Radkin said in his ear. She jumped to the ground, sheathed her sword, grabbed a discarded spear, and from the safety of the shield wall she started to pick off the Amalites.

Darian sheathed his sword and quickly reached up and broke off the head of the arrow where it stuck out. Then he pulled the shaft from his arm. He ignored the pain, pulled his sword again and kept fighting.

———•◆•———

It was late that afternoon before the battle was over. It was only then, looking around at the bodies, at the blood that covered her hands and body, that Jena was fully aware of the horror of what they had done. It was a bloodbath. The civilian population that hadn't been killed in the massacre had run into the woods to hide. She wanted a bath, and she wanted it now. She looked till she found Tarius, then cringed. Tarius was still in Katabull form and covered in blood from head to toe. Tarius had wiped the blood off her face with her hand, leaving her face a smear of red. Hestia stood beside her covered in almost as much blood and grinning like a devil.

Jena walked towards the assembled group and realized they were the leaders of the different troops, no doubt talking further strategy.

They had a map spread out on what was left of a wagon, and Tarius was talking. Jena walked up, wrapped her arms around Tarius, and lay her head on Tarius's back—the only part of her body that wasn't covered in blood. Then she just lay there silently. Tarius patted her hand reassuringly, but couldn't stop to comfort her in the middle of a strategy meeting, and Jena knew this.

"First we have to take care of our wounded. We have only ten, two of them serious," Tarius said. "Unfortunately both of our severely wounded are Katabull, so the sooner we can get them to Montero the better."

The other leaders quickly gave their tolls. In all, there were twenty-five casualties and thirty seriously injured.

"We will send the wounded back on one of the ships as planned," Hestia said.

Tarius nodded. "We will put the ships out in the harbor close enough that they can be here in minutes if we need to beat a retreat, but too far out to be easily boarded by Amalites. Fifty fighters will stay here in Armond burning the town and the dead..."

"Hold up, Tarius," Hestia said thoughtfully. "Let us not be too hasty in burning the buildings. If we leave a force to make sure the Amalites can't come in here and take over, we may be able to use the buildings in future. However if such an attack should come, and it looks as if our forces are being over run, let us then burn the town to the ground. The smoke of the burning will be a warning to us that all is not right."

"Good plan, Hestia. All right. We can make the civilian population carry their dead outside the town and stack them. That should serve as a warning to any Amalites who might think of riding in here," Tarius said. "We will stay here tonight and move out at first light as we planned. We will meet the other troops here, and together we will march to the Jethrik front."

"Tarius," Hestia cleared her throat a little. "Perhaps we should meet with the Jethrik leaders here at our rendezvous point. It is just inside Jethrik territory. They will know where the Amalites are and where we can do the most good. With their knowledge we will better our chances at success and stop them from killing our men by mistake."

Tarius took a deep breath and was silent. Jena, however, was not.

She walked around from behind Tarius. "You expect Tarius to meet with Persius and his lot to discuss strategy? Have you gone mad, Hestia?"

Tarius put a hand on Jena's shoulder. "She's right. It's the only way. Put us all together and let us discuss how best to kill the Amalites. I will do it. The real problem is that Persius will not meet with me if he knows it is me. Therefore, we must very carefully word our invitation so that he doesn't know it's me he is meeting with."

Jena stomped off in a huff. She went to find their wounded and see if she could help. She was surprised to see her father there among them. "Father," she said kneeling beside him. "Are you all right?"

"He's fine," Jazel answered before Darian could. "Didn't any one of you morons listen to my incantation? I specifically said 'If you do not wish to die, do not look into the sky.' Do I have to spell it out for you people? Do I have to specifically say, 'Don't look at the archers?' The specifics of the spell are that they can't get a good bead on you unless you make eye contact. There's no sense in having me along if you don't listen," she grumbled as she tended to Radkin's wound.

"You all right, Radkin?" Jena asked.

"Cracked ribs—that's all. But I'd be dead if it wasn't for your father," she said.

"It wasn't anything really," Darian said, blushing and looking at his feet.

"And with an arrow through his arm no less!" Radkin said.

"Wouldn't have had an arrow in his arm if he had listened to the spell," Jazel harrumphed. "I noticed that our good queen had three arrows sticking in her shield as well, so I guess this stupidity spans the classes."

Darian looked at Jena. "What about you, Jena? Are you all right?"

"It's a little overwhelming, but I'll be all right. Right now I'm more upset with what the Queen and the 'Great Leader' are discussing. They want to meet with Persius, and they want Tarius to be there," Jena said.

"I guess it makes sense that they would have to get together. Still, I can understand your misgivings," Darian said.

"Misgivings!" Jena screamed. "I *hate* him. I'm afraid he'll try to trick us to get at Tarius. I don't trust him."

"Jena, you don't have to trust him. Tarius can out-think and out-fight him in her sleep. If he wants to do her ill, he won't get the chance. There is nothing to worry about."

Jena nodded then asked,"Are you in much pain?"

"No... Ow! Damn!" Darian screamed out suddenly.

"Damn it!" Jazel screamed, throwing her hands in the air. "You have blown another of my spells."

"Word from the front, Sire," the court herald announced.

"Don't just stand there! Send him in." Persius steeled himself for still more bad news.

The herald ran into the throne room out of breath and knelt at the king's feet.

"What is it?" Persius asked impatiently.

"My king, word has come from our spies. The Kartik and Katabull armies have launched an attack against the Amalite seaports. All the ports have been destroyed, and they are moving inland destroying every Amalite stronghold they cross."

"Rise. Do we know who is in command of these armies?" Persius asked.

"They say it is Queen Hestia herself, and the Great Leader of the Katabull People who are in command. That the armies are huge and well armed and supplied," the herald answered.

Persius looked at Hellibolt. "It is good news, Sire. This may be just the help we need."

"Prepare my carriage and my guards. It is time for us to go to the front, Hellibolt."

They were three days out when they spotted a rider coming up fast. When he got close, they recognized him as a Kartik warrior wearing garish Kartik colors and black armor with silver studs. He jumped from his horse and started forward at a strong pace, leading his horse.

"Halt!" Derek cried out. He and his partner, Heath, were now in the king's guard, and Derek was the captain of this expedition.

"Do not try to stop me. I mean no harm. I am on my way with a message from my sovereign, Queen Hestia. It is to be delivered directly to King Persius," he said in broken Jethrik.

"Hold here for a moment."

The man stopped, and Derek rode back to the king's carriage. He relayed what the man had told him, and to Derek's astonishment, Persius stepped from the carriage and walked directly up to the young man with Hellibolt close behind him.

"I am King Persius, and I am on my way to the front. What message have you for me?" he asked carefully.

"Good Queen Hestia and the Great Leader of the Katabull nation do send this message. 'We have already taken hold of all Amalite seaports and are carving our way through their land. We wish to form an alliance with you that will serve all of our people. We will meet you in four days' time at Star Point. There we will discuss how best to fight the war against the Amalites.'"

"They wish to be our allies, then," Persius said.

"No, they wish you to be theirs," the man said with a smile.

"What is your name?" Persius asked.

"My name is Rimmy, and you must not detain me, for I am needed at the side of my leader," Rimmy said.

"Wait! I must ask you this one question before you depart. Is Tarius the Black amongst you?" Persius asked.

"I am assigned to my leader, and my leader's pack, and know nothing of other units," Rimmy answered. "Now I must go."

Persius watched him go. He led his horse a bit away from them before he jumped on and rode away. Some Kartik courtesy, he supposed.

"What do you want me to do, Sire?" Derek asked.

"Press on to Star Point. I really don't see what other choice we have."

"But what of Tarius the Black?" Derek asked.

"What of her? We can not risk shunning the Queen of the Kartik and the King of the Katabull Nation because we are afraid we might run into Tarius the Black."

Any Amalite stronghold that fell between the Kartik/Katabull army and their destination was utterly obliterated. Kartik scouts were the best, and no unit came up on an Amalite stronghold unprepared.

All five troops met at Star Point with few, or in the case of the Marching Night *no* further casualties, and all had destroyed their given ports and killed many Amalites along the way as well. Two troops had burned their ports to the ground before getting orders to the contrary, but everything else was going as planned.

When their spotters sighted the Jethrik king's procession, they prepared to greet their visitors.

Persius got out of his carriage and rode his horse with only minimal armor, a sign of good faith on his part. Kartik soldiers came out to help them with their horses and gear, showing that Kartik hospitality was as good as rumor said it was.

The man they had met on the road before, Rimmy, came to greet them.

"Queen Hestia and the Great Leader will see you now," he said.

Persius wasn't used to being summoned this way, but swallowed his pride and put his entourage together. In a few minutes he and his people followed Rimmy. He walked in front, flanked by Derek on his right and Hellibolt on his left and the others followed with all the pomp and circumstance they could muster on such short notice. As they walked through the camp, the Kartik people moved aside forming a line on either side of them, and Persius realized it must be some sort of custom. It was strange—like walking into a sea of people and then having it part before him. He was sweating and realized he wasn't looking in front of himself, but in every other direction. He was searching the crowd, looking for Tarius the Black.

Finally the crowd parted for the last time. He heard Derek gasp beside him, and his head snapped forward. The Kartik queen and the Katabulls' "Great Leader" sat before him. The queen was a tall, dark Kartik woman. She wore the same gaudy gambeson and black leather armor as her people, but hers was of a finer quality and there was a jewel-encrusted gold crown on her head. Hestia was a breathtakingly beautiful woman, but that was not the reason Derek gasped.

Sitting to Hestia's right on the Katabull throne was Tarius the Black. She was wearing much the same armor as the rest of the army, but hers—like the queen's—was of a finer quality. Her pauldrons and knee cops were shaped like skulls that seemed to glare mockingly up at him. Except for the fact that she was now obviously a woman and the multiple piercings, she really hadn't changed at all. He thought about his own reflection these days. No trauma had been visited upon him. No arrow had invaded his body nor sword cut his flesh, yet in the last six years he had aged twenty. While Tarius had aged not at all.

Jena stood on her right hand and Harris on her left, both also bearing the signs of power and authority afforded them in the form of gold rings and better armor. Tarius glared at him with utter contempt, but it was the looks he got from Jena and Harris that made his blood run cold. Looks of pure hate and utter loathing.

"What is all this?" Persius demanded, waving a hand in Tarius's direction.

Hestia answered him in surprisingly good Jethrikian. "I knew you would not come if you learned that the Great Leader of the Katabull people, my trusted ally and war lord, was none other than the woman you ordered killed," Hestia said. "I also thought that seeing as you have little if any respect for women, especially women in authority, that you would be more likely to come if you believed you were being summoned by at least one man," Hestia answered.

Persius noticed to his disbelief that the queen's own husband stood at her left hand with nowhere to sit, while her champion stood on her right.

Persius' own throne was carried forward, and he sat down heavily.

Tarius was still silent.

"Now is not the time for personal whims or grievances," Hestia said. "We all have one enemy. An enemy who will never rest as long as even one fighting man among them lives. As long as even one of their children follow their gods. Are we all agreed?"

"Yes," Persius said grudgingly. He hated to admit to Tarius's face that she had been right.

Tarius just nodded silently.

"It is my plan to take the land of the Amalites and split it evenly between your country and mine. We will enter into a solemn pact that we shall not allow the teaching or worshipping of the Amalite gods. Those who are caught in any such practice are to be punished by death—no exceptions. Tarius and I are in agreement on these points," she said. "Are they agreeable to you as well, Persius?"

Persius thought about it a minute then nodded. "It seems a good plan."

"Then all that is left is to plan strategy," Hestia said.

Persius nodded. Suddenly, Persius could stand her silence no longer. He glared across the empty space between he and Tarius. "Aren't you going to say anything?"

Tarius looked at him and smiled a sadistic smile. "What would you have me say to you? That I was right about the Amalites, and that you were wrong? That all this death, all this blood being shed now is your fault? That I find myself in the uncomfortable position of being allied with the person I hate most in this world? You know all that, so what's the point of rehashing it? Unlike you, I do only what is best for my people. I will put aside my feelings for you to do that, but know this Persius. I will be watching you." She stood up then.

"If you mean to kill me, do it now and release me from your awful curse!" Persius cried out getting to his feet as well.

Tarius smiled still larger. "I have no desire to kill you, Persius. Even if I did, a promise I made to one whom you take for granted stops me from doing so. Why would I kill you when living seems to cause you nothing but pain?"

They poured over the map. Tarius, Hestia and the rest of the Kartik leaders told what they knew of Amalite positions, and Persius, Derek and his men told what they knew. As they talked over positions and strategies, Tarius seemed to forget that he was her hated enemy, and just talked to him as she did the others. Jena, however, never once quit glaring at him, and neither, for that matter, did Harris.

Jena and Harris both stayed close to Tarius. In fact, Jena made sure that she and Tarius were in body contact at all times. Hard to believe that she had forgiven Tarius so completely. That she seemed to be more in love with her now than she had ever been before.

"We will bottleneck them and drive them into the field of the Battle of the Arrow," Tarius said. "You will deploy all your troops there."

"Why there? So that you can even be right about the very spot in which we fight them?" Persius asked hotly. "Why not the Valley of Grudon or the Plain of Tureen?"

"Where would you rather fight? On a battlefield where you have won, or on one where you have lost?" Tarius asked him, not looking up from the map.

"If you drive a defeated people into a battle on the very place they lost so horribly before, they will have no morale left," Hestia said. "Besides, it's the most logical place to make our final assault. That's why the Amalites chose it as the site from which to launch their campaign the last time you fought them."

Persius sighed and then nodded, admitting that on even this point they were right. Battle plans and strategies were hashed and rehashed until late into the night, but all the big decisions had been settled in a little less than an hour.

Persius couldn't sleep. Not too unusual, he hadn't had one decent night's sleep since he'd shot Tarius with that arrow. He wanted to sleep again. He needed to talk to Tarius. He wanted to try and apologize to her, but he couldn't have done that in front of everyone else and he didn't really know where to start. He felt the words would come when he saw her. What he really wanted was for Tarius to let him off the hook. To say that she forgave him for all that he had done. To say that she was partly, or even mostly to blame.

It wasn't hard to find the Marching Night's encampment, not with their skull banners and brightly colored flags. Getting in was another issue.

The man stepped in front of him, sword drawn and ready.

"I am Persius, King of the Jethrik. I am alone and unarmed. I wish to speak to her royal majesty, Tarius the Black," Persius stated.

The man laughed and held his sword up higher. He said something that sounded like a curse and pointed Persius back the way he had come.

"Now see here..."

"Are you insane, Persius?" a sleepy, half-dressed man asked.

Persius looked up at the man in shock. "Darian! Is that you?"

"Yes," Darian answered simply.

"We found your horse in Wolf Harbor. We thought you'd been killed and rolled for coin. How..."

"It's a very long story." Darian talked to the guard in Kartik, and he lowered his sword. Then Darian walked up to Persius, took him by the arm and led him a little away from the Marching Night's encampment. "OK... Walking through the Marching Night's camp at night alone, explaining that you are, well, who you are, and that you are looking for Tarius? Not your brightest moment. While Tarius is bound by oath not to kill you, none of them are, and they are very loyal... insanely loyal to her. Oh, and by the way, they hate you! You are the villain in their favorite story; the boogey-man that frightens their children."

"Darian, I ask again... What are you doing here?"

"OK. The short version. I went to Wolf Harbor looking for clues about Tarius, and therefore Jena. I ran into the Marching Night at a pub..." The short version was still very long. "... and so now I'm riding with the Marching Night. And no offense, Persius, but I intend to stay with them, and if I'm lucky enough to live I'll go back to the Kartik."

"I don't understand. Your daughter seems more taken with Tarius than ever, and after Tarius broke into your home, killed Jena's husband and kidnapped her!" Persius said.

Darian laughed nervously. "Well, that isn't exactly what happened. Actually, Jena killed Tragon and ran off with Arvon and Dustan to join Tarius in the Kartik. Seems Jena not only doesn't mind that Tarius is a woman, but actually prefers her that way."

"You lied to me, Darian," Persius said in disbelief.

"What was I supposed to do? Tell you my daughter had killed her husband and fled to be with your enemy?" Darian asked.

Persius sighed. "Tarius wasn't my enemy until I made her one." He found a rock, sat down and rested his head in his hands. "I wish I could take it all back. I wish I could go back in time and wipe it all away, but I can't. I want to apologize to Tarius."

"That's very noble, Persius, but Tarius is a person of action. Words mean very little to her, and I doubt there is any deed you could do that would win her forgiveness. She forgave me, but I neither revealed her to Jena nor shot the arrow into her. Do yourself a favor; go back to your camp and do not stray. There isn't a man or woman among the Marching Night or the Katabull Nation that wouldn't like to bring your head to Tarius on a pike," Darian said.

Persius nodded and stood up.

"I'll walk you back to your camp, just to be on the safe side," Darian suggested.

On the outskirts of the camp, Darian turned to walk back.

"Darian?" Persius called after him.

"Yes?" Darian asked turning to face him.

"Would you at least give her my message? Would you tell her that I know now that I was wrong. That I know it's not enough, but that I truly am sorry. That I wish her only the best," Persius asked.

"I'll tell her." Darian bowed deeply and walked away.

Persius went back to his carriage and lay down. He tossed and he turned, even more restless than he had been before. Hellibolt appeared seemingly out of thin air, sitting on the end of Persius' bed. Persius all but jumped out of his skin.

"Hellibolt! What in the gods' good names are you doing?" Persius screamed.

"Bringing you good news, but if you don't want it..." He raised his hands as if to snap his fingers and disappear.

"No, no! Please. I could use some good news," he said quickly.

"I have had a vision. In battle shall come your hour of redemption."

"What do you mean?" Persius asked.

"My words are clear. You must not hesitate. The moment will be fleeting, and if you miss it, then things will continue as they have been, and nothing will change," Hellibolt said.

"How will I know the moment?" Persius asked.

"You'll know it when it comes, and you must not hesiate even for a moment," Hellibolt said and then vanished again.

His words did nothing to help Persius sleep.

21

For six weeks the Kartik and Katabull army pressed the Amalites from the north while the Jethrik forces pressed them up from the south, pushing them east along the border. Finally they forced them into the valley of the Battle of the Arrow. The Amalites were badly out-classed and out-numbered now.

By the time they reached this point, Hestia was commanding her own forces, taking the left flank, while Arvon and his unit took the right.

The Jethrik line was still intact, but was slowly and steadily being pushed back. Just as Persius was sure they could hold no more, over the hills behind the Amalites came a solid wall of shields. Directly behind it were horsemen, so many that they seemed endless, and everywhere you looked there was a Katabull. Suddenly, the Amalites were being squeezed from front and rear. With the plateau on one side and the river on the other, they were left with no room to retreat. Those who remembered the Battle of the Arrow knew this formation. They'd been up against it before. It meant that Tarius the Black was in command, and she didn't believe in letting anyone retreat and escape from a battle alive. The Amalites were desperate and petrified.

Tarius gave orders to the whole Kartik/Katabull army, and her orders were screamed through the ranks from one unit to another.

Persius watched in glee as the Amalites were mowed down before the might of the Kartik army. He pressed his troops forward hard to make sure there was no chance for the Amalites to break through his ranks and escape. This time, there would be no Amalite survivors. No peace talks. No politics.

They were winning easily with very few causalities, and then like a whisper in the wind Tarius heard her name being screamed throughout the Amalite ranks. Before she had a chance to figure out what they had in mind, every Amalite warrior seemed to turn towards her and the Marching Night. Then they were running at them like a wave across the field. They knew her tactics, knew that she was blocking their retreat, and they were just desperate enough to try to get through her.

"Harris!" she screamed. He rode up beside her fast. "Take Jena, Hestia and the Marching Night and retreat; I will guard your back."

Harris looked at the wave of men and horses rushing towards them. "I won't leave you, Tarius."

"I would do it for you!" Tarius screamed. "Now go!"

He nodded and reluctantly turned, grabbing hold of the reins of Jena's horse.

"Marching Night! Retreat! Retreat!" Tarius called. She looked at Radkin who had moved closer to her. "I said go."

"You can't hold them yourself." It was Darian who spoke from her left-hand side.

She looked around her, and ten of the Marching Night had stayed to fight with her, knowing it meant they would probably die.

Tarius growled. "Then let's go after them. Charge!"

They charged fearlessly towards the wall of soldiers that came at them, and about a third of the Amalites broke and ran the other way, afraid to face the rabid-acting Katabulls and their legendary leader.

When they had beat their retreat, Jena looked quickly around. When she saw where Tarius was, she started to ride back, but Harris still held her horse's reins. Jena realized then what Tarius had done.

"No!" she screamed and tried to get her reins away from Harris.

"Be still. We have to think this out. We must go where we can do the most good. Arvon! Where is Arvon?" Harris screamed.

"He's with Tarius!" Hestia screamed. Tarius was deeply entrenched, unable to lead the army, and Hestia suddenly realized what that meant. She was in charge. "Rutson! Bring your troop right! Kartina! Bring your troop left!" she screamed and her orders were screamed throughout the ranks.

"Harris! Where do we go?" Hestia asked.

Harris looked quickly at the battle. "We go back the way we came and attack the Amalites at Tarius's back. "They won't expect it, and it just might work. Our exit will be clear if we must retreat again."

"Then let's go!" Jena said, giving Harris a heated look. Harris gave her back her reins, and they rode in.

———•◆•———

"What the hell are they doing?" Persius asked realizing they suddenly had no opponents. He rode up onto a knoll despite the protests of his guards, so that he could get a better look. He saw then what was going on. The Amalites were leading a full-fledged attack on the Marching Night. The Marching Night was blocking their retreat, and the Amalites were desperate. If they could get through the Marching Night, they could escape with their lives.

Persius knew then that the moment was at hand. "Come! We must save the Marching Night!" He took off ahead of the others, running into the battle straight for Tarius and her people. His men did not hesitate to follow their king.

Eldred went down, a sword blow to the head killing him almost instantly. Tweed was not far behind him, though he fought till his last breath. Tarius knew they had met their end. Arvon on her left side now looked at her.

"We aren't going home," he said slicing into an Amalite and killing him.

"Neither are they," Tarius swore through clenched teeth.

They were being consumed in a wave of Amalites. Darian was torn from his horse by the force of the spear that hit him in the chest; he disappeared under the horses' thundering hooves. Soon only Tarius, Arvon and Radkin were left, and then a spear blow knocked Tarius from her horse.

She went into a Katabull rage, running into the Amalites deciding to take as many of them with her as she could. She had just pulled one from his horse and slit his throat. She looked up in time to see a blade rushing at her head, and she dodged it, throwing the body she held into the path of the blade. A spear came at her from the other side, and she spun her sword quickly, cutting the head from the shaft. But this time the swordsman's blade was too close. She swung back quickly, but knew she wouldn't make the block, and if she rolled to the ground she'd wind up under a horse. This was it. The killing blow that she wasn't going to catch. She saw his blade and hers as if in slow motion, as if for a few moments all time slowed down. Then suddenly the Amalite's blade stopped, wobbled and fell, followed closely by its wielder. When he fell, she looked up. There sat Persius astride his horse with his bloody sword in his hand. He smiled at her, and she smiled back, never happier to see anyone in her life. She nodded her thanks, then she grabbed the dead Amalite's horse as it was closer than her own and jumped into the saddle. From here she could see what had happened. Persius had called his forces to her aid, and the Marching Night had come from the other side. Radkin and Arvon were still alive and still on horseback. They looked at her and seemed to breathe a sigh of relief before moving to either side of her.

The battle moved away from them, and Jena saw her father lying on the ground. She reined her horse in and dismounted, kneeling by his side.

"Father! Father!" Jena cried out.

He opened his eyes and looked at her. There was an Amalite spear sticking out of his chest and blood running from his mouth. "I guess I won't be going back to the Kartik with you after all," he said.

"Yes, you will," Jena cried. "You have to."

"No," he coughed. "I won't. She was going to die to save you, you know that don't you? I couldn't let my devotion to you be any less."

The light left his eyes. She had seen it before and knew what it meant. "No!" she cried out.

An Amalite had gotten separated from his unit and had played dead. He saw Jena and thought her an easy target, so he got up and ran at her. She jumped to her feet in one fluid motion and drove her sword in just beneath his ribs, pushed up and twisted. Just the way Tarius had taught her to do. She pulled her sword out, ran and jumped on her horse. Then she took off to join the Marching Night.

Seeing that Tweed was dead, Rimmy had become reckless, running away from their unit, and just asking to be killed. Radkin saw him go and raced after him. She dove into the fight beside him, bettering his odds. "What are you trying to do, you fool?" Radkin screamed, the tears streaming down her face. "Leave our children fatherless?"

Rimmy seemed to hear her words. Confusion crossed his features for a minute, taking the place of the Katabull rage.

"Rimmy, they lost Tweed today. You and I have to get home in one piece."

He nodded and followed her back to the safety of the troop of the Marching Night.

The Amalites were completely broken. Their last chance for victory had fled when the Kartik/Katabull army had come over the hill, and their last chance of escape was over as soon they had failed to break through the Marching Night.

They panicked and leadership crumbled. There was neither rhyme nor reason to what they were doing, and while they were busy running around like chickens with their heads cut off, the Jethrik and Kartik armies did just that. This time there would be no survivors. Their gods had once again promised a victory, and then failed to make good on that promise. What was more, they knew as they died that this army would not stop here. It would march across Amalite and wipe out their world till everything about them and their lives was totally and completely obliterated.

They had hoped to take over the world and make all praise their gods. But their gods had forsaken them, and the infidels would plunder their temples, and soon no one would be left to worship them.

The gods had no one to blame but themselves.

When they had counted and buried their dead, the combined army of the Jethriks, Kartiks and Katabulls marched across Amalite, killing every fighting man and priest they found there. They burned their filthy temples and broke their idols. They did not leave the land until the curse of the Amalites had been cleansed from the world.

22

They stood on the deck waiting for Kartik to come into view, and directly it did. There was a communal sigh when they first caught sight of the mountaintops peaking up out of the sea. Soon they would be home. When they stepped off the ship onto the docks, then it would feel like it was finally over.

The sail home had been a time of quiet reflection for them all. They had been physically, emotionally, and spiritually exhausted. The trip home had given them a chance to think about all that had happened. A time to heal from their losses and dwell upon their success. They were going home, but not everyone who had come with them was making this trip, and that made the voyage bittersweet. They had put the Amalites down and brought a lasting peace to their world, but at a very high price.

Jena was the first to speak. "I will be glad to be home," she said. She took Tarius's hand and looked at her. "Now that it's all over, I can tell you. Everything. *Everything* you said about war was absolutely true, but I'm not sorry I went. I'd do it again, and I know father felt the same way."

"I also wouldn't change my decision," Harris said. "Although in eight months my son will have grown and won't remember me."

"Gee! I wonder if Dustan has grown while I was away," Arvon said lightly.

"Perhaps he's forgotten you," Harris poked back.

"Oh, now I doubt that," Arvon said brushing his hair back with his hand.

They all laughed.

Radkin stood by Rimmy with her hand on his shoulder. "We lost Tweed, our household is short, and we will all feel the loss. We lost a lot of good warriors, but none died in vain. None were sorry to have died for the cause."

"I don't know how to tell our children," Rimmy said, his voice choked.

"The children will miss him, as we all will, but they are resilient. The children will comfort you, Rimmy, and you will feel better," Radkin said, gently patting him on the back.

"You will tell them about Tweed and make sure that they never forget him," Jena said.

"I will tell all the children of him. Of all of you. The fallen and the living," Tarius said. "I will say of Tweed that he, like Radkin and Arvon, Darian, Eldred, Frets, Jax, Jerrad, Lional and Kirk did not leave my side even when I had called a retreat. They did not leave me even though they knew that to stay would almost surely mean their deaths. I will say of Harris that he led the retreat in spite of the fact that he didn't want to. That in all the world, never has anyone had a better or more loyal friend. Of noble Hestia I will say that there was never a wiser queen, nor one who understood battle as well as affairs of state, a ruler who wasn't afraid to risk her own life to free her people from the threat of the Amalite scum. I will say of the witch Jazel..."

Jazel took a bow at the sound of her name.

"... that she wove many spells which helped us in our battles, and protected us from harm. Or that at the very least they would have if we would have but listened to her incantations."

"Thank you," Jazel said.

"I will say of Jena that no one fought as hard or as well, or was as good a lover."

Jena slapped her in the shoulder. "I'm sure the children don't need to know that last bit."

"Tarius, you promised that together you and I would make history," Hestia said, "and we have. We have changed the world, but here is something I have been wondering since we killed and disposed of the last Amalite warrior. With no war in the world and no enemy, what will become of Tarius the Black and the Marching Night?"

"I will attend to the leadership of my people. Jena and I, with Arvon and Dustan, will start our family, and we will raise our children. If evil again appears in the world, we will go and fight it before it has a chance to flourish, and in the meantime we will enjoy the peace that we have worked and sacrificed so much for," Tarius said.

All the Marching Night cheered.

"And, as I said, I will tell stories," Tarius said then added only half joking. "I truly believe that I am a frustrated bard."

"As long as you don't sing," Harris said pulling a face.

"I'm curious," Hestia said. "What stories will you weave of Persius, the King of the Jethrik?"

"Ah! Now you see, Hestia, the story of Persius is the greatest story of all. For it is the story of one who does a terrible wrong, but when his moment of redemption comes he seizes it and doesn't worry about the cost. His story will give hope to all who are burdened with guilt," Tarius said.

"And who will tell the story of Tarius the Black?" Harris asked.

"We all will," Hestia said.

Persius sat in his throne room. For the first time in years, the air smelled sweet to him. His heart felt lighter in his chest. These days almost everything made him smile. It was as if his soul had been returned to him clean and pure. He slept, and his dreams were sweet delight.

He must have been smiling again, for Hellibolt asked him. "Is there something that amuses you, Sire?"

"These days, Hellibolt, *everything* amuses me," Persius said. "I am not even annoyed that I have been waiting for Edmond and Justin for nearly an hour."

"The academy is at least half an hour's ride, Sire," Hellibolt reminded him. "Why did you send for them anyway?"

"You'll see," Persius said lightly. "I feel as if I have been reborn, Hellibolt. A dark cloud has been lifted from my spirit."

"Very good, Persius," Hellibolt said with an indulgent smile.

The court herald ran in. "Sire, Master Edmond and Master Justin, as you requested."

"Send them in at once," Persius said.

Edmond walked in carrying a scroll. Justin was right behind him.

"I'm sorry it took us so long, Sire, but I had to break up a fight on my way out the door," Justin said and added on a heavy note. "Master Darian always was better at dealing with the boys and their attitudes than I was."

"That's quite all right," Persius said. "Let me see the scroll. There are a couple of changes I want to make in the enrollment qualifications."

Edmond handed him the scroll reluctantly.

Persius opened it and read. "Here's the first one... Hand me a quill, Hellibolt."

Hellibolt produced a quill seemingly out of thin air, and handed it to the king, who began writing on the scroll. "No Katabull. How stupid a rule was that one? They are faster and stronger and better fighters. Of course they should be allowed to join the Sword Masters if they so desire. In fact, let us take a lesson from the Kartik. Katabull wishing to enter our academy don't have to meet any other requirements."

Edmond started to protest, and Persius held up his hand. "My mind is made up."

Persius read on. "Ah, here's it is." He started writing. When he finished he looked up at them and smiled. "If the women want to fight, then for the gods' sake, *let them fight!*"

About the Author

Selina Rosen lives in rural Arkansas with her partner, her parrot, Ricky, assorted fish and fowl – both inside and out, several milk goats, an undetermined number of barn cats and her dogs, Spud and Keri. Besides writing, editing, and taking care of the farm, she's a gardener, carpenter, rock mason, electrician (NOT a plumber), *Torah* scholar and sword fighter. In her spare time she creates water gardens, builds furniture, and adds to her on-going creation of the "Great Wall of Kibler."

Selina's short fiction has appeared in several magazines and anthologies including *Sword and Sorceress 16*, *Such A Pretty Face*, *Distant Journeys*, three of the MZB Fantasy Mags, *Tooth and Claw*, *Turn the Other Chick*, and *Anthology At the End of the Universe*. Her story entitled "Ritual Evolution" appeared in the first of the new *Thieves World* anthologies, *Turning Points*, and her second *TW* story, "Gathering Strength," appeared in the new *TW* anthology, *Enemies of Fortune*. Look for her new story, "The Big Trash," in the spring issue of HelixOnLine.

Her novels include *Queen of Denial*, *Recycled*, *Chains of Freedom*, *Chains of Destruction*, *Strange Robby*, *The Host* trilogy, *Fire & Ice*, *Hammer Town*, *Reruns*, and novellas entitled *The Boatman* and *Material Things* from YDP, and *Bad Lands*, a gonzo-mystery novel co-written with Laura J. Underwood from Five Star Mystery (Techno Books).

Her newest project is one that, hopefully, will be on-going for several years. Check out her website (below) for her continuing series, *The House*. It's posted in episodes – one per week for the first four weeks, then one or two per month depending upon demand.

In her capacity as editor-in-chief of Yard Dog Press, Ms. Rosen has edited several anthologies, including the award-winning *Bubbas of the Apocalypse*, *The Four Bubbas of the Apocalypse: Flatulence, Halitosis, Incest and...Ned*, *International House of Bubbas*, *Houston: We've Got Bubbas!*, and two collections of "modern" fairy tales—the Stoker-nominated *Stories That Won't Make Your Parents Hurl* and *More Stories That Won't Make Your Parents Hurl*.

You can contact Selina through her personal website or Email:

www.selinarosen.com
selinarosen@cox.net

Our titles are available at major book stores
and local independent resellers who support
Science Fiction and Fantasy readers like you.

**EDGE Science Fiction
and Fantasy Publishing**

Tesseract Books

Dragon Moon Press

www.edgewebsite.com
www.dragonmoonpress.com

Our titles are available at major book stores and local independent resellers who support Science Fiction and Fantasy readers like you.

Alien Deception by Tony Ruggiero -(tp) - ISBN-13: 978-1-896944-34-0
Alien Revelation by Tony Ruggiero (tp) - ISBN-13: 978-1-896944-34-8
Alphanauts by J. Brian Clarke (tp) - ISBN-13: 978-1-894063-14-2
Apparition Trail, The by Lisa Smedman (tp) - ISBN-13: 978-1-894063-22-7
As Fate Decrees by Denysé Bridger (tp) - ISBN-13: 978-1-894063-41-8

Billibub Baddings and The Case of the Singing Sword by Tee Morris (tp)
 - ISBN-13: 978-1-896944-18-0
Black Chalice, The by Marie Jakober (hb) - ISBN-13: 978-1-894063-00-5
Blue Apes by Phyllis Gotlieb (pb) - ISBN-13: 978-1-895836-13-4
Blue Apes by Phyllis Gotlieb (hb) - ISBN-13: 978-1-895836-14-1

Chalice of Life, The by Anne Webb (tp) - ISBN-13: 978-1-896944-33-3
Chasing The Bard by Philippa Ballantine (tp) - ISBN-13: 978-1-896944-08-1
Children of Atwar, The by Heather Spears (pb) - ISBN-13: 978-0-88878-335-6
Clan of the Dung-Sniffers by Lee Danielle Hubbard (pb) - ISBN-13: 978-1-895836-05-0
Claus Effect, The by David Nickle & Karl Schroeder (pb) - ISBN-13: 978-1-895836-34-9
Claus Effect, The by David Nickle & Karl Schroeder (hb) - ISBN-13: 978-1-895836-35-6
Complete Guide to Writing Fantasy, The - Volume 1: Alchemy with Words
 - edited by Darin Park and Tom Dullemond (tp)
 - ISBN-13: 978-1-896944-09-8
Complete Guide to Writing Fantasy, The - Volume 2: Opus Magus
 - edited by Tee Morris and Valerie Griswold-Ford (tp)
 - ISBN-13: 978-1-896944-15-9
Complete Guide to Writing Fantasy, The - Volume 3: The Author's Grimoire
 - edited by Valerie Griswold-Ford & Lai Zhao (tp)
 - ISBN-13: 978-1-896944-38-8
Complete Guide to Writing Science Fiction, The - Volume 1: First Contact
 - edited by Dave A. Law & Darin Park (tp)
 - ISBN-13: 978-1-896944-39-5
Courtesan Prince, The by Lynda Williams (tp) - ISBN-13: 978-1-894063-28-9

Dark Earth Dreams by Candas Dorsey & Roger Deegan (comes with a CD)
 - ISBN-13: 978-1-895836-05-9
Darkling Band, The by Jason Henderson (tp) - ISBN-13: 978-1-896944-36-4
Darkness of the God by Amber Hayward (tp) - ISBN-13: 978-1-894063-44-9
Darwin's Paradox by Nina Munteanu (tp) - ISBN-13: 978-1-896944-68-5
Daughter of Dragons by Kathleen Nelson - (tp) - ISBN-13: 978-1-896944-00-5
Distant Signals by Andrew Weiner (tp) - ISBN-13: 978-0-88878-284-7
Dominion by J. Y. T. Kennedy (tp) - ISBN-13: 978-1-896944-28-9
Dragon Reborn, The by Kathleen H. Nelson - (tp) - ISBN-13: 978-1-896944-05-0
Dragon's Fire, Wizard's Flame by Michael R. Mennenga (tp)
 - ISBN-13: 978-1-896944-13-5
Dreams of an Unseen Planet by Teresa Plowright (tp) - ISBN-13: 978-0-88878-282-3
Dreams of the Sea by Élisabeth Vonarburg (tp) - ISBN-13: 978-1-895836-96-7
Dreams of the Sea by Élisabeth Vonarburg (hb) - ISBN-13: 978-1-895836-98-1

Eclipse by K. A. Bedford (tp) - ISBN-13: 978-1-894063-30-2
Even The Stones by Marie Jakober (tp) - ISBN-13: 978-1-894063-18-0

Fires of the Kindred by Robin Skelton (tp) - ISBN-13: 978-0-88878-271-7
Firestorm of Dragons edited by Michele Acker & Kirk Dougal (tp)
 - ISBN-13: 978-1-896944-80-7
Forbidden Cargo by Rebecca Rowe (tp) - ISBN-13: 978-1-894063-16-6

Game of Perfection, A by Élisabeth Vonarburg (tp)
 - ISBN-13: 978-1-894063-32-6
Green Music by Ursula Pflug (tp) - ISBN-13: 978-1-895836-75-2
Green Music by Ursula Pflug (hb) - ISBN-13: 978-1-895836-77-6
Gryphon Highlord, The by Connie Ward (tp) - ISBN-13: 978-1-896944-38-8

Healer, The by Amber Hayward (tp) - ISBN-13: 978-1-895836-89-9
Healer, The by Amber Hayward (hb) - ISBN-13: 978-1-895836-91-2
Hounds of Ash and other Tales of Fool Wolf, The by Greg Keyes (pb)
 - ISBN-13: 978-1-895836-09-8
Human Thing, The by Kathleen H. Nelson - (hb) - ISBN-13: 978-1-896944-03-6
Hydrogen Steel by K. A. Bedford (tp) - ISBN-13: 978-1-894063-20-3

i-ROBOT Poetry by Jason Christie (tp) - ISBN-13: 978-1-894063-24-1

Jackal Bird by Michael Barley (pb) - ISBN-13: 978-1-895836-07-3
Jackal Bird by Michael Barley (hb) - ISBN-13: 978-1-895836-11-0
JEMMA7729 by Phoebe Wray (tp) - ISBN-13: 978-1-894063-40-1

Keaen by Till Noever (tp) - ISBN-13: 978-1-894063-08-1
Keeper's Child by Leslie Davis (tp) - ISBN-13: 978-1-894063-01-2

Lachli by M. H. Bonham (tp) - ISBN-13: 978-1-896944-69-2
Land/Space edited by Candas Jane Dorsey and Judy McCrosky (tp)
 - ISBN-13: 978-1-895836-90-5
Land/Space edited by Candas Jane Dorsey and Judy McCrosky (hb)
 - ISBN-13: 978-1-895836-92-9
Legacy of Morevi by Tee Morris (tp) - ISBN-13: 978-1-896944-29-6
Legends of the Serai by J.C. Hall - (tp) - ISBN-13: 978-1-896944-04-3
Longevity Thesis by Jennifer Tahn (tp) - ISBN-13: 978-1-896944-37-1
Lyskarion: The Song of the Wind by J.A. Cullum (tp)
 - ISBN-13: 978-1-894063-02-9

Machine Sex and other stories by Candas Jane Dorsey (tp)
 - ISBN-13: 978-0-88878-278-6
Maërlande Chronicles, The by Élisabeth Vonarburg (pb)
 - ISBN-13: 978-0-88878-294-6
Magister's Mask, The by Deby Fredericks (tp) - ISBN-13: 978-1-896944-16-6
Moonfall by Heather Spears (pb) - ISBN-13: 978-0-88878-306-6
Morevi: The Chronicles of Rafe and Askana by Lisa Lee & Tee Morris
 - (tp) - ISBN-13: 978-1-896944-07-4

Not Your Father's Horseman by Valorie Griswold-Ford (tp)
 - ISBN-13: 978-1-896944-27-2

On Spec: The First Five Years edited by On Spec (pb)
- ISBN-13: 978-1-895836-08-0
On Spec: The First Five Years edited by On Spec (hb)
- ISBN-13: 978-1-895836-12-7
Operation: Immortal Servitude by Tony Ruggerio (tp)
- ISBN-13: 978-1-896944-56-2
Operation: Save the Innocent by Tony Ruggerio (tp)
- ISBN-13: 978-1-896944-60-9
Orbital Burn by K. A. Bedford (tp) - ISBN-13: 978-1-894063-10-4
Orbital Burn by K. A. Bedford (hb) - ISBN-13: 978-1-894063-12-8

Pallahaxi Tide by Michael Coney (pb) - ISBN-13: 978-0-88878-293-9
Passion Play by Sean Stewart (pb) - ISBN-13: 978-0-88878-314-1
Plague Saint by Rita Donovan, The (tp) - ISBN-13: 978-1-895836-28-8
Plague Saint by Rita Donovan, The (hb) - ISBN-13: 978-1-895836-29-5

Reluctant Voyagers by Élisabeth Vonarburg (pb) - ISBN-13: 978-1-895836-09-7
Reluctant Voyagers by Élisabeth Vonarburg (hb) - ISBN-13: 978-1-895836-15-8
Resisting Adonis by Timothy J. Anderson (tp) - ISBN-13: 978-1-895836-84-5
Resisting Adonis by Timothy J. Anderson (hb) - ISBN-13: 978-1-895836-83-7
Righteous Anger by Lynda Williams (tp) - ISBN-13: 897-1-894063-38-8

Shadebinder's Oath by Jeanette Cottrell - (tp) - ISBN-13: 978-1-896944-31-9
Silent City, The by Élisabeth Vonarburg (tp) - ISBN-13: 978-1-894063-07-4
Slow Engines of Time, The by Élisabeth Vonarburg (tp) - ISBN-13: 978-1-895836-30-1
Slow Engines of Time, The by Élisabeth Vonarburg (hb) - ISBN-13: 978-1-895836-31-8
Small Magics by Erik Buchanan (tp) - ISBN-13: 978-1-896944-38-8
Sojourn by Jana Oliver - (pb) - ISBN-13: 978-1-896944-30-2
Stealing Magic by Tanya Huff (tp) - ISBN-13: 978-1-894063-34-0
Strange Attractors by Tom Henighan (pb) - ISBN-13: 978-0-88878-312-7
Sword Masters by Selina Rosen (tp) - ISBN-13: 978-1-896944-65-4

Taming, The by Heather Spears (pb) - ISBN-13: 978-1-895836-23-3
Taming, The by Heather Spears (hb) - ISBN-13: 978-1-895836-24-0
Teacher's Guide to Dragon's Fire, Wizard's Flame by Unwin & Mennenga - (pb)
- ISBN-13: 978-1-896944-19-7
Ten Monkeys, Ten Minutes by Peter Watts (tp) - ISBN-13: 978-1-895836-74-5
Ten Monkeys, Ten Minutes by Peter Watts (hb) - ISBN-13: 978-1-895836-76-9
Tesseracts 1 edited by Judith Merril (pb) - ISBN-13: 978-0-88878-279-3
Tesseracts 2 edited by Phyllis Gotlieb & Douglas Barbour (pb)
- ISBN-13: 978-0-88878-270-0
Tesseracts 3 edited by Candas Jane Dorsey & Gerry Truscott (pb)
- ISBN-13: 978-0-88878-290-8
Tesseracts 4 edited by Lorna Toolis & Michael Skeet (pb)
- ISBN-13: 978-0-88878-322-6
Tesseracts 5 edited by Robert Runté & Yves Maynard (pb)
- ISBN-13: 978-1-895836-25-7
Tesseracts 5 edited by Robert Runté & Yves Maynard (hb)
- ISBN-13: 978-1-895836-26-4
Tesseracts 6 edited by Robert J. Sawyer & Carolyn Clink (pb)
- ISBN-13: 978-1-895836-32-5
Tesseracts 6 edited by Robert J. Sawyer & Carolyn Clink (hb)
- ISBN-13: 978-1-895836-33-2

Tesseracts 7 edited by Paula Johanson & Jean-Louis Trudel (tp)
- ISBN-13: 978-1-895836-58-5
Tesseracts 7 edited by Paula Johanson & Jean-Louis Trudel (hb)
- ISBN-13: 978-1-895836-59-2
Tesseracts 8 edited by John Clute & Candas Jane Dorsey (tp)
- ISBN-13: 978-1-895836-61-5
Tesseracts 8 edited by John Clute & Candas Jane Dorsey (hb)
- ISBN-13: 978-1-895836-62-2
Tesseracts Nine edited by Nalo Hopkinson and Geoff Ryman (tp)
- ISBN-13: 978-1-894063-26-5
Tesseracts Ten edited by Robert Charles Wilson and Edo van Belkom (tp)
- ISBN-13: 978-1-894063-36-4
Tesseracts Eleven edited by Cory Doctorow and Holly Phillips (tp)
- ISBN-13: 978-1-894063-03-6
Tesseracts Q edited by Élisabeth Vonarburg & Jane Brierley (pb)
- ISBN-13: 978-1-895836-21-9
Tesseracts Q edited by Élisabeth Vonarburg & Jane Brierley (hb)
- ISBN-13: 978-1-895836-22-6
Throne Price by Lynda Williams and Alison Sinclair (tp)
- ISBN-13: 978-1-894063-06-7
Too Many Princes by Deby Fredricks (tp) - ISBN-13: 978-1-896944-36-4
Twilight of the Fifth Sun by David Sakmyster - (tp)
- ISBN-13: 978-1-896944-01-02

Virtual Evil by Jana Oliver (tp) - ISBN-13: 978-1-896944-76-0